ENTER SANDMAN

The Abominations Saga 1

END OF DAYS
BOOK 3

CERISE COLE

Spotted Horse Productions

Enter Sandman is a work of fiction. Names, characters, places, brands, media, and incidents are either the product of the author's imagination or are used fictitiously. Any resemblance to actual events, locales, or persons, living or dead, is entirely coincidental.

Copyright © 2021 by Cerise Cole

All Rights Reserved. In accordance with the U.S. Copyright Act of 1976, the scanning, uploading, and electronic sharing of any part of this book without the permission of the publisher and the copyright owner constitute unlawful piracy and theft of the author's intellectual property. Thank you for your support of the author's rights.

Cover Art by Spotted Horse Productions

Edited by Sarah Williams

TRIGGER WARNING

Enter Sandman is a slow-burn, paranormal romance where the heroine doesn't have to choose between her love interests.

Some aspects may be **triggering** for some readers. The series includes stepbrother romance, an abusive parent, a parent lost to cancer, incidences of domestic violence, bullying, and plenty of teen awkwardness.

DEDICATION

Hate is a monster that lurks in the backs of our minds. It makes us think we're justified - but we aren't. All hate does is poison us from the inside out, rotting away our happiness. Of all the things to fight against, this is the one that we are all destined to succumb to.

Forgiveness is the only solution, but it is a hard thing to find. Everyone has their own story. We all make mistakes - and yet love really can find a way, even in the darkest places.

PROLOGUE

GAVIN

"I should've died."

The words hung in the silent living room. My eyes were on the TV, but I was ignoring the Twitch stream. That probably wasn't how Deke had expected me to respond to being asked if I was ok, but it was the truth. Physically, I was good enough. Weak still, but fine. Mentally was a different story.

"Sucks, huh?" Deke asked as he dropped down to sit on the couch.

His eyes hung on me, and I could feel it. His voice was filled with honest concern. Bax and Lars were downstairs, working in the garage. Linda had taken Jess to run some errands. Right now, it was just the two of us, which made talking about this a little easier.

I'd almost forgotten about how close he'd come to dying in Bax's basement, but his words brought it right back. That was what he meant about it sucking. Deke knew because he'd been there. For some reason, the fact that he could understand made me feel a little less alone. Less like I had to keep this to myself. Unfortunately, I didn't know the right words in English to describe what was going on in my head. The whole thing was a jumbled mess.

"When she fixed you," I tried, "did you see the colors?"

Deke's brow creased. "Colors?"

"She's purple. Like those blacklights," I explained. "Bax is light blue. The color of the sky, almost. Lars is green, but not like leaves."

"Darker or lighter?" Deke asked. I couldn't tell if he was patronizing me.

"Brighter," I said. "Neon, but not quite."

"She mentioned that," he admitted. "The colors, I mean. Jess says the colors on your hands are because of the colors of your soul. She didn't tell me what shades, though. She did say that you're red."

I shrugged. "Dunno. Didn't really see myself. I just saw the silver cord. I was sure it would break, and then the purple ran down it from her. Blue and green came next, but it took a bit."

"When she healed you," he said, showing he was keeping up. "Lars said that Jess worked spirit magic on you. Same thing she did to me, which means she touched your soul, but you didn't have much left, so she used her own. She said something about making more, but I'm not sure how that works."

I waved all that off. "Cambion magic. She saved me, but she needed the cord to do it. We're all tied to her by those, and I know I sound like some idiot, but I saw it, Deke. I saw that cord, and I can't stop thinking about it."

"Ok." He leaned his weight onto the arm of the couch as he spoke. The whole time, his complete attention was on me. "Tell me about it?"

"I don't fucking know the *words!*" I snapped.

Deke just lifted a brow. "You're fluent in English, Gavin. If you don't know the words, you'll find others or we'll figure it out. I know it's hard to talk about this shit without feeling like you're putting yourself out there, but it's *us*. I need to know, ok? There's something about this quad that isn't like the rest, and I think it's what's going to keep the four of you alive."

"The bonds," I explained. "The cords. That's what those silver things were, but not all are silver."

"Which ones aren't?" he asked.

I shifted in my chair, not sure this was going quite right. Still, he'd asked. "Yours. The line between you and Jess is black. Rotted, maybe? But it didn't feel like that. It felt like a shadow. Like it was ignored."

"I'm not supposed to be bound to her," he reminded me, his voice taking on that instructor tone he used when telling us the bad things.

But I slammed my fist down on the arm of my chair. "You fucked her!"

"And that was a mistake," he mumbled.

"Was it?" I turned my complete focus on him. My jaw was set. I wanted to say more, but not until he answered.

Deke just leaned over his knees and lifted both hands to scrub at his face. "No." Then he sighed. "I am seven years older than that girl. I'm her fucking *mentor*. A position of power over her. She just got away from her abusive father. Girls like that want someone to tell them what to do, and you've seen her - she wants me to give her the answers. I don't want to be the next mistake she makes, and the three of you are good for her."

"So it was a mistake," I said, pressing him to pick a damned side.

"For her, yes," Deke conceded. "It was a mistake for me because I know better. I know I should keep my hands off. I just..." Closing his eyes, he tossed his head back. "Fuck! Yeah, I caved. Fucking sue me."

This time, I was the one leaning forward. "You know, after that shower you two shared, she stopped flinching. She stopped worrying about being so good all the fucking time."

"Instead, I am," Deke pointed out. "And what happened to you wanting her all to yourself, huh? Having to share with Bax and Lars was just so you could get something instead of nothing?"

"Fuck that," I grumbled. "That was before I died."

"You didn't *die*," he insisted. "She saved you, Gav."

"I still saw the fucking bonds," I shot back. "You don't get it. They swirl around her. My cord goes to her and it's wrapped all around her body. Bax's is loose, but it's trying to do the same. Lars' is so tight it's melting into her. Yours is fucking black. There's like a little hint of something in it, but the shadows cover it up. It's that thing!" I threw up my hands. "The hand holding. The kissing. The..." I groaned when I couldn't find the right words.

"The need to touch her," Deke whispered. "To be around her. That magnetism she has that makes me turn into a fucking idiot when she looks at me too long."

"That!" I said. "Magnetism. That's the word. It's the bonds, Deke. It's this thing that makes us work together, and I saw it. You're a part of it, but you're not. You're killing that bond and it's going to fuck her up."

He nodded slowly, as if taking that to heart. "When she woke up after healing you, her first words were that she needed more. She needed to touch me - or one of you. I feel like I'm a part of this quad in a way I never did with the others. Not even those women I was sleeping with."

"Because you're supposed to be," I told him. "There's a cord between you and her. There were more, but I didn't look where they all went. You have a bright silver one, but that goes to Tash, and it's small. Like the one between me and Bax."

"Bonds," he repeated. "Ok. I mean, if we're talking about magic and demons, bonds make just as much sense."

Oddly, that made me feel better. "Yeah?" I asked.

Deke lifted one shoulder in a weak shrug. "Sure. She makes magic. All four of you have magical powers in your hands. I can do ritual magic. Something ties the four Brethren together, right? It's some power, and bonds is as good of a word for it as anything else.

Otherwise, you wouldn't end up finding each other. You wouldn't be repelled by other quads. That's why I said magnetism, because it pulls the four of you together while pushing away any other Brethren."

It made sense. I wasn't fucking crazy! Tash had tried to say that my near-death visions had been nothing more than the brain's way of understanding my body shutting down. I didn't buy that, but this? The fact that we *were* tied together in a real way? It made sense. It made me feel like this wasn't my imagination. I wasn't some daydreaming fuck-up.

"So what are you doing about your bond with her?" I asked.

Deke groaned and turned away. "Gav, it's complicated."

"No, it's not."

"Yes," he insisted, "it is. Do you really want me crawling into bed with you and her? Do you want me luring her to mine to spend the night? How the fuck are you going to feel when you sneak up the hall and she's not there? It's fucking complicated, and my damned job is to make sure that the four of you are happy. Not me. Not my dick. I have to keep my Brethren working so we can close these damned seals before the Horsemen get out!"

"And she needs you!" I yelled. "Jess gives and gives and gives. Who gives back to her? Us?" I scoffed at that. "Yeah, trust me, it's a real hardship to get her naked. Sure, sometimes I make her coffee. Really puts me out. No one calls me a slut at school."

"They call you gay instead," Deke countered.

I grumbled under my breath, because he was right. "That hasn't happened in a while."

"And you're now crawling naked into a bed with how many guys?" he pressed. "Maybe I'm bad at math, but I can't figure out how you'd get someone else in that damned bed without a man curling up against you. So, you still think this is so important?"

"Yes," I mumbled. "You don't understand, Deke. It just is."

"So how about you explain to me why you think so," he snapped.

"I'm not fucking them," I insisted.

"You know that," he said, "and I know that. Shit, I saw enough to be sure of it."

"When you were getting your kicks," I taunted. "Spying on her because you want it, but don't want to admit you do."

"I want it!" he roared. "I also haven't forgotten how worried you were about someone thinking you're gay. I saw Bax 'helping' her suck off Lars. So tell me, do you *always* stay on the other side of her? How's that gonna work with one more man in your little orgies, hm? You're so damned worried about someone thinking you might be gay that you've never considered your situation means a whole lot of naked men around you. Then what, Gav? How the hell are you going to deal with it when someone's dick brushes your leg, huh? Maybe a moan beside your ear? Still think this isn't complicated as fuck?"

"I'll deal with it," I insisted. "She saved my life. The least I can do is make sure she has everything."

Deke sighed, sounding like he was giving up. "Why is this so important to you, anyway?"

"Because this only works if we're all together," I said. "Don't you fucking get that? Everyone wants to kill us. Demons, Martyrs, regular people, and probably more I don't know about. You're the one who said we're stronger together, and I saw it. I was dying and together they brought me back."

"Because it's about the four of you," he tried to explain.

"No!" Again, I slapped the arm of my chair. "It's five, Deke. You're bonded to her too - you're just letting it rot. If you want us to play this game, put our lives at risk, and everything else, then you can't play it safe while we risk it all. All or nothing. You're either in, or we're out. You don't get to fuck her once and ignore it. You can't lead her on, hoping we'll make up for it. This is us, and maybe it's fucked up - or gay, or gross, or anything else - but there's only one way it works. You're in, or you're not."

He shoved to his feet, but only managed to take one step. I was convinced he was about to storm out, yet Deke just stopped. His head dropped, and for a moment he just breathed a bit too hard.

"Fine. If I'm going to do this, then you'd better be damned sure you're ok with it. I'm not going to start something with that girl and change my mind because you get cold feet. I'm not about to break her heart because you teenagers have a tantrum."

"She needs this," I told him. "*She* does, Deke. Not me. Not you. Not Lars and Bax. Jess can't carry us all, but she'll try. She needs the bonds - including yours."

"How do I prove I'm all in?" His words were too soft.

"I don't know," I admitted.

"Because fucking her isn't what she needs," he added. "Jess isn't looking for sex."

"She's looking for a bond," I agreed, looking up at him.

Deke was looking back. "Yeah. One I tried to kill off. This is going to be weird, Gav."

I just shrugged. "I'm getting used to weird. Might not be easy, but we'll figure it out. I just really don't want to die again."

"You didn't *die*," he groaned.

My eyes went back to the TV. "I knew I was going to. I knew it, and all I could think about were the things I'd fucked up. The shit I wouldn't get to do. I don't want any of us to have those as our last thoughts."

"Everyone does," he countered. "That's the shitty part of dying, so how about we try not to?"

"I figure that starts with being all in," I told him. "Movie night in Bax's room tonight."

"I'll be there," Deke promised, "because, yeah, I'm in. Tash hates it, but I actually think you're right. I also think this is the dumbest idea I've ever had."

CHAPTER ONE

SPRING BREAK WAS BASICALLY OVER. That was my first thought when I woke up. It was Sunday, so we still had the rest of today, but the four of us had missed all the wild parties and drunken debauchery. Still, our stitches were out, our bodies were healed, and we were fine. I just wasn't sure we'd stay that way.

Demons knew who we were and where we lived. Not hard, since Bax had a bit of a reputation in town. Thankfully, the wards were holding - including my dad's. Yep, Ted Bailey had added an additional ring around the property to keep out something. I just couldn't tell what. Nor could Deke or even Tash. Dad's magic was so old and so powerful that it was beyond anything they'd ever heard of.

Great.

As I tried to force myself all the way awake, I was thinking about how I should figure that out today. Tash was out of town to get "supplies" of some kind. She'd left when the demons stopped testing the wards. Wednesday or Thursday. I wasn't sure which, since the days had sort of blurred together. Linda had been pampering all of us since last weekend, making up for us getting hurt, it seemed. Thankfully, she knew not to show up on our floor before noon and to always knock first. Then there was Deke.

My eyes cracked open to see his face right before mine. He'd actually spent the night last night. Ok, so we'd all just lain on the bed watching a movie, but he hadn't left. Now, he was lying right beside me, wearing nothing but his underwear. I knew because the man slept like he was trying to fight demons: violently.

He'd thrown the blankets off at least twice. Bax had tried to pull them back once, but that hadn't lasted long. And speaking of Bax, he was murmuring on Deke's other side, sounding like he was about to wake up. That was probably what had disturbed my own sleep, if I was honest - but I didn't mind. The view was so worth it.

Deke wasn't a "pretty" man. He had been at some point in his life. Now, he just looked hardened. The scar on the left side of his face was deep, and it matched the claw marks across the rest of his muscular body. His hair was a jumble of colors, from his naturally dark roots to the fire-engine red middle, and down to the yellow-blonde ends. I liked it, though.

Behind him was Bax, the sexy bad-boy of Hellam High. Everyone always said he was trouble with a capital T. He kinda was, but not for the reasons anyone suspected. He was also beautiful. The guy's body was a work of art, his deep brown hair always had that perfect tousled look, and his face belonged in every girl's fantasy. Add his family money to that, and it wasn't shocking that he'd ended up as both a man-whore and overly popular. He also never let people see much below the surface.

My eyes ran across them both, comparing them as I tried to find the motivation to sneak out of bed. Deke throwing around the covers would make that a little easier, at least. I could just slide down to the end without needing to crawl across anyone. Then, just as I was planning my escape, Bax murmured again, shifting closer to the warm body right in front of him: Deke's.

The best part, though, was how Deke snuggled back. I was biting my lips together, trying not to giggle at them. A pair of big,

ENTER SANDMAN

tough guys, and they were unconsciously snuggling each other! Cuteness overload was taking over when Bax moved his arm around Deke's waist - then down.

His palm caressed Deke's side, most likely thinking it was mine. Well, what they didn't know wouldn't hurt them, right? Except I barely had the thought before Bax reached even lower, sliding his hand forward, across Deke's hip, and down to... Oh my! Bax's fingers moved across Deke's dick, seeking, searching, and then gripping across the man's morning erection - but the wrong way. His hand was turned like he was reaching for a pussy, not a cock.

Still asleep, Deke caught his wrist, holding the hand there as he thrust into it. Bax made a noise like he was confused - and they both froze. Only for a few seconds, but it was enough. Both men were now awake, and Deke was still holding Bax's hand against his dick. Worse than that, Bax's fingers were curled under Deke's balls! I quickly closed my eyes, hoping that if they didn't know I'd seen it, then it wouldn't be quite as awkward. Well, or hot, but that was beside the point.

"Fuck," Deke breathed, shifting over fast enough to make the bed bounce.

Bax seemed to move the other way. "Sorry," he mumbled just before I heard his feet hit the floor. "I'm used to being beside Jess."

"Yeah," Deke said, sliding down the bed the way I'd planned to. "I should be up anyway. Tash comes back today."

"Right," Bax said, but cracking my eyes showed that neither man was looking at the other.

I didn't even need to see them to feel the tension in the air. It rippled across their voices, making those few words sound strained and almost angry. Their shoulders were tense. Their backs were both to the bed and each other. Deke was facing one wall. Bax was pointed toward the bathroom.

"I need clothes," Bax said, pushing to his feet.

Which was when Gavin groaned, tossing off his blankets. "You two make a lot of noise."

Deke's body tensed again. "Sorry," he said before marching to the door and leaving the room without another look.

Gavin just sighed. "Least he's trying." It sounded like that was meant mostly for himself.

It also sounded like he didn't have a clue why things were a little awkward. At least there was that! The best I could do was pretend to still be sleeping, which meant either keeping my eyes closed or only open a slit to see where they were. After a little wandering, Gavin had picked up his dirty clothes and headed to his room for a clean set. Bax rummaged through his dresser, finding something for himself, then headed into the bathroom. When both doors clicked, I let out a heavy sigh.

"Caught that too, did ya?" Lars asked, his voice a soft rumble beside my ear.

I rolled over to face him. "The tension?" I asked.

He smiled at me sweetly. "I was just about to kiss your neck when Bax started groping Deke in his sleep. Well, both of their sleep."

"And Gavin..." I said, remembering how worried he'd been about someone thinking he was gay.

Lars just rolled his eyes, then tugged me a little closer. "The whole thing is stupid."

"Being gay?" I asked, not quite keeping up.

"Being scared of being gay," Lars corrected. "You know, with my people, it used to be a sign of strong medicine. It's also natural, normal, and something to be proud of. Well, was. American culture has seeped into our tribal thinking a bit."

Immediately, a dirty thought flashed through my mind, making me giggle. "So, saying you're down for some hot guy-on-guy action for me?"

"Not really my thing," Lars said. "Also not scared of it, unless you forgot me grinding against Bax inside you?" He shifted his hips even closer, pressing his erection into my belly. "Naked men don't get me going, but if I happen to have a sexy little succubus getting me hard, I don't give a shit what my dick is touching."

"What about Bax?" I asked, making sure my voice was barely even a whisper.

Lars lifted his head, looking at the bathroom. "Is he in the shower?"

"Don't hear the water," I said.

"Probably jerking one out." Lars shook his head, then looked at me again. "And what about him?"

"He's not going to be all freaked out, is he? I mean, have you ever seen Bax get embarrassed?"

"I'm more worried about Deke," Lars admitted. "He was raised in Russia, and you know that's not really a thing there, right? Like, homophobia is so strong it's homicidal."

I just pressed my face into Lars' shoulder and sighed. "Almost makes me glad school starts tomorrow."

"Nerd," Lars teased. "Only you would be excited about school."

"Megan's not there anymore," I reminded him. "Where's the downside?"

"Uh, we can start with waking up at unnatural hours and end with homework." But he kissed the top of my head. "And there might be a bit of hating that I can't do *this*."

"Yeah..." Because I'd almost forgotten that part. "But Linda quit..."

"And immediately jumping in bed with my supposed stepsister doesn't really help her win that sexual harassment lawsuit, Jess." He huffed out a breath before wrapping his arms around me. "You know I love you, right?"

"Yeah, and I love you," I promised.

He nodded. "Well, then that's going to be enough. Mom's ok with this. Not good. Not quite excited yet, but - "

"Gavin almost died," I reminded him. "It's a little hard to be excited about anything after that."

"I meant us," he corrected. "She's doing pretty good with the whole demon hunting, risking our lives thing. Not being able to adopt you? That's the hard part. I'm blaming pregnancy hormones."

"I'm blaming her being too nice," I said. "Always sucks when guys assume hormones are responsible for how we think."

He opened his mouth, but before a word came out, the bathroom door opened. Lars jerked his eyes up, over my shoulder and a smirk took over his face. "Jerking one out in there or something?" he joked.

"No!" Bax snapped. "I was..."

I rolled onto my back and turned my head so I could see him. Bax's eyes dropped from Lars' face to mine, then he sighed.

"I was going to let you sleep in," he mumbled.

"Which means," Lars said around a laugh, "he *was* jerking one out."

"Like you don't do the same," I groaned, forcing myself to sit up. "But I need to pee!"

Both guys moved out of my way, leaving me a straight shot to the bathroom. The door was barely closed behind me, however, before I heard their voices start again. Naturally, it was Lars' that came first.

"Full disclosure, I was awake," he said.

"I wasn't," Bax grumbled. "Thought I was about to wake up Jess in the best way, and I was having a dream about her in a set of red lingerie, lying on the table. No, I don't know what table, but it was hot. And then that wasn't Jess."

"Deke," Lars said. "Yeah. Need me to smooth that over with him?"

"Nope," Bax said. "We're going to pretend like nothing happened, and you will not breathe a word of that where Gavin can hear."

"You're not gay," Lars assured him. "Shit. How many times have I wrapped an arm around you in the middle of the night?"

"You don't stroke my dick!" Bax hissed, sounding like he

wanted to yell but was struggling to keep his voice down. "Talk about embarrassing."

There was a long moment of silence. Long enough for me to finish my business, flush, and get my shorts back on. I headed to the sink, barely turning the water on because I didn't want the sound to mask what they were saying.

Then Lars finally said, "No. I just fuck Jess with you. And? Saying you're totally hands off with Deke now? C'mon. That's not going to convince him to try."

"I have a feeling he's pretty convinced," Bax assured him. "He's made a few comments. I just don't want to be the freak who chases him off."

"Freak?" Lars asked. "How so?"

"I fucking grabbed his dick!" Bax said, and this time it was much louder than a hiss. "Woke up with that shit in my hands like I was about to jack off, but not *my* dick. What the hell would you think if I'd done that to you?"

Lars made a noise like it was no big deal. "That you should sleep next to Jess tomorrow? Fuck, I dunno, Bax. I'm certainly not going to be worried about it."

"Gav will," Bax mumbled. "Never mind Jess!"

Lars just laughed. "Jess would think it's hot. C'mon, haven't you read any of her books?"

"Maybe..." Bax admitted.

Which was when I opened the door and headed out. Mostly because I couldn't hide in the bathroom forever. Both guys turned to look at me with very guilty expressions. Lifting my hands in defeat, I just turned for the door, intending to head back to my room so I could brush my teeth.

"Wait..." Bax groaned. "I'm sorry. I woke up badly."

I turned back to him and didn't stop until I pressed a kiss to his lips. "It was a good show for me, Bax. I will also swear I never saw a thing, don't know shit, and maybe try to get you and Lars to see if you can both fit again."

He dropped his head. "And now my dick's hard. Go, like, get dressed or something," he begged, turning me toward the door. "We're supposed to start training again today."

"Which means Gavin's back to normal?" I asked.

Bax just flashed me that sexy smile he did so well. "Maybe you should ask him yourself. I bet he has a coffee waiting for you already. Man's fucking whipped."

"So are you two," I teased as I left the room, raising my voice once I was in the hall. "Don't try to deny it! Whipped!"

"Fuck yeah, I am," Lars called back. "I'll do ropes and chains too!"

"Wrong kind of demon," I said before closing my bedroom door and ending that while I was still ahead.

CHAPTER TWO

TRAINING ENDED up being a shooting lesson. That meant packing up our gear, hauling it to the north side of the property - almost the exact opposite direction of the still-cracked seal - and setting it up. Then, Deke had us all shoot. The whole time he watched us, making almost no comments. It wasn't until we were packing up that I finally figured it out. He'd been checking to see if any of us would flinch.

Because we'd lost.

The demons had kicked our asses, and it had been pretty traumatic. I was sure some people would have a hard time coping with that, but there was one thing Deke kept forgetting: our entire lives had been traumatic. The four of us had all learned early on to push through it, simply because that was the only way to survive.

No, that didn't make it any easier, but it meant that being together helped more than anything else. We were no longer alone. We had each other to rely on. We also knew that if we had a problem, someone would listen. Never mind that I'd spent my life being beaten by demons. Well, just one. My dad.

We barely made it back before I realized that we weren't the only ones who'd been traumatized. Linda was waiting in our living room, wringing her hands as she paced between the kitchen and the couches. The moment we walked in, her eyes jumped to each of us like she was counting.

"So, everything's ok?" she asked.

"Just training," Deke assured her.

The heaviest breath tumbled from Linda's lungs. "The last time I heard gunshots in the distance, you came back carrying Gavin." Then she pulled in a breath. "So, dinner?"

Deke reached over to rub her shoulder gently. "The kids have to clean their weapons first."

"Can I help?" she asked.

"Sure. You can clean mine."

I just groaned. "No fair, Deke."

He glanced over, and our eyes met. It made his lopsided smile soften a bit. "When you've cleaned as many guns as I have, you can let someone else do it," he joked. "You, Jess, can't even remember how to put the weapon back together."

"And this is one of those things I can do for you kids," Linda said as she followed us all into the dining room.

"Wait..." Lars said. "Is the cleaning fluid safe for her?"

"It's just cleaning oil," Bax assured him. "Besides, it's not like she's going to eat it."

"Yeah, but the baby - " Lars tried.

"Is fine," Linda assured him as she claimed a seat. "Ok, someone show me how to do this."

So we did. Deke was adamant that we needed to be able to function on our own in case anything happened to him. That meant everything from taking care of our weapons to knowing how to lie with a straight face. The second part was easy. Over the last week, he'd been talking to us about things like avoiding the cops, explaining away the weirdness, and other "useful" tricks for hunting demons in a world that didn't believe in them.

An hour later, we had the guns pulled apart and were scrubbing pieces with the little brushes. Gavin was convinced that the cleaning fluid smelled like lemons, but I didn't agree. Sure, if you believed that cough syrup tasted like cherries, it might be the same, but only in the most distant and disgusting way possible.

Then the front door opened. Immediately, five of us tensed. Linda just turned in her chair to look back. The entrance beside the kitchen wasn't large, but after a few seconds, Tash moved past it. She paused, either seeing or smelling us, and changed directions, heading our way.

"So, you're all healed up enough to start training again, huh?" she asked.

"Sutures are out, wounds are closed, and even Gavin is doing good," Deke assured her. "How was the trip?"

Tash smiled at him, and I wanted to rip her face off. Only half of it was from jealousy. Maybe even a bit less. Mostly, I hated that she hadn't felt the need to tell us where she was going, what she would be doing, or why she thought it was important. Plus, the woman hated me.

But it seemed that a little time away had done her some good. "I have presents," she announced.

Digging in her coat pocket, Tash pulled out a jumble of something and dropped it in the middle of the table. Necklaces, I realized. All different kinds. One was silver, another was gold, and a few were made of leather, rubber, or something like that. Gavin leaned over and started separating them out.

"Do I want to know why you're buying us jewelry?" he asked.

Tash just pointed at the pile. "Those have been enchanted. There's one for each of us, and they will allow you to sense demons, cambion, angels, and all of the other abominations."

"How?" I asked as I reached for a delicate silver chain with a pendant that looked like an infinity symbol.

Lars grabbed one of the leather-looking ones. "Better question. Why?"

While Bax and Gavin debated over the necklaces they wanted,

Tash pressed her palms to the table and leaned over our dismantled guns and oil-stained rags. "You four don't realize this, but the number of demons at the seal last weekend? Not normal. We usually get between one and five. This entire town is crawling with demons, and they all look as normal as everyone else."

"Like Ted," Linda said softly.

Tash flicked a finger at the necklaces. "One of those is for you too."

"But I'm not fighting demons," Linda reminded her.

"Nor am I," Tash admitted. "Well, not normally. But if we want to know who's safe, then we need to start with *what* they are. The more demons there are in town, the more likely other things are to show up and hide among them. Other abominations. That's why the necklaces detect all of them, because while it may start with demons, I doubt it will stay that way."

"But I'm sure it has nothing to do with Jess being evil," Bax grumbled. "So is the baby, Linda. Just so you know. Tash is convinced of it."

Tash slapped her hand on the table. "Stop. Evil or not, you four just picked a fight, and wouldn't you like to know if the guy at the next pump is thinking about killing you while you're getting gas? Or maybe knowing if a kid in class is half demon so you can stay away from their parents at the next football game?"

"Football's over," Deke said, a devious little twist to his lips.

I wanted to giggle, because he was right. It also didn't matter. It was just his way of picking on her, which made me feel more like he was on our side now. Something had shifted since we lost that fight. I wasn't sure exactly what, but I no longer felt like I had to apologize for being what I was.

"You know what I mean," Tash said. "Look. You four are no longer a secret. Those demons know who the Brethren are now. That means they're going to want to get rid of you. The house is warded so they can't get in. Well, not without one hell of a fight. When you're at school, though?"

"If my dad could hide being a demon," I said, looking at the rest, "then just think about who else could be one. For all we know, half our teachers could have been at the seal."

"And it's easier to kill them if we know who they are," Gavin said softly. "Guys, we wanted this. We asked her to find a way to help us, and she has. Just because she has a problem with Jess doesn't mean this won't help us."

"He's not wrong," Lars admitted. "Even Ted suggested that we do this differently."

"You mean get all first-person-shooter on them?" Bax asked. "Organized hits to take them out on our terms."

"At night, not at the seal, and planned our way," Deke said, showing he was on board with this. "The first step is figuring out which humans were out at the seal as demons - hence the necklaces. This has nothing to do with Jess."

Linda reached her hand out to take a gold chain with a heart pendant. It looked like a locket. "How do you kids plan to keep from getting arrested?"

Yep, that made all of us pause. There was just something about having my stepmom help plan a murder that felt kinda wrong. Linda was amazing, but she was also the nicest woman I'd ever met in my life. She was the kind of mom who held our hands and told us it would be ok. *Not* the kind who cleaned guns and planned demonic hits.

"Is it..." Bax asked, looking over at the other two guys.

"Nope," Lars said. "Not just you. Mom, you realize we're going to shoot people, right?"

"Yes," she assured him, gesturing at the gun laying in front of her to make the point. "I also know that you kids will be so worried about all the exciting parts that you'll forget about the boring stuff that gets a criminal caught. I watch enough real crime dramas to be sure. It's always the stupid mistakes, like where you park your car, that get you busted."

"No bodies," Deke reminded her. "Demons dissipate. Plus, the quad can make people ignore them or leave them alone."

"So we just need to make sure there are no cameras," Linda said. "Those probably wouldn't be affected by magic. I'll head to city hall and see if there's a list. It should be public information."

"Most stores too," Lars pointed out. "Those won't be public."

"I want a list of demons," Tash said as if we hadn't just gone off on a tangent. "Everyone you four see that isn't human..." She turned to look at Deke and Linda. "The two of you as well. We need to see what's living among us. The eleventh seal has been cracked for much too long. The Order isn't happy about it - "

"I should probably try to explain to them," Deke told her.

"They don't care if your quad lives," Tash reminded him. "They want it sealed, and *now*. Deke, it cracked last summer. It's the end of March. The sands are shifting, and they're convinced it's this seal. Unless you want god-knows-how-many Martyrs showing up to help, then we need to start making progress."

"Just keep throwing ourselves at it until we die?" Bax asked.

"That is not what I meant," Tash assured him.

"No?" He leaned back and lifted his chin. "Maybe just throw Jess at them first? You know, since she's just an evil demon brat, right?"

"No..." Tash tried.

But Bax wasn't about to let up. "So, are you saying she's not evil now? No problems with the magic you taught her how to use? You're perfectly ok with her now that she saved our lives? Or are you still waiting for a chance to stab her in the back?"

"I just wanted to make sure that she was working for us, not them!" Tash snapped.

"Them," Bax said, pushing to his feet. "The demons, right? Because she wouldn't be able to help herself. Being half demon and all, what was it you said? She's prone to excess? Which, of course, means she'd fuck us over. I'm not sure how that works in your little head, since Jess's dad beat her and we love her, but - "

"But I wanted to make sure Deke didn't get stupid," Tash shot back.

Bax smiled, and it was a look that made it clear he was winning. "Stupid enough to help us? Stupid enough to use her magic as a weapon because we don't stand a fucking chance against demons? Stupid enough to worry more about winning than doing it the Order's way? What kind of stupid are we talking about, Tash?"

"Stupid because he stuck his dick in her!" Tash said.

Deke groaned, turning away to simply walk out of the room. I just pressed my hands onto my face, refusing to look at Linda. Gavin chuckled under his breath and Lars said nothing, but Bax *still* wasn't done.

"Because you're jealous, or because you'd rather the five of us just suffer in misery? In case you missed it, we're not playing by the Order's rules anymore. We're not going to simply kill someone because you tell us to. I don't give a fuck if they're a demon or not. My girlfriend's half demon, and I will let this world *burn* before I let anyone hurt her. And speaking of demons, I've been feeding the kids for you."

Tash sighed, dropping her head. "I bought a few things for them too," she admitted. "They're cute, Bax. I'm not trying to get Jess killed. I was trying to make sure she's stable. I pushed her to be sure she wouldn't break. Time and time again, she impressed me. I just want to make sure my family isn't going to pay for what hers does."

"Deke isn't your family anymore," he warned.

"Oh, he'll always be my family," Tash promised. "And no, I don't want to sleep with him. The four of you can quit worrying about that. I'm just here to make sure he stays alive." Then she turned and followed Deke out of the room.

"And I'm here to make sure we do too," Bax said, dropping back down into his chair.

Naturally, that was when Linda turned to look at me. "Did you have sex with him, Jess? And are the rest of you ok with this?"

"I... but..." I stammered.

Thankfully, Lars took over. "It's complicated, Mom. It also has to do with these marks on our hands, and we're figuring it out. I promise that we're ok."

"How old is he?" Linda asked, her eyes right on me.

"Twenty-five," I mumbled.

Linda just nodded. "Seven years isn't too bad." She paused to lick her lips. "And when you get tired of these guys keeping you up at night, I have a room upstairs for you to hide in."

"Really?" I asked. There was no way she'd make things this easy.

Linda just shrugged. "Every maternal instinct in my body wants me to have a fit about this. I want to tell you that you're too young, yell at Lars about being taken advantage of, and scream at those two - " She wagged her finger at Bax and Gavin. "- About relationships being more than just sex. I'm also sure that I'm wrong, you kids will get pissed at me again, and that it won't solve anything. So, this is me trying."

"She's not using me, Mom," Lars said.

"I know, honey," Linda assured him. "I also know that I was sure I was about to watch Gavin die on this very table, I saw you and Bax offer your own lives for him, and Jess made magic to fix him. I *know* that happened, but I keep wanting to say it was a dream, none of this is real, and try to convince you kids to act like kids - but you can't."

"I'm sorry," I told her, feeling like the worst person in the world.

"Don't be sorry," Linda told me. "Jess, this is when you should lift your chin and say it doesn't matter what anyone else thinks, because you know what you want, or need, or whatever." She looked down at the necklace in her hands. "You kids deserve to be happy, ok? However that makes you happy, and if this is it, then I'll figure out how to be happy for you. If it's not, I promise I will listen and help you all sort it out. I mean, that's what moms are for, right?"

"Best mom ever," Lars breathed, pushing out of his chair to head over and hug her. "Just convince Tash that Jess is ok?"

"And your baby sister too," Linda promised. "I just keep reminding myself that rules are for normal people, not the kind who save the world."

CHAPTER THREE

WE FINISHED WITH THE WEAPONS, got cleaned up, and headed to bed. School started again in the morning, and I wasn't ready for it. So, just to make my life easier, I picked out something to wear, checked my bag for my books and anything I might need, and then I crawled into bed and lay there.

Minutes ticked by. A door closed at the other end of the hall. I kept staring at the ceiling, even when I heard someone check their alarm ringtone. Next, I tried closing my eyes, but sleep still wouldn't come.

It wasn't just that my mind was on overdrive. It was simply that I didn't want to be alone. I missed the feel of the guys around me, the sound of their breathing, and that comfort that came from another person's mere presence in a room. So I gave up.

Slipping out of my bed, I didn't consciously choose where I was going. I simply headed down the hall and into Gavin's room. The entire floor was dark, but my eyes had already adjusted enough that I could see him flopped on his back in the middle of his bed. Slowly, he looked over at me, and a smile touched his lips.

"You too, huh?" he asked. "Can't sleep?"

I crawled under the covers and scooted over until I could tuck my head against his shoulder. "I needed something to cuddle with, I think."

His arm curled around my back, his fingers playing with the skin over my spine. "It's like touching makes it easier," he breathed. "Oh, and the necklaces work."

That last part caught me off guard. "What?"

Gavin just chuckled. "You are cambion." Using his other arm, he reached up to touch the masculine thing around his neck. "It's like there's some kind of focus on you, and I just was sure of it. As if I didn't know before, but in my brain, I almost heard the word, it was that clear."

I moved my arm so I could play with the long and narrow silver tube that served as the only ornamentation on his necklace. "Yours, Bax's, and Lars' almost look the same."

"Lars has two of the silver things," he explained. "Bax and I match."

"Beads," I said, offering the word. "I mean, I think that's what they're called." And then I yawned.

He chuckled softly. "And now you're tired." He hugged me just a little closer. "Go to sleep, *mi cielo*. I love you." He bent to kiss the top of my hair. "And thank you for saving me."

"I couldn't live without you," I whispered.

"I know," he agreed. "All or nothing. I'm not ready yet, but when I saw you on that ridge? When I knew you didn't mean to come back? It made me a little less scared to die, thinking that I'd still be with you."

I just pressed my face into his chest. "God, I love you, Gav. I also don't deserve you."

He wrapped his free hand around the palm on his chest - my left one. Slowly, his thumb traced the symbol scarred there. "I think this disagrees. We all deserve each other. It's why we're here." This time, he was the one who yawned. "Close your eyes. Let me just hold you."

I did. The feeling of being wrapped up in his arms was enough to make me finally relax. Before I knew it, I was asleep. If I dreamed, I didn't remember it. At some point, he rolled onto his side, so I shifted to match, spooning up against his back. That was the only thing I remembered until his phone began to softly jingle with a tone that gradually got louder.

Gavin moaned at it, but the volume kept growing, making it clear it wouldn't be ignored. Pulling away from me, he stretched to silence it, then came right back. Blinking, I managed to get my eyes to open, and wasn't surprised at all to find it was almost daylight. That meant time to get up for school.

"Why are we still doing this?" I asked.

"Because dropping out of school would get noticed," Gavin grumbled, forcing himself to sit up. Then he mumbled something in Spanish, and I was pretty sure one of those words meant "asshole."

"Who are you cussing about?" I teased as I rubbed the sleep from my eyes.

"Deke," he admitted. "No getting noticed. Half the demons in town already tried to kick our asses, but we can't get noticed by normal people."

"Because normal cops would throw us in jail for murder," I reminded him. "And we are talking about planning a few hits."

Gavin tossed off the blankets and got out of bed. "No bodies," he countered.

I let my eyes appreciate the way his boxers fit his ass. "Missing persons. That's almost as good as murder."

"Stop being right," he said, dropping his boxers to pull on another pair.

Yep, my eyes followed. Gavin wasn't all muscular like the other guys. He was fit, but like a swimmer or martial artist. Sculpted. He'd once said he didn't bulk up enough, but I disagreed. I liked the way he was shaped, including the deep creases at his hips that led right to his still morning-hard dick.

I was silently enjoying the view when a fist pounding on the door made me jump and Gavin's head snapped up. "It's Monday," Lars yelled at us.

"I'm up!" I called back.

And that made the door open. "Well, saves me a trip," Lars said as he smiled at me. "You know, you can sneak into my room too."

"Yep," I said as I slid out of the bed. "I also know that Gavin will let me sleep." As I walked past him and into the hall, I stuck my tongue out, making it clear I was picking on him.

But Lars caught my arm, stopping me. "Kiss first."

"Morning breath," I countered.

He just gave me a look like I should know better. So, giving in, I pressed a peck to his lips, which was enough to make him release me. It also put me in a pretty decent mood. There was something nice about this arrangement. I had three hot guys to gawk at, and they liked when I did it. Yep, I was living the dream.

Which was why I actually put some effort into how I looked that morning. My pants were tight the way Lars liked them. My shirt was soft but loose. My hair got left down, since I knew Bax preferred it that way. I put on my heeled boots that let me look Gavin in the eyes, and then I had a little fun with my makeup.

I was just finishing up when a soft tap sounded just before my door opened. My eyes checked the reflection, and then my lungs forgot to breathe. Grey sweats, one hell of a bulge, and a bare chest were the first things I saw. The scars told me it was Deke before I looked up to see his face.

"Coffee?" he asked, lifting a travel mug.

I turned on my chair to face him. "Thanks. Why are you awake?"

"Making sure my quad actually makes it to school," he admitted, his smile lopsided because of the scar on his face. It also looked like he wasn't all the way awake. "Which, I'd like to say, is a little weird."

"Why?" Because it wasn't as if school was a new thing.

He came the rest of the way into the room and closed the door behind him. "Because I feel like I'm too old to have a thing for a high school girl." And he held out the mug.

I took it, then took a sip. Yeah, that was a perfect cup of coffee, and my moan proved it. Deke chuckled once at my reaction, but he didn't move. The problem was that I didn't really know how to respond to what he'd just said.

So he kept going. "Tash and I had a talk last night. I made it clear that her comments about you won't be tolerated. You're a cambion. You're also Brethren and a part of this quad. If she can't accept that, then she can't accept me. She promises that she's ok with it." He paused to clear his throat. "I also made it clear that you're eighteen, and that means you can make your own decisions about who is or is not in your bed."

"What changed, Deke?" I asked. "You made it very clear that there wouldn't be anything else between us. I'm not picking a guy. I'm not going to stop being with them. What changed your mind?"

"You're *eighteen*," he growled, his hoarse voice making it sound even more intimidating. "You're putting on eyeliner to go to *school*. I don't give a shit if you're fucking Bax, Lars, and Gavin. In case you missed it, I kinda enjoyed watching."

"I was eighteen when you met me," I pointed out. "That hasn't changed, Deke."

He just sighed. "And you're still a *girl*. You're not even old enough to be a woman yet."

"Eighteen is still legal," I reminded him.

"There's a big difference between legal and grown up," he promised. Then his face winced and he huffed out a grunt. "No. That's not what I meant. You being cambion has never been a problem for me. You being in high school is. You being my responsibility is even more. I know I should keep my hands off you - and then, I saw you charge a demon in a basement with almost no training. I watched you fight so hard for your quad. You're not a little girl, even if you are still in high school. You are

Anathema, and this is me saying that I was wrong. You just have to figure out what you're going to do with that."

"Ok," I said, not quite sure how he expected me to respond to that. Taking another sip of my coffee gave me an excuse to change the subject to something safer. "What does Tash want the list of demons for?"

"Abominations," he corrected. "She wants to see what is really in this town. I can feel the demons, but that's all. With as many as were at the seal last weekend, there has to be more here. Witches, cambion, and so on."

"Why?" I pressed. "What is she going to do when she knows?"

"Figure out how to hit them tactically," he explained. "She'll make the maps, I'll make the plans."

I leaned back. "I'm not killing all abominations just because of what they..." I paused, seeing Bax ease my door open behind them. "...Are."

"We need to go," Bax said, glancing over at Deke's back and jerking his eyes right back to me.

There was definitely a little awkwardness still there from the other morning. Not that I could really blame Bax. I would be mortified if I'd started groping Deke in my sleep, and I'd fucked the guy. That didn't mean I had permission to do it again. Never mind the fact that it was Bax - or Deke.

"I'm ready," I promised, pushing to my feet, but I needed to make one thing clear. "I'm serious, Deke. The Order wants to kill me because of what I am. I'm not going to do the same to someone else who has no clue what they are. It's not fair, and it's not going to help us."

"Killing demons?" Bax asked, clearly figuring that out from what I'd said.

"Making a list of what's in Hellam," Deke corrected.

"Yeah, I'm with Jess on this," Bax said. "Those little shadows in my basement at the big house? Not evil. Jess? Not evil. So, if you want us to kill something, you make sure it's evil."

"I want to make sure that when you close the seal," Deke said, "you're not outnumbered. That's *it*. If I don't know what we're up against, who it is, and where they live, then our only option is to do the same fucking thing again and hope that this time it's not Jess who gets a set of talons in the back - because none of us can save her."

"We'll make a list," Bax agreed, "but I'm not just handing it over. In case you haven't figured it out yet, the Order's no longer running the show."

"We are," I agreed.

Bax gave me a proud smile, but Deke just sighed. "Hard to plan an assassination in the middle of the night if we don't know who and where, Bax. Trust me, or don't. I'm still going to do my best to keep you four alive."

"Because of Jess," Bax said, but there was something just a little too tense about his voice. Or maybe that was insistent. I couldn't be sure.

Deke threw up his hands and headed for the door, pushing past Bax to get through it. "This, Jess, is what I was talking about. Eighteen! Fuck!"

Bax just crossed the room to grab my bag. "Which means he's in a mood and it's time for us to leave. You ready for this?"

"Nope," I said. "I also have no clue how this necklace is supposed to work."

"Trust me." Bax pressed his hand to the middle of my back as he guided me up the hall. "It's pretty self-explanatory. You are a cambion."

Which didn't really help me at all.

CHAPTER FOUR

LARS DROVE to school that morning because Bax wanted to sit in the back with me. He kept his hand laced with mine until we pulled into the parking lot. Then he made sure to be the perfect gentleman, getting my bag out and carrying it for me. Since the weather was nice and it was the first day back after Spring Break, everyone was camped out in front of the school.

But before we could go near other people, we had to put on our hand coverings. Mine was a spandex support sleeve for my supposed tendonitis. Gavin had fingerless leather gloves in a very punk style. Bax didn't bother because his power didn't hurt people. It was Lars who usually had to be inventive. He'd been using the long sleeves of his shirts, but the weather was too nice to dress like that anymore.

Wearing a t-shirt showed off Lars' arms, and they looked so good. His muscles were just enough to be defined even when relaxed. His forearms were my favorite part, though. That I could see veins pressing against his copper skin only made them look better. The problem was that he didn't have anything on his hand.

"Uh, Lars?" I asked.

"I'm like Bax," he reminded me. "An accidental touch will just result in someone being fair. It doesn't hurt them. I'm also trying to learn how to control it. Deke said it was ok."

"What if someone asks about it?" Gavin wanted to know.

Lars grinned. "I'll show them the tattoo on my chest and call it a tribal thing. Usually makes people shut up pretty quick."

Which meant it was worth trying. So, together, the four of us headed for our usual table. Before we even made it there, I saw Shannon break off from her friends and make her way over. She reached us just as I hopped onto the metal table. Gav quickly claimed the spot beside me, leaving Bax and Lars standing before us.

"Hey!" Shannon said as she came over. Her smile was for me, but she included everyone in that little greeting. "You skipped all the parties?"

"Finished moving Linda's stuff around," Bax lied without hesitation. "That woman has some heavy-ass furniture."

Shannon just patted his shoulder. "Never thought I'd see the day when Bax Hale got boring." Then she grinned at me. "Dunno how you managed it, Jess."

"I had nothing to do with this," I insisted.

"Except for being the girl of my dreams," Bax countered. "Nope, nothing at all. Besides..." He smiled at Shannon. "We all know that I'd get myself in shit at a party."

"But maybe Jess wants to hang out and have fun with the rest of us?" she teased. "I actually came over here to let you four know that I'm dating Travis now. We kinda made out at Marie's party on Saturday, so it's not a secret."

"Good for him," Lars said.

"What about Linda?" Gavin asked. "If you're not with Shannon..."

"Then you can be with Jess," Shannon finished. "I mean, we all know Linda quit. Sucks, because she was cool, and that new idiot in the office is completely by the book, but still. It means you can stop pretending to be her brother now, right?"

"Not yet," Lars admitted. "Mom has a lawsuit. Sexual harassment stuff, because Mr. Garcia complained about Jess after Linda wouldn't go out on a date with him. Linda got written up for the fucking morality clause because she's Jess's legal guardian." He lifted a brow to make the point. His mom, my guardian. That was messy.

"Shit," Shannon breathed. "Fuck, I'm sorry. I just - "

"It's fine," Lars assured her.

"And it's not your job to worry about our mess," I added. "Shannon, I still don't know why you even care."

She ducked her head and smiled. "Well, Megan's downfall made it worthwhile. I dunno. I mean, captain of the basketball team or one of the bad boys? My reputation is doing pretty good right now." Then she waved that off, making it clear she'd just been joking. "Mostly, it's just because Bax and Gavin have always been cool to me."

I gave Bax a look because I *knew* he'd slept with her. He wouldn't talk about it, but there was just some casual acceptance between the two of them that I couldn't quite figure out any other way. Bax ignored me, although the curl to his lips made it clear he was aware of what I was thinking.

Gavin just chuckled. "You might as well tell her."

"You didn't?" Shannon gasped before smacking his arm. "Bax!"

"What?" he asked, dodging away from the hit. "I'm learning how to be a gentleman."

Shannon just groaned. "In tenth grade, Bax punched my ex for trying to sleep with me at a party. I was drunk. I was a virgin. He was drunk - the ex, not Bax. Well, Bax stepped up and was all heroic, then he took me home."

"My home," Bax clarified. "She was too smashed to go back to her place without her parents killing her."

"And he slept on the couch," Shannon finished. "The next morning, he took me home. I wasn't even old enough to drive."

"I'd just turned sixteen," Bax said. "Was pretty proud of being able to get myself around. I was just trying to show off my car."

"Bullshit," Shannon laughed. "You were being a gentleman. Of course, everyone said he fucked me, and Bax pretended like he had no clue what they were talking about. My best friend said I was with her, and yeah. Megan was pissed, and that started our little feud, which is why she started the abortion rumor later."

All the pieces were starting to make sense. "Wow. Ok," I breathed. "I just figured..."

"I'm friends with these guys," Shannon said. "Mostly because as much as they like to pretend they're pigs, they really aren't. Well, sorta."

"I'm a pig," Bax promised her. "I'm just honest about it."

"Gavin's not," I reminded him.

"Oh, and what am I?" Lars asked just as the first bell rang.

I hopped off the table and grabbed my bag. "My stepbrother, remember?"

"I am really starting to get a stepbrother kink," Lars joked. "I'm sure you've got a book like that, right?"

"Nope," I said. "But I am reading about some guy-on-guy stuff. There's a series by Kitty Cox, and I'll let you borrow it if you need ideas."

Shannon laughed as she stepped back. "Yeah, *I* need that one. Come to the next party, guys. It's more fun when you're there!"

"I'll think about it," Bax promised, lifting his hand in a wave as she left.

Lars picked up his own bag. "I just want to know when you have time to read, Jess."

"In class," I scoffed. "Not like I'm worried about my grades anymore."

But Gavin caught my arm before I could leave. "You forgot something, *mi cielo*."

ENTER SANDMAN

Turning, I stepped back into him. Both of my hands found his chest and I kissed that boy as hard as I could. He was ready for it, though. Our mouths met, our tongues swirled, and Bax groaned beside us. Lars just chuckled, but I didn't care about that. I couldn't get enough of touching Gavin.

It was like he made those fireflies come back. There was a rush, and while I wanted to call it magic, this was a very different kind. It was made from love and fueled by passion. I couldn't forget how close we'd come to losing him, and I couldn't talk about that at school, so I told him with my kiss.

"Ok..." Bax groaned. "Breathe, you two. We still have to be students for a few more months."

I pulled back and my eyes found Gavin's. "I love you."

"*Te amo tambien*," he whispered. "See you in third."

But when he stepped back, his hand slid all the way down my arm first, then our fingers felt like they got stuck. I didn't want to let go. I wasn't ready to be back here, trying to act normal again. For a moment, I felt the void between us as he turned away, but then Bax's arm came around my shoulders, pulling me against his side.

"I love you too, so you know," Bax said softly.

"It's not a competition," I assured him. "It's just..."

"I know." He rubbed my far arm reassuringly. "I can't forget the sight of him gasping on the table. I get it."

"Yeah." And I pressed my head against his shoulder. "It just feels like something changed in that moment, you know? Like, between us."

"Good or bad?" he asked.

I shrugged. "I want to say good, but the why makes it a little bad. I dunno. You and Lars didn't hesitate. And now all I can think is that we all shared something so big."

"Souls," he breathed, stepping away as we reached my locker. "Yeah, kinda explains why I can't keep my hands off you, huh? I mean, in a hand holding and hugging sort of way."

"Sure you do." I laughed as I traded out my books for my first class. We both knew he wanted a lot more than just hand holding. "And if you want to make it on time, you should probably get going." Grabbing my book for first period, I closed my locker and stepped back.

Bax just cupped the side of my face. "Fuck school." Then he leaned in and kissed me softly.

I relaxed into it. Bax was always the hard and fast kind of guy. He knew how to seduce and was damned good at it, but this was different. This was more, deeper, and filled with emotion. It was gentle, not meant to turn me on, but rather to make sure I knew how he felt - and I did. I felt the same way.

"I love you," I whispered as our lips parted.

He tipped his head to press his brow to mine. "I know."

We both laughed at the same time, but it was enough to let us split apart. "Get to class, Han Solo," I said as I turned in the other direction.

"Nerd!" he called back, but it didn't sound like an insult. Nope, he made that sound like the best compliment ever.

This was a good way to start school again. Maybe it was crazy, but I did like the new softness to my guys. Not that I hadn't enjoyed their arrogance and egos before, but I wanted both. It made me feel like all of this was real and actually happening to *me*. Like it was a dream come true.

I was smiling wistfully as I headed to my first class of the day, thinking about how much it sucked that Lars and I were still hiding our relationship. Some of it was just my own pride. I wanted to kiss all three of them in school and let everyone know I'd caught them. I liked the fact that I'd somehow gone from nobody to the girl with the three hottest guys in school. I also hated that I couldn't say three. I had to pretend like Lars and I were just friends, nothing more.

But as I turned into the main hall, it felt like a pressure popped in my head, making me look up. Not my ears or my nasal cavities, but my actual head! Gavin was wrong - there wasn't a word, but I somehow just *knew* that there was a demon near me. I couldn't stop thinking about it, so I turned back, scanning the student body, trying to figure out how I'd be sure.

That had to be my necklace. This was the whole reason we were wearing them, but how the fuck was I supposed to pick a person out of a crowd like this? And then I saw it. Like a spot of brightness or a bit more shadows - a sensation I couldn't even describe to myself - I found the person moving in the opposite direction.

I didn't think. I didn't stop to consider how dumb of an idea this was. I just hugged my book to my chest and turned around, following that moving blob of "different." Just to be safe, I hooked the fingers of my right hand into the sleeve hiding my left. If this went bad, I'd pull it off and let this monster see just how strong I was on my own.

Then he turned down a side hall. I couldn't tell who it was, but I saw enough to know it was a guy. Jogging to catch up, I went the same way. Down here, there were fewer students, and the grey shirt moving before me was definitely being worn by a demon. A familiar one. Oh, shit. I knew him!

"Travis?" I asked.

He paused, turning back with a smile on his face. "Hey, Jess. I didn't think you had a class this way."

I didn't care about any of that, because the necklace was screaming at me. It was adamant that this was what I was seeing, and yet the guy standing before me was the same friend who'd I'd talked to countless times before.

"You're a demon?" I asked.

His eyes went big and he hurried to close the distance between us. "Shh, we don't talk about that in school."

Which meant yes. It meant he *was* one, and I hadn't had a clue. What the actual fuck?

CHAPTER FIVE

TRAVIS WRAPPED his arm around my shoulders and guided me to the side of the hall, away from the students still heading to class. I went, but my mind was spinning. Of all the people at school, it was him? He'd been so cool with us. He'd known Bax forever, and I was pretty sure they called each other *friends*.

"Did you just find out or something?" he asked. "I was pretty sure Ted was trying to keep you out of all this, but when you started hanging around Bax, I wasn't sure."

"You know about my dad too?" I gasped.

He ducked his head and chuckled. "Yeah, um, he's a pretty big deal in our community. He guards the gate from the Brethren."

But wait. Things weren't adding up. "So if you're worried about the Brethren, then why do you talk to Bax?"

"Same reason you do," he assured me. "Look, if we know where they are, then they can't sneak up on us. I just figured that if we're friends - and Bax *is* pretty cool - then it might make him hesitate long enough for me to get away. If I know what he's doing, I can stay a step ahead."

My head was bobbing up and down on auto-pilot, trying to

rattle all of that into place. "So you know about the rest of the Brethren?"

"Yeah." He chuckled, the sound meant to be kind. "Unlike you, I was born hearing about all this stuff. I'm guessing you got a crash course recently or something? Just be careful. I'm pretty sure that Gavin, Lars, and that other guy Bax moved in make up this quad. I mean, Bax doesn't try to hide his mark at all, but - "

"Deke?" I asked. "No, he's the Sandman."

"The what?" Travis asked.

"Martyr," I corrected. "*I'm* Anathema."

Travis's hand dropped from my arm, his eyes went wide, and he stepped back. "But..." He blinked, then shook his head. "Ted's your dad. You're..." Then he dropped his voice. "...Cambion. Jess, we're what they hunt."

"Yes to being cambion," I said. "No to the hunting. Look, you remember when I was out for a week because Dad went to jail?"

"Uh huh," Travis said. "He started hanging out with a couple other greaters around that time. I sent Lars a heads-up to stay on his good side."

There was so much there. Travis was playing us? Well, not really, but it sure sounded like he was going out of his way to be nice to save his own skin. Never mind that I had no interest in killing him just because of what he was. Shit, we were feeding the babies in Bax's basement, for fuck's sake!

"Yeah," I breathed, deciding to just file all of that away. "Well, Dad came over that weekend and kinda lost his skin. Surprise, your father has four eyes, you know? But I've had this mark on my hand since I was fourteen." I lifted my spandex covered arm to prove the point. "Travis, they all know I'm half demon. I mean, they were there when I found out. Wait." My eyes narrowed. "You were at the seal?"

"I was not," he promised.

"But you saw the map," I shot back.

"I did," he agreed. "I recognized the seal almost immediately. I figured you were trying to scope out their plan too, since cambion are undetectable. I mean, you're sleeping with Conquest!"

"Did you tell the rest?" I demanded. "Was that why there were so many there?"

"Fuck," he huffed. "No! I told my guardians, and they told a few others - because we wanted to stay far, far away from that shit. Not all demons are looking to pick a fight, ok? Your father is the head of those who believe we should conquer the world, making it a new home for demonkind, but some of us like it just the way it is."

"So you weren't there?" Because if he'd been involved in any way, I was pretty sure that would put an end to any friendship we may have had. I needed to be very, very sure of this one thing.

Travis blew out a breath, stepped back, then flopped against the wall. "Jess, I'm eighteen years old. I've only had one molt. I'm a lesser demon, which means that any of those four - you four, I guess - could kill me on sight. I'll molt into a common around twenty, give or take. That's when I'll have enough power to be more than a minor nuisance."

"I don't really have the demonic orders down yet," I admitted.

"Minor are basically toddlers. Little kids. Light burns us at that age because we don't have solid enough bodies. Um, around ten to thirteen, we molt into lesser demons." He kept whispering the demon part. "It's like our version of puberty. Commons are next. They're basically adults, and greaters are the ones who've lived more than a human lifetime. Power grows with each molt. All I'm saying is that I'm about as weak as Megan, ok? No real superpowers. I can start a campfire, but that's the extent of my parlor tricks. I. Was. Not. There. Mostly because I don't want to die, and both sides would tear me apart. See, not all demons agree, and disagreeing with someone like your father is a death sentence."

"Disagreeing about what?" I pressed.

"This. All of this," he told me. "Look, I'm just trying to keep my nose out of shit long enough to graduate, get a career that will take me to the middle of nowhere, and then try to pretend like I'm a normal guy. That's *it*. I just don't want to go back there, because they will eat me. That's why my mom got me out, and I'd rather die than go back." He caught my arm. "Please don't tell them?"

"Who?"

"The Brethren," he whispered. "They'll kill me. It's what they do."

So I clasped his arm back, right at the bicep. "No, it's not what *we* do. Travis, I'm half."

"I'm whole," he countered.

"So? Are you evil? Did you try to kill Gav? If you weren't there, then you're fine."

But his head twitched. "Someone tried to kill Gav?"

"Yeah, but we got him put back together. Look, it was a bad Spring Break, and we all have these enchanted necklaces now." I touched the pendant at my throat. "So, unless you bail now, they're going to know. The moment they see you in the halls, there will be no question what you are. I'm also going to tell them, but I'm pretty sure they won't care."

"Shit," he breathed, tugging his arm back. "Fuck!"

"Just talk to us at lunch?" I asked, stepping back. "I dunno, truce until then? I'll give the guys a heads-up, and you can make your case or something? Because I have questions, Travis, and I think you're the only one who can answer them."

"Here?" he asked. "I mean, the cafeteria."

"Same place we always eat." Another step, because the halls were now empty enough that I knew the bell would ring any second. "We already know, so it's not like you have anything to lose, right?"

He pushed out a breath. "Ok. Lunch." Then he turned and hurried to his class.

I spun and started jogging the other way. Travis was a demon? Ok, a teen demon, and not one of the kinds who'd tried to rip us apart, but still. He'd said so many things, and so easily, that it meant he understood all of this stuff. What if he also understood my magic?

Shit, what if he could actually help us?

For me, it was hard to imagine that he'd suddenly become a horrible and evil person. I hadn't when I found out what I was. My father had always been an asshole. I honestly believed that nothing had changed except my awareness of who Travis really was. It would be no different than him telling me he was trans or something. The information might take a bit to get used to because of my preconceived notions, but it didn't change him. And if I could be half demon and not evil, then I had to believe that everyone could.

I made it to class after the bell had rung. I told the teacher I'd forgotten the combination to my locker, which earned me an eye-roll, but not a detention. Then, just to make sure that things didn't blow up between now and then, I pulled out my phone and sent all of the guys a text.

> **Jess:** Travis is going to talk to us at lunch. Truce until then. I'll say more when I see you.

I didn't get a response, but I didn't expect to either. Then, while my class went on about our latest lesson, I managed to tuck my Kindle onto my lap and sneak in a couple more chapters of *Converge,* that book I'd told Lars about. It made the class pass a lot faster, but I had to keep half my attention on the teacher. When the bell finally rang, I was up and headed to my next class with my mind still on Travis.

I didn't see another demon in the halls, nor anything else. When I got to second period, I dropped into my chair and waited, then waited a little more. Lars finally showed up and slid into the spot next to me before leaning closer.

"What is going on with Travis?" he asked.

"Demon," I whispered.

Lars' eyes flared. "What?"

I just nodded. "He wasn't there on Saturday. Look, I felt something and followed it before first period - "

"Alone?" he asked.

I gave him a disgusted look. "Yeah, but I was ready to bare my palm, ok? I'm not stupid."

He lifted his hands in surrender. "Fair point, but do you really blame me for being twitchy?"

"No," I conceded. "I'm kinda the same. All I know is that he's a lesser, he wasn't there, and he doesn't agree with my dad. I told him we have a truce so we can talk at lunch, because he looked like he was ready to bail."

"And he just offered this up?" Lars asked.

"No," I admitted. "Um, he thought the Brethren were Bax, Gav, you, and Deke. He assumed I was trying to get on your good side. Like, eavesdrop to get intel and make you like me so you might not think about what I am."

Lars just nodded his head slowly. "There's so much wrong with all of that."

"I know." I reached over for his hand. "But he knows this stuff, Lars. What if he might know my stuff too?"

"Like, how to do... it?" he asked, not wanting to say magic with people all around us.

I nodded. "I just think it's worth asking, and how many times has he helped us?"

"But we still don't know who took that video that pissed Ted off in the first place," he reminded me. "Was that an insurance policy?"

"He was there," I pointed out. "Can't take a video from a car if he was right there with us."

"No, you're right," Lars agreed. "I'm just worried about Gavin and how he's going to handle this."

"We all are, but Gavin's not the weak one here."

"You're not either," Lars pointed out. Then he realized what I was hinting at. "Shit. Bax?"

I bobbed my head in a silent yes. "They're friends. They've been friends since like ninth grade. I know firsthand how much betrayal hurts, so maybe you can work on that?"

"If you make sure Gav's ok," Lars said. "And Travis is cool, but if I have to pick sides?" He pointed at me. "So if you think we should give him a chance, then I'm ok with it. If you decide he needs to go, then I won't hesitate."

"He didn't ask to be born," I reminded Lars. "He's no different than me."

"You don't know that," he countered. "I know you're fine, but people lie, Jess. All kinds of people. They promise they won't have another drink, won't hit you again, and everything else. I'm not blaming what he is any more than I'm blaming what you are. I'm just saying that people suck, and Bax is right about one thing."

"What's that?" I asked.

Lars smiled. "I will let the whole world burn to take care of you. We all will. That's why we work. If Travis is on the wrong side, he can burn too."

"I'm actually ok with that plan," I decided just as the teacher walked in.

CHAPTER SIX

THE MOMENT I made it into third period, Gavin wanted to know what was going on. That made me think Travis had been avoiding the guys all day. Smart move, in my opinion. But before I could answer him, Mr. Garcia started class. The man's eyes hung on me and his face looked even more grumpy than usual. Most likely because he'd been told that Linda really was suing the school district for his sexual harassment of her.

But with my teacher watching me like a hawk, I couldn't exactly talk to Gavin. The moment our class was over, I canted my head toward the hall, Gavin nodded, and we both hurried out of the room. We were barely through the door when his arm found my waist, pulling me against his side.

"What's going on with Travis?" he asked. "Most of all, why do we need a truce?"

I waited to answer for a bit, until we weren't packed together with so many people. Oddly, Gavin didn't push. His pretty olive-colored eyes kept sliding over to check on me, but he didn't complain. The moment I felt it was safe enough, I leaned in and lowered my voice.

"After last week," I said, "how are you feeling about demons in general?"

"They aren't my favorite," he admitted, but it was with a little smirk. A weak one, but it was still there. "Why, Jess?"

"Because I figured out how the necklaces work, Gav. Travis is one."

Gavin's feet stopped hard, and his arm around my waist made sure I stopped with him. "What?"

"Locker," I reminded him. "We need to put our things away. I talked to Lars in second, and he's going to warn Bax, but I want to be there when Travis comes to talk to us."

Gavin's head moved, but I couldn't tell if that was a nod, a shake, or something else. It looked more like he was trying to digest what I'd just said and it didn't taste good. Still, he started walking again, letting me lead him to my locker.

"Gav?" I pressed when he was quiet for a little too long.

"I died, Jess," he said. "A demon killed me."

I shoved my bag into my locker then turned to face him. "I know. That's why I didn't want you to walk into this without knowing. Still, it's Travis."

"Was he there?" he asked.

"No," I assured him. "That was my first question too. I was going to touch him if he was, but he said he's just trying to get out of here. He's not much more than the shadows in the basement, ok? Just a kid, kinda like us."

He pushed out a heavy breath. "Yeah. I guess I just thought I'd have a little more time before I had to think about that again."

"I know," I said again, catching his hand and lacing my fingers with his. "And I know we're all trying to pretend like we're fine, but it's ok not to be."

He just nodded slowly. "I'm alive."

"And my fireflies are coming back," I promised. "The more I'm with you guys, the easier it is to reach them. There's one of him and four of us, and I will not let him hurt you."

Gavin chuckled at that. "I'm supposed to be protecting you, Jess."

"It goes both ways," I assured him. "I kinda prefer us protecting each other. Gav, I don't want to be a weak little girl. I don't want to be the pity case. I want to be a badass hero who can fight her own battles with her equally strong men at her side, ok? Besides, I saw it. When the demon hit you, I'd just looked over. You were protecting us. You had your turn. Let me have this?"

"Bax was right," he said, moving a little closer. "You're not fragile. You look like it, and you aren't the way I imagine a badass woman to look, but you're not fragile." He reached over my head and closed my locker. "I'm ok."

"I want to know what a badass woman is supposed to look like," I teased.

Gavin just wrapped his arm around me again and turned us toward the cafeteria. "Combat boots," he said. "Hates makeup. She's supposed to be a... shit." His brow furrowed. "Not butch. Not manly. The girls who like boy things?"

"Tomboy," I offered.

He nodded. "One of those. She doesn't care about being popular, hates anything cool, listens to weird music, and is a loner."

But my eyes narrowed. "Have you been reading my books too?"

"Yeah, uh..." He flashed me a boyish grin. "I just wanted to see where the people go during sex. Some of the words are stupid, though. I don't like turgid. It doesn't make me think of dicks. Slick is a good one, though."

I huffed out a laugh. "Gavin!"

"What?" he asked, clearly teasing me. "Lars and Bax said I should. Then Deke said something about - " His mouth snapped shut.

"About what?" I pressed.

"Touching," he mumbled. "If we're with you, and he's there, then where we fit and how we might touch."

"It's not gay," I assured him. "And if it is, so what?"

"I'm *not gay*," he insisted. "I'm with you. They're with you. I've seen the bonds, and I know this is how it works best, but I don't want to fuck a guy!"

"So don't fuck one," I told him. "You aren't required to crash with the rest of us, you know. I keep ending up in your room."

"No, I like that," he assured me. "It's just..." Then his breath fell from his lungs, his eyes closed, and his feet paused.

We'd just rounded the corner into the cafeteria, and I felt it too. Demon. Whatever enchantment Tash had gotten on these things worked a little too well. There was no way to ignore it. My eyes scanned the area, and I found Travis talking to Shannon. Beside me, Gavin took a deep breath, recovering from that, and we both started walking to our normal table again.

"It's not that insistent about you," he admitted. "I just know it's you. That? It's a warning."

"Good to know," I said as we made it to our table. "But we're not done with that other topic."

"Which other?" Lars asked, clearly having heard.

"Personal!" I huffed before smiling to make sure he knew I wasn't upset.

Lars just thrust out his lower lip and nodded. "Ok. I can take a subtle hint." But his eyes jumped over my shoulder.

Beside me, Bax lifted his head, but before he could turn, Travis found the last empty chair at our table and slid into it. The guy looked nervous, and I couldn't honestly blame him. Lars, Bax, and Gavin were all looking at him in a new way - like they wanted to rip his arms and legs off.

Travis's eyes jumped across their necks. "Ok," he said. "So, I'm guessing I should just put it out there. I'm a lesser. Um, Bax, I know you have the crown of Conquest. Jess said she's Anathema." Then he looked at Gavin and Lars. "I thought it was you three guys and that other one."

"Deke," I clarified for the rest.

"No, he's our Martyr," Bax said. "How long have you fucking known, Travis?"

"Remember that night our freshman year when we were all hanging out at the creek? Like, the football players were having a big party, and we were drinking beer down in the cattle pasture?"

"That was like the second time we ever talked," Bax said.

Travis nodded. "Yeah, but that's when I saw it. I mean, you seemed cool, but I was going into sports, hoping to get a scholarship to college. I mean, it's not like we have that shit on the other side of the gate, so it sounded fun."

"Wait," Lars said. "When did you come out?"

"Shit," Travis breathed. "I was little. I dunno, like six years old? Maybe five, almost six. Right around there. I know I ended up in the basement of Bax's place. It's kinda the closest spot to get out of the light."

"And light hurts," I added.

Bax was nodding. "How do you know to go there, and how do you get in?" he asked.

"Someone usually points us that way," Travis explained. "No, let me start at the beginning. The Pit of Hell? Yeah, it's not that big. It's packed. Bigger things eat smaller ones, so we hover around our mothers. Most of my brood became a snack. When the crack showed again, my mother pushed me out. I had a sister make it through too, but she died on this side. A common was herding us toward the house, but we didn't understand. There aren't stars down there. No trees. It's a completely alien world, and then we're back in darkness."

"The basement," Gavin said softly.

Travis nodded. "Yeah. From there, we're gathered up, checked out, and then sent to live with guardians. They pretend to be our parents. The problem is that we can't look like kids until we're around human puberty, and then it's pretty inconsistent. We have to molt first, so we can get enough power to do that sort of magic."

"Making a body," Bax realized. "So how old are you?"

"Eighteen," Travis assured him. "I also didn't have leukemia as a kid. I wasn't in and out of hospitals. That was the story my guardians - who I call my parents in public - told everyone. It's also why I didn't go to public school until ninth grade."

"Were you there?" Gavin asked, his voice oddly detached. "You saw the map. You knew what day. Did you tell them? Did you try to kill us?"

"No," Travis promised. "I saw Saturday, and I told my guardians to stay away. Look, I have no interest in killing anyone."

"So why did you get to be such good friends with me?" Bax asked.

"Because I hoped like hell that maybe it would make you give me a chance," Travis said. "When I first saw your mark, I knew what it was. Conquest. We learn that shit pretty early on. Brethren kill us. We don't stand a chance until we're greaters. I thought you were cool, I actually enjoy talking to you, and I hoped like fuck that our friendship might be enough for you to tell me to run instead of killing me." He swallowed, clearly nervous. "And I thought Jess was doing the same thing."

"Why?" Lars asked.

Travis gave him a look like he was stupid. "Because she's the Devourer's kid. She's a cambion. That means she's one of us, not one of you."

"She's ours," Gavin said, and the warning was obvious.

"And I'm not brave enough to piss off Ted," Travis assured him. "Look, I'll drop out of school today and head out of town. I'll tell my guardians, and they'll vanish too. We're not looking to pick a fight with you. We just want to survive, ok?"

"And you can't do that in Hell?" Bax asked.

"No," Travis said. "The strong get stronger and the weak get devoured. That's how Ted got his name. He earned it in the Pit by eating his way to the top. He killed everyone he could, grew, molted, and kept going. They say that by the time he made it up top, he was a greater who'd had an extra molt. He's not someone we fuck with. If Ted talks to us, we say 'yes, sir,' and kiss his fucking ass."

"Because of his magic?" I asked. "Is that what makes Dad so strong?"

"Among other things," Travis admitted. "He has a lot of magic, and he's perfected what he uses, but he's also strong. His form is lethal. He has no qualms about who he hurts. He has survived, but he's not interested in teaching others how to do the same. He only cares about making sure he doesn't die."

"What about your magic?" I asked.

That made all three of my guys look at me. "What are you doing, Jess?" Bax asked.

"Travis has to have magic, right? All demons do?"

"We do," Travis admitted. "It's how we make our human bodies. The problem is the size. Think of it like a glass. As a minor demon, we have little sippy cups. They don't hold much, but it's all we need. As a lesser, I have more, but it's a coffee cup. When I molt into a common, I'll have a sixteen ounce glass, right? Well, as a greater, I'll get one of those supersized things. Sixty-something ounces, and more if I can keep pushing it. I have magic, but what good is it? I can push the magical elements a bit, but I can't do much before I'm worn out."

"But you know how it works," I said. "Do you know how mine works?"

"Shit," Gavin said. "You were a force of nature out there, Jess."

"And I barely know what I'm doing," I reminded him. "Tash is going off of what we've seen mages do, not what we know is possible."

"I know a little," Travis said. "I know you take the elemental magic and cast it like a witch. Fireballs and shit like from video games. Lightning bolts and things like that."

Lars sat up a little straighter. "She can cast lightning bolts?"

"Yeah..." Travis said, looking at all of us.

Because Bax was starting to smile. Lars looked a little shocked. Gavin looked like he approved of this idea. Me? I was starting to make plans.

"So, you willing to help the enemy?" I asked.

Travis narrowed his eyes. "You?"

"Me," I agreed. "I need someone to explain all of this mess to me, and I have a feeling that the Order of Martyrs is full of shit. They hate me. We don't know what I can do. I want to close the seals so the Horsemen don't get out, and I can't do that if a couple dozen demons are trying to kill me first."

"Full immunity for me and my guardians?" Travis asked.

"What will you do with it?" Gavin asked.

"Gav, we just want to live. Yeah, I'd like the seal to stay open, because I know there are a hundred more kids in there like me. I also understand about the Horsemen. Those fuckers will kill all abominations, so the seals have to be closed - but I got out. I'd like to stay out. I like blue skies, and trees, and girlfriends! I just want to live the same way you do. That's why I wasn't at the seal. I'm not going to try to stop you from closing it."

"And when Ted finds out you're helping us?" Lars asked.

Travis blew out a breath. "Then I hope that the Brethren really are stronger than demons, because I'd be fucked either way. I mean, shit. A quad is supposed to blow into town, deal with that shit and move on. You're not supposed to go to school with me!" He paused to lick his lips. "Or be people I'd call friends."

"After school," Gavin said, "come to our place. Sounds like there's a lot my girl needs to know."

"Gav?" I asked. "Are you sure you're ok with this?"

He just pointed at Travis. "He knows how your magic works, Jess. If he can help you learn anything, then yeah. Maybe it'll make it easier when Lars gets cut down, or Bax." Then he caught my hand. "Or you. I can't heal you, so if this means you're safe, then I'm definitely ok with it."

"And no need for combat boots," I said, trying to make it a joke.

Gavin actually chuckled. "I like you in heels better."

"Then I'll be there," Travis promised. "I might be scared shitless, but I'll still be there."

CHAPTER SEVEN

The rest of the day felt like it dragged on, but we made it through. The moment the last bell of the day rang, we all headed to my locker, packed away our books, then hurried to the car. Bax said that he'd reminded Travis to come to our place and made sure there wasn't basketball practice today, so we wanted to get there first.

It was a little weird to coordinate talking to a demon around his basketball practice, though. It was crazy to think that a few months ago I'd been worried about my grades and going to college. Back then, my monsters had been abusive people. Now, they were actual demons. My life had become a paranormal romance novel!

Which was kinda cool, if I was honest, but it did nothing to prepare me for how to deal with this. Still, since we'd made it through school, that meant we'd be back in training. So the moment I got home, I went to put on some athletic wear. The guys split for their own rooms, clearly intending to do the same.

Seeing us all pile through the house made Deke give us a confused look. Bax just yelled that we had a friend coming over in a bit, and then I was in my room. From the sounds of doors shutting, the same was true for the rest of them. I'd just pulled on my sports bra and was standing there in my panties when I heard a knock at the front door.

Cursing under my breath, I yanked on my pants and scrambled to get a shirt. I pushed my arms into the sleeves as I headed to my bedroom door, but I could hear someone moving up the hall. Ok, so Travis would be let in. Ducking my head through the hole, I pulled my shirt down my ribs and made it into the hall just as the front door opened.

"Hey, is Bax..." That was Travis's voice.

"Demon!" Deke snarled.

Travis yelped. I was running that way. Another door opened behind me in the hall, making it clear I hadn't been the only one listening, but Travis was retreating.

"Shit. Knew this was a bad idea. Fuck, I'm going!"

"Travis!" I yelled, hoping to get him to stop.

I made it onto the front porch area to see Deke with his sword in his hand, making his way down the stairs. Travis was back on the ground and hurrying to his car, but Deke was in full attack mode. I didn't even think. I just rushed down before him and shoved both hands into his chest, making our Sandman stop.

"Travis, it's fine!" I yelled.

"He is a *demon*," Deke snarled.

I just nodded. "Yeah. Kinda why I asked him to come over. I need someone to tell me about that crap, and you don't know it."

Deke grabbed the side of my neck with his free hand - hard - pulling my face right up to his. "They're not your *friends*, Jess."

"And I'm not evil," I reminded him, lifting my chin just a bit. "He's just a lesser. Not even something for you to worry about, right?"

His eyes dropped to my throat and his jaw clenched. "That boy dares to step out of line..." he warned, his rough voice sounding a little too much like a growl.

But Travis had turned around. "Let her go!" he yelled.

And then he pushed. A rush of air hit us hard enough to shove me back. Deke had to let go to keep us from falling on the stairs. For a heartbeat, we both leaned, and then the air was gone. I looked down to see Travis braced and ready. Deke didn't even bother with that. He lifted the sword in his right arm and moved to chase the little demon off our property.

Bax's hand dropped onto Deke's shoulder, holding him back. "Easy, Sandman. He gets a pass for that."

"Like fuck he does," Deke snapped.

"You having your hand around Jess's throat?" Bax countered. "No, I'm with Travis on this. Besides, he's our guest. This is still my place. Put your dick away and get over it. He's not evil."

"He's a fucking demon," Deke shot back.

"Yeah, and you're a Martyr," Travis said. "You've killed more people than I ever will."

"Demons aren't people!" Deke yelled.

I just smacked his chest. "Fuck you, Deke."

"You're not a demon," he reminded me. "Cambion are different."

"Oh, *now* I'm different? Is it because I have a pussy? Or because you need my magic? Ever stop to think that maybe Travis is here to explain that magic to me?"

Gavin just cleared his throat. "He's our friend."

Deke's head dropped down to his chest in defeat. "Fine, but only because I know you can kill him." Then he turned and stormed back upstairs.

"Sorry about that," Bax said as he headed down.

I followed, with Gavin right behind me, and Lars stepped through the front door, making it clear he'd been right there, waiting. Travis just pushed out an anxious breath, then scrubbed at his face. The guy looked like he'd just had the fright of his life.

"He's on your side?" he asked.

"Yep," Lars said. "He's the one training us."

"He tried to choke Jess," Travis said. "I wanted to push him back, but..."

"He's protected," Gavin said. "Martyrs have a minor resistance to magic."

"So do Brethren," Travis said. Then he huffed out another heavy breath. "Ok, my heart's racing now. I was sure this was a set up for a second there."

"It's not," Bax promised, tilting his head at the stairs. "Want to come up, have a beer or coffee, and talk about this?"

Travis chuckled, but the sound was dry. "That's not going to happen."

"Why?" Lars asked absentmindedly.

But the moment he said it, I understood. "Because the place is warded against demons. Dad could barely make it in, and Travis can't cross the threshold."

"Yeah," Travis admitted. "So you know, there's also a revulsion ward around here. I turned up the driveway and wanted to go right back home." He licked his lips. "That's demonic."

"Dad," I mumbled.

"Probably," Travis agreed. "It's his kind of magic."

So Bax gestured around the corner. "Well, we have a yard and chairs over here. Probably more comfortable than standing in the drive."

"Thanks," Travis said as we all began to head toward the back yard. "I'm sorry, but this is weird. The whole thing. The fact that I'm even talking to you, let alone here is insane. You're supposed to kill me."

"And you're supposed to kill us," Gavin pointed out.

"Actually, I'm supposed to run," Travis admitted. "Commons and above fight. I don't stand a chance against your hands. I probably shouldn't be telling you that, but - "

A woman's voice cut him off. "What the fuck?!"

It came from the garage, and Tash followed right after with a gun already in her hand. I didn't even think - and neither did the guys. The four of us just moved to shield Travis. It was Gavin who grabbed the guy's arm, holding him behind us.

"Move," Tash ordered.

"Put it down, Tash," I said. "He's here to help me."

"He's a demon," she said, letting go of the gun with one hand so she could touch her necklace.

"Figured that out," Lars assured her. "Hence his help."

"Move," she said again.

From the shadows of the garage, Linda made a noise before hurrying out. "Put that weapon down, Tash. You will not point a gun at my kids!"

The muzzle dropped a bit. "Linda, that's a demon."

"I don't give a shit," Linda said, the profanity like a whip cracking. "If you shoot my kids, then I will shoot you."

Surprisingly, that made Tash chuckle. Lowering the weapon the rest of the way, she turned to look at Linda. "Do you even know where we keep the guns?"

"I helped clean and put them away, so yes," Linda assured her. "I don't necessarily know how to aim one, but I'm sure I could figure it out. Now, stop terrorizing the kids."

"What's going on?" Travis asked.

Lars chuckled. "Yeah, Travis, meet my mom. Mom? This is Travis, he's a friend from school and a demon. He's here to help Jess."

"With her magic?" Linda asked.

Travis just tossed up his hands and started walking toward the grassy area we called a yard. "I'm done. That's it. Everything I thought I knew! Fuck!"

"Wait, wait, wait..." Lars said, running after him. "Trav, it's cool. Mom knows about Ted too. She was there."

The other guys followed, but I wasn't about to just leave Tash to try something worse. As they disappeared to explain the way of things around here to Travis, I marched right up to Tash, reached over, and flicked on the safety for her gun. She didn't try to stop me, but she didn't look pleased either.

"What are you four doing?" Tash demanded.

"The necklaces work, Travis is a demon, and he's been cool with us for long enough that I'm willing to take a risk," I explained. "You don't know anything about how my magic works. I'm not about to ask my dad. We just learned that I'm not powerful enough to stop all the demons in Hellam, which means we have to try something else, right?"

"Right," she said, sounding like she was waiting for the other shoe to drop.

"This is something else," I said. "He wasn't there, Tash. He's already said that some of the demons don't care about us closing the seal. They know we have to because of the Horsemen. They also know it needs to crack because of the kids. Did you know demons eat each other?"

"I did," Tash admitted. "That's how your father earned his name. He ate Martyrs and Brethren too."

I made a face because that was just disgusting. That it was my dad somehow made it worse. "Regardless," I said, refusing to think about that too hard, "the ones who get out young just want to live. I'm sure some of them are bad, but not all of them. I mean, I'm not evil. I don't care if you agree, because we're the Brethren here. You're supposed to be helping us, not the other way around."

"You're supposed to be helping the Order," she reminded me.

I just smiled deviously. "Oh, c'mon, Tash. The Order? How many times do we have to go over this? Maybe we'll be team 'Martyr' when they change their stance on abominations. But until then, what exactly is the Order giving *us* to make us think helping them is a good idea? We're the ones with the power. We're the ones who can do this, and there won't be another quad until we die, right?"

"And if you don't play by their rules, the Order will remove you," Tash warned.

I caught that one little word she'd used. "*Their* rules." Lifting a brow, I made sure she realized what she'd said. "And their rules mean that the ones who work the hardest get shit on the most, right? In case you haven't figured it out yet, I know how to play the good girl. That doesn't mean I want to be one. I'm tired of having people push me around and threaten me to get their way."

"He's still a demon," Tash said. "Jess, you have no idea how dangerous that boy is."

Linda finally decided to speak up. "More or less than the kids?"

When Tash canted her head and grimaced, I knew that Linda had just hit on something. Tash didn't want to admit she was right. She also wasn't ready to accept Travis, though.

"Tell yourself that we're using him," I suggested. "Tash, it doesn't matter if he's our friend or enemy. I'm a cambion. I have magic that saved both Gavin's and Deke's lives. I was able to get us out of there when everything went wrong. I need to use this, right?"

"You do," Tash conceded.

"And you don't really know about it. You can research what effects have been seen, but you have no clue how to help me make them happen, right?"

"Right," she grumbled.

"Travis does." I let that hang between us to make the point. "He's scared, he was ready to run, but he not only showed up to help, he also tried to push Deke off me."

"What," Linda snarled, "did that man do?"

I lifted a hand, calming her down. "He was being emphatic, Linda. That's it. Travis just thought he was going to hurt me and tried to help. That counts for something, right?"

"That man!" Linda groaned, turning back for the garage. "First, he's sleeping with a teenager, and now he's pushing her around? You tell those boys I'll bring down snacks in a bit. First, I'm going to give Deke a piece of my mind."

Tash sighed around a chuckle, the sound a little weary. "Which means I'd better go save him. Just... Be careful, Jess?"

"I promise I won't let anyone hurt my guys, Tash."

That made the corner of her lip curl higher. "And how many are you claiming now?"

"All of them," I promised. "I'm still deciding whether or not you're worth fighting for."

"I'm ok with that." Then she turned to follow Linda.

I made my way around back. That had actually been easier than I'd expected. It also made me think that Tash wasn't a complete bitch - just mostly one.

CHAPTER EIGHT

When I reached the guys, they were all sitting in the middle of the grass, spread out in something like a circle. There was a spot between Gavin and Lars, so I took it. When I eased myself down onto the grass to sit cross-legged, that put me right across from Travis. He'd paused whatever he was saying when I showed up.

"So, do they want to kill me?" he asked.

I shrugged. "Tash is a bitch, but I think she gave in. Linda basically told her off, and those two are friends."

So Travis looked at Lars. "And your mom is honestly cool with all of this?"

"She doesn't really get a choice," Lars explained. "She was there when Ted turned into a demon, hacked at my side, and tried to take her and Jess home. Mom's also pregnant with Ted's kid, which makes things complicated."

"Is that why you and Jess are still on the down-low?" Travis asked.

"How many people know about that?" Bax asked.

"A lot of people suspect," Travis admitted. "Lars keeps putting off any girl who hits on him. He says he's hung up on an old girlfriend, but really?" He looked between all the guys. "Who's going to turn down a piece of ass for some girl a few states away?"

"Not me," Bax said. "But I'll do it to make sure I don't lose the one I've been chasing."

"Exactly," Travis said. "And the one girl he can't have is Jess. So there are rumors. Megan put it in everyone's head."

"Fucking bitch," Gavin grumbled.

"Wait," Travis breathed, his head snapping over to me. "Is that why she suddenly dropped out of school and fessed up to her mess? Was it you?"

"All of us," Gavin said. "Remember when I beat up Collin? Yeah, that's what started all of it. Someone gave Megan a video of the fight. Megan showed that to Ted. He got pissed and shoved Linda. Jess tried to stop him, and she didn't have on her brace, so there was a lot of touching."

"And she didn't know she was one of us," Bax explained. "We were looking for a guy."

Travis was nodding at all of that. "Makes sense. And Olivia Porter took the video. A few weeks ago, she told Shannon that if she didn't stay away from me, she'd show it to the cheer coach."

"What?" I gasped, because Olivia was the last person I would've suspected.

Travis grunted like he wasn't impressed. "Yeah. Those two don't get along. I'm not sure why, but they've been one-upping each other since freshman year. Well, Shannon asked to see it, playing it up like she couldn't believe I'd do something like that. She said she replayed it, zoomed in on it, and when Olivia got tired of hovering over her shoulder, she deleted it."

"Nice!" Bax said.

"Shit," I breathed. "Remind me to never fuck with your girlfriend. She's got guts."

"No kidding," Travis said. "Shannon's a little intimidating, but in the best way. She's honestly amazing."

He sounded half in love with her already, and it was kinda cute.

Granted, Shannon was stunning. She was also popular, was the kind of girl who'd go places, and didn't need a guy to be happy. In other words, she was everything I wanted to be. That was probably why I was so confused by her friendship, but I liked it.

Never mind that Travis had just solved the mystery of the video. No, that didn't make it go away, since Megan had a copy of it, but at least we knew it was just normal, petty crap. It had nothing to do with our abilities or anything demonic. I was willing to call that a win. I was also pretty sure that Collin was no longer a problem, so the whole ordeal was nothing more than history now.

"Ok," I said, changing the subject back to the real reason he was here. "What do you know about demon and cambion magic, Travis?"

He blew out a breath and leaned back onto his hands. "Well, it's elemental. There are five elements though, not four."

"Earth, air, fire, water, and spirit," I said, making it clear I knew that much.

Travis nodded. "And they can be combined. Spirit is life energy, basically. So, healing for us. Now, the difference between demon and cambion styles is that our magic has to come from something. Yours can be called to you."

"Clear as mud," Lars told him.

Travis lifted a hand, showing he'd explain. "We rely on what already exists. So, to make a body, I need to have earth magic. I can use dirt, plants, and other organic materials to build a skin, and spirit magic to resize myself. Right now, I fit, but when I molt again, I'll be bigger than a human form, so there's a little compacting magic going on."

"How long does it take?" Gavin asked. "When Ted came in, he burned off his skin pushing through the wards."

"Shit," Travis huffed. "He made it inside *there?*"

"Broke down the front door," Bax admitted. "When he crossed the ward line, his skin basically burned off."

"Ok," Travis said. "First off, that's incredibly powerful. Not magically, either. Just pain tolerance and sheer strength. Those wards are like cling wrap: clear but tangible. They flex a bit, but there's something elastic about it. They also feel like fire ants. Millions of pinpricks of pain when we touch them."

"How do you know?" I asked.

He laughed once. "We have lessons. My guardians have been teaching me about this since they took me in. Most kids learn colors and numbers. Demon kids learn about Brethren, wards, and gates along with it."

"Gates," Bax said, catching that word. "You mean the seals?"

"I mean the thing they seal," Travis corrected. "The seals you're so worried about are like police tape on a gate. The gate is how we get in and out. Right now, that gate has a hole in the bottom. Well, it's not the actual bottom, because it's set in the ceiling, but the analogy works. As often as the seal has been cracked, the demons inside the Pit have managed to chip away at the gate until there's a hole. Not a big one, but big enough for a common to fit out. A greater could probably squeeze through it, but it would be a very tight fit. The kids, however..."

"And with the seal cracked, that's how the shadows are coming out?" I asked.

Travis smiled. "So you've seen them, huh?"

I nodded. "We've been in Bax's basement. We're also feeding them. Um, we kinda killed a pair of commons down there."

That made Travis sit up. "What? No!"

"They came at us," Gavin snapped.

"I'm sure they did," Travis said. "You're Brethren and they were trying to protect the kids! Fuck! That means no one moved them. I need to..." He leaned to pull his phone out of his pocket.

Bax snatched it from his hands. "Talk first, Travis. No offense, but we just had a pretty big fight with a bunch of demons, so we're a little twitchy."

"Ok." Travis sighed, pressing his lips together like he was thinking hard. "You've heard about the underground railroad for

Black people trying to escape slavery, right? Same idea. Around the seals, we find a place to stash the kids where they won't get hurt. Every seal, Bax. There's a group of demons, usually commons or greaters, who come to collect them, move them into safe places, and find them homes. Demonic homes, where they can adjust to life up here."

"Refugees," I realized.

Travis nodded. "Yeah. That's all we are. Ok, not *all* of us. You have to understand. Hell? It's one continuous place. There are chambers and corridors. It's like caverns, and it's deep. It's also not big. We're talking the size of a single town."

"Which is pretty big," Lars pointed out.

"Not for a world's population of people," Travis said. "Overpopulation is a problem, and something no one considered when making that place. Getting from the Hellam seal to one in Europe isn't equivalent distance. It's more like driving through a high crime neighborhood. Distance is warped by magic because the Pit isn't really a place. It's more of a dimension. Same with Heaven, I'm sure. But if the kids are out but no guardians are coming to pick them up, that's a problem. They'll starve, Bax. It'll take a while before anyone figures out that the guardians are behind schedule, and then longer to be sure that they aren't coming. We don't really travel in groups, because that's a good way to get dead!"

"We're feeding them," Bax assured him.

"Just... I know this sounds stupid, but if you can, give them cat food?" Travis asked. "It has a few things they need."

Bax chuckled. "We gave them options, and they all liked the cat food. They're on that expensive special stuff. The natural raw diet crap. It's what they all liked."

"Nice," Travis said. "We, um, our systems aren't developed yet at that age. They're basically toddlers to about ten years old, but they're larva. Like a caterpillar before it becomes a butterfly. Completely different inside."

"I've got a regular shipment for them," Bax promised. "Tash even opened a window on the wooded side of the house so they can go outside at night without being burned by the light from it during the day. We're trying to take care of them."

"Good. Yeah. And I need to tell my parents so they can put out the word and make sure someone comes to get them," Travis said, grabbing his phone back. His thumbs immediately began moving. "You're feeding these ones, but what other gates were those demons supposed to go to? What about the kids at the next place?"

Then he tilted his phone so Bax could see the message. When Bax nodded, Travis hit send. In my opinion, that was proof that he was honestly on our side. Well, side might be the wrong term, but at least he wasn't our enemy. This was more of a situation of culture clashes. Just one problem. He'd never finished talking about magic.

"What about the elemental stuff?" I asked. "You kinda got off on a tangent."

"Right," Travis said. "Jess, this is a lot. I mean, I'm not an expert, and most of this is just stuff I know. It's like the sky being blue, right? You just know it is, not necessarily why it is."

"I can see that," I admitted.

"But demonic magic comes from what's here. Yours can call it to you. We make fire from things that will burn. We move the earth, bring forth the water, and so on. We use the world to our advantage. Trees become spears, as an example. You, however, can create it. That's the power of a little humanity. You want fire? You make fire. You want ice, you remove the heat and add water. Mix and match the elements. I can turn a lake into daggers of ice, but you can turn the air into the same thing. I make the ground buck, but you can create stakes of rock, dirt, or even wood."

"Useful," Gavin said.

"Which means it's all about the creativity," I realized. "It's figuring out what is possible and imagining it hard enough before I do it - or learning to imagine a lot faster."

"And being able to use that element," Travis said. "Most of us are only strong in one or two."

Lars just leaned over his knees. "Jess has them all."

"All?" Travis asked. "Spirit too?"

"It's how she saved my life," Gavin said.

Travis's breath slowly slid from his lungs. "What happened?"

"Demon put his fingers through my back," Gavin said. "Long fingers. Sharp claws. I was dying. She made me stop."

Travis just nodded his head slowly, but his eyes were on the ground. "Yeah. I'm sorry, man. Look, I don't want to fight with you four. I also don't want to be in the middle of this because I don't want to help kill my kind."

"But - " I tried.

Bax lifted his hand, stopping me. "We don't either. Maybe every other quad has killed demons on principle, but that's not us. Jess is cambion, and I don't give a shit. She's not evil, and I'm pretty sure you aren't either. Our powers are supposed to save the world, right?"

"Or destroy it," Travis said. "Depends on which side of this fight you're on."

"Yeah, well, I don't think there's a conflict," Bax said. "We're supposed to save the world from the fucking Horsemen. We'll kill assholes who hurt people. Don't care if they're demons, witches, or humans. I also don't care if they're Martyrs, Travis. Jess is an abomination, and we're with her. Not *just* with her until shit hits the fan. We're completely with her. If you really just want to live a normal life, have a family, and do whatever demons in human bodies do? Man, I'm so cool with that."

"Why?" Travis asked. "The Martyrs will just kill you off and get another quad."

Gavin chuckled, and the sound was a little demented. "Let them try, Travis. Let them fucking try."

CHAPTER NINE

Travis continued telling us what he could. It seemed that making a body took as long as it took. The limiting factor wasn't the spell, but rather the magic available to do it. For Travis, it would take about an hour. For someone like my father, it would be minutes. For a minor demon, it was impossible because they just didn't have enough magic available.

It was also why demons were cautious with casting magic. It seemed they couldn't just pull it in like I could. Demons were made of magic. They consumed it rather than siphoned it. They ate other creatures, including each other, for that reason. Thus, getting a demon to cast magic at us would drain them in ways that normal combat wouldn't.

But all of that made a few things obvious. First, Travis wouldn't be shedding his human skin without a very good reason. An hour-long ritual might not seem like much, but he'd have to have enough magic first, and that could take days to regenerate on his own. Never mind that an hour-long ritual was still a lot of work. I knew because of Tash's magic lessons with me.

Second, my dad was kinda terrifying. He'd eaten his way to so much magic that his body had grown into an extra molt. He was basically a super-greater demon now, and had magic unlike anything that had been seen before. Third, it meant that stripping someone's human appearance wasn't really that big of a deal, because while it might be a lot of work to fix, it *could* be done in a day.

The most important thing, though, was that we'd been fighting them wrong this whole time. Because Brethren - and the Order - didn't understand demonic magic, they didn't know how to make it hard to use. For thousands of years, quads had shot, stabbed, and hacked at the demons they wanted to kill. Those demons had tough bodies that could take a lot of abuse. They were basically supernatural tanks. Their magic, however, was strong but limited. We needed to hit them in a way that negated their physical strength and would force them to rely on magic. Magic that I could block.

Eventually, Deke made his way over and told us all to come into the shop. Bax said that wouldn't work, but Deke assured him that he'd just fixed the wards. The front half of the garage was no longer locked off to demons. The rest of the house was, but since Travis was helping, Deke had made adjustments. After sharing a look, the five of us climbed to our feet, but I was trying to figure out the catch.

Then Deke offered his hand to Travis. "Deacon Vose, this quad's Sandman. Most people call me Deke."

Travis accepted the offer and shook. "Travis West, high school senior, captain of the basketball team, and lesser demon." He let go, but for a moment he didn't move. "And that's it?" he finally asked. "We're just cool now?"

"A little over a week ago," Deke told him, "we got our asses kicked by over two dozen demons. They know who these four are, and *where* we are. Needless to say, when a demon shows up on the doorstep, I expect the worst."

"Yeah..." Travis said, dragging the word out. "And grabbing Jess by the throat?"

"Is why I don't want to kill you," Deke admitted. "I wasn't hurting her, just making her look at me, but you still tried to protect her."

"Deke's a little emphatic," Bax explained. "We've mostly taught him to stop yelling all the time, but it's like living with a drill sergeant."

Deke laughed once. "Considering that I'm supposed to get you four ready to survive all of this, I'd say it's a good enough description." But his eyes shifted over to me. "Linda insisted on snacks. Said she's thrilled that you and Lars have friends over. They set up a table in there."

His eyes looked like he was ready to strangle someone. It made me want to laugh, but I could imagine Linda trying to be the perfect mom regardless of what Travis was. She'd spent her whole life waiting for the moment when she could entertain her kids' friends, so it made sense. The only problem was that none of us really wanted to be mothered.

"Well," I said, heading that way, "we have some useful stuff already. We've been planning these attacks all wrong, Deke."

He moved to my side, letting the rest of the guys follow. "How so?"

"Demons eat magic," I said. "I pull it from the world around us, which kinda makes it feel unlimited. It isn't, but it means I have a bigger reserve than a demon."

"Uh huh." He glanced back at Travis. "And how much does a lesser demon have?"

"So little that Jess could squish me like a bug," Travis said, proving he overheard. "I'd never try to have a magical fight with her. I can, however, take a hit. It's why I was so good at football. I'm fast. If she's trying to hurt my body, I'll survive."

"And you're just offering this up?" Deke asked, making it clear he still didn't trust the guy.

Travis paused as I walked into the garage. Sure enough, Linda had been domestic again. There was a metal patio table set up along with some plastic chairs. I was pretty sure I'd seen this set on the far side of the barn, which meant someone had moved it. Clearly, I wasn't the only person to realize that.

"Mom!" Lars snapped when his eyes hit it. "What were you thinking? You shouldn't move that!"

"Tash helped," Linda said as she set down two paper plates with little cracker sandwiches on them. "She's also getting sodas for all of you." When she stood up straight again, she was grinning. "I may have mentioned that hosting company fell under my new job description and that Deke and Tash are just guests."

"Nice," Bax said as he pulled out a chair. "You three joining us?"

"Still weird," Travis said as he sat down.

I took the spot beside him, pinning him between me and Bax. Lars moved to my other side. We had to scoot the chairs around a bit to fit Gavin beside Bax and leave room for everyone else. Deke pulled up a toolbox and sat on that. Not worrying about anyone else, he leaned his elbows onto the table.

"Why are you helping, demon?" he pressed.

"It's Travis," the guy reminded him, "and just because I'm a demon doesn't mean I agree with every other demon in the world. We do have political divides, you know. Humans have Democrats and Republicans. Demons have world domination and peaceful coexistence. I'm a PC demon."

Lars ducked his head and snorted out a laugh at the bad joke. I had to press my lips together, but the fact that PC also stood for politically correct went right over both Deke and Gavin's heads.

"So you don't care if we close the seal?" Deke asked.

Travis wavered his head from side to side. "Yes and no. Look, I know it has to be closed. I also know it won't stay that way, so it doesn't matter."

"Why not?" Deke pressed.

A look of confusion crossed Travis's face. "They never do."

ENTER SANDMAN

"But why not?" Deke asked. "The seals are supposed to be permanent. The spell on them is supposed to make sure of it, and yet they keep cracking, and faster each time."

"I don't know shit about that," Travis promised. "I just know that the Pit is bursting at the seams. I know that your super-special spell isn't that impressive. Maybe we've learned better magic? No idea, but it's pretty easy for a group of greater demons to crack it, Deke. When I got out, I remember the circle of them casting together."

"The magic doesn't feel right," I told Deke. "When you started that ritual, it was impossible to ignore, and it felt wrong."

Tash joined us, pulling up a chair just to drop into it and ask, "What if it's just because your magic is the antithesis of ours?" Then she set a six-pack of cold bottled Cokes beside the sandwiches.

"Don't think so," Travis said. "I mean, angelic magic is our opposite, and it's suffocating. It's not..."

"Discordant," I offered, reaching for a drink. "Deke's spell felt like it had gone off, like spoiled meat."

"Good analogy," Travis agreed.

"Wait," Gavin said. "So you can just feel, or smell, or taste this magic?"

"The spells," Travis clarified. "Keeping with the analogy, it's like walking into a kitchen. You can smell when a meal is cooking, but not when the food is still in the fridge and cabinets."

"And when it's done," Bax said. "So does this mean you know when Jess casts her magic?"

"Not really," Travis admitted. "If I'm right beside her, sure. Keep in mind that her magic 'reads' just like mine. There are about fifty demons in Hellam right now, give or take. Most of us use some amount of magic every day." He tapped his chest to show he meant his body. "That's a lot of demon magic, so a little bit from a cambion won't really stand out."

Linda wheeled over an old computer chair that had been

parked at the workbench. "Which means she's an even better weapon than we thought. Now, how many of these fifty-odd demons do you know?"

Every head at the table turned to look at her, but Linda was watching Travis. The guy stammered a few times, but no real words came out. Linda just smiled at him kindly.

"Approximately is fine, young man," she assured him.

"Some," Travis finally managed to get out. "Just like I know people at school, but I don't really *know* them. I know if they're a sophomore, or in band, or things like that. I know who most of the demons in town are, but we're not friends or anything."

"Do you know who wants to kill us?" I asked.

"And who was there the other weekend?" Gavin added.

"I can guess," Travis said. "Why?"

Linda nudged the plate of snacks at him. "Because my kids are pretty strong, but they can't fight everyone at once. If they're going to get that seal closed, then they'll need to kill them in smaller groups."

"Not the best tactics," Deke grumbled. "Linda, he's one of them. He's not going to just tell us who we need to pick off."

"Actually," Travis said, "if you'll promise to leave the rest of us alone..." His eyes jumped over to Bax. "I know the greaters. I know which side they're all on. The rest shouldn't be a problem with your abilities, at least from the stories I was told."

I caught that last part. "You heard stories about us?"

"Yeah," Travis said. "All my life, I've heard about how dangerous each of you are. How you can negate our demonic strength, forcing us to be as weak as a human. How your abilities are unstoppable. I mean, my guardians used that crap to tell me that if I stayed up too late, partied too hard, or anything else, that the Brethren would catch me."

Tash scoffed. "Telling stories about our enemies is a common way of keeping kids in line. It's no different than how we were taught that demons are searching for the Martyr's temple and will kill all of us when they find it."

"They are," Travis said dryly. "Those who want to take over the world think the Horsemen are a lie and that destroying the training ground you people use will give us the ultimate advantage. They know it's in a poorly-populated area, and they're pretty sure it's cold."

"Shit," Deke said, looking at Tash quickly before he turned back. "Travis, if we promise you and your family will be safe, can you help us find the demons who want us dead?"

His sudden change said a lot. Probably more than he wanted, and Travis's expression made it clear he'd noticed. The guy's eyes dropped to the table, but his lips curled a bit. He was planning.

"Which means you really need me," Travis said. "So, if I say someone's off-limits, then that's it. They're off-limits. That includes the ones who get the kids, the ones who raise us, and all of the peaceful coexistence demons. The ones wanting world domination? I'll tell you who they are, but that's my deal. I know you killed the babysitters in the basement. I don't know how many kids are starving to death right now in other locations because of it, so that's my line. If you want my help, then you have to help me back."

"Tell them to talk to me," I said. "We're trying to take care of the kids, but the demons jumped us."

"Why were you down there?" Travis asked.

It was Bax who answered. "We were going to herd them back to the gate at night. We had no idea that was their safe house. All I knew was that I had monsters in my basement and I didn't want to hurt them if I didn't have to. The adults attacked us, Travis. One almost killed Deke."

"Which is how I learned I can heal people," I said.

Travis dropped his eyes to the table. "This isn't going to be easy, you know. My people hate you. All four of you."

"And I'm a cambion," I reminded him. "If you don't want to tell them I'm also Brethren, then I'm ok with that. I'm still a cambion."

"Ok," he agreed. "What's the worst that happens? We all die?"

"Pretty much," Gavin said. "Sounds like that's what will also happen if we don't try, though."

"Yeah," Travis agreed, "but the four of you were supposed to be who killed me. I'll find out who was there, but I'm not giving you all the names. You'll have to prove to me that you're not coming after us indiscriminately."

"And those bedtime stories," Tash added. "I want those too."

Linda just nudged the plate. "And you kids eat. I know you're hungry. At least act like teenagers while you're trying to save the world!"

"Might as well," Lars said, reaching for one - because it wasn't like this could get any weirder.

CHAPTER TEN

Travis stayed a while longer. Mostly, he talked about demonic society, trying to help us all understand that they weren't bad people. I may have asked a few questions to help that along, but no one seemed to mind - especially not Travis. Gavin was quiet, although he didn't seem pissed off. It was more like he was weighing all of it.

When Travis finally left, we headed up to do homework and have a real dinner. That led to another discussion of what we'd be doing, how we could handle this, and it kept coming back to the same thing: assassinations. The guys preferred to think of it like video games. We were going to make tactical strikes against our enemies.

But none of this was easy. I'd killed a demon, but he'd *looked* like a demon. I hadn't killed a person before! Bax had an even bigger problem. He refused to believe that demons were evil just because of what they were. He wanted to be sure someone had been at the seal before we planned a hit. Never mind that we were talking about actually planning hits!

It didn't take long before Deke lost his temper. Slamming his hand down onto the table, he snapped at Bax to get his head in the game. These were the people who'd almost killed Gavin! Bax shot back that Travis wasn't. That led to an argument that only ended when Deke left the table in the middle of it.

And I couldn't stop thinking about all of it. That night, I was once again lying in my bed, staring at the ceiling and not tired at all. I thought about sneaking into Lars' room, but then what? Getting laid wouldn't answer any of my questions. Going to talk to Bax would only make more. I'd already spent the night with Gavin, and would my guys start to feel ignored if I spent two nights in a row with him?

So I closed my eyes and tried to sleep. I got close too, but then my mind turned back to that weekend. I remembered the demon on the rock who'd tried to grab Deke. The one who'd shoved his fingers through Gavin's back and picked my boyfriend up like he'd weighed nothing. Then I thought about the fear in Travis's eyes when he realized he'd been exposed.

Bax had to be right. Demons weren't evil simply because they were demons. There was one main thing that made me feel like I wasn't inherently evil: I'd fallen in love - three times over! That meant I had to have some slice of good in me, right? That meant the same had to be true for others. My father was an asshole, but so were plenty of people.

But Deke also had a point. Demons wanted to see us dead. Even Travis had been ready for the worst. It sounded like demon stories made us into the boogie man - and for good reason. Thus, the good ones wouldn't be too nice to us either. This was a lose-lose situation no matter what we did.

So how could we be sure we were making the right choice? How could Bax convince himself that the person we were killing deserved it? How could I be a part of this? Not for moral reasons, but the physical ones. I wasn't as strong as the guys. I had no experience with stealth or breaking in. I also really didn't want to go to jail. If we got arrested, the guys would at least be together.

Me? I'd get slapped in some girls' wing with people much meaner than me and a hand that would kill with a touch.

I eventually rolled over to see two a.m. on the clock. This wasn't working. I couldn't just lie here alone and sleep. I was too spoiled, too used to being around my guys. So, if everyone else had been ruled out, that left only one person to make me feel better. Deke would know what to say so I could find some sleep.

Slipping out of bed, I didn't worry about getting dressed. I just headed down the hall to the last door on the opposite side. There, I tapped. It took a moment before I heard noise inside the room. A few seconds after that, the door cracked open. Deke stood on the other side with his tri-colored hair sticking in all directions, wearing only his underwear.

"Jess?" he asked.

"I don't want to go to jail," I blurted out.

With a chuckle, he pulled the door open as wide as possible. "I can't sleep either."

"You look like I dragged you out of bed," I admitted as I stepped in.

He pushed out a breath as he reached up to finger comb his hair into something resembling order. "I'm trying to figure out what to do about that demon."

"Travis?" I asked.

Deke caught my shoulders and steered me toward his bed. "Sit," he ordered before moving to grab one of the two chairs in his room. "And yes, Travis. That fucker came onto the property, Jess! That means he made it through the initial wards."

"He said he had an urge to turn back," I explained. "Sounds like Dad's wards are working, but since we invited him, it overrode that."

"Which is another stupid thing," Deke grumbled. "What were you four thinking? Inviting a demon here!"

"He's our friend!" I insisted.

"I was under the impression that you didn't have friends until you started hanging out with these guys," Deke countered. "Are you involved with this kid?"

"No, Deke," I huffed, aware that this conversation was not making me either relaxed or tired. "Travis is with Shannon. Shannon was pretending to be flirting with Lars to keep my relationship with him from causing problems for Linda."

"And this guy's ok with that?" Deke lifted a brow as if I should know better.

"He's nice!" I said. "We also didn't know he was a demon until I saw him this morning. Yesterday morning. Whatever!"

"And how much information did you just give him about our weaknesses?" Deke asked. "That boy knows our plan, your lack of training, and how many more things that give them an advantage? Now he's going to help us decide who we're going to kill. I thought *Gavin* was Bax's best friend. Has he already forgotten how close Vengeance came to dying because of a demon?"

"No," I breathed. "None of us can. It was also me, not Bax, who invited him, ok? Gavin too. We were all on board with this because it's Travis. Besides, I need to learn how to use my magic."

"Which means that demon now knows how weak you are," Deke said. "Don't you get it, Jess? I'm just trying to protect you."

"Me?"

"All four of you," he clarified. "But yes, you. Do you think it's easy for me to forget what you did? That I was in the same situation as Gavin and you just fixed it. You were right there, willing to throw your life into mine."

"And Tash thought I was stealing time from you," I mumbled.

He leaned over and caught my chin. "Look. That kid seems decent enough. The problem is that I've seen too many demons try to be nice. In the end, they always turn on the Brethren."

I let my eyes close as I leaned into his hand. "I don't know if I can just shoot people, Deke."

"You can," he promised. "Jess, you can do anything. You held off the demons long enough for me to get the guys back. You fought as hard as any Brethren I've ever heard of. You aren't some weak little girl."

"I just don't wear combat boots," I mumbled, thinking about my talk with Gavin.

Deke's thumb swept across the side of my face. "Doll, you do. Well, work boots. Close enough. You also wear those cute ones with the heels. So?"

"No," I said, leaning back to pull my face from his hand. "It's about the characters in my books, you know? So many of the 'strong' women hate being girly. I kinda like it."

"Girly works for you," he promised. "But why did you really come in here?"

"Because I couldn't sleep," I admitted. "I spent last night with Gavin, and I need to sleep, but I know Lars would get me going and Bax would get me talking."

Deke pointed at the pillow. "Then lie down and keep talking. If you're sitting up, then you're not relaxing, and that means not sleeping."

I grunted at him, but I also obeyed. Deke's sheets smelled like him. They were wrinkled and messy, but that reminded me of him too. His bed was cool, making me think he'd been out of it for a bit. I noticed all of that, but I didn't pull the blankets over myself. I wasn't quite ready to sleep yet.

"Deke? Are you mad at Bax?" I asked out of the blue.

He leaned over his knees and groaned. "I'm annoyed with him," he admitted.

"Because of me?" I asked.

His head snapped up, those storm-grey eyes of his finding mine. "No."

"Because of Travis?" I asked.

He bounced his head from side to side in a gesture that wasn't really an answer. "A bit. I'm pissed he put us all at risk."

"It was me," I reminded him. "I'm the one who promised Travis a truce until we could talk. I'm the one who wanted him to explain demon magic. It was me, Deke. Don't take it out on Bax because of what happened the other morning - " I snapped my mouth shut because I wasn't supposed to have seen that.

"Fuck," Deke grumbled, shoving to his feet to walk to the far side of the room.

I rolled onto my back and scooted up, convinced I'd just said the wrong thing. I was just about to apologize when Deke grabbed his phone and started tapping at it. Confused, I just watched as he finished and set it back down on the dresser out of reach from the bed. Then, he made his way around the foot of the bed and crawled in on the other side. Once there, he lay with a body-sized gap between us and let out a heavy sigh.

"I'm not pissed about the grabbing incident," Deke admitted. "I'm embarrassed. I'm also worried about Gavin."

"Why?" And I meant the Gavin part.

Deke seemed to understand. "I'm not sure he's as fine as he's pretending," Deke said. "He keeps saying he died. He didn't die. You saved him before his heart stopped."

"But that doesn't mean it didn't feel that traumatic," I pointed out.

"I know." He rolled onto his back, then laid his arm out. A glance made it clear that was an invitation for me to come closer. "You aren't sleeping because you have this need to be close to your quad," he said. "It seems to work with me too, so come here, doll."

"Is this weird?" I asked.

He jerked his head in a come-here motion. "Everything about this quad is weird, so I'm getting used to it."

"And you told me to keep my hands to myself," I reminded him.

"No, I told you it couldn't happen again," he corrected. "I was also wrong, doll. Gavin chewed me out the other day because he said he saw our bonds. He says I'm already tied to the four of you, and damned if it doesn't feel like that. I *want* to touch you. I keep reminding myself that one moment in the shower doesn't mean shit, and that you have three guys who treat you like a princess. You deserve that, Jess. You also don't need me fucking it up."

I gave in and slid closer so I could curl against his side. "Why would you fuck it up?"

Deke closed his eyes and turned his head to the ceiling. "Because of what happened the other morning," he said, the words so soft.

"But Bax thought you were me," I reminded him. "You probably thought he was me. It was an accident."

"I didn't think it was you," Deke admitted.

I forgot to breathe for a moment. "Grace?" I asked, naming the woman from his last quad that I knew he'd cared about.

"Jess, I knew it was Bax. I wake up enough at night to know where I was."

My mind jumped back to the way Deke had grabbed Bax's wrist and thrust into his hand. "Oh," I breathed.

He murmured as if I was on the right path. "Bax is straight. Gavin's homophobic."

"And you're not straight," I realized.

He finally turned to look at me again. "I'm not. That's how Tash became my big sister. It's why she made me cocoa and helped me believe that everything would be ok. Growing up as a bisexual boy in the Order of Martyrs? It is not something we talk about. Or a lesbian."

The air slid from my lungs. "Tash?"

"Mhm," he admitted. "She doesn't want to sleep with me, Jess. She might want to sleep with you. It was the secret we had, and it tied us together. It's how I knew I could trust her when we found out what your father is."

"Why didn't you two just say something?" I asked.

"Gavin," he said, making that an answer. "He's made no secret of the fact that he has a problem with it. He was beaten by his father because he wasn't manly enough, and it worked. Gavin learned that he has to be strong, sexual, and toxically masculine. Why do you think I smacked those boys around when you started coming over? Why I was worried about him shoving you into the snow and kissing you? Because that's what boys do when they think girls are just here to be their playthings."

"Oh," I whispered. "So you like Bax?"

Deke just chuckled, and it was hard enough to make my head bounce. "I keep telling myself they're boys."

They. Not him, but they. I noticed that. "You said I was too young too, but you still gave in."

"Gave in," he reminded me. "That's very different from seducing or making a move. And yes, I've lain right here and jacked off a few times - and I wasn't always thinking of you. I'm also the Sandman."

Another change. He wasn't calling himself our Martyr anymore. Deke had embraced the fact that he was our Sandman. The rules had changed, and he was trying his hardest to embrace them. I just wanted to help.

"So, saying you'd cave if Bax or Lars walked into your shower, huh?" I teased. "Gonna steal my boyfriends?"

His entire body stilled. I couldn't even feel the rise and fall of his breath, but the pounding of his heart shook his rib cage. "No," he finally said. "Jess, I'm bi. That doesn't mean I'm stupid. Most guys are not ok with the idea of another man checking them out. Your guys are also straight."

"Well, Lars says he's fine with it. He doesn't understand the problem because of how he was raised. I guess Cherokees are a little more open-minded or something." I tilted my head up so I could see his face. "I also kinda have a guy-on-guy fetish, but that's probably creepy, huh?"

"Eighteen," he mumbled, sounding like he was talking to himself. "You had to fucking be eighteen. All four of you. Old enough to be legal, young enough to have no clue what you're doing in life."

"So teach me, Deke," I pressed.

"No, doll, I think you're teaching me." He curled his arm,

pulling me closer against his side. "I'm not going to steal your boyfriends. I grew up believing that admitting my attraction to men would get me hurt, if not killed. When I came to America, I made sure to enjoy the 'sinful ways' of this country. Yes, I mean I fucked a lot of guys. I fucked a lot of girls too, back when my face was in one piece. I'm not really worried about where my dick goes so much as not being alone. But more than that, I don't want to cause a rift in this quad. The four of you are too good together."

"But you're a part of us," I reminded him, reaching over to trace one of the scars across his chest.

He pressed his hand over mine, stopping the touches. "The replaceable part. Jess, the four of you are the most powerful quad I've heard of. You are a force of nature. Together, you can close the seals and push the demons back to Hell - if you can survive long enough to learn how to fight. If half your quad is worried about me instead of staying alive, that's not going to happen."

"That's not fair to you," I pointed out.

"I never asked for fair," he promised. "I'm also very happy with a beautiful girl who is sometimes too wise for her years, and other times is so young that I want to keep her safe. Now close your eyes, doll. Let me take care of you. Go to sleep and I'll chase off the bad dreams. That's what a Sandman does."

"Do I at least get a kiss?" I asked, hoping it might even work.

He smiled, but that was all. "No, doll. With you, kisses lead places. Close those big brown eyes and sleep. Someone has school in the morning, and I already set an alarm."

CHAPTER ELEVEN

Deke only tossed twice all night. Both times, it was when I pulled away from him. Once, I heard him mumble like he was trying to talk in his sleep. I curled up against his back, hooked my calf over his knee, and he quieted almost immediately. When the alarm went off the next morning, I found myself with my face pressed into his chest and his arms wrapped tight around me.

"Doll," he said, his voice even more rough than usual. "School."

"Drives you crazy, doesn't it?" I teased. "That I'm still in high school."

He actually chuckled. "Makes me feel like a dirty old man. Knowing you've slept with at least three guys makes it a little less like I'm corrupting you."

"What is it with you guys and numbers?" I asked as I sat up.

The alarm was still going off, so Deke reached down, jerked his dick into place, then got out of bed to silence the noise. What he didn't do was answer me. At least not until he was on my side of the bed and tossing back the covers.

"We're supposed to like our women submissive and delicate," he said, offering me a hand to help me out of bed like a gentleman. "Innocent usually helps with that, or so a lot of guys think."

"Oh, so that's what gets you going?" I slid to the edge of the bed so I could find the floor. Then I stayed there, letting go of him to scrub the sleep from my eyes.

"No," he admitted. "I liked that you're a mule. You were completely forgettable until you told me you weren't leaving. I could tell you were scared - and now I know that was because of me acting like your dad. I also knew that fear didn't make you flee. That, doll, is what gets me."

"I'm done being scared," I told him as I finally stood. My intention was to head for the door, since my clothes were all in my room.

But Deke's voice caught me just as I reached for the doorknob. "No, Jess, you aren't. It won't stop you, but you will still be scared. The next time one of us gets hurt, you'll be scared. There *will* be a next time. Just know that I don't respect you any less for it. Being fearless isn't what makes you impressive. It's that even when fear is smothering you, you refuse to give in."

I had to pause for a moment to let that sink in. Then I glanced back to see him standing by his bed, still in his underwear. Those scars on his chest proved that he knew what he was talking about. The lines across the left side of his face made it clear he couldn't forget. Deke had known fear, so I had to believe him. Both about me and it happening again.

"Thanks," I said. "For the bed, the words, and that. Even if you think it's just your job, it still helps."

His eyes jumped to the side, but he didn't budge. "Go to school, Jess. Oh, and see if that demon has a name for us yet. You may trust him, but I don't."

"Not all demons are bad," I reminded him.

"But they're not all good either," he countered. "Get that hot little ass out of my room so I can jack off already."

Yep, I laughed. I also went. Gavin caught me in the hall, the crease on his brow making it clear he was confused about why I'd been in Deke's room. On principle, I decided that I wasn't going to tell him. I had too much on my plate today, and while talking to Deke had helped me fall asleep, it had also added a few more things to deal with.

First off, Gavin. I remembered how pissed he'd gotten when Collin called him gay. He'd almost refused our relationship because he didn't want to be involved with the guys. Then again, he hadn't run away screaming after the first time we'd all ended up in a bed together.

I didn't think Gavin was homophobic. I was pretty sure he thought he should be. If he didn't want to get bullied, then he had to make it clear he was straight. If he wanted to be seen as a man, that meant he needed a woman. All of it was bullshit, but that was how he acted sometimes. Or acted like he was supposed to act, if I was honest.

Because Gavin had been a virgin until a few months ago. He was in love with me, and I was pretty sure he was straight. All of that was fine, but if Deke and Tash weren't straight, then we had a problem just waiting to explode. Granted, Deke had said something about toxic masculinity, and that meant Tash would be fine. She was a lesbian, and two women together was supposed to be hot or something.

As if I had any room to talk. How many of my books had a guy-on-guy kink? Yeah, a few of them. I'd already had sex with two guys at once. Three, if I counted Bax being in the living room too. I was basically living the dream, but just thinking about Bax and Lars kissing sounded incredibly sexy. Or Deke and someone. I didn't even care who. I just wanted to grope them while they did it.

Needless to say, it took me a little longer to get ready for school. I was also the last one in the truck, and my eyeliner was not looking its best today. Maybe that was due to my pink cheeks? Because the moment I saw Bax and Lars, my mind went right into the gutter.

"What?" Lars asked.

"Nothing!" I insisted.

"Period stuff," Bax teased.

"Shot," I reminded them. "Don't do that anymore. Try again, Bax."

It was Gavin who got closest. "She spent last night with Deke."

"Oh!" Lars said, twisting in the passenger seat to see me. "So, that's happening?"

"It was talking," I assured them. "I had questions. Mostly about going to jail for murder, because at least the three of you would end up in jail together."

"And we have these powers for a reason," Bax reminded me. "We'll be fine, Jess. We're also going to make sure to plan everything first."

"Just feels wrong," I grumbled.

"I know," Bax agreed.

Gavin reached over for my hand, lacing his fingers with mine. "Killing them at the seal doesn't bother you, but hunting them down in town does?"

"No, it's more that they'll be at home, and home is supposed to be safe." Then I heard myself. "Ok, it's stupid. I also hate that they'll look like people, not monsters."

And I hated that I didn't know what was going on with my guys, my love life, and all of that, but bringing it up would lead to questions. Those questions would bring out things that would only make it worse, so I'd focus on the little problems for now.

"We still have to kill them," Gavin said. "One way or another, we need to close the seal. You heard Tash. It's been open for almost a year. We tried. We failed. If we want to try again, we need to make sure we're not outnumbered, and this is the only way to do it."

"Won't they know it's us?" Lars asked. "I mean, demons start dying, and the first place I'd look is us."

"But the barn is secure," Gavin countered.

"And they won't know how we're going to hit," Bax said, "or

when. It's not a fair fight - and I'm ok with that. We need to hit them at night, in their homes, and only when we're ready."

"Fuck," Lars groaned, tossing his head back. "School is really going to get in the way."

"We need to make sure we do our research," Bax said, ignoring Lars. "Look, Travis is cool and all, but how do we know that he hasn't been lied to? If we're going to take these things out, then let's make sure we're doing it right. You three ok with that?"

"Completely," I assured him.

Lars nodded, but Gavin was a little too quiet. I turned to look at him just to find him staring at the floorboards. Lars turned to see him, and I was pretty sure Bax was watching too.

Finally, Gavin said, "Not all demons are bad. Demons tried to kill me. It's hard. I want to kill them all, but if all demons are bad, then Jess has to be bad too, and she's not. I just can't imagine a good one."

"Travis," Bax offered.

"We don't *know that*," Gavin said. "Deke's right. We need to be careful. Travis was your friend because he knows what you are. He's been spying on us for how long? He knew what Jess was before she did, but he didn't say anything. Can we really trust him?"

"We weren't a quad when he first saw my hand," Bax countered. "Hell, I hadn't even met you, Gav. He assumed Deke was one of us, not Jess."

"And?" Gavin asked. "Doesn't change that he was spying."

"What would you do?" Lars asked. "If you saw your mortal enemy, and he had no idea he was supposed to hate you, what would you really do, Gavin?"

"The same," Gavin admitted. "I just don't want to get stabbed in the back again."

Literally. He meant what had happened at the seal, and I didn't blame him at all. "I won't let it happen," I told him.

"No," he groaned. "Jess, I don't want to be a pussy either. It hurt.

It sucked. I fucking hate that I still dream about it, but I'm not going to cry about it. I'm going to *do* something!"

"Whoa, hold up there," Lars said. "Gav, being freaked out because you got shanked by demon talons isn't anything like being a pussy. It's called being human."

"And you're not freaking out," Gavin said.

"I wasn't lying on the table," Lars told him. "Look, you're a fighting machine. You're badass with a gun and hand-to-hand. You're not a pussy. You're also not a robot who feels nothing. Don't try to act like it. Not fucking cool, man."

"Let's just agree to do our research," Bax said. "That means we'll plan this right, we'll make sure no one gets stabbed in the back, and we'll take our time until we're all comfortable with the hit, ok?"

"Yeah," Gavin agreed, and the rest of us nodded.

Which made that the working plan. So, when Travis showed up to sit with us at lunch, we were all waiting for the worst. Any version of the worst that we could think of. This whole Brethren thing had us doubting the people we'd trusted just weeks ago. It had reminded us that we were very mortal, and there were a lot of things out there that wanted us dead.

"I have a name you'll want," he said, leaning in to keep his voice down. "When I got home last night, I told my guardians what's going on. They think I'm insane and want nothing to do with this. However, my 'mom' said she knows who attacked Gavin. It was Ted's friend, Greg Hamsted."

"What?" I gasped, because that was a name I knew well.

Travis nodded. "Yep. I'm trying to get the names of the greaters who were there that night. I know that Greg and Ted were. My mother says Greg was in bad shape for a bit there. He got hit hard. When she asked what happened, he told her some punk kid had broken two of his fingers, then winked, but it sounds like he almost died."

I nodded slowly, remembering the demon I'd grabbed, hoping

to kill. I'd had to let it go to get Gavin out, but it had collapsed. They took a few seconds to dissolve, but I'd assumed it was dead. Clearly, I should've held on a little longer. Fuck!

"His mom works at the pharmacy," Bax said, unaware that the asshole should already be dead.

"And this," Travis said, pushing a piece of paper into the middle of the table, "is where he lives." But he wouldn't take his hand off it. "I need your word, Bax. If I help you, then you leave myself, my guardians, and the other PCs alone."

"Is that really what you call yourself?" Gavin asked.

"No," Travis admitted. "We don't have a name, but it works well enough so you know who I mean. This isn't a stretch. Jess knows who her father hangs out with. It won't be hard to find out where he lives. I just need to be sure that it's not going to come back on us."

"We promise," Bax assured him.

"Or from them," Travis clarified. "If they realize I'm a traitor, they'll tear me apart as fast as the four of you will. Look, I should be running for the hills. I should have my shit packed and be on my way to New York or someplace where I can get lost. I also want to get my diploma and go to college. So if shit goes sideways, I'm out."

"Don't blame you at all," Bax said, snagging the paper from under his hand. "Look, if this is the guy who fucked with my best friend? Yeah, he goes first."

Travis licked at his lips. "And they'll expect that. They know you're licking your wounds. They know they fucked you four up. They think it's worse than it is."

"But Dad helped me get away," I breathed.

That made Travis's head snap over. "What?"

I nodded. "He put up a wall of fire so they couldn't overwhelm me. I shot him, but it didn't seem to hurt, and then he let me go with Deke."

"The rest think the fire was yours," Travis said. "Ted said you shot him, knocking him out for a bit. We all heard that story."

"Fucker's playing both sides," Gavin growled.

"No," Lars said. "He's still trying to get his women back. He thinks that if he can kill us off, then there's nothing stopping him from claiming Linda and Jess."

The thought made my blood run cold. "Then Dad's on the list too," I decided. "I know he's stronger, and he's not going to be easy, but I'm not going to give him a chance to keep abusing Linda, the baby... or me. Not ever again."

CHAPTER TWELVE

When we got out of school that afternoon, the first thing we did was head to the wrong side of town - the side where Greg lived. The address Travis had given us was a little brick house in one of the older neighborhoods. The paint was flaking, the porch was cluttered, and no one was around. The car in the drive, however, matched the one I remembered coming to my house.

No, it wasn't proof, but it was a pretty good indicator. We didn't try to stop and do a stakeout. We simply drove down the street at a nice, slow, residential pace. That all four of us turned to stare would've been comical in any other situation, but that was where we'd commit our first murder. It was the site where we'd have to plan this big hit.

Gavin pulled out his phone and snapped a few pictures. Then he started typing like he was sending some kind of ranting text. When he was still going by the time Bax had made it back onto the main road through town, my curiosity was killing me. Not wanting to interrupt, I leaned to steal a peak, seeing nothing more than a document of some kind, and it was filled with a wall of Spanish text.

"What are you doing?" I asked, giving in to my curiosity.

"Notes," Gavin explained. Then, "Shit." With a chuckle, he put the phone down in his lap. "I can't speak English and write Spanish. I was just trying to write down the things we'll need to know. Windows, neighbors, and those things."

"Best entrance is probably the garage," Lars said. "His bushes are overgrown which means we wouldn't be seen going in."

"Have to be careful of door cams on the neighbor's places," I pointed out.

Bax scoffed at that. "Jess, those people can't afford them."

"And they're not that expensive anymore," I told him. "I'd thought about one for our place, when I was still with Dad. We can't rule it out, and Linda had a point with that. If someone catches us on camera, then all of our special skills won't matter. We'll get arrested."

"They dissolve, though," Gavin reminded me. "No dead bodies to worry about."

"But a pile of dust might be suspicious," I countered. "A missing person? That will get noticed. Do we really want to risk it?"

"Let's give it all to Deke and Tash," Bax decided. "They've done this before, and they're trained in how to make it smooth, so they can plan it."

With that decided, we headed home. It wasn't a long drive, but this time it was a quiet one. Before Spring Break, it had felt like the four of us were always on the same page. After, I kept worrying that we all had very different ideas about how to handle this. Gavin wanted to fight. Bax wanted to get answers. Lars was mellow enough to go with the most logical decision.

The problem was that I didn't want to do *any* of this. Just weeks ago, I'd thought I was the luckiest girl in the world. I had magic, I had the three hottest and most amazing guys in school, and I finally had a home where I felt like I belonged. Now, I kept feeling like it was all about to be ripped away.

Soon enough, we pulled into the driveway. All of us grabbed

our bags, but my mind was on overdrive. From what Deke had said last night to the way Gavin was hyper-focused on this hit, I felt like I needed to do something, and one thing was easiest. So, as the guys headed for the house, I called out.

"Hey, Bax?"

"Yeah?" he asked, turning back and stopping when he saw I wasn't following. "You ok?"

"Can I borrow you a second?" I begged.

"Gimme your bag," Lars said, walking over with his hand out. "I'll take your things upstairs."

I passed it over, along with an appreciative smile. Bax offered his as well. Lars took it, making a production of being put out, but I knew better. On the stairs, Gavin jerked his chin at me in that male way of silently asking if everything was ok. I smiled back, hoping he knew that meant it was - or would be.

"What's up?" Bax asked when the guys reached the top of the stairs.

"A lot," I admitted. "Is it just me, or are things weird all of a sudden?"

"Weird how?" he asked, walking me around the corner of the house and toward a more private area of the yard.

"I don't know," I groaned, "but you and I seem to trust Travis. I'm not sure Lars and Gavin do."

"Which makes sense," Bax assured me. "Jess, they don't have to always agree with us. Hell, we don't have to agree with each other."

"Yeah, but - "

"No," he said, easing me around to face him. "That shit fucked with Gavin hard, ok? He's trying to figure out how to deal with it, but that doesn't make it go away. He saw his entire life flash before his eyes. I saw my best friend almost die. I know it wasn't easy for you or Lars either, but you haven't spent as long with him as I have. That guy's like my brother, ok?"

"No, I get that," I promised. "It's just that I feel this tension, you know?"

"Have you ever considered that it's you?" he asked.

In truth, I hadn't. He could also be right. I felt so conflicted about all of this. That was what had kept me awake the night before. It was why I'd gone to Deke for some answers, even if I hadn't really gotten any. Even worse, the number of questions piling up were doing more harm to my mental stability than helping.

So I stupidly blurted out, "What's going on with you and Deke?"

Bax's entire body heaved, like he was trying to figure out how to suck in a breath, run away, or something. Maybe like I'd punched him in the gut. It looked like that was the last thing he'd expected, and I wanted to take the question back as soon as it was out of my mouth.

"Never mind," I said, turning to walk away.

Bax grabbed my arm, stopping me. "No, ask," he told me, sounding like it was almost painful to say that. "Jess, it was an accident, ok? I was asleep. It doesn't mean anything."

"I know," I promised. "But you've been different lately. Like, you wouldn't look at him in my room the other morning, and now it's all about Travis and finding these demons. Never mind Gavin! I just..."

He dropped his chin to his chest and sighed. "Your mind is going a million miles an hour, just like mine," he realized. "Let's start with the easy shit. I grabbed Deke's dick. I was asleep, I thought I was going to be groping you, and I didn't. It was embarrassing as fuck. I'm not really used to getting embarrassed, and I have no idea how to apologize to him. I mean, does that make it better or more weird? Never mind that we just got him involved, you know?"

"But why is that a big deal?" I asked. "Why are the three of you so invested in getting Deke to sleep with me?"

He looked at me for a little too long, his eyes jumping from one of mine to the other. I waited while he licked his lips, then pushed a hand over them. I didn't get the impression that he was trying to evade my questions - if my rambling even counted as such - but more that he was trying to figure it out himself.

"Gavin says he saw bonds when he died," Bax explained. "He didn't die, and *I* didn't see any bonds, but that's how he kept saying it. He's kinda stopped talking about it lately, but I don't think it's because he's forgotten."

"I think the bonds are part of my magic," I admitted.

"I don't," Bax countered. "The moment he said bonds, I knew exactly what he was talking about. From the moment I kissed you, I've felt something bigger and more powerful than any other girl I've been around, Jess. Deke says we're drawn together, and I think those bonds are what does it. Gavin said he saw colors, and they matched our hands. You said that's the colors of our souls, right?"

"Yeah..."

"Well, then doesn't that mean we're destined to be these things? I will be Conquest. I could never have been a Vengeance. I get activated or I don't, but I can only be a Conquest."

"Are Conquests always light blue?" I asked.

His mouth opened like he was about to answer, and then just closed. A moment later, his brow creased. "I don't know," Bax admitted.

"Another fucking question," I grumbled.

"What's up with the questions?" he asked.

"It's like every time I think we're getting ahead, I ask something and come back with five new questions and no answers," I said. "Like last night, when I wanted to know about how we're going to stay out of jail and why this isn't murder. Next thing I know, Deke's all telling me about how he's..." This time, my mind stepped in before my mouth went too far. "Uh, going to make sure that doesn't happen," I finished lamely.

"And what were you really going to say?" Bax asked, seeing right through me.

I wrinkled my nose and shook my head. "It's not important, ok?"

"Jess, you're stressing the fuck out, and the first thing you asked me about when we got alone was the other morning. Something's going on with you and Deke. I'm getting the impression that me groping him got in the way of that and now you're all over the fucking place, so let me help?" He clasped both of my arms and stepped a little closer. "I love you, and I might not know how to fix everything, but I don't want to just be a dick and bank account, ok? I want to be a good boyfriend, and that means listening, if nothing else. I'm trying to answer your questions, but you have to actually ask them first."

I nodded. "Gavin's freaked out at the thought of anyone thinking he's gay," I said. "But that's the problem, because what if someone in the house is? What if that's going to make all of this blow up, and then where will we be? Where will *I* be? I mean, my dad isn't just a greater demon, he's a greater-greater demon, and he helped me even after I shot him, but he's never helped me before so he clearly wants something, and we're going to end up killing demons who look like people. My luck is shit, so I'm going to go to jail for this, which is not how to save the world - and now you're being weird with Deke, and I don't know how to *fix* any of this because each time I try, I just - "

Bax's mouth landed on mine, silencing the vomit of words. I sucked in a breath, shocked that he'd done that, and his tongue flicked in to tease mine. Something in the back of my mind let go, my body relaxed, and I leaned into him. His lips moved again, and this time I was there, kissing back, forgetting about all the other shit I'd been worried about a second ago, because this was real.

Bax loved me. This arrogant, beautiful guy was all in. He'd done everything I could dream of to prove he was serious, and even now he wasn't trying to get me to shut up and go away. He just kissed me, taking his sensual, slow time about it. When his hand moved to the back of my head, a moan got caught in my throat. As if that was a sign, he gently pulled his mouth away.

"That's my girl," he praised. "Now tell me what's really bothering you, Jess."

"Deke's bi and Tash is a lesbian." Yeah, I caved immediately, but only because I needed to talk about this with someone. "Gavin's so against being gay that he beat up Collin. What's he going to do to Deke?"

"Wait," Bax begged. "Deke's into guys?"

I jiggled my head in a nod. "That's why Tash took him under her wing. After what happened the other morning, I've been worried about how Gavin will react and if this is going to make a mess of things."

"Why didn't he say anything?" Bax asked.

Which was when I realized that Bax might not be ok with this either. "It's cool, though, right?"

"I fucking grabbed his dick in my sleep, Jess," he said. "Shit. That makes this even worse. Gavin doesn't know what happened. I'm pretty sure he was asleep, but Deke knows I didn't mean it, right?"

"He knew you were asleep," I promised. "He's more freaked out about how he reacted. Bax, how do we make Gavin ok with this?"

"Shit," Bax breathed. "Look, Gav was raised that it's not ok. Not for religious reasons, but because of what happened. Being gay makes a guy weak. He was put in the hospital for being weak - and he almost died. If he's strong, then he doesn't get hurt, but it means he does the hurting." He turned halfway back toward the house. "Fuck!"

"What?" I begged.

Bax just kept going. "What about Lars? Does he know?"

"About the grab or Deke? Because the grab, yes. Deke? No. Not that he'd care, though."

"You can't be sure of that," Bax countered. "Look, it's not like with girls. Y'all make out and it's hot."

"Same with guys!" I huffed. "Shit, you've read my books. Hello, chick porn. I'm kinda into some guy-on-guy stuff, and if you can make girls kissing into a thing, then there's no reason I can't do it back. I mean, that little glimpse of you all cuddled up next to him, and that many muscles? Kinda like a dream come true for me. Right up there with you and Lars at the same time - which was hot as fuck, ok?"

Bax visibly relaxed at the change in subject. "Yeah. We need to do that again."

"We do, and Lars doesn't care," I told him. "He told me. Lars is fine. I'm hoping you're going to be fine. I also like Deke, Bax. I honestly do - which is why I screwed him in the shower! This is all supposed to be perfect, and I feel like it's going to fall apart any minute."

He leaned in and kissed my forehead. "We will never fall apart. We're bonded, Jess. I don't care who Deke fucks. I'm not even worried about grabbing him. I'm embarrassed, and I was worried that he'd think I was gay and be grossed out. He's not, so that's three out of four. Four out of five if I count your kinky little ass."

"Funny," I muttered. "But Gavin's not going to be ok with this, and it will come out. Probably at the worst time."

"Then we bring it up now," Bax decided. "I'll see how freaked Gavin would be about someone in the house being gay. While we deal with that, I'll tell Deke that we need to plan this mission well, so he - "

"It's not a mission," I broke in.

"It's a mission," Bax assured me. "Think of it like a mission. Those are demon spies, masquerading as humans. You are not going to murder them because this is an act of war. Most of all, I promise that we will make sure that Greg is evil before we take him out. If he's the one that put his talons in Gavin, then we're just helping with a little revenge."

"Ok," I conceded.

"Piece by piece," Bax told me, "we'll tackle all of this. I know it feels like a lot, but we can do this, and I'm going to be right beside you the whole way. We've made it this far. Somehow, we'll figure it out, because Gavin's right. We have a bond, and no matter what, that *will* hold us together. Maybe it's a magical bond. Maybe it's just that we're all in love with the same girl. Doesn't matter. It's going to work out."

"I just hope you're right, Bax. I really do, because losing the three of you scares the shit out of me."

"Me too," he agreed. "Me fucking too."

CHAPTER THIRTEEN

WE EVENTUALLY MADE IT UPSTAIRS. Both Lars and Gavin asked if I was ok. I assured them I was. Overwhelmed, but I was still ok. Then I changed into my workout clothes, because I was supposed to have a magic lesson with Tash. Since that had been what kept us all from dying at the seal, it felt even more important than it had before. Plus, Travis had given me some new ideas to try.

I headed to the ground floor, to the room where she'd put up the protective circles. There, I waited. When it seemed like I'd been sitting there for an hour, I pulled out my phone to check the time. No, it hadn't been an hour, but it had been fifteen minutes. The clank of something in the shop made it clear I wasn't alone, so maybe Tash just didn't know I was down here?

I headed that way only to find Deke. "Hey, where's Tash?" I asked. "I'm supposed to have a lesson."

Deke pulled out his own phone and sent off a text. "Feeding the kids, I think," he said as he tucked that back into his pocket.

A second later, a short little tune played from beside the protected room. Deke just groaned and headed to it. Sure enough, when he moved the door from its fully open position, there was Tash's phone, stuck in a rack. He picked it up and offered it to me.

"So, she probably doesn't even know she left this here. You want to head down to the big house and let her know what time it is?" he asked.

I took the phone, putting it into the pocket on my other leg. "Does she get stuck over there a lot?"

"More than she'd admit to anyone else," he said, flashing me a smile. "We still ok, Jess?"

"We're good," I promised. "Just..." I bit my lips together, trying to find the right words. "All of this got hard for me, Deke."

"I know, doll," he said, reaching up to cup both sides of my face. "You're supposed to be worried about grades and popularity, not the fate of the world."

"Or murdering people," I mumbled.

His thumb teased the line of my chin just below my lips. "Then we'll train you until you can handle it. I'll make sure that your reflexes are so good that it won't matter if you freak out. The seal's already open, which means that taking our time to get this right isn't going to change anything."

"What if the other cracks?" I asked.

"Then we'll need a strong quad to stand against the Horsemen," he told me. "I'll also make you a plan. Nice, easy steps so you can focus on the next one. Right now, it's just a lot, and you don't work that way. You like bite-sized pieces and we just dumped a mountain on you."

That. He'd just figured out my problem, and the relief from it was almost palpable. Letting out all the tension in my body with a huff, I leaned into him, pressing my head against his chest. Deke didn't hesitate before his arms wrapped around me. Lately, that had been happening more and more. Touching him wasn't weird. It was reassuring, and I really did feel like he would take care of me.

Maybe he wouldn't protect me, but I could do that myself. So could Gavin. Bax would help me feel brave and confident enough to keep going, and Lars would remind me that it was ok not to be ok. The four of them felt like they buffered me, but that was the thing. Every day since we'd lost that battle, it had started to become four guys. Not just my three, but all four of them - and I liked it. I didn't want to lose this before I truly had it.

"Spend the night with Lars tonight," Deke said. "I'll make sure he knows it's a sleeping visit, but I think you need it. Bax tomorrow, because touching us seems to help you as much as it does us. Now, go find your magic instructor and burn out all of this anxiety. That's all the planning you need to worry about today. Magic, relaxing, and sleeping with your boyfriends."

"Thanks, Deke," I said as I pulled away. "I'll get better at this."

"I don't care," he promised. "I like powerful more than perfect."

That put a little spring into my step as I headed back out of the garage and down the drive. It wasn't a long walk, and the weather was gorgeous today. The sun was out, but it was still early enough in the year to be nice instead of hot. Come May, it would change, but that was about a month away.

When I reached the mansion, the front door was open. Not standing wide open, but just a crack. That meant the alarm wasn't on either, which was a good thing. I'd never memorized the code, but it seemed Tash had. Making my way in, I tried to remember how we'd gotten to the basement last time, because this place was huge.

Turning left led me to an area that looked about right. Halfway down the hall, one of the doors was open, and when I reached it, I saw stairs. Those led down, but no lights were on. I paused at the top to let my eyes adjust, knowing the minor demons were so sensitive to light that it burned them.

While I was looking at the darkness, waiting for it to be more than just a single shade of black, I heard a woman's giggle. Carefully, I made my way down. Yeah, without any lights, it was dark enough to make a child have nightmares. The swirls moving among the blackness were creepy - and I knew what they were. Then again, maybe that made it worse, not better.

And in the middle of the main room, I saw her. Tash was lying on the floor with about a dozen demonic children piled all over her. The woman giggled again as she tried to pet one. They all had different shapes, and none of them were solid, but they reminded me of adorable little monsters. The kind that should be made into toys instead of nightmares.

"Tash?" I asked when I was all the way down.

She sat up quickly, making the minor demons scurry behind her. "Jess? What are you doing down here?"

"We're supposed to be having a lesson," I reminded her. "Deke tried to text you, but you left your phone in the shop."

"Shit," she grumbled.

"Friend?" one of the kids asked.

"Yes, she's a friend," Tash assured it. "She's also half demon. Her dad is the Devourer of Hell."

At that name, most of the kids dropped into a crouch or clung to Tash. One of them hissed! I just lifted my hands, making it clear I wasn't coming closer.

"And I don't like my dad," I said, pitching my voice so it sounded as gentle as possible. "He used to hurt me. Tash and my friends helped keep me safe."

"Cambion," something said beside me.

When I turned to look, I found an almost lizard-shaped thing moving toward me. Its body was long and low, but its head reminded me of a cat more than anything else. It even had the pointy ears. Without fear, it began to weave between my ankles, checking me out.

"I am," I admitted.

Tash just draped her arms around her knees, not bothering to get up. "They're curious," she explained.

"They're lost and confused," I added. "Travis was telling us about what it was like when he got out. He was young, but he still remembers it clearly."

She nodded. "Jess, you can't trust him."

"I also can't trust you," I shot back. "Travis hasn't tried to hurt us, but you make no secret of what you want to do to me."

"I was testing you," she insisted.

I grunted at that. "It's a good excuse. Sounds all noble and shit, but it's a lie. You were trying to keep Deke away from me. You wanted to get rid of my quad quickly, before Deke could get attached. How about we don't lie to each other for a moment, because that - more than anything else - will let me trust you."

She patted the spot beside her. "Sit."

I lifted my chin. "Why?"

"Because the kids like company and looking up at you sucks," she said. "Jess, just sit your ass down and let's talk?"

I huffed in frustration, but I did make my way over to hand her the phone she'd left in the shop and then sit. Not beside her, but close enough that we could talk without yelling and yet still dodge if the other tried something stupid. No, I didn't really expect her to attack me, but I also wasn't about to pretend like we were besties.

"Deke let me know that he told you about us," she started out. "He also said you don't seem to care if he likes guys, even if that's him checking out your boyfriends."

"I don't," I admitted. "That's not to say that *they* won't. Lars is fine, but Gavin isn't, and Bax seems to be worried about what Gavin might think more than anything else."

She nodded. "And me?"

"What about you?" I asked. "We both know exactly what those guys would say. Something about lesbians, hot, and can they watch, right?"

She ducked her head and let out a breath that sounded like it wanted to be a laugh. "I mostly meant how you feel."

"Oh." I hadn't actually considered that. "I don't think I do, Tash. I mean, I'm not into girls, but you are. So are the guys. It's...

There's..." I had to stop so I could figure out how to say this. "It's nothing. It's normal. It is what it is. I don't have an opinion about that any more than I do your eye color."

"Nice," she muttered. "Well, that makes one thing easier. So, what had you so bothered that you spent the night with my little brother last night?"

That was the first time I'd heard her refer to Deke as her *little* brother. It wasn't much, but something about it made me feel like she was finally letting me in. Maybe she *had* been testing me. I had a feeling it was more true that she'd been pushing herself, but either way, she seemed to be honestly trying. The least I could do was try back.

"I'm worried I'll freak out when I have to kill a human," I admitted. "Everyone's talking about how the best way to even the odds is to assassinate the toughest ones in their homes or on our terms, right? But that means they'll be people, and just the thought of breaking into a house, killing someone, and then going to school the next day seems..."

"Intimidating," she finished for me. "But you fought back so hard at the seal."

I nodded. "I didn't have another choice! I mostly pushed them away, though."

"I saw a lot of fire," she countered.

"But that was when they were trying to kill one of the guys!" And I groaned, because I knew I wasn't saying this well. "Tash, I read books where people fall in love, not where there's a lot of blood and gore. I'm not cut out for this. How many times did I freeze instead of helping? What if we get in the middle of this and I do it again? What if one of these demons rips apart Gavin, or Bax, or Lars?"

"Jess," she tried.

But I was on a roll. "I'm just freaking out because I don't want to be what you said. I want to take care of my guys - even Deke - but I'm worried about using magic wrong because the Martyrs are going to come after me, or killing these people and liking it because my dad's a demon. And - "

"Jess!" she barked, interrupting. "Shit. Ok, I'm sorry. Fuck."

But the volume of my name had made my mouth snap shut and my head lift to see her. Tash pushed her hair back with both hands and then sighed. For a moment, I felt like I'd just made all of this worse instead of better.

"I am thirty years old," Tash finally said. "The Order pulled me out of Slovenia when I was six. For as long as I can remember, demons were evil, abominations were selfish things that wanted to exterminate humans from the world, and fighting back was the only way we could stop this. I was taught to hate you," she told me. "Just like Germans learned to hate Jews, white supremacists hate Blacks, and so on."

"I know," I mumbled.

"You really don't," she said. "Jess, look at how easily you accept that Deke and I aren't straight. That's been our biggest secret, because it would've had us killed in the temple. You just shrug it off. You don't know how to hate like that, so you don't get it. They said the right things to use my own fears against me. Deke learned better from working with his early quads, but I'm trying. This is me *trying*. All my life, you've been my enemy, and yet no matter what I do, you've refused to treat me as shitty as I've treated you."

"I don't want to be like my dad," I said, doing my best to explain.

She nodded slowly. "And instead, I'm acting like him. I'm *trying*, Jess. Deke's helping. The four of you? You're helping the most. These kids are adorable, and there's nothing evil about them. That means the Order's wrong. You're right. I've proven it to myself, so now I have to change all of my habits, and I'm going to fail at it. I'm going to suck at this. I'm going to take two steps forward and then slide back three - but over the last few months I've learned one very important thing."

"What's that?"

She leaned forward, looking right in my eyes. "You are not evil.

You're not going to suddenly become a monster. I was wrong, you were right, and Deke will train you to handle everything else. Trust your guys, because they do love you. I don't know how you make that work, but you are. I'm trying to not be like the people who terrorized me as a kid, and I suck at it. So stop worrying about everything. Most of this isn't your problem to solve. It's mine. It's Deke's. It's the guys'. Just worry about learning magic and how to fight off something bigger than you."

I nodded. "Which is kinda what we're supposed to be doing right now."

"Yeah," she agreed, finally pushing herself to her feet. Then she offered a hand to help me up. "Let's go do that, and when I'm an unfair bitch to you again, call me on it, ok?"

I accepted her hand. "Promise."

CHAPTER FOURTEEN

Tash's words made me feel better. Not perfect, and not like all the problems were gone, but I did feel better than I had before. Working with magic helped more than anything, though. Travis had mentioned ice and lightning. I honestly had no idea where electricity fell in the whole elemental scheme, but I was willing to try.

I started with sparks. I messed up with frozen rain instead of falling ice daggers. Tash had suggested a whirlwind to hold someone in place by slinging them off balance, and I added that to my repertoire. After an hour of trying to think of new and inventive ways to make magic, we eventually gave up, but I felt like I'd actually accomplished something this time.

The next day at school, Travis handed me a list of things I should be able to do. Simple ones, he said, and the list looked like a bunch of moves from a video game. Fireballs, ice balls, rolling earth, quicksand, and more. When I asked him about it later in the halls, he suggested that I watch some anime or game trailers to get visual inspiration. As a cambion who could use all of the elements, if I could see it in my mind, I should be able to make it happen. I didn't really need to worry about what element made it, just what it would look like when it happened.

But while magic practice was important, it wasn't the only thing I needed to work on. Now that the days were getting longer, Deke had added another lesson to our daily routine. While I learned magic, the guys learned to fight with knives. They were the long survival type, but their practice weapons were rubber things that looked like some kind of Halloween prop. Deke said he'd found them on Amazon.

His theory was that if someone dropped a gun, they'd need a backup weapon. I had magic as mine. The guys, however, only had their hands. A knife might be enough to push a demon back, but it would only be helpful if the guys could actually do some damage with them. Even better, he taught them how to work in pairs, with someone watching the other's back.

Every other day, we headed to the berm on the north side to do more shooting. Our guns now had silencers on them. That made them shoot a little different, but not enough for me to notice. They also weren't silent. The bang had become more of a pop, but it should be enough to keep us from panicking a neighborhood when we did our "missions."

Deke also added more than silhouettes for us to shoot at. The guy had picked up a box of cheap frisbees. Once we were "warmed up" he would call a name, throw one, and see if we could put a hole in it. Sometimes we managed. Most times we didn't. Still, it made me feel a lot better to be learning how to shoot a moving target. Day by day, we were getting better. More confident, if nothing else.

And then there was our biggest lesson. Hand-to-hand combat had become even more vital after that fight. It was how we'd keep distance between ourselves and any demon who tried to hurt us, so we had to do it every day. The moment I was out of my magical practice sessions, I headed to the lawn to join up with the guys, and we worked on dodging and blocking. A lot of it was getting away more than anything else - and I still sucked at it.

Friday evening, I was working with Lars while Deke helped Gavin and Bax. My stepbrother was pushing me, refusing to let up. He punched full force, so I ducked. The moment my head was down, he kicked, and his knee came dangerously close to my face. I grabbed his leg and shoved, pushing him off balance, but Lars was quick enough to grab the back of my shirt.

Together, we crashed down on the grass, laughing. He pushed out a heavy breath, making it clear he'd had to work for that, but I was panting just as bad. Taking the excuse to catch my breath, I shifted a bit, getting closer, and Lars reached down to twine his fingers with mine.

"You're getting good at this, Jess," he said.

"I feel like a mess," I admitted.

"I promise you don't look like..." But his words trailed off as his eyes focused on something behind me.

I couldn't help myself. I turned to look, just in time to see Bax and Deke going at it. In all the time I'd been training, I'd never seen Deke fight like this. Bax was pretty good at the hand-to-hand stuff. Not as good as Gavin, but their styles were different. Gavin was agile. Bax was strong. Deke was both.

Sitting up, my mouth fell open as I finally realized what we should look like when doing this. The punches were solid. The blocks were full hits. Those guys would probably have bruises when they were done, but in that moment, I realized we were no longer fumbling. Maybe we weren't perfect, but it seemed Deke had managed to take the four of us from high school kids to badasses.

"Wow," I breathed.

Lars moved behind me. His arm wrapped around my hip and his chin came to rest on my shoulder as he watched with me. A few times, he made appreciative noises.

"Deke's been getting a lot more intense in our knife sessions too," he explained.

I turned my head to see him. "Am I going to be able to keep up?"

"You already are," Lars promised. "I promise I'm not taking it easy on you, and you're wearing my ass out." He grinned. "I don't just mean in bed either."

"Hush!" I laughed, knowing he was joking.

Mostly because I'd been doing more sleeping at night than anything else. Talking was a close second, and yes, I'd told Lars all about my worries. Like always, he'd convinced me it would end up ok. He didn't care about Deke's or Tash's sexuality. He and Bax were supposedly talking to Gavin about his homophobia. Lars had talked to Deke about having Travis help with my magic lessons, and our Martyrs were carefully planning our first hit with no rush on it.

Things were being handled. I just had to focus on learning magic and getting passing grades at school. That was it, and the bite-sized pieces helped more than I wanted to admit. Seeing that we weren't as far behind as I'd feared helped even more. We could do this. We might be teenagers, but Bax looked like some kind of special ops assassin - if there was such a thing. He looked like someone I would not want to pick a fight with, at least!

And then it happened. Bax went for a counter attack, Deke blocked hard enough to make Bax stumble, and the pair crashed to the ground. Deke somehow got Bax's hands pinned, using the rest of his body to hold Bax on the ground. They still struggled, but after a few seconds, Bax just relaxed.

"I give," Bax panted.

Deke laughed at the phrase, then just flopped down. The guys were lying half on each other, but clearly exhausted. I was just about to get up when Deke flinched, rolling off Bax quickly. Even more confusing, Bax just laughed, and hard.

"Fuck off," Deke said, making it clear I was missing something.

"So Jess isn't the only one who gets you hard," Bax managed. "Need to go take care of that, Sandman?"

"No." And Deke pushed to his feet, still breathing hard as he yanked his dick to a different angle. "I need you to do that again with Gav."

"The sparring or the getting hard part?" Bax taunted as he sat up. "Dude, it's cool."

"We are not going there," Deke said, gesturing for Bax to get up.

"Going where?" Gavin looked at Deke as if he wasn't impressed at all. "Are you seriously hard from that?"

Deke just gestured to his crotch. "Yes." Then he crossed his arms. "Increased heart rate and friction do that to a lot of guys. It's pretty natural, so don't be shocked when you end up with a boner in the middle of a fight."

"Happens to me all the time," Lars called out.

"Because you're with Jess," Gavin said. "Not natural with another guy."

Bax just pointed at him. "That's the shit I was talking about. Not cool, Gav. Doesn't make you look like you have bigger balls."

"I'm not gay!" Gavin snapped back. "Not my fault I don't want someone to think I am."

Deke just tossed up his hands and started walking toward where Lars and I were sitting, trying hard to let that blow over. "Up!" Deke ordered. "We're not done yet. More blocking, less talking."

But Bax had shoved to his feet, and his complete attention was on Gavin. "You're being a dick, Gav. Pull your head out of your ass already. It's not funny, ok?"

"Why, because I don't want to fuck some guy?" Gav asked.

Deke spun back around and across the lawn yelled, "Because I do. Is that what you want to hear? No, that's not why I get hard when sparring. Has nothing to do with wanting to fuck Bax. Still happens."

"What?" Gavin asked.

Lars lifted his chin. "I do it too. Not into guys, and it doesn't just happen with Jess. I've had my dick crushed against Bax a few times because the fucker's stronger than me."

I just dragged both hands down my face. I didn't like that everyone had just turned against Gavin. I also hated that Gavin was so stupid about this one thing. I honestly had no idea how to fix it, so I just stood there like an idiot while the guys yelled at each other.

Gavin was just looking at Deke. "You're joking, right?"

"I'm dead fucking serious," Deke told him. "I'm bi, which means I like men."

"No," Gavin said, as if that could somehow change Deke's mind.

But Deke wasn't about to give up. "Yes."

He marched back toward Gavin, making the rest of us follow. I wasn't sure if this was about to turn into a real fight or just a screaming match, but both of these guys looked just a little too pissed.

"I fuck men," Deke said. "Call me gay if you want. Won't change a damned thing. I'm still here. I'm still going to make sure that the four of you are good enough to close that seal, and then the next one. It's also none of your damned business."

The moment he was close enough, Gavin stepped in and shoved. "Then stay the fuck away from me. I don't want you grabbing my dick."

Deke rocked with the push, slapping Gavin's hands away. "You're the one who said all or nothing. *You* told me to step up. I was trying to stay out of your mess, but you *demanded* that I make an effort. Still happy about that, Gav? Still think this is a good idea?"

"You didn't say you were a queer," Gavin huffed.

Deke smiled, but it was a cruel look. "You didn't say you were a bigoted asshole. Guess we're both to blame. So what are you going to do about it, Gav? Are you out now? No more worries about the bonds or how that works?"

ENTER SANDMAN

"Fuck you," Gavin snarled.

"No," Bax said, pushing in between them. "He's right and you know it. Either you're scared because you want it, or you're scared because you're an idiot. Neither's a good look, and I'm pretty sure Jess isn't impressed right now."

"I'm not," I admitted.

But Deke just leaned into Gavin's face a little more. "I'm bi. Tash is a lesbian. We're not going away, so you figure your shit out. I made it very clear that adding another person would get weird. You said you were fine with it. You taking that back now? Because I'm not changing my mind. I'm not putting Jess in the middle of *our* issues. Stop acting like a little boy and grow the fuck up." Then he turned and stormed away. "Lesson's over."

"Faggot!" Gavin called after him.

Bax didn't hesitate. He swung, catching Gavin right in the jaw. "That just went too far," Bax snarled. "If you don't want to be in the room with him, then fine. You want to be the odd man out, then that's your call. You call anyone names like that again, and I'll beat it out of you."

Gavin slowly reached up to touch his chin. "Asshole."

This time, I was the one pushing between them. "Can we please not fight each other?" I begged. "Gavin, it's not a big deal."

"It is!" he insisted. "How many times has he looked at my ass?"

Lars just huffed out a laugh. "I love how you assume your ass is nice enough for him to look at. Maybe he's been checking out mine?"

"Same shit!" Gavin insisted.

"But I'm ok with it," Lars said. "If Deke wants to grab a handful, I might even get hard. Doesn't fucking matter to me. I'm man enough to not care."

So Gavin looked at me, a little desperation in his eyes. "You understand, right?"

"Not really," I admitted. "Gav, it's no big deal. So Deke likes guys. I do too. I don't see why this is a thing at all."

"He slept in the bed with us!" Gavin insisted.

"And?" I asked.

For a moment, Gavin just looked at me as if I'd spoken some foreign language. Then, between one breath and the next, he shoved away from us and started walking toward the barn. I turned to follow, but Bax grabbed my arm.

"He needs to figure it out," Bax said, his voice gentle.

"But we all just ganged up on him," I pointed out.

"No," Bax assured me. "I've talked to him a few times, and he's not about to budge without a fight. Let him fight, Jess."

"It's how Gavin deals with things," Lars told me.

"But I don't want to lose him," I insisted.

"So you'll lose Deke instead?" Lars asked. "This has to get fixed, sweetie. One way or another, and none of them will be pretty."

"But you can't make Gavin be ok with it," I pointed out.

"That's where you're wrong," Bax told me. "We can. We will. I'll talk to him, but he doesn't need to be babied, Jess."

"He almost died!" I reminded them both.

Lars nodded at me. "Yeah. And that's not going to be the last time. If he's worried about stupid shit like this, it might go from almost died to *did* die. How about we sort out our shit before it blows up in our faces, ok?" He reached out to hook his fingers with mine. "And it is *our* shit. We're a quad. We'll find a way to make this work. May not be perfect, but we will figure it out."

"Ok," I breathed. "I just don't know how."

"I do," Bax promised. "This is my problem to deal with. Not yours, babe. Believe it or not, we guys can do things without you making all the decisions." Then he pulled me closer. "Just focus on the magic. We'll deal with the dicks."

CHAPTER FIFTEEN

THAT EVENING WAS TENSE. Deke headed upstairs to avoid us. Gavin ranted about how he hadn't done anything wrong, but Bax and Lars kept shutting him down. I couldn't take it. I hated all of this. The only reason I didn't snap and scream about it was because of something Tash had said.

She'd pointed out that I'd never learned how to hate. When she'd said it, I thought she was wrong, but the more I thought about it, the more I realized she had a point. I'd been scared of my dad, but I hadn't hated him. If I had, I would've found a way to get out. I wouldn't have tried to protect him, like when I'd asked Linda not to call the cops.

I wanted to say I hated Megan and Collin, but it wasn't the same. I hated them for what they'd done. I'd started out liking them both, but they'd ruined it. I'd never hated them because of something out of their control. I was pretty sure I had my mom to blame for that. She'd always told me to walk a mile in someone else's shoes before I judged them.

As soon as we were done eating, I claimed I had homework, so headed to my room. I did, but I wasn't honestly worried about it.

Then, just as I opened the door, before I could even step through, I heard Lars' voice in the living room.

"You know you just chased Jess off, right?"

"I didn't do anything," Gavin insisted.

Bax didn't agree. "You've been pissed about Deke since we finished training. In case you missed it, she likes him. Just think about how pissed you'd be if someone said shit about Jess fucking four guys."

"It's different," Gavin mumbled.

Which meant he wasn't ready to budge, and I just didn't have the emotional energy to deal with this. Bax said he'd handle it, so I was going to trust him. He'd known Gavin for years. That meant he should know how far to push him before Gavin exploded. And yet my stomach was still in a knot.

I felt like we were falling apart. In every relationship I'd ever seen, the moment people started bickering, it fell apart. Or worse, it turned abusive. Complaining turned to fighting, and fighting always led to breaking up. I'd been dumped enough times to be a pro at this.

Deke had warned us that this wouldn't work. I couldn't just date everyone at the same time and expect it to be more than a fling. Someone would get mad, someone would be a favorite, or someone would feel left out. I hated to admit it, but he'd been right. I was in love with Gavin, but I hated that he felt like this. I also had no clue how to make those things fit together! How could I love a guy who treated someone else like this? If I stopped loving Gavin, what would that do to Bax? Should I just call the whole relationship off, tell them we were just friends? Date Lars and just Lars so I didn't tear Bax and Gavin apart? Tell Deke it was impossible and go back to the four of us being happy?

I had no answers and I hated all those options, so I opened a book and started working. I finished one class and started on the next. Just as I was ready for the third, a soft tap sounded at my door. I didn't get the chance to respond before it opened and Deke stepped through.

"Hey," he said, keeping his voice down.

"When did you come back downstairs?" I asked.

He didn't move from his spot right in front of the door. "A second ago. I also heard them still talking in the other room, but didn't see you in there."

"Using the mirror again?" I teased.

He let out a weak laugh, but it was just one. "Jess, this isn't going to work."

My blood stopped. My lungs forgot to breathe. A million pinpricks raced across my skin, starting at the back of my neck and rushing toward my fingers and toes. His words echoed my own thoughts, but I hated them so much more when he said it.

"Oh," I breathed, closing my book.

Deke blew out a long breath, then finally took a step toward me. "How did Bax know about me?"

My eyes dropped to the comforter beneath me. "I kinda told him."

"I see." Then Deke sat down by my legs. "I wish you hadn't done that."

"He said he'd deal with Gavin," I explained. "They've been friends forever, and I didn't know what else to do. I feel like something's broken, Deke."

"Well, it is now," he grumbled. "Look, you and your quad work. I'm the problem here."

"No," I told him. "Gavin's the problem. I don't know why this freaks him out, but - "

"Because it's weak," Deke explained. "Women get fucked, and women are supposed to be weaker than men. If you're not doing the fucking but receiving it, then you're a pussy. Being a pussy is weak." He shrugged. "I kinda grew up in the same environment. Trust me, I know exactly what he's thinking, because I thought it about myself."

I reached over for his hand. "And it's stupid. I am not weak, Deke. I don't have a dick, and I don't care. I've been hit harder than most of those guys. I mean, Gavin wins if we're comparing, but so? Dad used to beat the shit out of me and I took it. That's not weak."

"It wasn't smart, though," Deke countered. "You should've turned him in."

I tugged at his hand, making him look at me. "I had nowhere else to go. I made a plan, I was going to get out, and I was going to do it in a way that would let me stay far from him. So what if it wasn't the way you'd do things? See, Bax said something, and I kinda like it. He said we don't always have to agree."

"But you have to be able to work together," Deke countered. "If I'm just the Martyr, then it doesn't matter if Gavin hates me for being queer. I'll still teach him. I'll use his hate and rage to make him lethal."

He'd gone back to calling himself a Martyr. I didn't like that. It felt like a position, not a title. Sandman was something that fit with us. Conquest, Vengeance, Judgement, Anathema, and Sandman. That made us five. Martyr was what we called Tash, and it didn't matter if she stayed or left.

"You said you wouldn't do this," I grumbled. "Outside, you told Gavin you were all in, and now you're back out?" My voice was slowly getting louder, but I didn't care. "No! You don't get to make me like you, let me fuck you, tell me no, then yes, then no again. I am not a *goddamned yo-yo*, Deke!" And I yanked my hand back.

He came halfway with it. His hand landed by my hip, and Deke leaned in, preventing me from sliding to the other side of the bed. "I'm trying to make the right decision, Jess. You don't love me. I don't love you. We fucked, and I have a feeling you can walk away from that easily enough."

"It's not about the sex," I told him. "Don't you get that?"

He didn't move away, but he did drop his head. "Yeah, I do."

I lifted my hand and wrapped my fingers around his bicep. "What are we doing, Deke?"

ENTER SANDMAN

His grey eyes found mine. "I don't know. What are you doing, Jess? What exactly are you thinking?"

There was no more than a foot between our faces. Not too close, but close enough that the deep, raspy sound of his voice made my heart beat a little faster. A million thoughts ran through my mind, but I didn't have an answer for him. I didn't know how to explain what I felt.

I liked Deke. He made me feel safe when my world got too insane. He pushed me, making me feel like I could be someone strong. He was sexy even with his scars. Then there was the pure, raw manliness of him. The way he took what he wanted, pushed when he needed, and didn't automatically expect me to be too fragile to take it.

I liked him. Everything about him. Even the fact that he was into guys was a bonus for me. I couldn't explain why, but it made me feel like the sides were a little more balanced, like I wasn't surrounded by nothing but horny guys. Dumb, sure, but I still felt that way. Deke understood me, and I didn't know if that was because he was bi or older, but it was still there.

And I still didn't have an answer to his question, so I decided to muddle through. "I thought we were getting to know each other. I assumed that when you spent the night last weekend, it meant I had a chance. I don't know, Deke, because you told me it wouldn't happen, then you came in here Monday morning and said you'd changed your mind, and now you've changed it back!"

"I didn't change it!" Deke snapped, his voice just a little too loud. "I'm *trying* to make this easy on you."

"But I like you!" I shot back, matching his volume.

And my door opened. Immediately, the pair of us jerked apart and turned to see who that was. Bax stood there, tensed like he was ready to do a little of his own yelling. His eyes jumped from me to Deke and back, then his shoulders relaxed.

"Today is not the day, Sandman," Bax said.

Deke shoved to his feet. "This is why it can't happen, Jess.

Maybe you can make three guys work, but the four of us won't happen. I'm the odd one out."

He headed for the door, but Bax blocked his way. "I don't care who you fuck, Deke."

"And yet you just outed me to Gavin," Deke countered. "He does care, and the only one paying for it is Jess."

Bax just crossed his arms, making it clear he wasn't budging. "When they call you a Martyr, this isn't what they mean."

Closing his eyes, Deke let out a long sigh. "And how are you handling my big secret, Bax? Think that I'm nothing to fear now?"

Bax dropped his arms and stepped right into Deke's chest. Then, his hand landed on Deke's crotch, cupping it gently, and Bax lifted a brow, refusing to look away. "You want to thrust again? Or would you rather we flip this around, hm? You don't get me hard, but so? How many times have you walked in on me? How many times have I fucking cared, Deke? I've had my dick grinding against Lars' and liked it. Sure, Jess was in the middle, but what's the difference? I. Don't. Care."

Deke just reached down and carefully removed Bax's hand from his crotch. "And?" he asked.

Which was when I stood up and moved to ease them apart. "Guys, this isn't helping. Bax, Deke thinks he overstepped, and Gavin's not helping. You all but made that happen out there! You're the one who basically outed him, and now Gav's losing his shit."

"He needs to," Bax said, palming the back of my head to make me look at him. "That's how he deals. He's going to be a fucking idiot, but I'll make him get over it."

"And you'll trash Deke in the process?" I asked. "Talk about a rift. Jesus, Bax!"

Deke hooked my chin, turning my face so I looked at him. "Stop worrying about me. I've had a lot worse than some kid calling me a fag."

"She's worrying about her," Bax said. "She's trying to make this sound all sensible because she doesn't want you to start ignoring her."

I inhaled to say something, but there was nothing to say, so the air just slid back out. My shoulders dropped, and I knew I was losing. This wasn't going to happen. Deke was determined. Bax was stubborn. Gavin was freaking out. My perfect little world was imploding, but had I really expected anything else?

But Deke refused to let me look away. "I'm trying to help you, Jess."

"I don't want your help," I insisted. "I don't want to be managed. I don't want to be fucking protected!"

I had no idea what I was thinking, but both of these guys were holding me between them, cradling me, sheltering me, and I was sick of losing out because it was what was safest. So, grabbing the front of Deke's shirt, I pulled him closer. Doing so made me turn, and Bax's hand fell away from my head. Then, before either guy knew what I was doing, I shoved my mouth to Deke's and kissed him as hard as I could.

"That's my girl," Bax breathed.

Deke kissed back, thrusting his tongue into my mouth, but his hands pulled mine away from his shirt. Easily, he forced them up and out, even with my shoulders, while he pushed me back. I was pretty sure Deke was trying to get me off him. It felt like he was ready to turn away now that I didn't have my fingers clenching his shirt, but I collided with Bax's chest. Another set of hands - Bax's - closed on my wrists, and he pulled my hands behind my head.

Deke let go. I was pinned, both of these men pressing into me from different sides, but for a moment everything paused. My big move had just backfired, but Bax wasn't letting go of my wrists. My elbows were up by my ears now. I could feel Bax's dick against my ass, quickly getting harder. Before me, Deke was breathing heavily. I couldn't tell if it was rage, passion, or fear. It also didn't matter.

"Now this," Bax said, his voice just a bit deeper than normal, "is not at all how I expected this to end up. Tell me, Jess. You like to be held down?"

"Yes," I breathed, my eyes locked on Deke's.

"And you said you're not evil," Deke growled right before his mouth was on mine again.

Bax just leaned in to whisper in my ear, "I like holding, so I think this is going to work out very, very well. Deke, lock the door."

CHAPTER SIXTEEN

THE MOMENT DEKE stepped away to lock the door, Bax let go of my wrists. I was almost disappointed, but his hands immediately moved to my waist, tugging my shirt higher. It seemed this was happening. Deke had come in here to tell me we couldn't be together, and now Bax was making this work. I was so ok with this idea.

I also wanted to be kissed, not just fucked, so when Bax pulled my shirt over my head, I turned to face him. My mouth found his. My hands dropped down to tug at his shirt the way he'd pulled at mine. His reached around my back, quickly releasing my bra. I yanked his shirt over his head and tossed it away so we were both topless. Together, we both reached down for the other's pants. Bax was faster, and as he pushed at my waistband, he looked over at Deke.

"You just going to stand there, or are you going to help?" Bax asked.

"This is such a bad idea," Deke said.

So Bax bent, my pants hit the ground, and I'd barely stepped out of them before he spun me back around. "This," he told Deke, "is a great idea. Tell me, do you think she's wet yet? Because I'm going to hold her while you check and see."

Feeling a little mischievous, I bit my lower lip and pushed my hand down. As my fingers slipped between my own folds, I watched Deke, aware that the bulge in the front of his jeans was growing. His eyes were locked on my hand, and he stood there breathing just a little too hard, but the man refused to move.

"I can't do this," he said, but it came out more like a growl of desire.

"You've already done this," Bax reminded him.

"Not with you!" Deke snapped.

So Bax let me go and shoved off the last of his clothes. "Yeah?" he asked as he got his socks off and the pants away from his ankles. "Because you might look at my dick?"

Yep, I could see what he was doing. Conquest was conquering, and I wanted to help. Turning sideways, I reached over to stroke Bax's length just as he stood back up. Now it was Bax staring at Deke, daring him, taunting him.

"I don't care if you touch. I also don't think you want me. I'm pretty sure we're both hot for the same girl, and I kinda like this group shit." Bax pulled my hand from his dick and took a step back. He tugged me with him, stopping when he reached the edge of the bed. "I don't care if you watch, touch, or stick your dick down her throat," Bax said, "but we're doing this."

"Jess?" Deke asked, a hint of insecurity tinting his voice even as he tried to hide it.

I just pushed Bax down so he was sitting on the bed. "All or nothing, Deke."

"Turn around," Bax whispered. "Give the boy a good view, Jess. Spread those knees..."

One of his hands on my hip guided me down. The other, I couldn't feel. When I lowered myself, I realized it was on his own dick. Bax lined himself up, then pulled. My hips dropped, he filled me, and I gasped with the sensation. Before I could do more than that, my boyfriend grabbed both of my elbows, pinning them behind my back.

That shoved my breasts out. When Bax spread his legs, opening me so Deke could see our connection, that was when the man finally gave in. Reaching behind his neck, he pulled his shirt off in a fluid motion, dropping it to the ground even as his feet finally moved. Bax used my arms to lift me up and then back down, taking his time about pumping me onto his body.

I could feel my nipples getting hard. I couldn't look away from Deke's face. Yes, Bax felt good inside me, but the hungry look in Deke's eyes was the same one he'd had in the shower. This man was feral, and I loved the way it felt when he was focused on me, so I gave in. My head fell back against Bax's shoulder. My breasts were begging for attention, the peaks like hard rocks now. I could feel my pussy throbbing around Bax's dick, but he was moving slowly, tormenting me until a whimper slipped out.

"That's my girl," Bax praised. "Gonna let him play with you?"

"Yes," I gasped. "Or beg if he doesn't hurry up."

Deke kicked off his shoes, and then just dropped to his knees before me. "Fine. You win, Bax."

And then he kissed me hard, reaching up to run his calloused palms across my nipples. Fuck, but that was what I wanted. I twitched at the sensation, driving Bax deeper into my body. The grunt from behind me was worth it. Bax managed to shift his grip so he was holding my arms with one hand, and then I felt him lean back.

That was so he could brace. Shoving a hand down onto the bed allowed him to thrust up into my body. My feet were on the floor, letting me almost hold myself up, but I was truly at their mercy. Deke kept kissing. His hands went from caressing to flicking and pinching my nipples. Then I felt his lips curl against mine.

"All in, right Bax?" he asked as he lowered himself onto his heels.

Bax exhaled hard. "Yeah. Show me what you got, Deke."

So Deke leaned in, pushing his face right against my pussy. My legs were wide open. He was also kneeling between Bax's knees. At first, I didn't feel more than the heat of his breath, and then Deke's tongue slid onto me from the bottom up - and Bax let out a deep groan before slamming into me harder.

"Fuck, that's good," he panted. "Lick her damned clit like that."

Deke did, the tip of his tongue hard when it flicked across me. I wanted to grab the back of his head, but I couldn't. Not without pulling free of Bax's grip. I also couldn't balance, which meant I was at their mercy. Both of theirs, and I loved it. As Deke continued to torment me, licking, sucking, and teasing my clit, Bax kept pumping.

My body felt like it was on fire in the best way. Sparks shot across my nerves, my pussy was stretched and full. The feel of Deke's shoulders between both mine and Bax's legs was erotic. The motion of Bax beneath me was sensual. It all felt so damned good, and I just wanted more. I wanted it all.

Then Deke reached up to grab my breast. He used it almost like a point of balance, but his fingers teased me. Pinching the tip between his middle finger and thumb, his index finger swirled across my nipple. I couldn't hold back the moan. Between that, his mouth, and Bax's dick, my body couldn't handle it all.

My hips bucked, pressing my pussy down onto Bax and further onto Deke's face. Neither man seemed to care. If anything, it encouraged them. Deke ducked his head again, and then I felt his tongue at my entrance, licking across Bax before he came back to make me gasp with another round of the sweetest flicks and sucks.

Over and over, they sucked and fucked. I didn't know how we'd ended up here, and I honestly didn't care. Just minutes ago, Deke had been trying to tell me this couldn't happen, and now it was. Somehow, Bax had done this. I wanted to say for me, but I wasn't completely convinced it was *just* for me. This felt like more, like something bigger, as if Bax needed it as much as I did. Not the touches, but the connection.

The bond.

The thought hit me as Deke began to suck, ravishing my clit inside his lips with the tip of his tongue. Paired with everything else, I couldn't hold off. My orgasm hit hard, with almost no warning, and my body arched into it. Bax grabbed my shoulder with the hand that had previously been holding my arms. As I came, he kept thrusting, pumping into me hard as the waves of pleasure took over my body.

Deke just chuckled and leaned back, using his hand to wipe his face. "Oh, give her a little break. I felt that orgasm throbbing through her clit." Then he stood and began opening his pants. "Slow, Bax. Let her cool off, then bring her back for us."

"Oh, I think I like it when you play," Bax teased. "Breathe, Jess. Yeah, just like that, baby."

Because breathing was all I could do. My body was sure it couldn't take anymore, but in the best way. Bax's long, slow strokes kept me from coming down completely, but they also didn't make me feel too sensitive to enjoy it. My arms were now free, and I didn't want to stop touching.

Shifting a bit, I managed to reach behind me to hook my fingers around Bax's neck. His hands moved to my waist, his grip moving me the way he wanted. I liked that, the way it made me feel like he couldn't get enough of me. Rolling my hips, I made it clear that I could take a whole lot more. My eyes, however, were locked on Deke.

His pants hit the ground and my eyes dropped to his dick. Deke's hard, thick dick. The scars looked like decorations on his body, outlining the hard lines of his muscles. I caught the corner of Deke's lips curling into something like a smirk, and then he wrapped his own fingers around his shaft and pumped once.

"Tell me you suck dick, girl," Deke taunted as he moved a little closer.

I reached out and wrapped my fingers around the base of his shaft. "I love to suck dick, Deke."

That was all he needed to hear. Deke's hand landed on the back of my head and he pulled me closer. My lips parted, but before I could even lick at that swollen head, he pushed in. The man gave me enough time to work with him, but gentle wasn't Deke's way.

I looked up as I pushed my lips down as far as I could go. Deke, however, was watching Bax. When I began to slide off, that was when he finally looked down - and Bax took over. His hips thrust upward, burying his dick into me. I felt my breasts bounce with the impact, and my breath rushed out. Deke just smiled and then pulled me back down onto his length.

They did it again, then one more time, finding the rhythm. Then, the pair began to move in opposition. Every time I gave up inches of Deke's dick, Bax filled me. When I leaned in to suck back more, Bax withdrew. It made me feel like we were all working together, as if this wasn't just about pleasing me, but also about me pleasing them.

And then I added my hand. My palm slid over his slick length in time with Bax driving into my body. I needed to moan, so I did, not caring that his dick muffled the sound of it. Beneath me, Bax groaned, reaching down to play with my clit as he kept going, driving into me a little harder with each thrust.

"Deke..." he warned.

"You gotta get her off first, Bax," Deke said, giving a little push with his hips so that his dick pressed deeper into my mouth.

"Was waiting," Bax huffed as his hand began to move faster on my clit, "for you."

Deke just dropped his eyes to me. "That's my girl," he breathed, something tender in his rough voice. "Just take it, doll. Stop trying so fucking hard and just fucking take it." He began to move his hips, sliding through my lips. "Feel his body under you. That cock inside you. Good, huh?" And again, he pumped into my mouth.

"Oh, god," Bax groaned. "I'm gonna cum so hard, Jess."

"Shut up," Deke told him. "Stop talking and fuck her like you mean it. Hard, Bax. I want to see those tits bounce as I fuck her face."

His hand on the back of my head pulled, but Bax obeyed too. The pair of them began pounding into me. Deke used short little thrusts, never even hitting the back of my throat. Bax just let go, taking what he wanted. As my men filled me, they lost control, and this was what I'd been wanting.

Their touches were amazing. The feel of their hard dicks was a turn-on, but nothing was as sexy as the feel of them both wanting to lose themselves in my body. Each man moved differently. They were nothing alike, and yet I had control over them both by just giving in. That was what turned me on the most. It was what made me feel so good. The knowledge that these gorgeous, amazing, confident men wanted me this much ignited something in my mind.

I wasn't sure if it was the boost of confidence, the taboo of what we were doing, or something else, but I loved this feeling as much as the sensations of my body. It made me feel beautiful, and I wasn't used to that. It made me feel wanted, and that was all I'd ever dreamed of. Combined with Bax's hand teasing my clit and the view of Deke's eyes slipping closed with pleasure, I didn't even try to hold out.

My body tensed, a tremor of pleasure warning me I was close. Bax felt it and fucked a little faster. Deke began to move slower. I didn't even care that they were no longer in time. I just wanted to make sure I didn't bite down, bend the wrong way, or screw this up somehow. I wanted to feel them both lose control, but they were determined to make me do it first.

I groaned, feeling my legs tremble. Deke jerked his dick out of my mouth just as I came. My body tensed, my back arched, and a deep groan fell from my lips. Bax only managed to thrust one more time before he lost it. Deke stepped back, his eyes running over both of us as he took over, stroking himself a few more times before grabbing the tip of his dick and just groaning. Cum filled his palm.

"Fuck," Bax breathed, flopping back onto the bed. "Yep, I'm done."

I eased myself off of him only to roll onto the bed beside him. With a chuckle, Bax pushed at my legs, turning me a bit so I was almost the right way on the bed. Deke just shook his head at us and headed into my bathroom. He didn't bother closing the door, so when he bent over the sink to rinse off his hands, I could see him. All of him. Every hard, scarred, elegant line of him.

"Hey," Bax called at him. "Bring a cloth for Jess?"

"Warming up the water," Deke assured him. "Figured you teenagers wouldn't worry about that."

"Fuck off," Bax said. "You're not that much older than us."

Deke walked back out, carrying a cloth. "Seven years. That's a long time, Bax." Then he passed me the cloth. "You ok, doll?"

"I will be if you say that's going to happen again."

Deke bent to grab his underwear out of his pants. "Pretty sure that's not my call."

"Oh, is it mine?" Bax asked. "Because I have a serious threesome fetish. Really want to try a foursome, but have a feeling Gavin won't get all close and cuddly with me and Lars. You, however..."

"I was trying to show you that this won't work," Deke said.

Bax began to chuckle. After a moment, he shifted himself so he could lie beside me, but the chuckling didn't stop. When he finally had his head on the pillows, he took the now-used washcloth from my hand and wiped off his softening dick.

"If you mean all but sucking me off? Yeah, not seeing a downside. If you mean because you try to be rough with Jess, that's her call." And then both of them looked at me.

"I want to fix Gavin," I said.

"What if Gavin can't be fixed?" Deke asked. "It's not like he has a chip in his paint. He's scared of the idea of another man being into him. He's *scared*, Jess, and that doesn't go away with the snap of a finger. So then what? Do you really want to risk pulling your quad apart because you need another dick? You already have three."

"Four," I told him. "In case you missed it, I just had your dick too." Then I scooted back a little more so I could use my pillow as a backrest. "And if Gavin's not ok with this, then he's not. I can have a thing with him and then you three. Two separate things. I won't let it pull us apart. None of us, Deke."

"I'm with her," Bax said. "I'm also staying the night, so I'll apologize in advance if I grab your dick."

Deke dropped his head and scratched at the back of his neck. "Ok. All in. Well, for as long as she'll take me, I am."

"Good," I said, moving over so he could join us. "I need someone to cuddle with. I'm tired of feeling like we're fighting."

"Not fighting," Deke promised as he unlocked the door and turned off the lights. "I think we're all just trying a little too hard to take care of each other."

"Which isn't a bad thing," Bax promised. "Might get loud, and maybe a little ugly, but it doesn't have to be bad."

CHAPTER SEVENTEEN

That weekend was a little tense. Gavin had heard us fucking, so it wasn't a secret that Deke and Bax had been with me. He tried to ignore it, brooding a bit, but Bax wouldn't let him get away with that. Sometime on Sunday, Gavin finally exploded, yelling at Bax about how he'd picked Deke's side instead of his best friend. Bax made it clear he'd picked me. Just me. The rest was for Gavin to deal with.

I tried to talk to him, spending Sunday night in Gavin's room. It helped, but things were just a bit awkward. The tension around this meant I didn't feel sexy, but Gavin wasn't really any better. We just talked, and it helped more than I wanted to admit. He asked me how I could be ok with Deke wanting to fuck men, and I countered with him getting turned on by two women making out. Surprisingly, that actually made sense to him, but he had a bigger problem.

"It's just that this means they're right," he mumbled into the top of my hair.

We were lying on our sides, chest to chest, and he was hugging me close. I tried to look up, to see if there was some hint of what he meant on his face, but I couldn't. He had his chin resting on the top of my head so all I could see was his neck.

"Who's right?" I asked instead. "And what are they right about?"

"That it's gay," he admitted. "It was one thing when they joked about it but I knew better. Now I don't."

"Do *you* want to fuck Deke, Gav?"

"No!" he said, answering almost immediately.

"Then it's not gay," I told him. "Besides, you've lived with Deke for how long?"

"But I didn't know he was checking out my ass," Gavin tried to explain. "How many times have I walked around this place in my boxers? Fuck, just a towel!"

"Nothing has changed," I soothed. "Deke isn't going to rape you. If that was the case, he would've months ago."

"But I heard about the morning groping," Gavin admitted. "Bax said that's how he found out."

I kissed the hollow of Gavin's throat. "In case you missed it, Bax was the one doing the dick grabbing."

"Deke humped his hand!"

I just started laughing. Part was the stress of this mess. Part was the use of the word "humped." Mostly it was the futility of it all. Ignorance bred fear. Fear turned to anger when it was pushed too hard. Over the last few months, we'd all been through a lot, and my options were to laugh or scream.

"He pressed into someone grabbing him," I managed to say. "Someone, Gav. Deke was asleep, so he didn't even know who. This whole thing is fucking stupid, ok? From what I heard, you're the one who told Deke to spend the night that night. Not me. Not Bax, and not Lars. It was you."

"But I didn't know," he reminded me.

"So?" I asked. "I mean, you just assume that he wants you. Maybe he thinks you're ugly. Besides, if you had known that Deke was a little more kinky than you, would it then be ok for him to cut me out? Have you simply decided that this mess of a relationship we're doing is too much? What's really going on?"

Gavin leaned back to see my face. "I don't know how to do this," he admitted. "I don't hate him. I just don't know... I don't want..." Closing his eyes, he groaned. "Never mind."

Then he tried to roll over, but I wasn't going to let him get away with that. I grabbed Gavin's shoulder and tugged him back to face me. "I like Deke, ok? I like you too, so don't you dare make me choose."

"No..." he promised, facing me fully just to cup the side of my face. "Where I'm from, being gay means bad things. It means getting beat up or chased out of church. It means parents kicking kids out. It means priests doing things to little boys."

"All over Spain?" I asked.

He shook his head. "I don't think so. My dad always said there were big cities that ignored sinful things like that. I think it was just my area. Like, my parents and their friends." He almost ended there, then mumbled, "Maybe just my church."

"Gav? Did something happen to you with a priest?"

"No," he assured me. "But I knew other guys. One of the ones who beat me up."

I nodded slowly, letting that sink in. "So you think that gay means rape, and rape makes you a bully. I can see why that freaks you out, but Deke isn't going to rape you. Shit, he was bullied because of who he likes."

"Yeah?" he asked.

I nodded. "That's why Tash took him under her wing. She protected him because we all need someone on our side."

"Yeah. I just don't know how to act," Gavin admitted. "When Deke's around, I keep thinking about it, and then I stop thinking about you. I know we have these bonds, and I know that's important. *He's* important, Jess. To you, to us, I'm not sure. It's just hard to think of him being gay as being ok."

"He's not gay," I corrected.

"Whatever!" Gavin said. "Into guys. I don't want another guy touching my dick."

"Ok." Because that settled that. "When Lars brought up the idea of all of us dating, you said you weren't ok with sharing like that, so we'll make it work."

"And that's all?" Gavin asked. "You're not mad at me?"

"I'm disappointed, but not mad," I assured him. "Gav, I like the group stuff. I love that I could roll one way and cuddle with you, or roll the other and press up against someone else. You don't, and that sucks, but we'll make it work. I still love you, and I don't want to lose you over this."

"You will never lose me," he promised. "Never, Jess. I just need to figure it out, but you give up so much for us. The least I can do is try to understand, and I am. It's just not working."

"That," I told him, "is why I fell in love with you. It's ok for it to be hard. It's amazing that you're willing to try."

"For you," he said, "I will do anything. *Te amo, mi cielo.*"

We fell asleep not long after that, but his words helped. They took away that fear that had been bothering me for days now. I didn't need us to be perfect. I just needed to know that we were real and not going anywhere. I needed to stop feeling like what was good for me might be bad for everyone else.

The next day, Gavin made a point of saying good morning to Deke before we left. At school, Travis gave us a few more names of various demons who he knew lived in town. Unfortunately, he had no idea who had been at the seal, but assured us he'd find out. He also passed me a list of the ones who'd stayed home because they didn't want to fight. Those didn't come with addresses, but Travis did give me a warning.

"If any of them get hurt by you four, I'm done."

I couldn't blame him for that. Not all demons were evil, but that didn't mean they were all good. The same was true for Brethren, it seemed. Somehow, we had to prove to Travis that we weren't like the quads that had come before, and this was how. The demons who hadn't hurt us shouldn't be hurt by us.

And while I completely understood Travis's reasons, that didn't mean he couldn't lie about it. There could be some demon coup going on that we were being pulled into. He could be giving us names of humans to save his own skin. There were hundreds of reasons why he might simply pretend to help us, and none of them would be easy to prove.

So we began taking trips around town when we got out of school to verify the information he'd given us. None of us wanted to plan a hit on a person just to find out they were human. At that point, it wouldn't even matter if we killed them or not. Breaking into a house just to have our necklaces stay silent would be almost as bad.

For the next two weeks, we alternated between scoping out as many people in town as possible and planning the mission to take out Greg. We found plenty of demons in Hellam, and most were on Travis's lists. Some were buying groceries. Others were getting gas. For the most part, they looked like completely normal people.

The lists were given to Deke. He promised he wouldn't just hand the names over to Tash. Our combat lessons moved from the yard to the mansion, and we started learning how to clear rooms and watch each other's backs. Our shooting days became more frequent and our list got longer. Bit by bit, my magic was getting better.

In other words, we may have gotten our asses kicked at the seal, but that didn't mean we had to tuck our tails and hide. Things were still awkward between Deke and Gavin, but there was no more name calling. Sometimes, Gavin would flinch from Deke's touch, but he was now apologizing for it. Deke hated it, but he didn't bitch.

Somewhere in there, I started texting Travis for advice - the magical kind. I'd ask him how to make a spell to cage something, and he'd give me an idea. If I couldn't figure out what mixing two or three elements together could do, he'd explain to me the pros, cons, and list a few examples. A few times, he even came over to demonstrate.

His spells were small and tightly controlled. Mine were big and powerful. Travis could take a hit, and his body was almost indestructible, but his "mana pool," as he called it, was tiny. The term worked well for the guys. It seemed it was from some game they all knew - or a few of them - so they easily grasped the concept.

Which was how I ended up learning how to play some of those games. Regenerating my health and mana gave me a whole new appreciation for how this worked. It was also weird to think of my magic as obeying the rules of game mechanics, but it was mostly an analogy.

During this time, my grades dropped. Bax got called into the office because he was all but failing English. Lars got in trouble for falling asleep in one of his classes. Gavin was still just a little too quiet, but he managed to stay out of trouble. Linda tried to convince us to just do enough to get by. She was adamant that we'd want our high school diplomas later in life. The sad thing was that none of us tried to correct her.

Because this was my future. This was what I'd be doing from now on. I was a demon hunter, a cambion mage, and the most lethal of the Brethren. The five of us were the last line of defense for this world, protecting it from the Apocalypse. It no longer sounded insane. It didn't feel like a joke or a fantasy. Somewhere between New Year's and the second half of April, Deke had turned us from high school kids into Brethren.

But on a Friday morning, as we were all piling into Bax's SUV to head to school, Linda came out of the garage dressed a little too nice. We all paused, but Lars turned back to her.

"Mom?" he asked. "What are you doing? Please tell me you're not going to a job interview?"

"No," she assured him. "It's my last meeting with the attorney.

You kids have been so busy, but I'm still working on my divorce. It's being finalized on Tuesday, Lars."

"Do you need me to go to court with you?" he asked.

"No," she assured him. "It's just a quick thing." But her hand dropped to her belly where the bump was just starting to show. "My attorney knows Ted was abusive, and he promised to walk me back to my car. I'll be fine, and it's a courthouse. What can Ted do?"

"Burn it down?" Gavin suggested. "We should go."

"You should be in school," Linda scolded. "Go act like normal kids. Let me handle this. Today is a routine meeting. We're just making sure we have all the documents we need and the attorney is going to update me on the thing with the school board. Sounds like they might want to settle."

"Ok," Lars said, pulling open the SUV's door, but he paused before getting in. "We might be out late tonight, so you know."

"Why?" Linda asked. "What are you doing?"

I stood up on the far side of the vehicle so I could look over the roof. "We're going to get pizza."

"And?" Linda pressed, because she knew us too well.

Bax chuckled, clearly thinking the same thing. "And we're counting demons. Supposed to be a ton of people hanging out at the Slice after school. Everyone's planning senior skip day, so we're going to go have fun and act like kids."

"Then eat something while you're there," Linda said. "I'll tell Deke and Tash that we'll have an evening to ourselves."

Then she waved and climbed into her car. The four of us settled into the SUV, but Bax let Linda leave first. As he backed out of his parking space, he casually asked, "She's just a little too ok with this."

"Coolest mom ever," Gavin said.

Lars and I just shared a look. She was absolutely amazing, but it was still weird. Linda was just too nice to be caught up in the middle of this, and yet we couldn't keep her out of it either. I wanted to say she didn't really understand, but I knew that was a lie. The woman had been working with Tash for days on our assassination mission! She was as invested with all of this as we were.

"Bad time to mention that she's the beneficiary of my will?" Bax asked as he headed down the drive.

"What?" Lars gasped.

Bax just nodded. "There's a stipulation in there for all of you, but Linda is who will inherit all of this. I just figured that she'll need it to take care of the baby."

Lars reached forward to clasp Bax's shoulder. "Thanks, man. Doesn't sound like enough, but feels nice to know she'll be taken care of."

"That's why we work," Gavin said, sounding almost like he was talking to himself. "It's why we're going to make it through this, because no matter what, we will always take care of each other."

"Exactly," I agreed, hoping he was right.

I didn't honestly believe we'd make it through this alive, but I was certainly willing to hope, because we were almost ready to start taking out demons. Just a little over a week from now, we'd get to see if our training actually worked.

CHAPTER EIGHTEEN

The four of us had become inseparable, so it surprised no one when we grabbed a booth together at the Slice that afternoon. Bax knew everyone, so he charmed the guy working in the kitchen to make us the most pepperoni-and-cheese-covered pizza possible. While we waited for that, other students began to make their way in.

Tina Carter, one of the soccer players, showed up with a notebook, a pen, and a stack of surveys. Clearly, she was the one organizing all of this. When she saw Bax, the girl smiled, looked away, and her cheeks turned a little pink. Gavin chuckled, smacking Bax's arm to make it clear I wasn't the only one who noticed.

"So," Tina said, raising her voice so everyone would pay attention, "Senior Skip Day, this year, will be on May third. We need to decide what we'll be doing instead of school." Her eyes jumped over to Bax.

He just shook his head. "I'm not doing a party, Tina. Moving Linda in kinda nixed the underage drinking."

"Crap," the girl breathed. "Ok, does anyone else know where we can have an all-day event and bonfire? It's a Friday."

While they started talking about who had land, whose parents would be gone or not care, and bickering about the best way to make this work, Lars tapped my shoulder. Subtly, he pointed to the windows, his finger aimed at where the gas pumps stood outside. I turned, expecting to see a friend. Instead, a wave of awareness hit me: witch.

The guy's truck was old and looked like it had been hit a few times. He was young, maybe twenty, but probably less. His clothes were dirty, but the most shocking thing was that I was pretty sure I knew him. Well, knew of him. I swore I'd seen him at Collin's place, working with the dairy cattle.

"He lives on Collin's ranch," I told the rest. "I don't know his name."

"Could be useful," Bax pointed out. "I mean, Tash seems to use witches a bit."

"Do we do anything?" Gavin asked.

The rest of us shook our heads. "Deke once told me that messing with witches is a bad idea," I explained. "That's an angel's job. Never mind that he hasn't done anything wrong."

"Kinda what I thought," Gavin said. "I mean, about the wrong, not the angels."

Then our pizza came. The four of us dug in, barely paying attention to Tina's best attempts to wrangle the motley gang of students into agreeing on anything. Some wanted to start early. Others pointed out that skipping meant sleeping in, so noon should be fine.

"What do you think, Bax?" Tina asked.

Bax groaned at being called out, but turned to see her. "I think that if you plan this earlier than noon, no one will show up but the people here. I think that even noon is a bit early. Half the senior class will trickle in around three and stay all night. Most parents aren't going to be ok with their kids skipping, so a few will hide out there, but not as many as you're hoping. We like to be lazy, Tina."

"Can you get alcohol?" she asked.

Bax shrugged. "Maybe. Pretty sure I'm not the only one."

"But you can get kegs," a guy pointed out.

Bax chuckled at that. "Ok. I'll make sure there are at least two, but I'm not paying to get the entire senior class smashed."

"But are you actually coming?" Tina asked.

The answer to that didn't come from Bax. It came from Shannon, who'd just walked in the door. "Lay off, Tina. If he shows, he'll be with his girlfriend."

Tina's eyes jumped over to me, her jaw clenched, and she looked away almost immediately. Thankfully, she also changed the subject again, but I'd caught that glare. Shannon seemed to as well, because she rolled her eyes as she made a straight line to our table.

"Hey," she said, squatting down at the end. "Have any of you seen Travis?"

"Not since lunch," I admitted.

Shannon just nodded. "Yeah, I'm starting to think he's avoiding me. He's started eating with the four of you, and he keeps having things come up in the evenings when he's supposed to see me. Did I piss him off or something?"

"He's been busy," Gavin told her.

"I think his parents are dealing with something," Lars explained. "He's been a little vague, but that's why he keeps talking to Bax."

"Money," Bax lied. "Don't say anything to him, though?"

"Not a word," Shannon promised, but she looked relieved. "I've been trying to think of how I screwed this up already."

Bax just picked up his phone and began typing. "Just bad timing. You're fine, Shannon. He's into you." Then he tapped the screen and smiled. "I also told him to get his ass over here."

Shannon patted Bax's knee. "Thanks. Owe you one. It's just that, um..." She looked at Gavin and Lars. "Cover your ears or something." Then, with a smile, she kept going. "We kinda, um, went all the way, and then it's like he's ghosting me."

"He's probably nervous as shit," Lars told her just as Bax's phone dinged.

"And, he's officially not ghosting you," Bax announced. "He said he just needs to finish up, but he'll be here in five minutes."

The reality was that he'd probably been doing research to get us more names of demons. Possibly fighting with his guardians about even talking to us. I wasn't sure, but before I'd realized he was a demon, the guy had been completely into Shannon, and now he was involved in our mess.

I was just thinking that it meant we needed to help out when another customer walked into the Slice. She was in her late twenties, maybe early thirties, but that wasn't what caught my attention. It was my necklace screaming, "cambion," in my mind. When the four of us all turned to look in the same direction, I knew it wasn't only me.

And the cambion wasn't the woman. It was the three-year-old little boy holding her hand.

"Who's that?" Gavin asked.

Shannon twisted to see. "Charlotte? She works at the Dollar Store. Why?"

"Is she married?" Lars asked.

"Live-in boyfriend," Shannon said. "Guys, why?"

"Because she looks familiar," I told her. "We had someone come onto the property the other day, but I don't think it was her. Different hair."

"Kid's cute, though," Lars said.

"Aww," Shannon teased, "you're the family type?"

"Not really, no," Lars assured her. "I'm also not an only child, so I like the ones that aren't screaming."

Shannon continued to pick on him for a bit, yet my mind had just gone off on a tangent. Had my own mom been like that lady? Did she know what I was? Had she known what Dad was? Did that woman have any idea of the power her son would be able to throw around?

Probably not. I tried to join in with the conversation at the table, but I was stuck on that one thing. Grabbing a slice of pizza, I shoved that in my face to give me an excuse for missing half of what was going on around me. Shannon was normal. She was perfectly human. She'd just said she'd had sex with Travis!

What if something failed? What if a condom broke or her birth control was fickle? What if Travis got her pregnant? We'd been so focused on the demons coming out of the gate that I hadn't stopped to think about what it would mean for the ones who stayed here. They wouldn't all just match up together. Hell, I didn't even know if they had female demons!

I was sure they must. If there were mothers who had broods, they had to. Travis's "mom" was a demon, and that made me think she wasn't just wearing a woman's body to blend in. It was just that I'd never seen one. If I had, I hadn't realized it, but that didn't mean all demon men would only hook up with demon women. I was proof of that!

But the necklaces we wore had an extra benefit I hadn't thought of. The moment Travis pulled into the parking lot, I knew. The warning for demons was a *lot* more intense than the one for cambion or witches. It also gave me enough time to say I needed a refill and to slide out of the booth. I'd almost made it to the soda fountain when the guy in question walked in.

"Hey, Travis," I said, tilting my head in the universal symbol for him to come over.

He looked at our table, probably seeing Shannon, then gave in. "What's up?"

I didn't say anything until I had some soda pouring into my cup. Even then, I kept my voice down. "Heard you and Shannon kinda took the next step."

He laughed once. "Yeah. Um, I really like her. Please don't give me a lecture about moving too fast?"

"More about accidents," I admitted. "What do you think she'd do if her kid was like me?"

"Nothing," he assured me. "Most of you have no clue. You're invisible when you aren't screwing around with the elements. You also don't just happen upon that crap. Supposedly, only like one in a hundred figure out what they are, and of those, half don't believe it's possible."

"So, normal?" I asked.

He nodded. "Usually. Kinda why you're so terrifying. You not only know and believe, but you've trained. I'm also being smart, ok? She wants to go to college, and raising a kid would screw that up."

"And accidents happen," I hissed.

"And abortion is still legal," he reminded me. "Adoption, too. Fuck, I'll step up and be a dad. I might be what I am, Jess, but I'm not a dick, ok? Takes two to tango, I really enjoy tango, and I *like* that girl."

I turned my spandex-covered hand, making him aware of it. "I'm just trying to figure out how this and that work together. If we do nothing, and you make things like me, where does it end?"

He leaned into my ear. "Angels," he whispered. "They'll make sure the balance never gets out of line. There's also a whole lot more of them out here than there are us."

"And yet I've never seen one," I countered.

"You're in Hellam," he reminded me. "This is our gate. Means it's one of the few places we're not hunted by them. Why do you think we stay? A few witches use us as cover because our numbers scare off the fuckers, and the witches get a break because of it. Jess, we're not winning. We're not taking over. We're fucking scraping by. We're also not the bad guys."

"And I assume angels are?" I asked.

He lifted a brow and canted his head. "*I* think so. If you'd ever met one, you'd probably agree. Bax, Gavin, and Lars might not, but you would. It's like being a bunny trying to live in a lion's den. There's only one way that ends."

"Ok," I said, giving in. "You should also know that Shannon thinks you're ghosting her. The guys kinda said that your family's having an issue, and Bax said you'd been talking to him more because of money."

"That fucker," Travis groaned. "Ok. Thanks for the heads-up. I'll have to figure something out."

"Taxes," I told him. "One of your parents didn't have enough taken out, IRS is on your ass, and you know he's loaded. Bax is helping out, and you're trying to make sure he knows you appreciate it."

The smile he gave me had nothing at all evil in it. "Thanks, Jess. I mean it. I really don't want to screw things up with her."

"Then take her to Senior Skip Day," I told him. "Spoil her. When we text you, tell us you're busy. Shannon is probably the most amazing girl I've ever met, so don't you dare screw this up!"

"She wants to be a vet," he told me. "I mean, that's a lot of college, but I kinda like it."

I groaned around a laugh, and turned him toward our table. "You are a goner, Travis. Complete mush, but it's working for you."

"Kinda like your thing is working for you," he said. "Friends, Jess?"

"Definitely," I agreed just as we reached our table. "So," I said, making them all look up at me. "I just informed Mr. Busy that if he ghosts you, I'll chop his balls off."

"That's what I'm talking about," Shannon said, lifting her fist toward me.

I tapped mine against it, tossing a warning look at Travis. He just lifted his hands in surrender, backed up two steps, and grabbed a pair of chairs for himself and Shannon. Pulling those over, he made it clear that they were definitely going to be hanging out for a while.

And while we talked, laughed, and acted like teenagers, he also managed to point out a few more demons and cambion to me. Over the last few weeks, we'd confirmed every single name he'd given us. Both the bad demons and the good ones. He'd also gone out of his way to help me learn how to use my magic. As far as I cared, Travis had proven himself. That meant he really was a friend. I just hoped our friendship wasn't a massive mistake for either of us.

CHAPTER NINETEEN

None of us really cared about Senior Skip Day. In truth, it had been an excuse to hang out and check on more people in town - a reason that wouldn't raise any eyebrows or draw attention. The problem was the man sitting in a booth at the back. I didn't notice him at first, and I couldn't say when he'd shown up. My necklace didn't care about him at all, and yet something about him was a little creepy - enough that even Shannon noticed.

He didn't watch the other students. He wasn't concerned about his meal or the staff working there. Every time I looked up, the guy was watching the six of us. Even worse, he wore a long sleeve - and it was a little too warm outside for that to be normal. The creep could've been hiding track marks or racist tattoos for all I knew, but something about him felt a little off. Travis agreed, saying he was definitely walking Shannon to her car when we all decided to leave.

The man just kept sitting there.

Lars told Deke about it as soon as we got home. Deke said there was nothing to be done now, but to keep an eye out for more people watching us too closely. If we were drawing too much attention, it would complicate our hits on the greater demons in town, and we were almost ready. We had the guns, the ammo, the magical attacks planned, and even our entry and exit mapped out. This would be our first assassination, so we'd run through it dozens of times, and now we only had a week left.

I had a feeling that the only reason we were waiting was because of Linda's divorce. Deke had learned the hard way that we wouldn't rush out to die without making sure that woman was taken care of. She wasn't mom to all of us, and yet she was. She'd stepped up when we needed her most, gave us the comfort of home, and somehow made us feel like all of this was ok.

So when Tuesday rolled around, I was a bundle of nerves. Linda said the court proceedings shouldn't be a big deal, but it was my dad she was divorcing. He wasn't used to losing, and the man had made it clear that he wasn't ready to give us up. Considering that she'd made the mistake of telling him she was pregnant?

I couldn't take my eyes off my phone. I kept waiting for some emergency notification that she was headed to the hospital - or worse. I wouldn't put it past my father to kill her in one of his fits of rage. But there was nothing. Class after class passed, and my phone stayed silent. Not even the guys texted me.

All through lunch, I kept checking. My anxiety was growing. Thankfully, I wasn't the only one. Lars was just as bad. Bax and Gavin seemed to understand, keeping the topic light and not picking on either of us for looking at our phones every two seconds. Linda had said her case was in the morning, so what was taking so long? Had there been a complication? I wanted to text her to make sure she was ok, but what if she was in court? What if that got her in trouble?

The rest of the day crawled. I couldn't focus on my classes. I couldn't even get into my book! My guts were twisting, my hands felt clammy, and I found myself zoning out, trying to imagine this working out the right way. The problem was that I couldn't. In my mind, I was braced for a million ways it could go wrong, because I couldn't actually imagine something going right. There had to be a complication. Nothing ever worked out easily for me.

Then, just as we were leaving our last class of the day, both Lars' and my phones vibrated with a notification. He reached into his pocket. I had to pull my bag around to get mine. Just as we made it into the hall, both of us swiped to unlock our screens and our feet stalled out in unison. The text was from Linda.

> **Linda:** It's over! The divorce is final, and my last name is once again McKay! Sorry it took so long, but things got a little complicated because of the baby. I'll tell you about it when you get home because I didn't want to bother you kids in the middle of school. Also, my attorney had some papers for me to look over with that sexual harassment settlement. It's a good day! It's over! I'm officially divorced!

Without thinking, I threw myself at Lars, wrapping my arms around his neck in the biggest hug possible. "It's ok! It all worked out!"

He picked me up and spun me around, laughing like he was just as excited as I was. "Fuck, that sucked," he groaned, putting my feet back down. "But it's done. Sounds like - "

"Surprise, surprise, she *is* dating her brother." The snide voice was from Mr. Garcia. Lars set me down, but my Spanish teacher was glaring at us as he passed. "Good thing that's on camera. I tried to tell the school board how you are, Jessica, and now I have proof of it."

"Proof we got good news?" Lars asked, making Mr. Garcia pause to turn back.

"Proof that the rumors about the two of you are true," the man clarified, his eyes jumping over to me. "You just can't help yourself, can you? Two boys aren't enough. No, girls like you? I've been teaching long enough to know your type."

"My... type?" I huffed, feeling all of the joy at hearing the divorce was finalized evaporate.

I'd been anxious all day long, braced for the worst, but this wasn't it. That man! How dare he all but call me a slut in front of everyone at school? He was supposed to be a teacher - an example! Never mind what he'd done to Linda. Then again, the two things were more related than I wanted to admit.

"So, you have a problem with me dating someone, Mr. Garcia? Don't you think that should be my guardian's problem?" I taunted.

I watched his jaw clench. "I think you're setting a poor example for the other girls in this school. Everyone thinks that you're such a good little student, but look at you. Your grades are falling. You are not the model student people say, and it all happened when you stopped living with your father."

"The father who beat me?" I shot back. "So, you're trying to say that you condone child abuse, is that it? You have a problem with me - now that I'm eighteen - living with Linda because she's divorced? Because she's nice? What's the issue, Mr. Garcia, and how is my love life a part of it? I'm just dying to hear this."

The man scoffed. "So Linda's all alone now? I told her this would happen."

"Yeah, hence the hugging," Lars told him. "Her divorce just went through. We don't have to worry about Ted anymore..." He took a step closer to Mr. Garcia, stopping so his shoulder was blocking me like a shield. "And Jess isn't my stepsister."

"She still has two boyfriends," Mr. Garcia countered. "This is what I was trying to help with, but your mother had to blow it out of proportion. Now, she's teaching that girl to act the same way: to use these boys, take advantage of them, and then whine when she gets what she deserves for it."

"Deserves?" Of all the words he could've picked, that was the worst one. "So are you saying I deserved it when my father beat me hard enough to break my arm? Are you saying Linda deserved to be sent to the hospital by him? Are you saying that we women need to be abused to behave? Is that it?"

"No!" he snapped. "I'm talking about discipline, manners, and maybe taking you to church, young lady. The way you've been acting is irresponsible! I offered to help Linda. She did nothing but whine about her problems, but this is what you call equality, isn't it? Women get everything and men end up paying for it one way or another."

A crowd was starting to gather. Ok, maybe my voice was a little too loud, and the fact that both Lars and I were facing down a teacher without shame may have drawn a little attention. I also didn't care. I didn't have to be good anymore. Lars wasn't my brother anymore. Most of all, this asshole would not get away with talking about Linda like that!

"Did Linda deserve it when you blackmailed her for a date? Did she deserve to be written up for some bullshit lie when she refused your offer? Is this what women deserve, Mr. Garcia?" I could feel those fireflies inside my chest bouncing around like they were hornets. "If we don't do what some man wants, we fucking *deserve* what we get?!"

As I screamed the last word, something happened. I couldn't even begin to explain what, but I felt it. Like a release of pressure, the magic escaped, but all I cared about was this man telling the damned truth. Linda had just gotten her divorce, and it still wasn't over. My happy moment with Lars had been ruined because Mr. Garcia had to step up and say something.

Time and time again, the good things in my life were ripped away just as I dared to believe in them, and I was so over it. It wasn't fair. I'd done nothing to deserve this, and neither had Linda. None of us had! I also didn't have to just shut up and take it anymore. Let him come at me. Let him tell my father. I didn't care who I pissed off or if they liked me. I had my guys, and they'd already proven they'd stand with me when things got hard.

ENTER SANDMAN

"You will not use that type of language in front of me!" Mr. Garcia bellowed, daring to take a step toward me.

But it wasn't Lars who stopped him. Bax slipped through the crowd and braced up in his path. A split second later, Gavin was there. The guys had staggered themselves the way we'd been taught, putting me at the back. No, not to protect me, but because this was where I was the most useful.

"Answer the damned question!" I screamed, so angry that I couldn't control myself anymore.

"Yes!" Mr. Garcia yelled back. "I told her I'd take care of that problem, but I expected something back. What's wrong with that, hm? Just look at you! You're off the rails, Jessica. I'm going to have you suspended for this, and then maybe Linda will realize that she made the wrong choice. She made a fool out of me! She thinks I wanted to be her friend? Ha!"

"Shit," Lars breathed, turning around and trying to push me back. "What did you do, Jess? Why is he saying that?"

I didn't know what was making him answer. I also didn't really care. I just wanted everyone to know that I was *done*. Linda wasn't here to stand up for herself, and how many times had she stood up for me? Now it was my turn. For Linda, for myself, and even for Megan. I had once told Lars that for girls, there was never a good choice, but I'd been wrong. As the surge of magic coursed through me, I realized I'd found it. The right choice was to stop running, stop hiding, and start fighting.

"Oh, so it's ok when a guy screws around, huh? You think Linda should sleep with you because you'd do something nice, but if she did sleep with you, then what? Is she a whore? A slut? How dare I have two boyfriends? What did you say about Megan? Oh, but I'm sure you didn't have a problem with Oliver knocking her up and refusing to take responsibility, right? Because it's not *about* responsibility!" Lars grabbed me around the chest and started pushing me back, but I resisted. I wasn't done yet. "It's about having a dick! It's about thinking you're stronger, bigger, more popular or something else! It's about abusing those who can't fight back and shaming them when they try to resist, but I'm done taking it, Mr. Garcia! I'm done with being abused! I'm - "

"Jess, shut the fuck up," Bax growled as he pushed between me and Lars.

Then he bent and scooped me over his shoulder. My head hung down toward his ass, my feet were kicking before him, and Bax didn't care at all. Lars just huffed in surprise, but Gavin was moving, bending to grab my bag with one arm and Lars' elbow with the other.

That was how we made our retreat. No, I didn't scream about it, but I did struggle, wishing Bax would just put me down! I'd been winning, didn't he see that? Linda was free and clear now. I wasn't related to Lars anymore. Most of all, I didn't have to be a good girl anymore, so why shouldn't I just say what I thought? Why did I have to keep being so damned *good?*

"Shut down the damned magic," Bax growled when he reached the parking lot. "Jess, I don't know what you're doing, but Travis said magic, and now Mr. Garcia is spilling his guts? Quit while we're ahead."

"Shit," Lars breathed. "Is that what she did?"

"Put. Me. Down," I demanded.

Bax stopped and eased me to the ground, his hands finding my shoulders. He didn't step away.

"Jess," he said, a gentle warning in his voice, "I don't know what pissed you off, but - "

From behind us, Oliver's voice interrupted him, calling out, "What the fuck, you bitch!"

CHAPTER TWENTY

GAVIN GROANED deep and low as he turned back to face Oliver. The guy was storming toward us, and while other students were in the parking lot, most of them were headed home. It looked like the scene I'd just made in the halls had delayed everyone a bit, but now it was starting to break up. Oliver, however, was intent on the four of us.

Behind him, a pair of girls giggled and pointed. To the side, a couple of guys were watching, grins on their faces like they were laughing at him. At that moment, I realized that my little rant had just outed him, and while the rumors may have been swirling quietly, I'd basically turned up the volume to full screech in the halls.

I also didn't care.

"Got a problem?" I asked, turning to face him.

Bax just groaned, and unlike Gavin's warning sound a second ago, this came across more like he was pained. "Let it go, Jess. You've already made a big enough mess."

"No," Lars said. "She deserves this."

That was all I needed. That one little bit of support made me feel like I wasn't out of line. Lars understood. He'd been just as stressed as me all day long. We'd both been forced to hide our relationship because someone might not like it. The one time things started going my way, and these idiots thought they could just bully me a little more and I'd go back to being nice and quiet Jess? Not gonna happen.

"Why'd you have to bring it up?" Oliver asked. "You got a problem with Mr. Garcia, then you yell at him. I'm fine with that, but now everyone knows what that trashy little slut is saying about me."

"Because you knocked her up," I shot back. "Oh, but she's the girl, so she's the only one who has to deal with it, right?"

"It's not fucking mine!" Oliver roared.

"Did you *fuck* her?" I asked. "Did you stick your dick in her?"

"So did everyone else," Olivier insisted. "Doesn't mean it's mine. Shit, she fucked Collin while he was still with you. Figured you'd say she had it coming."

"No one has it coming!" I threw up my hands in exasperation. "Why don't you get that? Saying she had it coming is her shirt getting ruined or her mascara running. It's not a goddamned baby, Oliver. It's not you calling her a slut for doing the exact same thing you did. It's not everyone at school calling me a whore because I've slept with half as many people as Bax has!"

"A lot less than half," Bax pointed out. "But hey, I got a dick, so that makes it ok, right?"

Oliver's mouth hung open as he looked from me to Bax, and then over to Gavin. "Yeah? Well, fuck all of you. Coach is going to kick my ass off the team now. You just ruined my life, Jess. All four of you might think this is funny, but - "

"What about Megan's life?" I asked. "Did she *deserve* to have it ruined? Hey, she got you off. Is this how you pay her back? Leaving her high and dry with a kid, no support, her dreams of college or a future ruined, and not even someone to talk to about it?" I stormed forward three steps before Bax grabbed my arm, preventing me from getting in Oliver's face. "Did Linda deserve it? Did I deserve it? Is that how this works? We have vaginas, so it's ok for you to shit on us? Not anymore, Oliver. Maybe I'm pissed at Megan. Maybe I'm fucking around - but you are too. Maybe I'm a bitch, but so fucking what?!"

"And maybe you want to ruin your life," he screamed, "but my parents will kick me out."

"Then you should've thought about that first, or do something about it now! You did this, Oliver. You tried to get me to go to that party with you. You planned this, so don't think I have any sympathy for you."

"Yeah?" he asked. "And you've been fucking your step brother since then, huh? Just spreading your legs for every guy on the Hale ranch? Is that why you're pissed? Because you're just as much of a little cunt as Megan?"

"That's my fucking girlfriend!" Gavin roared, pulling back his arm.

But I was just a little faster. The magic was still there. The anger was still begging for a way to let it out. The fact that Oliver couldn't even admit he was wrong fueled it. I didn't think. I didn't plan. I barely even envisioned the reaction, but months of training together kicked in. As Gavin braced to swing, I pushed - and as hard as I could.

Oliver's feet left the ground. His body flew back like he'd been shot from a cannon. There was just one little problem with all of this. It wasn't how Oliver landed on his ass so hard that his head bounced on the concrete. It wasn't the whimper of pain that came from him or the way so many people turned to look.

It was that Gavin hadn't swung.

"In the fucking car," Bax growled, turning me and pushing me towards his SUV hard enough to make my feet start moving.

Lars followed, pressing his hand to my back. Gavin and Bax moved in behind us, and the four of us walked with a purpose. We didn't run. Nope, Deke had trained us to never flee a scene. We stormed away, making it look like we were the victors. It didn't really help, though.

Maybe there wasn't a crowd around us, but this was the student parking lot right after school. I hadn't even traded out my books! We hadn't dawdled to check our lockers. I'd lost my shit on Mr. Garcia, then on Oliver, and most of the school was either still headed to their cars or waiting in line to drive out of the parking lot.

They'd all seen.

I should've been mortified or paranoid about it. Instead, it just felt good. It was like that pressure valve on Lars' car, and when he released it while the engine was still hot, the water shot straight up, burning everything it touched. Right now, that was me, and I liked it. For once, I hadn't just shut up and let the guys stand up for me. I hadn't apologized or pretended like I was wrong. I'd yelled, made a scene, and told everyone what I thought about this bullshit.

It was the last step in killing the good girl.

Old Jess was gone. New, cambion-Jess was here, and I liked her a lot more than the version of me who'd been helpless. This girl didn't need combat boots to kick ass. She had eyeliner and magic powers. She had a gun, three boyfriends, and hunted demons. She was the kind of strong female who didn't take shit from anyone and would come out victorious. The kind I read about, longed to be, and had finally become.

The moment I was in the back seat of the car, Lars moved to sit beside me. Bax was driving. Gavin was in the passenger seat. There was no fucking around, and none of the guys seemed happy for me. If anything, they were all a little too intent on something.

"What?" I asked.

"You just shot a guy halfway across the parking lot," Gavin said, "with *magic*."

"And a shit ton of people were looking," Lars added. "Jess, what the fuck?"

My mouth flopped open and I looked at all of them. "You didn't expect me to take that, did you?"

"No," Lars promised. "We also didn't expect you to throw out magic! Fuck, there could be a Watcher around, or some kid could tell a parent. Deke said not to get noticed, and that? Yeah, that's gonna get a lot of notice."

"I'll say I did it," Gavin told them. "I hit him fast. They'll buy it."

"Fuck," Bax grumbled, thumping the hell of his hand onto the steering wheel. "This is going to be bad."

"We'll handle it," Lars assured him. "We always do."

I leaned forward, between the front seats, "I can - "

"No!" Gavin snapped. "You've done enough."

"Hey!" Lars barked at him. "You don't get to say shit, Gav. You put your bullies in the hospital. Jess didn't. She's shut up and taken this for long enough, ok?"

"What set you off?" Bax asked, catching my eyes in the rearview mirror.

"Linda," I admitted. "Her divorce went through, and when I hugged Lars, Mr. Garcia said that was proof we were together, and he just said it like Linda was to blame."

I was starting to feel bad about what I'd done now. I'd tried to stand up for myself, and clearly I'd fucked that up too. Damn it! But this wasn't fair! How many times had Bax made a scene and everyone laughed it off? Lars had shown up and joined right in. No big deal. Gavin beat the shit out of a guy with his motorcycle helmet, and that was fine - but I do this and I screwed it up?

No. I didn't deserve this. Linda didn't deserve this. Lars didn't deserve this for sticking up for me, or even Megan for doing the same thing as the rest of us. It felt like I was stuck playing by different rules than everyone else, and I was not ok with that.

"Why is it ok for you guys to be dicks to everyone else, and the one time I try, you're all pissed?" I demanded.

"Not pissed," Lars said.

Before he could add more to that, Bax sighed, lifting a hand. "It's not that, Jess. It's the magic."

Gavin turned in his seat to look at me. "And twice! Not just with Mr. Garcia, but you sent Oliver flying. One, we could explain away. Both? You are out of control! What the fuck, Jess? What part of not getting noticed did you not understand?"

No. Just no. He was the last person to talk to me that way. After all the stress he'd put me under, the drama about Deke and Gavin wanting our relationship to still work, he treated me like this? Never mind that I'd saved his life. My *magic* had! The same magic he was now pissed off at me for using?

"Oh, I'm out of control?" I asked him. "What about you, huh? How many times have you lost it, but when I do it, it's a big deal?"

"I made sure no one else saw," Gavin snarled.

"And I can't take any more of this!" I yelled back at him. "I have bent over backwards for you, Gav. When do I get to be the one who's happy? When do I get to stand up for myself? I can't throw a punch like you. I'm not about to pull a gun out at school. Fuck that. No, all I have is magic, and everyone wants to kill me for it. You were supposed to be on my side. You were supposed to make me happy and not just pile on top with everyone else." I huffed in frustration and flopped back in the seat. "Every time I think things are going to be ok, it just gets fucked up. Maybe you should just put me down like everyone's saying."

"That is *not* what he's saying, Jess," Bax insisted.

Gavin just cursed under his breath and threw himself against his own seat. Lars pushed out a breath, then turned to face me. Gently, he reached over for my hand, linking our fingers together. His thumb swept against the side of my hand.

"You ok?" he asked.

I nodded. "I'm just..." I could only shake my head, because I didn't even have a word for this feeling. So, I tried something else. "It's not fair, you know?"

"What's not?" Lars asked.

ENTER SANDMAN

I gestured to where Gavin sat in front of me. "This. It's all falling apart. Either I have to just take it when people treat me like shit, or I'm acting like a demon. I don't want to be like my dad!"

"You are nothing like your dad," Lars promised.

I nodded, making it clear I understood. "Then why am I so pissed, Lars?"

With his free hand, he reached up to smooth my hair back. "Because one person can only take so much, Jess. Because you've never been allowed to lose your shit before? Because I'm pissed too? I dunno, but it's ok. Just keep the magic toned down, ok?"

I jiggled my head in a weak nod. "Ok. I'll try."

"But yell as loud as you want," he said softly. "Even if that's at me."

CHAPTER TWENTY-ONE

THE REST of the ride back home was a little tense and very quiet. Thankfully, when we made it upstairs, the tone was a lot lighter. Deke and Linda were in the living room, sitting diagonally from each other and talking softly. Tash was in the kitchen making a drink. When the four of us piled in, they all stopped and turned, but it was with smiles on their faces. We couldn't say the same.

"Everything ok?" Linda asked.

Lars just took over. "Little issue at school, but your divorce is really done?"

"It is!" She beamed, looking like she was honestly excited about this. "Now, there were a few complications..."

I dropped my bag by the door and headed for a chair. The guys did the same. In the time it took for us to sit down, Tash came in and handed Linda a drink. I couldn't tell what it was supposed to be, but something was frothy at the top. That made Lars sit up.

"What - " he tried to ask.

"Root beer float," Tash assured him. "Indulgent, non-alcoholic, and she deserves it."

"Thought it was beer," he grumbled around an awkward laugh. "Sorry, Mom."

"You're fine," Linda assured him.

"So, there was a complication?" I pressed. "But it's all ok?"

Linda nodded. "It's finalized. The problem is that in the state of Oklahoma, they don't like finalizing a divorce while a woman is pregnant. The attorney Bax hired for me pointed out that we split up because Ted hurt me, that I didn't even know I was pregnant at the time, and went to the hospital for sutures and a concussion. Ted has a history of aggression, and his therapy worked in our favor." She paused and looked over at Bax. "And because of my new job and a certain letter, I was able to prove that I'm financially stable without Ted's income - or lack of it."

"Wait." I looked at Bax too. "What letter?"

He glanced down at his hands. "Um, I kinda signed a form stating that my estate would handle any financial issues for both Linda and the baby until the child is eighteen."

"And..." Linda pressed.

"Oh, they know about the will," he assured her. "I mean, who else am I going to leave this to? My dad? Not likely."

Linda blew out a big breath. "Well, I appreciate it, but I'm also not going to take advantage of you. I'm pretty sure you have no clue how much money you're talking."

"About a month's income," Bax said. "I mean, that's what my financial guy said. To pay your wages for twenty years? Yeah, that's about what the company is giving me in a month. I dunno, I figured it was worth it."

"Thank you," Linda told him. "I can't..." She let the sentence trail off, reaching up to dab at her eyes. "Oh, stupid hormones!"

We all chuckled a bit, which gave Linda the chance to steal another sip of her celebratory drink. My mind was still going, though. The divorce was done, she was single, but what about my dad? She hadn't really mentioned that yet, and I got the impression no one else was going to ask, so I had to.

"Dad doesn't get custody of the baby at all?"

Everyone fell quiet again and turned to look at me. Linda wobbled her head from side to side, looking like she was trying to figure out how to answer that, or maybe that it was complicated. Either way, I really wanted to know.

"Jess, your father has been trying very hard lately," she told me. "He didn't fight me in court, and he could have. He could've tried to insist that I stay married to him until the baby was born, or demanded updates from my doctor's visits." She paused to lick her lips. "He also said that he knows he was wrong. He admitted that in court, which means it's recorded. He can't take it back."

"So?" I asked.

"It gives me leverage to make sure your sister doesn't ever have to live with him," Linda explained. "Jess, he admitted that he hurt me - and you. What he did to you is why the judge allowed this to be finalized. Your father isn't getting custody, but that also means he won't pay much for child support."

"But you're covered," I insisted, gesturing to Bax so she'd know what I meant.

"Financially," Linda agreed. "The question is how your sister will feel about not having her father in her life. What happens when she has a teenaged tantrum and demands to know him? It's not as easy as you're making it out to be. This little girl is probably going to be just as strong-willed as you are. Ted is going to be in some part of her life, and I'd like to make sure that's a safe one."

"Yeah, but - "

"No, let me finish?" Linda begged. "Jess, I know this hasn't been easy. I know you think I should just cut him out and pretend like it never happened. The reality is that my daughter might have other ideas. What happens when she runs away to see him? What happens when someone in town tells her who her father is? It's not like it's a secret. She will find out, she will have opinions, and I'm willing to bet she'll do something about it."

"Yeah," I begrudgingly admitted. "Probably."

"But," Linda went on, "you are right. It's just been hard for me to wrap my mind around the fact that the man I fell in love with isn't the man he turned out to be. I want to give him another chance the same way I did for you. Here's the other thing you probably haven't thought about. I'm older than you, Jess."

"Ok?" Because I kinda knew that.

"I was raised that marriage is a commitment, and that I'm supposed to be the one to fix this. I wanted to try counseling. I kept thinking that I should go through all the steps before I made a decision. You and your generation see this differently. Every generation, it gets a little easier for a woman to stand up for herself, and while I thought my generation was the independent one, it seems I was wrong. This has been hard. Ted and I weren't married that long, and I kept thinking it was all my fault. I don't know, maybe everyone does that, but with a baby in the middle of this, I just felt like I had to try."

"Yeah, but he was going to hurt you," I countered.

Linda slowly bobbed her head. "I know. I'm trying to say that you were right, Jess. I was wrong, and I'm still trying to accept that. It's not easy to let go of all my ideals. I wanted a family. In my mind, that was a husband and kids. I got the kids, but I lost the husband. I don't want to be the only adult in my family. I don't want to be a single mom - money or not, Bax."

He just lifted his hands in defeat before he could say a word.

So Linda kept going. "Jess, in the course of this divorce, I've realized just how long this has been going on for you, how hard it has been, and how helpless you must have felt. I'm sorry. I really am. I want to make sure that this baby never has to worry about that, but if I make her father into something we avoid, she'll seek him out because of curiosity. So, I talked to Ted after court."

"What?!" Lars gasped, nearly standing in shock.

"In the courthouse, with security present," she assured him. "Ted is sorry. He's trying to make things right, but he doesn't understand. He thinks that a single kind act will erase what he's done to you, and I explained that it's going to take at least four years, maybe longer. That's how long it took for us to get here, after all, with him abusing Jess. He has to atone and prove that he's changed, not just *say* he's sorry. I am your mom, Jess." She looked at the guys. "And all of you. Maybe not your real mother, and it's complicated, but I am going to do my best to be mom to you all."

She paused to pull in a deep breath. "And that means dealing with Ted. It means helping you hunt demons however I can. A few months ago, I never would've believed any of this, and now the four of you are taking shooting and knife fighting lessons. You, Jess, have magic! This is hard for me. It's never going to get easier, but I don't care. I love you kids, and I will support you. I will do everything in my power to protect you, even if that means I'm the one who gets arrested for it."

"Not gonna happen," Deke said. "For the baby, if nothing else."

"Because they can't raise a kid," Tash pointed out. "Linda, you need to get that thought out of your head. At any time, these four could be on the run, and that's not a good way to raise a baby."

"I'm just saying," Linda assured us, "that I'm all in. And maybe I lashed out when I found out that Jess and Lars were dating too, but this is a lot." She looked between the Martyrs as if seeking their agreement.

Tash nodded her head. "It is. Deke and I grew up knowing about this, but most quads resist it at first. We always hear them ask if it's a joke."

"But not these four," Deke said. "They already knew."

"Because we've had these for a while," Gavin said, lifting his left hand. "Hard to think it's a lie when we've spent years trying to figure out why we have it."

Linda grabbed her drink and took another long sip. "Well, sometimes it's easier to stick our heads in the sand. I think it's like being a kid and hiding under the covers, hoping the monsters will just go away. It makes no sense. Blankets aren't a shield, but if we can't see it, then it must not be able to see us, right? That was how all of this felt. If I refused to accept Jess and Lars, then I could still do an adult adoption with Jess. If I refused to see that Ted was abusive, then he'd stop hurting us. It's stupid, but it's what I was doing. I'm also trying to stop."

"But it's over now," I assured her. "You're divorced, and the house is warded, so Dad isn't a problem anymore."

"Sadly, it's not that easy," Linda explained. "Never mind the rest of this!"

"Speaking of the rest of this," Bax said, looking over at Deke. "We had a slip today at school."

"Two," Gavin said.

I felt the air sliding from my lungs as they all looked at me. I wanted to explain, but what could I say? I hadn't even meant to do anything to Mr. Garcia. I'd just wanted him to admit the truth. I'd been so stressed - still was! - and he'd picked the wrong moment to say something. That was why my timing had been off, but did it matter?

"What kind of slips?" Tash asked.

"Jess did magic," Lars said.

"And kinda tossed a guy about fifty feet," Bax added.

"What?!" Deke roared, shoving to his feet.

"Not fifty feet," Gavin said quickly. "Not that far, but his feet left the ground."

"Did anyone see?" Deke demanded.

"Yeah," I breathed. "Kinda everyone. It was in the parking lot."

"What the fuck were you thinking?" Deke asked.

"Hey," Linda snapped.

"No," Tash said, thrusting out a hand to make Linda stay out of this. "How many witnesses?"

I could feel my throat closing. I'd screwed up bad. The more questions they asked, the more aware of it I became. This was so bad. Super bad. Bad bad.

"Like, most of the school," I mumbled.

"Fuck!" Deke growled.

My heart was now beating faster. I'd tried to stand up for myself for once, and clearly I'd screwed it up. Crap. What now? I had to do something, anything, to make this better. I could feel a tingling in my fingers. My ears were starting to ring, and my throat was so tight I was sure I was about to suffocate.

"I..." The word came out as a squeak. "I'm sorry!"

And just like that, all of the pride I'd had because I'd stood up for myself vanished.

CHAPTER TWENTY-TWO

"What happened?" Deke demanded, his eyes locked on me.

I had to swallow twice before I could get my voice to work. The growl in his voice was intimidating, and I knew I'd screwed up. Hell, I'd pissed off Gavin, and he'd never been mad at me before - but I'd just wanted to stand up for Linda! I hadn't really meant to mess with Mr. Garcia. I'd screwed up my timing with Oliver.

"Um..." Fuck, my pulse was pounding so hard I could hear it in my ears. "I didn't mean to, but Mr. Garcia was trying to say that me hugging Lars was..." I looked over, hoping for a little help because slutty wasn't the right word, yet it was all I had.

Lars' blue eyes were waiting. Clearly, he noticed the panic in mine, so he took over. "We got the news that everything was ok with Linda - and you have to understand that we'd been stressed about it all day. Well, she hugged me, I kinda spun her around, and that man saw it. He started talking about how it was proof, and he meant the lawsuit."

"Which the school board is already trying to settle," Linda assured us.

"Yeah, but Jess got mad," Lars went on. "He said something about deserving, and she kinda went off on him. Started asking what she deserved, and what you deserved, and even what Megan deserved."

"Stupid bitch," Bax grumbled under his breath. When my head snapped over to look at him, he winced. "Not like that, Jess. I agree that what's happening to her isn't fair. I don't have a single problem with what you said, but she's still a bitch."

"Yeah," I admitted. "She kinda is, but that shouldn't make it ok for Oliver to screw her over."

"Doesn't," Deke assured me, "but I just want to know about the magic."

"I got mad," I explained, "and the fireflies turned into wasps, and then something released, and Mr. Garcia started admitting to it."

Tash stepped over beside Linda's chair. "With witnesses?"

"Yeah," I mumbled. "And I said something about Oliver getting Megan pregnant and then trying to say it wasn't his, but Bax and Lars kinda got me out of school. I didn't even get my homework, you know?"

Bax chuckled. "I threw her over my shoulder and carried her out. Figured that would distract from a teacher admitting that he'd sexually harassed someone in the office. Seems to have worked."

"Then Oliver followed us," Gavin said.

I nodded. "And I tried to do what we'd talked about. Gavin pulled back to punch him, so I tried to time it, but I got it wrong."

"I hadn't hit yet," Gavin said. "I was planning to just threaten him."

Deke was slowly nodding his head the whole time we talked. His eyes were locked on the floor, making it clear he was listening and actually thinking about what we'd said. I had a feeling that wasn't a good sign, and his next words proved it.

"How many people saw?" he asked. "You said most of the school, but are we talking five hundred people? Twenty?"

"About a hundred," Bax guessed. "Of those, there's no telling how many were actually looking, but I'm pretty sure at least ten were."

Then Deke lifted his head, his stormy eyes landing on mine. "What happened, Jess?"

"It just..." Yeah, saying it just happened didn't really answer his question. Crap. "I was mad," I mumbled under my breath.

"Why?" he pressed.

"Because of all of this!" My heart was racing again. Everyone was looking at me, and I could feel it. "Don't you get it?"

"No, doll, I don't." He licked his lips. "What happened, Jess? What made you mad? What made you lose control?"

"This!" I shoved to my feet, turning to face him. "All of it. Every bit of it. And the one time I get something good, Mr. Garcia ruined it. I mean, I'm not allowed to have nice things, right? I get away from my dad only to find out he's a demon and now people want to kill me. Everything that's good gets screwed up, so maybe Tash was right. Maybe I should've just run when I had the chance."

I turned, intending to go to my room, but I didn't make it. The moment I walked past Tash, her hand snapped out to grab my bicep, jerking me to a stop. The woman didn't even look mad. She simply watched me.

"I was testing you," she reminded me.

"And Dad?" I asked. "Was he testing me too? Deke doing his yo-yo thing? Is that just a test? Mr. Garcia trying to blackmail Linda is a test? It can't *all* be a test!" And I yanked my arm free, intending to finish storming from the room.

"Jess!" Deke bellowed. "I was trying to make your life easier."

"Yeah? And what about Gavin?" I asked. "Was he trying to make my life easier?"

"Shit," Gavin grumbled. "Jess, I'm sorry. I don't even know what I did!"

So I rounded on him. "You hate Deke now. I happen to like him. And we used to have something perfect, but I should've known better. Deke warned me. He said this whole relationship with us wouldn't work. Tash said that I'd become evil, and maybe that's what I did, but - "

"No," Linda said, calmly setting down her glass. "Jess, you will go sit down. Deke, your ass needs to be on that couch too." She turned to look at me, making it clear she meant it. "Tash, find a chair, because I'm sure you're a part of this too."

"Linda, I just..." I gestured to my room, hoping she'd let me go.

The woman simply pointed at a cushion. She didn't bother saying a thing. So I went to sit. All of us did. The moment we were all settled, Linda looked at Deke.

"What did you do, Deke?" she asked.

He sighed. "I'm bi. Tash is a lesbian. It's how we became friends. Gavin found out, and he's a little homophobic." Deke shoved his hand over his mouth. "So, just as I thought it was safe to start a relationship with Jess, Gavin had a problem with it, so I tried to back out."

"Gav's not homophobic," Bax said. "May sound that way, but that's because it's the only way he knows to talk about it. He's confused, and he learned when he was young that hating it was safer for him than anything else."

"I'm trying," Gavin said. "I just..."

"Wait," Lars begged. "Those are all the details. Jess, what's the real problem? You always deal with the shit that gets thrown at you. What's really going on?"

I began picking at a thread on my jeans. "I don't want to have to deal with it."

"Ok, but you've been tense for a couple of weeks," he countered. "Talk to me, sweetie?"

So I pushed out a heavy breath. With Linda watching us, I knew I couldn't say no. I couldn't just storm out of here and try to pretend like this hadn't happened. We'd taken on a full "family discussion" mode, and those never went well for me.

"I tried to fix it," I told Lars. "I thought that if I told Bax, then

Bax could talk to Gavin, and then I could focus on my magic, and Travis knows how to do that, but Tash hates him because he's a demon, and - "

"I don't," Tash said, interrupting my ramble. "Jess, I don't hate Travis. I'm wary of him because he's a demon, and demons hate us. I'm worried that he might be trying to take advantage of you, but he seems ok. He's been helping you more than I ever could. We changed the wards in the shop because he's ok."

"Oh." Well, there went one little piece of stress on me.

The problem was that as it dissolved, it felt like a million pounds had been taken from my shoulders, but there was still so much left. I couldn't focus, couldn't concentrate, and couldn't relax because the perfect was gone. I was unconsciously bracing for the worst, and the worst just kept coming. All that was left was for my guys to dump me for being a psycho chick.

Linda just looked over at Gavin. "Do you have a problem with who Deke loves?"

Gav's mouth opened like he wanted to answer, but at first nothing came out. Then he made a few false starts. "Uh... I mean... If it's me! And if it's Jess, yeah!"

"So you don't think Deke should date Jess?" Linda pressed.

"No!" Gavin insisted. "I mean yes. Yes, Deke should date Jess, and no, that's not what I meant. It's just that we have to. Well, not have to, but she needs us to, and we like her, but I'm not gay!"

"Who ever said you were?" Linda asked.

He looked over at Bax, clearly looking for some backup.

"Aw, man," Bax groaned. "Talk about awkward." He still pulled in a big breath and turned to Linda. "He's worried about what might happen if or when more than one guy is in a bed with Jess at the same time."

"I see," Linda said, but the corners of her mouth were just a little too tight. "Do you think someone might slip and stick their dick in your ass, Gavin? Are you worried you might accidentally swallow someone's balls?"

Yep, I choked. There wasn't even a laugh to it. This was pure, simple, mortification. And yet, somehow, hearing Linda ask that so calmly made me relax a bit. Maybe a lot. There was just no way to be pissed, stressed, and freaking out when the woman who was all but my stepmother was talking about my boyfriend accidentally swallowing balls!

Beside me, Deke had his face in his hands. On the other side, Lars had his jaw clenched, clearly struggling not to laugh. Gavin's face was so red that it had reached his ears, and Bax just looked exhausted. That was kinda how I felt. It was like all of this stupid crap had just built up so high that I was drowning under it, and I was simply too tired to fight anymore.

"Do you?" Linda pressed. "Clearly, you aren't worried about some guy seeing you naked, Gav. So it's not that. Do you think Deke would just accidentally have sex with you?"

"No," Gavin mumbled.

"Then what is so scary about it?" Linda asked.

"I don't know!" Gavin snapped. "It's gross. It's..."

"So, you haven't tried anal sex yet. I see." Linda had to clear her throat, but her stoic facade was slipping. "Did you care about the women Bax used to date?"

"Fuck," Bax corrected. "If we're being blunt, Linda, then let's be blunt."

"I don't care who he fucks!" Gavin snapped. "Unless he's cheating on Jess, then yeah. But that was before we knew her."

"Exactly," Linda said. "So why do you care about who Deke fucks?"

"Because he's supposed to be with her!" Gavin insisted. "He has a bond with her. I saw that bond when I died, and his is rotting. How can he be with her if he wants a guy?"

"No," Deke said, slicing his hand through the air to stop that line of thinking. "That's not how it works, Gav. I don't say I'm bi to get one of each. I just don't have the same issue you do. I happen to know when a guy is good-looking. Sometimes it turns me on.

Sometimes it doesn't. I also know when a girl is good-looking. Same thing with them. Me being bisexual doesn't mean I'm going to run out and get a boyfriend and mess around. I've already talked to Jess about this!"

"Oh," Gavin said, glancing over at me.

I nodded. "He did."

"Sorry," Gavin muttered.

"I wish you'd just talk to me about it," Deke said. "This has been stressing Jess out for days. Look, her entire life has been turned upside down, and maybe you boys don't get it, but her plans are gone."

"Fuck," Lars breathed.

Deke nodded in agreement. "Yeah. This is hard for her. You three are so busy thinking about getting laid, and she's over here worrying about learning magic, learning to shoot, learning to fight, keeping her grades decent, staying away from her father, trying to figure out if she's evil, and everything else we've dumped on her plate. This isn't a fucking video game for her, ok?"

"Plus," Linda said, her calm voice breaking in, "I'm betting that none of you have realized that Jess has never been allowed to do that. If she acted out like that..." She gestured to where I'd been standing when Tash stopped me. "Her father would've hit her. If she yelled at a teacher, he would've whipped her with a belt. She couldn't have fun, couldn't misbehave, and if she tried, she was punished. Of *course* she's going to mess it up when she tries. That young lady stood up for not only me, but also herself today. None of you can understand how hard that had to be for her." Then she looked at me. "But I'm proud of you, sweetheart."

"But I messed up," I reminded her. "I'm not supposed to let normal people see magic!"

"We'll handle it," Tash assured me. "Believe it or not, I agree with Linda on this. Jess, these guys don't get it. They've been allowed to be loud and messy for their entire lives. They don't understand how hard it is to hold your ground. We don't expect you to get it right the first time, you know." Then she looked at Deke. "And you?"

"Tash..." Deke tried.

"No, Deke," Tash snapped. "I told you not to do this. I warned you about getting too close."

"I was already too close when you said that!" he shot back.

"I know," Tash admitted. "So stop yanking the girl around, ok? Maybe the five of you are a mess, but you're a mess that seems to work. Even when it gets ugly like this, it's still working, Deke. These kids? They're the strongest Brethren I've ever seen. If Gavin's right and these bonds matter, then you're not helping anything by holding back."

"You've already gone there," Linda pointed out.

"Mom!" Lars groaned.

"I know how sex works," Linda reminded him. "It's kinda how I got you." Then she pushed herself out of the chair. "And Jess? You're coming upstairs with us. I think these boys need to have a little heart-to-heart talk." She ran her eyes over all of the guys with that expression moms had that made their kids obey. "And you *will* talk. Figure it out, boys."

"Yes, ma'am," Deke mumbled as Bax and Gavin nodded in agreement.

"I'll make sure of it, Mom," Lars promised.

CHAPTER TWENTY-THREE

WHEN WE MADE IT UPSTAIRS, Linda led me into her living room. I hadn't been to the third floor in a while. She'd done a lot of work, and the place was looking pretty homey. Then I sank into the couch. Oh, it was comfortable. Almost good enough to make me forget the insanity of the last couple hours.

"Are you ok?" Linda asked me.

I nodded quickly. "Kinda mortified, if I'm honest."

"Well, I'm not your mother, am I?" Linda asked, a sly little smile on her lips. "And I think this is working out well for me. I can play the mom card when I need to, and the not-the-mom card when that one works better."

"Be nice to her," Tash said as she walked over with a pair of cups. "It's tea, not coffee," she warned before passing me one.

"Thanks?" Because why was Tash making me a tea?

The woman just headed back to the kitchen to grab a third cup from the counter. "Don't you remember talking to grownups about sex at that age, Linda?"

"No!" Linda laughed. "I was a virgin until I went to college - which is why I ended up a party girl."

"Well, it's mortifying," Tash said as she claimed the seat across from us. "Never mind that Lars is your son. Those boys are so busy thinking with their dicks and trying to show what big men they are that it's never dawned on them that this is going to be hard."

"Like typical boys," Linda said, giving me a smile to make it clear I was included in the girl talk.

But my head felt like it was on a merry-go-round. I couldn't keep up. "Am I in trouble?" I blurted out.

"No," Linda assured me. "You, Jess, are under a lot of pressure, and it sounds like you're cracking a little. Your boys are being stupid, which is only making it worse. And here's the thing that none of them will tell you: you are allowed to have a meltdown. You're allowed to feel all of this, to be confused, angry about what you've lost, and pissed off because of something they do."

"But I don't want to screw things up with them," I tried to explain.

"It's not screwing things up," Linda assured me.

"It's also ok to not let them walk all over you," Tash said. "Jess, being their girlfriend doesn't mean you have to be a doormat. You are allowed to get mad, to make them apologize, or even to have a tantrum. So are they. That's how relationships work."

"Oh."

But in my world, that wasn't true. Mom and Dad hadn't really fought. At least, not where I'd been able to hear. I hadn't been allowed to talk back without Dad smacking me. When I'd gotten mad at my boyfriends and complained, they'd dumped me. Even Megan had gotten sick of me complaining about my dad too much. It had always been safest to just say nothing.

"Sounds like you didn't have a problem talking to that teacher," Tash pointed out. "So it's not that you have a problem with confrontation. What's going on in your head, Jess?"

I carefully took a sip of the tea, then set it down on the coffee table before me. "I screwed up at school, and no one's mad at me."

ENTER SANDMAN

"Would being mad make you feel better?" Tash asked. "Would it change what had happened? Would it undo the past?"

"No..."

"Exactly," she said. "You know you messed up. You know how you made at least one of those mistakes. The other was a power you didn't know you had, and I'll pick your brain about it more when you don't look like someone's about to kick you. But, from everything that was said down there, there is one thing that stands out. You've reached your limit, Jess. I want to know how I can help."

"But you hate me," I reminded her.

"I do not," Tash insisted. "Jess, I wanted to hate you. I tried to hate you. Unfortunately, you're kinda hard to hate, because you are right. You're not evil. You've worked harder than any other Brethren I've met in my life. You've come along faster, and on top of all of that, you're more powerful. You're also a pretty decent girl."

"Who's trying hard to grow up," Linda added. "Your father didn't let you, so now you're making up for lost time the same way I did. Believe it or not, I do understand that. I also want to help." She bit her lips together, and set down her own cup. "Jess, you can't do things the way I was taught is right. That doesn't mean you shouldn't be allowed to live life to the fullest. You're going to assassinate demons, fix supernatural seals that hold back Hell, and stop the Apocalypse. I think having four boyfriends pales in comparison."

"Three," I corrected. "Deke keeps trying to say that it can't happen."

Tash groaned. "Because of me. Ok, I'll talk to him tomorrow. If Gavin's right and you five have a bond, that has to mean something. Maybe it's because of your magic that he saw it, or maybe it's something unique to this quad. I honestly don't know, but I believe it's real, and I think it's important." Then she flicked a finger in my direction. "But the real question is, what do you think?"

"Uh..." I looked at Linda.

"Deke's attractive," Linda offered. "Bax has a reputation for making the girls giggle. Gavin is a sweet boy at times, and a damned idiot at others. And I'm a little biased about Lars."

"Lars is cute too," I admitted. "But it's more than that. Lars is amazing. He's my best friend in the world, and he always knows when I'm stressed out, or freaking out, or if I just need to talk. He's like... He makes me feel safe. And Bax? He tries so hard to be a pig, but he's really not. The more I get to know him, the more I realize that being some shallow man-whore was mostly an act. I mean, yeah, he had sex a lot, but he wasn't the jerk everyone made him out to be."

"I'm actually not that shocked," Linda said.

"And he makes me feel brave," I continued. "Gavin makes me feel strong, which is kinda weird because he's not the most muscular."

"He is the best fighter," Tash assured me. "Gavin has natural talent and the skill from his mark. I think strong is a good word for him."

"Yeah, but it's not just like, physical strength," I tried to explain. "It's emotional and mental too. He doesn't care what people say about him usually - except for this stupid gay thing!"

"To me," Tash said, leaning forward over her knees, "it sounded like he was more worried about Deke cheating on you than anything else."

"That, but it's all of it for him." I grabbed my tea and took another sip. "See, he was bullied because people assumed he was gay - he's not - and his dad hated him because he wasn't manly enough. At thirteen! So, 'being gay' is being weak, and being weak means getting hurt. The only thing he knows of gay sex sounds like priests molesting boys, and those boys took out their anger on him because he was weak, so it became a vicious cycle."

"I'll talk to him," Tash promised. "Might be easier coming from me than Deke."

I glanced over at Linda, then back, not sure if I should say anything. The levels of awkwardness had been maxed out for me today.

"She knows," Tash assured me. "Linda probably knew about me and Deke before you did. I didn't want us to have any misunderstandings, so I figured I might as well dump all the complications on her at once."

"And I have no problem with someone being gay, lesbian, bisexual, or anything else," Linda promised. "So, you can tell those boys that if they experiment, I'm not going to think it's weird. Most kids your age do."

"I don't think that's going to happen," I assured her.

Linda just shrugged that off. "The real question is what you think about all of this. Jess, how are you really dealing with your life being turned upside down?"

My teeth found my lower lip, and I couldn't quite figure out how to answer that for a little too long. When I did, it was the dumbest thing ever. "I'm not going to college."

"I know," Linda admitted.

"But that's what I've spent my life working toward," I reminded her. "It's all I had. I don't know how to do anything else, or what comes next, and Deke said he was going to make me a plan, but I still don't know the next step, and I feel like I'm stuck in a room, trying to clean it, and I just don't know where to start! I'm not sure what I'm supposed to do!"

Linda caught my hand, making me twist to face her. "You are supposed to fall in love with those boys. You're supposed to do something stupid at least once in your life, and it's usually a bad sex story. You're supposed to close the seal out there, become a kick-ass monster hunter, and save the world, Jess. You are supposed to be a Brethren strong enough to live until this baby is born so you can help me raise her."

I nodded quickly. "I'm trying."

"Which means you can't worry about all of it," she insisted. "Right now, nothing else matters except assassinating Greg. That bastard stuck his claws in Gavin, and you kids are going to make him pay for that. Nothing else - not me, the house, school, or anything else - matters right now. This hit is all you should focus on, ok?"

"Yeah, but what about me throwing out magic?" I asked. "I mean, what's the downside of that?"

"Martyrs," Tash said. "There are Watchers in Hellam, Jess. Only abominations do magic, and all abominations must die. That's why we don't want you using it outside of missions."

There was that word again: missions. Maybe they had a point, though. Calling them missions made it sound less like murder and more like a strategy in a war. Like a planned move that I was just carrying out.

"Ok," I breathed. "Just worry about killing Greg."

"And Jess?" Tash asked, making me look over at her. "There is not a damned thing wrong with you standing up for yourself. If those guys don't like it, then we'll stand with you."

"Don't let your father have any more control over you," Linda said gently. "We left him. Both of us. He can't hurt us anymore, and he certainly can't make us be weak, submissive, and quiet women, right?"

I reached for my cup. This time, I cradled it in my lap as I leaned back and got comfortable on the couch. "I don't want to be the good girl anymore."

"Then don't be," Linda said. "You know, when I grew up, I realized something. All those rules to make us be so good? All they're really doing is making us be obedient. They teach us that we can't say no, we can't do anything that might hurt someone's feelings, and we need to bend over backwards to make everyone else happy. Strange thing, though. The people who get ahead? They don't do that. They advocate for themselves. They know how to say no. They will scream from the rooftops when they want to be heard, not sit down and shut up. So, Jess, scream. That will make me more proud of you than anything else, ok?"

"Ok," I promised. "Thank you." I almost left it there, but there was one more thing I had to say. Probably the biggest one. "And you're not my real mom, but that doesn't mean you aren't my mom, Linda. I..." I had to swallow, and I couldn't take my eyes off the tea cup I was holding. "I love you like my real mom, and I'm so glad I got you."

"Oh, sweetie," she breathed, leaning forward to wrap me and my half-full tea cup in her embrace. "I love you too, honey. Nothing is going to change that. You are not alone, and you're not failing. You're just learning how to spread those wings, ok? So you spread them as wide as you can."

I nodded. "I'm trying my hardest."

"No," Tash told me. "You are succeeding. I'm proud of you too."

And for some reason, that felt just as good as when Linda said it. It seemed I hadn't messed up as bad as I thought. Maybe I could actually do this. All of this.

CHAPTER TWENTY-FOUR

I STAYED upstairs with Linda and Tash for most of the night. Lars came up to check on me at one point. Linda shooed him back downstairs, but he said the guys had all talked and were sorting out their mess. He also apologized. I wasn't sure what he was sorry for, but I told him it was ok anyway.

Eventually, I headed back downstairs. The TV was on in the living room, but I didn't check to see who was watching it. The guys were all quiet, which wasn't that unusual. Mostly, I just wanted to change into something relaxing since things had blown up right after school, but the moment I stepped into my room, I realized I wasn't alone.

Gavin was lying in the middle of my bed, looking at the screen of his phone. When he heard the door, he looked over - then quickly sat up. For a moment we just watched each other, my mind trying to decide what I should say first. That I was sorry? But I wasn't. That I hadn't meant to hurt him? That was more true, although I wasn't sure if he was hurt. That I might have overreacted? Maybe, but my long talk with Linda and Tash had erased my guilty feelings about that.

ENTER SANDMAN

Gavin solved my problem by speaking first. "I don't hate Deke," he blurted out.

A tense breath rushed from my lungs and I nodded, stepping the rest of the way in just to close the door behind me. "But you hate that he's bi, right?"

"No," Gavin groaned, closing his eyes like this wasn't going how he wanted. "Jess, I've been trying." He turned, setting his feet on the ground, then shoved his head into his hands. "I don't know how to say this, but I've been waiting for you so I could."

"Say what?"

"I like you, ok?" He glanced up. "I've liked you for a while, and then I fell in love with you, but I still like you too." He made a face because that clearly wasn't quite how he'd meant to say that. "I mean, I don't feel like I have to be with you. I want to, so that's the like part. I feel right with you. That's the love part." And a grimace crossed his face. "I'm not doing this right."

Maybe not, but he was being cute, and it was enough to put a weak smile on my face as I walked over and sat beside him. "I don't think I handle stress well, Gav."

He shrugged that off. "I was a dick. You're not supposed to handle that well. I'm also sorry."

So I leaned my head over to rest on his shoulder. "Deke said this wouldn't work, you know. All of us? Someone would get mad, someone would get jealous. I used to think that it would all miraculously work and we'd be happy forever after like in one of my books."

"Who says we can't?" he countered. "I can slap your ass, call you a slut, and, um..." He flashed me a boyish smirk. "I think that was when the other guy put his dick in her mouth."

Giggling, I flopped back on the bed. "So you've been in my Kindle, huh?"

He reached over for the phone he'd dropped on the bed and turned the screen to me. "Lars put in the password so I can see them." The Kindle app was open, and from the few words I could see, I recognized that book.

"Pretty sure none of those guys are calling Violet a slut," I pointed out as I sat back up.

"No, that was the other book where they called her a slut. This one has the guys dating each other." He dimmed the screen and put the phone back down, but his eyes wouldn't meet mine. "I asked Deke if he'd read it because it's easier for me to ask questions about the book than him. And he said he would, so I'm finishing it. I think Deke's more like Cy, though. He's all tough but soft."

"And you?" I asked.

He shrugged. "I want to be like Crimson. He's cool, and he can joke about it, and he's not worried, but that's the thing, Jess. I am worried. I feel like I'm doing something wrong if I say it's ok, because my father used to hit me if I didn't go after gay guys. He said that if I saw a butterfly like that I should beat his ass so everyone knew I wasn't one."

I just nodded, assuming that butterfly was his best translation without using a slur. "So... What does this mean?"

"Deke says that you need a plan, right?" he asked. "So this is my plan. I am going to be ok with Deke. It's going to take a little work, and I'm going to mess up, but Deke said he'll tell me when I'm being a dick. That means it's my lesson, not yours. When he yells at me for being an asshole, you're going to ignore it. We're not mad at each other - well, not for more than a minute or so - and it's my problem, Jess. You just have to worry about understanding your magic, so things like Mr. Garcia don't happen."

"Ok," I said, because he had a point.

"And Lars has been telling me about how the Cherokee and other American Indians see Two Spirit people. That kinda helps. I mean, I'm not into God and all that. I went to church, but I hated it, and his version makes it sound better. I don't understand how Deke could think guys are pretty, and that's gross, but I don't have to."

ENTER SANDMAN

"Which part is gross?" I pressed.

"Guys," he told me. "We stink, and we're hairy, and I like tits. I really like pussies." His eyes jumped up and a smile took over his lips. "But you like guys, and that's ok. Doesn't seem weird that you have sex with them, so I'm working through it. We need Deke, and I think Deke needs us. See, I keep thinking that we're all going to die, right?"

"Uh huh..." I just nodded my head, because that change in topic didn't make sense to me yet. "But I don't want to give up. I don't want to just say it doesn't matter because we might get killed."

"Me either," he agreed. "That's my point. We have these bonds, and we aren't doing things like the other quads, so what if that's the difference? What if they failed because they didn't work on their bonds? What if they thought it was too gay? What if our Sandman is that big of a deal, and Deke is what will save us? That's what I saw, Jess. The bonds? Deke is tied to us, and we're all tied to you. We have to be all in, and I may not know how to do that with Deke, but if he can try with you, then I can try with him."

"Oh, Gavin," I breathed, reaching over to cup his face and make him look at me. "You are the sweetest guy I've ever met, you know that? I don't want to tell you that you have to feel a certain way. I mean, that's what my dad did to me."

"You're not," he promised. "I love you, Jess. I can't stop thinking about you, and I'm always watching you because you're so beautiful. I can't get enough of your smile, but you don't do it as much lately. I noticed, but I don't know how to make it better, and I don't want it to be because I'm stupid. My dad was the one who said this was wrong. My dad said I was a piece of shit, and fuck him! I just didn't want Deke to think that he could have a boyfriend and yank you around, you know? But he said it's not like that."

"So you two talked?"

"Yeah." He pressed his cheek into my palm. "We all talked. We never used to, you know. Before you came around, we would practice, then play some games, talk about hot chicks, and maybe have a beer. Now we're always talking about emotions and shit. Stuff I always thought girls did, not guys. Lars says it's stupid that we can't, and there's no reason guys can't feel shit too. Like, we can be sad or need reassurance, and that doesn't make us pussies."

"He's right," I pointed out. "I mean, I do that, and I don't think I'm a pussy."

"It's different," Gavin mumbled. "Girls are supposed to."

"So are guys!" I snapped. "Gavin, that's bullshit. Why can't you do the same shit as me, and how the fuck does it make you *weak* to face something head on? Whether that's how you feel or a demon, it shouldn't matter. Fuck, you guys are screwed up."

"Just me," he admitted, sounding a little ashamed of it.

"So we unscrew it, right?" I offered. "I don't want to say it's ok, because it's really not. There's nothing ok about making Deke feel bad for who he is, or Tash, or me because I'm part demon, or Travis because he's all demon. It's just like someone saying you suck because you're Hispanic. That would be shitty."

"Yeah, but I'm European, so I don't really get that." He shrugged. "I know what you're saying, though. I also know that the only reason I was mad at school was because I was worried. I wasn't mad that you were mad. I was mad because if anyone saw that, then they'll come after you, and I don't want that. If they try to kill you, I will destroy them, Jess. We all will, and that's what's going to make us stronger than the other quads. We're fighting for each other. They were just fighting for the world."

That sounded completely backwards, but he still had a point. There was something about saving the world that sounded noble and heroic, but also distant and pointless. It didn't really matter to me. It wouldn't make my life better, and why should I care about all these people who'd done nothing but shit on me?

Fighting for him, however, felt bigger. It felt more immediate. I knew I'd do it without hesitation. If someone tried to hurt Gavin, nothing would stop me, and I'd already proven that at the seal battle. I had a feeling the same was true for Lars, Bax, and Deke, although I hadn't needed to worry about that yet. One day, I probably would, and I hoped I would be the kind of woman who wouldn't hesitate.

Because they were the most important things to me. These guys had accepted me as I was even when I hadn't. They'd shown me that I wasn't a loser, they'd stood beside me when things got hard, and I loved them. Every day, I loved them a little more. It was this feeling in my chest that was so similar to magic, but butterflies instead of fireflies. I loved Linda too, but she was a mom, and that was like a steady ember that gave me just enough to keep going. These guys were like lightning rods.

"I'm sorry I got mad," I told Gavin.

He scooted a little closer. "Get mad, Jess. I do it often enough that I can understand. Yell, scream, or throw people across parking lots. I don't care. I will still love you, and maybe I'll get mad too, but it doesn't mean I don't love you - or them. Those guys are like my brothers." He chuckled. "I've been practicing. You see how easily I said I love them?"

That made me giggle, but before it could become a full-fledged laugh, I leaned in and pressed my lips to his. "Stay the night in here, Gav?"

"Yeah," he promised. "And I'm going to be ok with Deke. I might be weird, or do something stupid, but I'm ok. I'm just learning, the same way you had to learn not to be good. The same way Bax is trying to learn how to be a boyfriend."

"So what's Lars learning?" I asked.

He shrugged. "I don't know. How to keep up with me?"

Wrapping my arms around him, I pulled Gavin down to the bed. "Keep telling yourself that, Gav."

Gently, he reached up to brush the hair back from my face. "Then it sounds like I need more practice. Good thing I'm staying all night. Gotta be the perfect man for my girl, right?" Then he leaned in and kissed me. "Because you deserve to have someone try."

"I have four of you doing that, Gav."

"Mhm," he agreed. "And I don't see anything wrong with that."

CHAPTER TWENTY-FIVE

The next day at school, the guys were a little extra attentive. I really didn't think I'd had that big of a fit, but it seemed they wanted to make sure it didn't happen again. At lunch, Bax asked three different times if I was doing ok. Gavin was being a little extra sweet, doing everything from getting me my favorite candy bar to holding my hand when I didn't need it for anything else. Lars? He rolled his eyes at them, but I had a feeling it was because he wanted to do the same. Instead, he made sure that my class with Mr. Garcia had gone ok.

It had, actually. The man didn't say a thing to either me or Gavin. Not in class, and not in the halls later in the day. When school was finally over and we headed home, it felt like it had been a pretty good day. The best part was that only one person asked about what Gavin had done to Oliver.

He'd lied so smoothly about martial arts and push styles that I was pretty sure we had that covered - at least until we made it out to the SUV. Unlike yesterday, we'd dawdled at our lockers long enough that most of the other students had left. That made the white rental car parked at the back just a little more obvious. I couldn't see through the window well enough to make out the person inside, but there was definitely a shadow sitting in the driver's seat.

Were we being watched? Was Tash right and the Martyrs were already in town? Unfortunately, the chances of that were good, so we hurried home and made sure to update Deke. He told us not to worry about it. What was done was done, and if they weren't trying to talk to us, we should still be ok. Besides, it could've just been a parent waiting to pick up their kid, parked far enough away to not embarrass them.

I kept thinking about it through my magic lesson. When we headed over to Bax's house for our run through of the hit that was coming up this weekend, I didn't have time. We also did pretty good, if I was honest. Neither Deke nor Tash were able to trip us up, which meant we were ready. Deke promised us one more run tomorrow, and then we'd take the rest of the week off while he finalized the last few details, like the weather and other things that could change between now and then.

As a group, we were walking back to the barn, chattering about the parts we were proud of. Bax had clothes-lined Deke in the second-floor hallway, forcing out a very ungraceful sound when Deke had hit the ground. Gavin had flipped Tash without a problem, securing her before she could reorient herself. Lars had been the one to figure out which room they were in, using subtle sounds to track them down.

And me? I'd done pretty good with closing doors and holding them shut. I'd avoided using any fire or water powers because I didn't want to ruin the gorgeous mansion. But air was easy and convenient. The best part, though, was that I'd figured out that doors and locks counted as earth magic, which meant I could unlock things without a key if I focused hard enough. That was going to be very useful!

Deke was thrilled that we wouldn't need to break a window or shatter a door to get in. Either one of those would give Greg a chance to brace for our attack. If I could unlock the door - and Deke planned to have a crowbar as backup in case I couldn't - then this should all be easy. We'd get in, take Greg out in his sleep, and get out before anyone even knew we were there. One greater demon down, which meant one less to fight back when we tried to close the seal again.

And then my phone rang.

Confused, I pulled it out to see Travis's number on the screen. He didn't usually call me, though. At most, he texted, and even then, we kept it pretty minimal. His parents weren't thrilled with the idea of him talking to us, and the other demons would only be worse. After all, we were the bad guys. Never mind the complications of a Martyr finding out what we were doing.

So I swiped to answer. "Travis?"

"I need help," he croaked, his voice so harsh that it barely sounded like him.

My feet froze. "Shit, where are you?"

That had the attention of my guys. They all stopped and turned to face me. Thankfully, they didn't start talking. With as rough as Travis sounded, I wasn't sure I'd hear him over their questions.

"The shop. Bax's," Travis said. "Greg got me."

"Travis is out by the shop," I relayed to the rest. "Greg attacked him." Then back to Travis, "Is he still there?"

"No," Travis promised, and I shook my head so the others would know the answer too. "He just left. Jess, my legs are broken." He pulled in a shaking breath. "Please help me?"

That last part came out as a whimper, and the sound punched me in the gut. "We're coming for you, Travis," I promised, walking again and stretching my legs as far as they could go. "Just stay out of sight in case he comes back, ok?"

"He won't," Travis promised. "This was a lesson. He left me alive on purpose, otherwise he would've eaten me. Just..." His breath shook again. "I'm on the side. Please come, Jess. Please?"

"I'm on the way," I assured him.

Deke jogged ahead to get his truck. It was four-wheel drive, so it could go across the fields without a problem. The rest of us hopped into the back without bothering to change. We were already armed and ready for combat, so there was nothing else we needed - and hopefully we wouldn't need any of this.

When we arrived, Travis was leaning up against the side of the small building. His legs were laid out before him as if he'd dragged himself to that spot, and the guy was covered in blood. I was pretty sure that most of it was his. Claw marks scarred his side. His face and arms were bruised and battered. Whatever Greg had done, Travis had clearly tried to fight back.

"Travis?" I called as I hopped over the side.

"Fuck," Deke snarled as he climbed out of the cab. "You boys secure the area. Make sure this isn't a trap. Jess, let's get him into the bed of the truck."

"No, no, no, no..." Travis mumbled, slowly shaking his head. "Hurts."

"And it's gonna hurt a little more, baby demon," Deke told him. "I don't want her healing you out here. She'll be too vulnerable." He moved to Travis's side and squatted down. "Jess, grab his things. Travis, arm over my neck or I'm throwing you over my shoulder."

"Just like a damsel in distress," I told my friend. "It's ok. I can fix you. I'm sure I can."

But when Deke lifted, Travis cried out, unable to hold it in. His poor legs dangled in the worst way, making my stomach turn. That was just not right. What the fuck had Greg wanted from him that had been worth this? That asshole! I was seething in my head as I grabbed Travis's bag and a water bottle from where they'd been dropped a few feet away.

"Anything else broken?" Deke asked as they reached the back of the truck.

"Not that I..." Travis paused to cry out again. "No," he finished.

"Then scoot back a bit," Deke said before letting out a piercing whistle. "Time to go!"

ENTER SANDMAN

I jogged back, but when I reached the bed of the truck, Deke grabbed my waist and lifted, helping me in. I immediately crawled over to Travis's side, wanting to help. When I turned back to thank Deke, he'd already moved on. Like some kind of precision strike team, the other guys hopped in the back, moving to brace Travis, and then we were driving out of there.

"What happened?" Bax asked, moving around to help me hold Travis in a sitting position.

"Greg was waiting for me after school," he said. "I got out of practice and he was parked behind my car. Told me to get in. I wasn't dumb enough to say no, but he knows I've been talking to you four. He's pissed. He said I'm a traitor and he was going to kill me, so I told him I was spying." He paused to yelp as the truck hit a pretty impressive bump. "I said I was trying to find out when you were hitting next. Told him I thought Jess was doing the same, which was why I tried."

"But he knows what I am," I pointed out.

Travis huffed out a weak laugh. "But I shouldn't. I made it clear that the four were Bax, Lars, Gavin, and Deke. He said I'm an idiot, but if I could get you away from them, then he'd let me live. It's the only reason he didn't eat me, because he was going to. Sounds like they need magic."

"Which means your dad wants you," Lars told me.

I nodded. "Yeah, kinda sounds like it, but fuck him. If he's gonna let his friends do shit like this? Just no."

"This is why they think demons are evil," Gavin said, sounding almost like he was talking to himself. "They hurt their own."

"So do fucking Martyrs!" I snapped.

"I know," Gavin assured me. "But this is their excuse. This is what the Order tells the members. Demons are so evil that they eat each other." He looked at each of us. "They don't say it's for magic. They call it cannibalism and use our disgust to build their hate."

"It's pretty gross," Bax told Travis.

"Fuck," Travis huffed, trying to make it a laugh. "I won't do it, but I don't care about magic. I just want to be human - or as human as I can." Then he leaned his head back, finding Bax's arm to rest against. "Most of us regenerate it on our own, but it's slow. Consuming another abomination makes it faster. They started eating demons because in the Pit, there's nothing else. It used to be wraiths and devas."

"Don't even know what those are," Bax assured him, but the tone of his voice was soothing. "Hurting?"

Travis nodded, but we were coming up to the house now, so it wasn't much longer. "Greg stomped on my legs. He said I'll never play sports again. He knows I just want to be normal, and he's making me pay for it, so fuck him. Fuck all of them!"

Then Deke stopped the truck. Just like before, we all made our way out, but the guys had this. Gavin lowered the tailgate. Bax and Lars eased Travis closer to the edge. While they worked on getting him out of the back without pulling on his legs, Deke made his way to the side.

"Jess," he said, reaching up to help me down.

"I'm fine," I assured him, hopping over the side of the truck bed on my own.

Deke still stabilized me when I landed. "We're taking him to the garage," he told the guys before turning me to the side. "This kid isn't human, Jess. I don't even know how this is going to work for you, so when do I pull you off?"

"When he's healed," I told him.

He ducked to look right in my face. "When do I pull you off, Jess? When is it too much?"

"I don't know, Deke, but this happened because he helped us. That demon is suffering because he wanted to help. So don't you try to tell me not to fix him, ok? Don't even think about talking me out of this."

"And if you burn yourself out like you did at the seal? Should we wait to hit Greg, giving him a little longer to prepare? Take the risk that he'll kill a kid next? What do you want me to do, Jess?"

I lifted my chin and looked right into his eyes. "I want you to trust me, Deke."

He just grabbed my left hand. "Then don't touch him with this. That boy isn't one of us. He might be your friend, but I'm pretty sure that won't protect him from Anathema."

"Shit." Because he was right. I'd almost forgotten, and it was sheer chance that I hadn't touched him with that hand. "Call Linda? My sleeve is on my makeup table."

"Don't start until it's on," Deke warned, tipping his head for me to go on while he pulled out his phone.

CHAPTER TWENTY-SIX

IN THE GARAGE, the guys had laid Travis out on a pile of plywood like it was a table. That didn't give me a lot of room to work, but I'd make do. A jacket had been folded over to work as a pillow for his head, and my three guys were all clustered around him. In the light of the shop, the poor guy looked like he was lucky to be alive.

"I have to wait for my sleeve," I said when I came closer. "I'm also going to need to touch his skin."

"Jess?" Lars asked.

"Other hand," I assured him. "I don't know why, but it always feels like I need to touch someone to heal them. My other magic isn't the same."

"Internal," Travis explained. "Spirit works through contact. Eye contact, audible contact, or touching. Doesn't matter, but if you want to influence them, you need to make contact." He let out another shaky breath. "Please tell me you're strong enough to do this?"

"I'll make sure of it," I promised just as the elevator dinged.

We all looked over to see Linda, Deke, and Tash coming out of it. Evidently Deke had gone upstairs after talking to me. He also had an armload of supplies. Wash cloths, it looked like, and maybe clothes? Linda was holding out my sleeve like it was the miracle cure, and in a way it was.

"Thanks," I told her, taking the sleeve without touching her so I could pull it on.

"How do I help?" Linda asked.

"Just stay out of her way," Deke called over. "Tash? He's going to need water, preferably not freezing. Soap if we have it, because she doesn't heal away the blood." Then he set his stuff down and moved closer. "And I think I'll have to help with this."

"It's not that bad," Travis promised. "I'm not dying. I just want to play football in college. That's all." Then he pulled up his shirt, exposing his belly. "Ready when you are, Brethren."

"Close your eyes," I warned. "I'm kinda new at this."

Then I laid my hand against his chest, just under his sternum. It took less than a second before I felt it, and the need to fix him pulled at me. I pulled at all the power I could find, sucking it into me - and reached for my friend's soul. It was there, vivid in its own way, but nothing like the rest of ours. The guys had colors that shined so brightly. Travis? His soul was black, streaked through with deep orange that swirled in the mists.

I didn't care. I pushed what I had right into him, digging my "fingers" into his morbid color. Beneath my hand, Travis twisted in pain, his body struggling to get away from the torment I was causing, but I could almost sense his legs. The breaks were like a disconnect. The wounds on his sides were bright spots of orange. All of it needed to be fixed, and if I could just tweak his soul a little bit, sampling it, then I could put him all back together.

So I pushed. The sound of Travis screaming was loud, making my ears ache. He fought, trying to get me off him, but the guys shoved him back down to the wood. Bit by bit, I could feel it working, but something felt off, like it was fighting me. Maybe calling to me was more true. A deep song, begging me to twist just a bit, let go, and take what I wanted.

That was demonic power. It was the difference between his magic and mine, but it knew me. It was daring me, egging me on for just a little more, and I was happy to give it. Travis would play football again, or basketball, or anything else he wanted to. He'd chase his girlfriends around, play games with his kids, and be a very normal man when I was done.

"Shit, his legs," Gavin breathed.

"Is it working?" Travis asked.

"Yeah, man," Bax assured him. "She's fixing you, but relax."

"Fucking hurts!" Travis groaned, sounding like he was trying his hardest not to fight me.

Then Deke's voice took over. "Gav, push up his pants. She's never been able to let go on her own. Bax, check the claw marks. Lars, see if there's anything on your side. When it's fixed, we'll pull her off if we have to."

I just kept pushing. It was as if Travis's soul was some kind of resource I could bend and stretch to make more of. Tash had been worried about me stealing it, but that wasn't what I wanted. It was to know it, to understand it, and to use it. To fix him with his own life, not mine. Not that of my guys.

And they were all shining around me. I could almost feel where they moved. Sky blue, electric green, raging red, and royal blue - it was as if they were being offered to me. And while I worked, I paused to look. This time, I saw the bonds Gavin had been talking about. Thick silver cables connected each of us, swirling through the colors the same way the orange did in Travis's black.

So many cables. So many connections. Each one was a slightly different shade, but they were all silver now. The one from the royal blue was a darker shade, and the one to the red was pulsing. I had no idea what that meant, but Gavin was right. We were bound together.

Among those was something else. Smaller threads that spun off me and away. One went to Travis's blackness. It was no bigger than a pencil, but it still connected us. That was how I was pushing my magic into his soul. It was how I was fixing him, able to reach who he was and make a difference.

Because whoever had said that I stole life to repair the body had been wrong. I used life. Mine, theirs, or someone else's, it didn't matter. From like to like. The less I used, the longer this took, yet I could make more. With one of my mental hands, I did that. The other kept working on Travis's brilliant orange wounds, struggling to reach a homogenous mixture of colors.

"That's good!" Deke barked.

"No!" I snapped. "Wait."

Oddly enough, they did. Travis was still groaning, but he was no longer screaming or writhing. I could feel the tension in him, but he'd stopped fighting. Still, his legs weren't quite right. Close - so close - but if I gave up now, he'd lose his dreams the same way I had. I was so sick of our goals being destroyed for the benefit of others. If I couldn't go to college, live to be old, or anything else, then at least Travis should be able to.

So I pushed just a bit more until something clicked into place. Travis gasped hard enough to lift his back away from the plywood even as I forced myself to let go - but that was easier said than done. The lure of his soul kept calling for me. The temptation of that power was like a drug, begging me to take a little more. It would be so easy to do. The power of this guy was right there, within my reach. I could steal it from him, but why?

Forcing my power back, I released him. It felt like it took an eternity, but the moment I was out, a wave of exhaustion hit me. My knees buckled and I knew I was going down, until strong arms wrapped around me. I opened my eyes to see Lars right there, easing me to my rump.

"Jess?" he asked.

"He'll play football," I panted, nodding to show I was ok. "They fucking use us, tear us up, and never care about what we want. Martyrs, demons, it doesn't matter."

"Shh," Gavin breathed, kneeling down at my side. "We know,

Jess. I promise we know. That fucker tried to kill me, and we're going to make sure he pays, but rest first."

I nodded, leaning into Lars so he'd wrap his arms around me. Over his shoulder, I watched while Bax and Deke checked on Travis, helping him to sit up. The first thing the guy did was look over at me.

"Thank you," he said, and there was so much emotion in those words. "I wasn't sure if a cambion could do it, but you're..."

"What?" Deke demanded. "She's what?"

Travis licked his hips. "Cambion inherit the power of their demonic parent. Well, the potential, although most never touch it. Her father is the fucking Devourer of Hell. He's not just a greater demon. He's something new. He's a nightmare. You think you understand, but none of you do. If our molts make us exponentially stronger? Yeah, do the math. Ted is like five greater demons in one - and she's just as strong."

"Fuck," Bax breathed, turning to look back at me. "I knew you were badass, but damn, Jess. Trying to make a guy feel inadequate, or what?"

That was enough to let the rest of us laugh. Linda and Tash moved in with a bucket of warm water, a bar of soap from the shop bathroom, and a dozen clean washcloths. Travis used those to wipe the blood off his arms. Linda grabbed one to clean his face, pointing out that he couldn't see it. And then, when he was finally considered good enough, he was told to take the clothes to the little bathroom and change.

Travis scooted to the edge of the wood and carefully got down. First he tested one leg, then the next, seeming a little surprised when they actually held his weight. After he took his first step, a strangled breath fell out, sounding almost like a sob. The guy just nodded and kept walking, but I saw him reach up to wipe at his eyes before he closed the door behind him.

"Greg's going to die," I told the rest. "Fucking with us is one thing, but Travis?"

"Should I be jealous?" Deke asked.

"Fuck off," Gavin snapped. "That's her friend."

"Uh huh. So were you three," Deke pointed out.

"Stop!" I demanded. "No, Deke. I don't steal my friends' guys, and Shannon is pretty much the only cool girl I know now. The problem is that this happened because of us! Travis helped me, and this is what he gets for it? Why would anyone else help us? Why would he ever want to help us again?"

"Because you just fixed him?" Tash offered.

"And not helping the kids," Linda pointed out, "would keep him from getting hurt again. Jess just paid Travis back. No, I'm with her. That boy suffered."

"What did he tell that demon?" Tash asked.

"No," I warned her. "Don't you start being a bitch again. You just got cool, Tash. No need to ruin it now." Then I looked at Deke. "Travis said that Greg left him alive on purpose."

"He did," Travis said as he came out of the bathroom. "He wanted to know why I was helping the Brethren. I told him it's the four guys." He pointed at Deke to make it clear who he meant. "Said I thought Jess was trying to get information for her father the way I am for my guardians. We need to know when you four will hit next. Greg offered to let me live if I kill Bax, Gavin, and Lars." He lifted a brow at Tash as he made his way back toward us. "Not Jess."

"And what are you going to do with that?" Tash asked.

With an arrogant smirk, Travis stopped right before her. "I'm going to make sure to tell Greg that there's a party some night, and that I'll try to take out Lars first." He looked over at Lars. "In theory, you should be the easiest since everyone knows Bax and would have questions."

"Makes sense," Lars admitted.

Gavin just chuckled. "So, like, Friday?"

"I can do that," Travis agreed.

Tash just threw her hands up in the air. "He could be playing you, for all you know!"

"After getting his legs broken?" I shot back. "How far are you willing to go for a scheme, Tash? Want me to break your legs so we can see if you'll lure in a greater for us? I mean, it would be the perfect ambush, right?"

"Pass," she grumbled.

Which proved my point. "Exactly. Travis is helping us. Get used to it."

"I'm fine with that," Tash shot back. "I'd say the same thing about another Martyr, Jess. What you four can do? When you're going to do it? How? That stays with us. The more who know, the easier it is for someone to figure it out. Secrets only stay secret if no one knows."

"I'm not about to ask," Travis assured me. "If I don't know, I can't admit it if they try to torture me. I'll still make sure there's a party on Friday, and we'll let it be known that you're all going. I suggest Linda catch you doing something and ground all of you that afternoon. Let Shannon know what, and she'll spread the word."

"Thanks, Travis," Bax said. "Now, how are we getting you home without making this worse?"

"My car's still at school," Travis said.

"I'll take him," Linda offered.

Tash just groaned and headed toward the back half of the shop. "Let me get some guns. Just in case, you know. The last thing we need is some demon getting his claws in you, Linda."

I just pushed myself to my feet and headed over to where Travis was standing. "Be careful, ok? I don't want you to get caught in the middle of it. You can get pissed at us next week if that's easier."

"No," he decided. "That fucker broke my legs. My legs, Jess. And he did that because he knew it would matter to me. I didn't want to pick sides before, but he left me no choice. I'm all in."

"And I'm going to make sure he pays. First my boyfriend, and now my friend?"

Travis just ducked his head and chuckled. "Demons aren't friends with Brethren."

"Weren't," I corrected. "Fuck the rules, Travis."

"Yeah," he agreed. "Fuck the rules."

CHAPTER TWENTY-SEVEN

Linda and Tash got Travis back to his car without a problem. The next day, he was at school and said everything seemed fine. He hadn't seen Greg, but that didn't make me any less pissed at the man. Bax was just as bad. He and Travis had been friends for a while. Greg was just some loser in town, living off the system just like my dad. Funny, that.

But things calmed down after that. At one point, Mr. Garcia tried to call me out in class for talking to Gavin. I just looked at the man, lifted a brow, and pulled out my phone. As casually as possible, I asked him if I needed to record this for the lawsuit. It convinced him to forget that the two of us existed.

And then the week was over. Shannon made a big production of saying she couldn't wait to see us at the party that evening. Bax wrapped his arms around me and said he had a plan to see his girl get drunk, and he meant me. For some reason, that was the part that was surreal. I was hunting demons and learning magic, but the moment those words came out of his mouth, it was as if this semester had never happened.

Last fall, I never would've imagined Bax Hale being committed to anyone. Now, I couldn't imagine him sleeping around. I couldn't imagine that a girl like me could end up with a guy like him - or Gavin, or Lars! Not that anyone knew I was with Lars, but still. These three guys were amazing.

Oddly, it wasn't just that they were the hottest guys in school. Sure, I still thought that, but it was so much more. They were badass, cared about how I felt, and were honestly everything I'd wanted in a boyfriend, or three. Never mind the fact that I had all three of them. No, I wasn't completely sure what was going on with Deke and me right now, but with what we had planned for tonight, I decided to allow myself just a moment to appreciate that this mess wasn't all bad.

In fact, it was pretty amazing. Maybe it was a little messy too, and definitely stressful, but if I had it all to do over again, I would definitely do it the same. I could barely even remember what it had been like to live with my father. The specific incidents stood out, but the boring day-to-day stuff had become a distant blur. Now, I had this. I had my quad, my Sandman, our pseudo-mom, and whatever Tash was.

So, on the way home, I decided to say something. "Guys? You know how bad the seal battle got?"

"Uh, yeah," Gavin said, because he'd been the one to get hurt the worst.

"Well, I just wanted to say that even if things go bad, I'm still glad this happened."

Lars reached back for my hand. "Me too, Jess. I actually like being a demon hunter."

"It's weird," Gavin said, "and getting speared sucked, but still worth it."

"I dunno," Bax joked. "Shit, easy women, tons of parties, and feeling like there was no point to my life?" He caught my eyes in the rearview mirror. "You know I'm kidding, right? Besides, I'm pretty sure that nothing else would've convinced us to share our girlfriend with each other, and I'm kinda enjoying this deal."

"Me too," I agreed, leaning back in my chair. "So, you three had better be careful or Deke will have to console me tonight, and I might make him do that naked."

"Shit," Lars laughed. "Jess, you should probably make him do that anyway. The guy needs a push, and we'll be fucking wiped. I have a feeling Greg isn't going to go down easy."

"Don't really care," Gavin said. "Gonna shove my hand through him and see how he likes it."

"Chopping off his balls would probably be easier," I pointed out.

"Do not want to see his balls," Gavin said, then grinned at me. "Old man balls."

"Demon balls," Bax added.

Lars just turned in his chair to look at me. "I think they're obsessed with balls. Sounds kinda gay like that." Then he smacked Gavin's leg.

But Gavin was still smiling. He wasn't pissed, wasn't trying to say that he wasn't gay, or anything like that. Clearly, he'd made a lot of progress since I lost my shit on Monday, and it almost felt like the guys were trying to make sure I knew it. Probably because they'd been talking about it when I wasn't around, which was oddly sweet. Gavin had said he'd try, and he had.

Which meant I was ready for this. Completely ready. All that was left was to wait for nightfall.

Around five, Bax texted Shannon to let her know we were grounded. Busted for talking back to Linda. Shannon knew better, but now she had a text to show others. She sent back a message about how much that sucked, and how he finally got free just to screw it up. He promised we'd go to another party later, and that was that. Our alibi was covered.

Then we waited a little longer. Around ten that night, all five of us began gearing up. Linda and Tash were staying home for this one, but Deke was going to be the getaway driver. Like us, he went armed. If we got pulled over, we were so fucked, so we had to play this tight.

ENTER SANDMAN

We all had a set of black fatigues. In truth, it was a thin long-sleeved shirt and a pair of cargo pants. Over that went a tactical vest. In there, we had the basic medical supplies like a pad to stop bleeding, gauze, tourniquet, and so on. Then there was spray paint, just in case we had to mark doors or where we'd been. They were the miniature cans, though. The rest of our pockets were filled with ammo. Most of it was silver bullets, since pure metals were supposed to hurt demons. We also had a clip of blessed bullets, and we might need all of them since Greg was a greater demon.

At one in the morning, we finally left. The streets in town were mostly quiet. The stoplights were abandoned. There was no one to care that we'd packed ourselves into Deke's truck as tightly as we could. He had the one vehicle that people wouldn't immediately recognize, and a blue full-size pickup? It didn't exactly stand out in Oklahoma.

When we made it to Greg's neighborhood, we didn't pull into his drive. Instead, Deke went a block over, backing his truck into the driveway of a house that was for sale, and from the overgrown lawn, had been that way for a while. It was diagonal from Greg's place. Then he shut his truck off.

"Ok, earbuds for everyone?" Deke asked.

We all put them in, then Bax started a group phone call. No, it wasn't as high tech as we'd like, but it worked. Our phones also went into our tactical vest, and we all spoke up to make sure we could both hear and be heard. With one last check of the guns, and two more of the houses around us, we finally climbed out.

"I'm listening," Deke said through our earbuds as we headed into the vacant backyard. "When you're done, let me know and I'll have the truck running before you get here. Bax? Your job is to make sure Jess can get over the fence once she's used her hand."

I grunted, hating how it sounded like I was weak.

But evidently that went across, because Deke added, "It saps your strength, Jess. Just not taking any chances. That's it."

"Better," I told him just as we reached the corner. "Ok, one of you guys look over and see if the neighbors are all asleep."

Gavin immediately hopped up on the slats of the privacy fence and peered over. "All houses are dark. Greg's fence is chain link, so watch the sound when you come over." Then he was gone on the other side.

Lars went next, then I followed after him. Thankfully, that chain link was positioned just right to let me step down and jump to the ground. It also was pretty stable. When Bax hit the ground behind me, we were ready. Everything around us was perfectly silent. The crickets were just starting to sing at night, and a bird called in the distance, but that was it. From this neighborhood, I couldn't even hear any traffic.

As a group, we headed toward the back door of the house. There was a large window in it, the kind that took up most of the top half, so we made sure to stay to the sides. Once there, Gavin leaned in to make sure no one was moving inside. When he nodded, that meant it was my turn.

I pressed my hand just over the doorknob and reached for my magic. Metal and wood fell under the element of earth. If I could imagine it, then I could make it happen, so I worked hard to imagine the locks on the door all gently unlocking. Tumblers would turn, deadbolts would slide, and the clicks would be soft and hard to hear. First, I heard the one on the handle. Immediately after that, a heavier thump proved that the deadbolt had obeyed too.

"Ok, it's open," I said.

All four of us drew our silver guns, the silencers already attached. Carefully, Gavin turned the knob until the latch released, and then Bax went in first. Gavin was next, and I followed, with Lars bringing up the rear. We made it three whole steps inside before a shadow filled the entrance to the kitchen. Greg roared and what had been a chair or a stool smashed into the cabinet beside Bax.

ENTER SANDMAN

The first pop was louder than I expected. In the silence of the quiet of night, it felt like everyone had to hear when Lars' gun went off. The bullet slammed into Greg's shoulder as we all activated the powers of our hands. Purple, green, blue, and red, the light filled the outdated kitchen, but none of it slowed down the greater demon.

"You!" he roared.

"Fuck off," Gavin snarled as he jumped in, throwing a punch to Greg's face.

Immediately, Greg turned to focus on Gavin, and the agile fighter spun, putting Greg's back to us. I wasn't brave enough to shoot from my angle, but Bax could. He put a pair of slugs into Greg's side as Gavin jumped back. I watched as Greg jerked when each one hit, time feeling like it moved in slow motion - and then the demon was running after Gavin.

"Shit," Bax breathed. "He's going up the hall."

The three of us ran after them, but as soon as we reached the living room, Lars grabbed me to yank me back. "Us first!" he growled. I wanted to scream something at him, but later. Now was not the time.

Thankfully, the house was small. Gavin went through the main area of the house and right up the hall to the bedrooms. He was fast enough to get a lead on Greg, and the stupid demon was so arrogant that he didn't seem to think we were a threat. I rounded the corner just in time to see Bax grab one of Greg's arms with both hands. Lars caught the other a moment later, and like a switch had been flipped, the demon became very, very still.

The boys shoved him against the wall, knocking a picture off in the process, but none of us cared. As I stormed toward him, intending to end this once and for all, Gavin stepped between us, his focus on Greg.

"Remember me, asshole?" he asked, lifting his gun to Greg's face.

"You're the little shit I crushed like a cockroach," Greg sneered.

Gavin just smiled. "Yep. Hope this hurts."

He pulled the trigger. Gore sprayed, catching Bax across the face, but I knew that wouldn't be enough. We'd learned that lesson the hard way. So, before he could heal, I shoved my hand against Greg's collapsing body and pushed with all I had. I wanted him to die as painfully as possible. I wanted to kill the man, the demon, and everything else.

At first, I wasn't sure if it was working, but this felt right. For the first time, I could feel the magic coursing through my hand the same way it did when I touched the elements, and I opened myself fully. If I'd gotten this power because of my father, that meant I should have a lot, and I wanted to burn this motherfucker from the face of the Earth.

His body began to dissolve, turning to powder in the guys' grip. That meant it was working, but since he'd been unconscious already, there was no last breath, no reaction. The man just dissolved the same way the demons in Bax's basement had.

"It's done," Lars said, and I heard that through both my ear and the earbud on the other side. "We're headed out, Deke, and Bax is a mess."

"Hurt?" Deke asked.

"Nope," Bax said, "but we do not want to get pulled over. I'm doing all I can to keep anyone from caring about this, but drive nice and slow."

As he talked, Lars grabbed my shoulder and turned me back for the same door we'd come in. Bax pushed Gavin after me. There was nothing else to say. We'd done it. It hadn't been perfect, but we were still alive.

And winning. We were definitely winning.

CHAPTER TWENTY-EIGHT

DEKE DROVE HOME SLOWLY, and we didn't talk about it. The truth was that we weren't excited. We didn't want to cheer or gloat. The feeling was more like completing a big test at school: relief that it was over. It was also a lot to take in.

I stared out the window the whole way, watching the sleeping town pass by. It seemed so peaceful out there, which was odd for a place filled with demons where we'd just killed a man. And he had looked like a *man*, but he'd made it easy. From the moment Greg had attacked us, I hadn't had a chance to worry about anything else. My guys had been in danger. I hadn't even gotten the chance to think about Travis and what Greg had done to him. It had all just happened too fast.

When we got home, Linda and Tash were waiting. Both of them looked worried until the last of us made it inside, and then Linda hurried over to Bax. She reached up to check his face and neck, but he caught her hands.

"Not mine," he promised. "No offense, but I'm going to go wash this off."

"You too, Jess," Deke said. "When everyone's clean, meet me at the kitchen table."

I didn't understand why I had to be one of the firsts until I began pulling off my clothes in the bathroom. My entire right arm was covered in things I didn't want to think about, the gore smeared by the thin fabric of my shirt. Evidently because I'd been moving in, I'd been just close enough to get a bit on me too. I was pretty sure that Lars and Gavin had something gross on their clothes as well, but that was ok. It wasn't their blood or brains, and Greg was dead.

When I walked out of the shower, Linda was waiting with a basket for my dirty clothes. Tash wanted my weapons and vest. I handed those over, and then headed to the kitchen. I could still hear the water running in Bax's room, but just as I left the hall, Tash thumped on Gavin's door and yelled for him to get clean.

Then I turned into the dining room. Deke was sitting at the end of the table where he usually ate, but the moment he saw me, he pushed to his feet. Two steps brought him to my side, and he palmed both sides of my face.

"Are you ok, doll?" he asked, his voice tender, not worried.

"Yeah," I promised. "I'm ok."

He leaned in and kissed my brow. "Good. I figured you wouldn't want a beer, so I made you a cocoa." Tilting his head, he gestured to the cup in front of where I usually sat.

Something about that was perfect. More than perfect. I really was ok, but I remembered Deke telling me that a good cup of hot cocoa was supposed to make us feel like everything was going to be ok. Seeing it, remembering that story, it felt like the mental hug I really needed.

"That's actually perfect," I said, heading around him for my chair.

But he caught my hand, stopping me. "Hey, if you're ok with it, I wanted to come check on you later."

"I'm fine," I promised.

ENTER SANDMAN

"I know, and not that kind of check. I can wait if that's better." He let me go and stepped back so I could get to my chair.

"No, tonight's good," I promised. "I have a feeling we're all just going to want to pass out now that the adrenaline is fading."

"And it's almost three in the morning," Deke said. "Sit. Drink."

So I did. Deke had a cup of coffee by his chair, but the guys had beers waiting for them. It also didn't take long before Bax wandered in. Gavin wasn't far behind him, and Lars was only a few minutes later. We'd barely sat down before Linda and Tash were back, making this a full family meeting.

"Ok," Deke said. "Greg is gone, and that's one greater demon that we don't have to worry about, but what happened? I heard fighting, and our plan was to catch him off guard. Where was the slip?"

"I don't think there was one," Lars said. "Jess opened the locks, we slipped in just like we trained, and the guy met us in the kitchen by trying to smash Bax with a chair."

"Fucking saw a shadow and dodged," Bax said. "No lights on in the house. No reason to think he was awake. The fucker was just there."

"Ted sat in the dark a lot," Linda offered. "He'd camp out by the window, just watching what happened outside. Maybe they sleep less?"

"Dad *used to* sleep fine," I assured her. "Or at least he used to go to bed like normal and get up like normal. I don't know if he actually slept. I wonder if they're all just on edge?"

"Which means we need to plan for that," Gavin said.

Deke was nodding. "Yeah. We also need to give it a little time. We don't want to hit anyone tomorrow, since they'll all be braced, and if we keep doing this on the weekends, they will catch on."

"Fuck school," Bax said. "I mean, what's the worst that happens? We sleep through class?"

"No," Linda said. "I do not want you kids driving around town if you're exhausted. That's a good way to get killed in a normal car accident!"

"She's got a point," Tash told us. "However, I'm more worried about the four of you. How are you holding up? How do you feel about what you did? Anything we need to train more on, or any concerns about the nightmares you'll have?"

"Nope, I'm good now," Gavin promised. "Fucker's dead, and that feels pretty nice."

"You were a fucking badass," Bax told him. "Guys, you should've seen it. Greg came at me, and Gav jumped him, punched him, and basically took aggro."

"Then he pulled him down the hall so we could get in formation," Lars said, the guys using their video game terminology. "Was perfect."

"And you, Jess?" Tash asked.

"I couldn't get a shot off because Gav was right on the other side and you warned that these bullets could pierce a body, so I followed, and when Bax and Lars pinned him, I got a good grab and dusted him."

"Dusted," Deke said, sounding amused. "Nice. I like it."

"But I don't think shooting them is going to work," I pointed out. "I mean, we saw how long it took to kill a common that way. The trick is going to be getting our hands on them. Bax and Lars subdued him somehow, and - "

"I conquered his need to fight back," Bax explained.

"I convinced him it was only fair for us to get our turn," Lars added.

I nodded to show I'd heard them. "And that worked. The issue is that with a demon moving around, that means we have to be careful not to shoot each other, and this just seems like it's the least efficient way to kill demons ever. I mean, we're supposed to beat these things, right? Travis has all these stories about how demons are scared of us, but we're not really any better than a normal person with the right weapons."

"I'm pretty sure Greg would say your hand is a lot more lethal," Tash countered.

"Yeah, but besides that," I groaned. "And why me? Anathema is the killing weapon? Why not Conquest, Judgement, or most of all, Vengeance!"

"You're not a normal Anathema," Tash admitted.

"Most don't kill with a touch," Deke explained. "Not that we're complaining, but the mark on your hand is for the most powerful variant, and you're more lethal than any I've ever heard of. Yes, part of that is your cambion magic, but not all of it. Normally, it's Vengeance who has the power to destroy demons, but it's more of a stun and less a killing touch."

"So I can stun too?" Gavin asked. "I need to practice that."

"I'll see what I can find," Tash assured him.

"I can do that," Linda offered, "because the kids are right. Is there something we're missing? Travis sounded like he was sure that the Brethren were terrifying, but the kids make it sound like their training is carrying them through most of this. If they can have some ability to make them even stronger, shouldn't we look for that too?"

Deke and Tash shared a look across the table. They didn't say a thing, but it was the kind of glance that spoke volumes. Deke shrugged, Tash shook her head, so Deke sighed. I honestly had no clue what that meant, but thankfully they didn't intend to keep us in the dark.

"It feels like there's a lot we don't know," Deke told us. "Lately, Tash and I have been talking about this. We only have records for about the last hundred to a hundred and fifty years. I was told that the previous journal for this quad was lost in a battle, and all the records with it."

"But," Tash said, "it seems the same is true for every quad. All eight of them. Demons act like we are the most terrifying thing, and the Order says that's because we're the only thing that can kill them, but it doesn't add up. With you four, that's even more obvious."

"Wasn't like this with my last quad," Deke admitted. "They were vicious in a fight, but except for distracting and maybe persuading witnesses, their powers weren't very useful."

I picked up my cup and cradled it. "These are all parlor tricks, though. I mean, it's useful with witnesses and to get ourselves out of trouble if we're not subtle enough, but for demons? There just has to be more. I want to ask Travis about it. He said he'd heard stories."

"I don't want you to tell him too much," Tash said.

"No." Bax shook his head. "I hear what you're saying, Tash, but fuck that. Look, the Order's rules are bullshit. So far, everything we're *supposed* to do is in the Order's best interest, but not ours. Kill Jess, as an example. You're supposed to teach us that all abominations are evil, intent on taking over the world, and should be killed on sight." He paused to look at the two Martyrs in the room. "Am I wrong?"

"No, you're not," Deke admitted.

Bax nodded once. "And we never would've known anything else if it hadn't been for Jess. Because she's ours and she's a demon, we won't kill her. Now, we have a demon helping us - and getting his legs broken because of it - and you think we should, what? Worry about him?"

"What if he's playing you four?" Tash asked.

"So?" Lars countered. "What, he might find out that we want to kill the demons? That we're going to close the seals? That Jess is a badass, we have an extra Sandman on our side, and that we're going to assassinate every greater demon until we can close the seal? Where's the downside, Tash?"

"When the demons aren't where you expect, fight back in groups, and the seal battle happens in someone's home in the middle of town!" Tash thumped her fist on the table to make her point. "Then what will you do?"

"I'm stronger," I reminded her. "And from the sounds of it, Dad doesn't want them to kill me. That makes it easier for me to kill them, and they won't expect me to be stronger. I also don't think Travis will betray us, and we have to try something else."

"Doing it over and over," Linda said softly, "and expecting different results is the definition of insanity."

"Fuck," Tash grumbled. "Yeah, I know. You're right."

"Just Travis," Gavin said, his words directed at the table. "If he suggests someone else, then we'll feel them out, but let's just start with Travis."

"I'm ok with that," I told him.

"Same," Lars agreed.

"Makes sense to me," Bax said.

We all looked over to Deke. "What?" he asked. "In case you four haven't figured it out yet, I'm not calling the shots anymore. I also know that."

"Maybe not," Gavin said, "but you're still one of us. Means you get a vote too."

"Then Travis is in," Deke decided. "Sorry, Tash. That boy has done nothing but stick his neck out for them. I think he's really their friend."

"And he's always been a good boy," Linda said. "We need to find a way to let him come over for dinner."

Tash just leaned forward and thumped her head on the table. "Ok! I'll see if I can work up some kind of exemption ward, or something. Means we're back to hitting the books, Linda."

"And the four of you," Deke said, "are off to bed. I suggest you sleep."

"Yeah," Gavin said as he sucked back the last of his beer. "No offense, but I'm going to my own bed."

"Same," I agreed.

Bax just looked at Lars and smiled deviously. "Need someone to cuddle with, big boy."

"Fuck off," Lars laughed. "I'm buying you a damned teddy bear or something. And no, I'm going to take up as much space on that mattress as possible. Pretty sure I pulled a muscle in my ass shoving that fucker against the wall."

"Advil!" Linda called as we all got up and the guys headed out of the room. "And I'll cook breakfast in the morning. Or afternoon. Whenever you four wake up. Night, kids, and I'm so glad you're still alive."

"Love you too, Mom," Lars said as he passed her, reaching down to rub her arm.

"Yeah, love you, Mom," Bax added, clasping her shoulder.

"*Te amo, mi madre*," Gavin said, bending to kiss the top of her head.

I paused to take the last sip of my cocoa, using that to hide the smile that was trying to take over my face. Then, setting my empty cup on the table, I followed the guys.

"Love you, Mom. Night." And I leaned over to hug her.

Linda just sniffed. "Good night, Jess." But the moment I rounded the corner, I heard her breathe a laugh. "I'm crying now."

"And smiling," Tash said. "Pretty sure those kids mean it, too."

"Yeah," Linda agreed. "And that's why I'm crying. You two had better keep them alive."

"Doing my damnedest," Deke promised. "Now go to bed, ladies. I'll get the dishes."

CHAPTER TWENTY-NINE

I HEADED TO MY ROOM, changed into a tank and shorts to sleep in, brushed my hair, then turned out the lights and crawled into bed. I was tired. Exhausted was a better word for it, and yet my mind refused to stop spinning. I wasn't freaked out by the killing, but I kept running over all the little ways it could've been better or how good we'd done. The thoughts just wouldn't slow down, and hence I couldn't quite fall asleep.

Outside my room, I heard the sounds of the house calming down. Nothing really stood out, but the sounds grew softer and less frequent. It helped. Just as I was ready to close my eyes and try sleeping, my bedroom door opened and Deke slipped in. He'd changed into a pair of sweats and a t-shirt, and his hair was wet, so he'd showered too.

He paused halfway to my bed. "Jess?"

"I'm still awake," I assured him.

He made his way over to the bed, sitting down on the edge. "You did good tonight, you know."

I moved back a bit, making room for him to get comfortable. "I didn't really do much, though. Every time I thought about using magic, it was pointless. Lars shot before I could blow him back, then Gavin pulled him into the hall. I was going to make the floor trip him, but Lars pulled me back and the guys subdued him."

"In, out, and done," Deke said. "Nothing wrong with that. I bet if you ask those guys, they'll all feel the same way. They barely did anything, but if each of you does a bit, it works. Fuck, the four of you just work."

"Yeah." I smiled into the darkness. "We kinda do."

"Which is what I wanted to check on," he said. "Gavin's been amazingly decent with me this week. He even told me to read a book."

"The Shades of Trouble series?" I asked.

Deke chuckled. "Yeah, I'm on book three now. But we've had a lot of talks about it. Gavin felt bad for one of the characters, and I explained how I was as a kid, and that one guy's lines - um, the model?"

"Ashton," I supplied.

Deke chuckled. "Yeah. Well, it helped. I can't say it's good yet, and Gav still says some pretty stupid shit, but I'm used to that. I don't want you to get stressed out because my feelings might get hurt."

"It's not that," I tried to explain. "It's that I hate the idea of him not being ok with you, or any of the guys having a problem with each other."

"But that's what people do, Jess," Deke explained. "Maybe someone wants to vote one way, and someone wants to vote the other. Maybe Bax likes the color blue and Lars likes green. Makes it hard to decorate a room or paint a car. People don't always agree, and that's ok. The part I want you to focus on is that we're all trying. Tash is trying to accept Travis. Linda is trying to accept that you're not a little girl and you are sleeping with her son."

"Bax and Lars?" I asked.

He chuckled. "Bax is trying to learn that he's a lot more than a pretty face and a big bank account. He doesn't complain because he knows how lucky he is, but that doesn't mean he believes he's a good guy. All his life, he's been told he's a piece of shit and that only his father's money gets him out of trouble." He paused to chew on his lower lip. "Lars is so worried about making you happy that he's not willing to ask for anything for himself. He has to learn that he deserves to demand a little too."

"And you?" I asked. "What are you trying to figure out, Deke?"

He blew out a breath. "That I have a thing for a high school girl. I mean, shit, you don't look like a little kid. You put on mascara and lipstick, and you could be twenty. You don't act like a little kid. You face down your issues with the kind of determination that it took me years to learn. Then, every time I start thinking of you as a woman and not a girl, you turn around and act like a teenager again, and I realize that's not fair of me."

"I'm sorry," I mumbled. "I'm really trying!"

"No, no, no," he soothed. "That's not what I'm saying. You're eighteen. You are supposed to act eighteen. There isn't a damned thing wrong with that. I'm just worried that I'm going to push you too hard and you're going to give in because you don't know how to say no." He reached over to brush a strand of hair from my neck. "Do you remember one of the first talks we had? I told you that if you ever needed help saying no that I'd help. The problem is that I can't do that if I'm involved with you. I can't be your trusted mentor and a guy you're fucking. It just doesn't work."

"So, you're saying it's over again," I realized.

"I am not," he corrected. "I'm saying that I'm trying to do the right thing, and fuck if I know what that is. I get so damned jealous when I hear you talk about your three boyfriends. Three, Jess. That means not me. I want to scream that I'm standing right here - and then I realize that I can't, because how can I be the buffer you need if I'm a part of that group?" He paused, let his head drop, and then sighed. "When you walked into the dining room tonight, I swear to god, I didn't want to kiss your head."

"Deke, I didn't follow you into the bathroom because I'm hard up," I reminded him.

"No, you're eighteen and horny," he countered. "Your hormones are taking over your brain, and you have no one to tell you that you have to behave anymore."

"And you've been nothing but amazing to me!" I sat up and scooted back so I could meet his eyes in the darkened room. "Has it ever dawned on you that my problem is that I don't feel like I deserve this? I'm the nerd that everyone overlooks - and now I'm not. I am dating the three hottest guys at school, and they are so much more than that. I mean, I started liking them because they're cute, but then they have to be amazing too? Of course I fell in love with them, so how dare I ask for more? But seeing your reflection in that mirror? I..." I blew out a breath as I tried to find the right words. "You take care of me, Deke. Even if that's screaming and storming at me until I can figure out that it's ok not to be scared. And I cried in front of you!"

"I'm sorry," he whispered, reaching up to cup my cheek. "I hated that I had to push you that hard."

"No," I insisted. "Deke, I'm saying that I trust you enough that I could. That I wasn't ashamed of being weak. Fuck, I like you! Why is that so wrong? And if it is, why can't I stop?"

"Same reason I can't," he said softly. "The more I'm around you, the more I like you. I just don't want to be that creepy old guy hitting on a sweet and innocent young girl to take advantage of her."

"Pretty sure I'm not sweet or innocent," I countered.

"You are," he assured me. "Jess, you are the sweetest girl I've talked to in a very long time. You're also innocent because you're only eighteen. You haven't had to deal with a lot of crap I'm already tired of. People dying, to start. Taxes! I'm not talking about sexually, doll. I'm talking about the kind of innocence that makes it hard for girls like you to say no to men like me."

"No." I told him, feeling my lips curl into a smile. "See, I can do it."

He chuckled. "Yeah. Fuck. You are amazing."

Then he fell silent, his eyes holding mine, but even though his mouth twitched he didn't say anything for a little too long. The silence began to stretch until it was almost uncomfortable, and he dropped his eyes to the blankets over my lap. I watched as his hand clenched and then relaxed, but I didn't know what to say either.

Deke finally gave in. "I feel something for you, you know." He grunted softly. "Shit. That's a lie. I'm falling for you, Jess. I like you, and a lot more than I should, so what the fuck am I supposed to do with that? I promised Gavin I was all in, but I don't want that to mean pushing myself on you."

I leaned forward, intending to kiss him, to make it clear *he* wasn't doing the pushing, but he caught my arm, stopping me.

"No, talk to me," he begged. "If you start kissing on me, it's not going to make me feel less like a piece of shit. So, tell me what you're thinking, ok? Embarrassing or not, I promise I can take it."

"I don't know what I'm supposed to say," I groaned.

"Supposed to," he repeated. "Jess, that's what I'm talking about. You're supposed to say what you think, what you feel. I don't ever want you to say something just to make me happy. I just want to know if you're looking for a little extra dick on the side, maybe someone you can talk to in the middle of the night who's safe, or something else. In your head, where is this thing going with us? Not them. Not all of us. Just you and me."

"I don't know," I admitted, crossing my legs under the blankets and honestly thinking about this. "See, that's the thing. I keep waiting for you to say no, say this can't happen, or something like that. I'm pretty good at rejection, because I've never been allowed anything else, so maybe I'm overwhelmed. Maybe I'm like a kid in a candy store. I dunno, Deke, but I like you. I like that I can come talk to you and you listen. Fuck, you usually answer. I feel like, um, remember when Linda talked about being a kid and hiding under the blankets?"

"Yeah?" He sounded like I'd just lost him.

So I plowed ahead. "You're the blanket, Deke. When I need to hide, or recover, or get a moment, I always find myself looking for you. Lars comforts me in one way, but you do it in another. I know that probably sounds stupid, but I like this."

"Just like this?" he asked.

"I like the spending the night parts too," I admitted. "And I really approve of the shower sex. I just don't want to be greedy. I don't want to force you to be with me when you could have a real girlfriend, you know? And I kinda feel like that's what I'm doing. Because I like you, those guys are going to pressure you until you have to say yes, and then you resent me and all of this blows up. I mean, that's partly why I've been so stressed, because every time something goes wrong, I keep waiting for the catastrophic failure."

"Nothing catastrophic," he promised, leaning in to catch my chin and lift my face up to his. "I want to be a boyfriend. I get that you're not giving up the others, and I don't honestly blame you. Those boys are cute. You're cuter."

"Me?"

He chuckled. "Yes, Jess. You. See, I'd like to be the boyfriend who manages this mess for you. The guy you can come to when Bax is looking at another girl, or Lars hasn't talked to you in days because he's trying not to get in your way, or even when Gavin is flipping between being so disgustingly cute and dumb as fuck in the same sentence."

I leaned into his shoulder and giggled. "Yeah, that sounds like them."

"But does it sound like me?" he asked, his rough voice just a little deeper when it was beside my ear.

"Boyfriend?" I asked, looking up.

He nodded. "Boyfriend. The guy who can kiss you outside this room - or the bathroom. Maybe one who can sneak in to help you shower. Possibly a shoulder to snuggle up against when you don't want to fuck and just need to be held."

I tugged at his shirt, revealing a band of skin at his waist, then trailed my finger along a pale line. "Can I play with your scars when I do that cuddling?"

"Doll, you keep moving your hand that way and this won't be cuddling."

So I swept my finger under the waistband of his sweats. "Well, if it's not just cuddling, then I guess that would make you a boyfriend, huh?" And I lifted my chin just a bit more, all but daring him to kiss me.

Deke leaned in, pushing me back, but he kept his mouth a hair away from mine until my back was on the bed and he leaned over me. "I'm going to take care of you, Jess," he swore. "No matter how you answer, I am all in. So officially your boyfriend then?"

"Yes," I breathed.

His mouth finally found mine, and I never wanted him to stop. My fingers fisted in his shirt on one side and I grabbed the waist of his pants on the other. This was not going to be a quick kiss, because I had no intention of letting him stop.

CHAPTER THIRTY

I PULLED WITH BOTH HANDS. One went up while I pushed the other down, needing to get Deke out of these clothes. He chuckled against my lips, then reached behind his neck and yanked off his shirt. That got dropped beside the bed even as he came back for another kiss.

This one was a little deeper and a lot more passionate. His tongue swept through my mouth, claiming it as his own. I relaxed, giving him complete control. Again, his lips caressed mine, and again his tongue explored. Just as a soft moan sounded in the back of my throat, Deke wrenched the blankets from between us, tossing them to the far side of the bed.

Then he stepped off the bed. "You sure about this, Jess?" he asked.

I sat up and pulled off my shirt, throwing it the other way. "Positive."

A crooked smile touched his lips. "Then take off those shorts too, doll, because I have every intention of getting between your legs a whole lot more."

I loved the way his voice turned husky when he said that, so I decided to be a little evil. Taking my time about it, I pushed both my shorts and panties lower, stopping halfway down my hips. "I need those sweats on my floor, Deke."

"That's my girl," he praised, dropping them to the ground without taking his eyes off me.

Damn, but he was sexy. Not beautiful, though. Deke was too harsh for that word. Masculine fit, and everything about him was definitely all male. From his broad chest and massive pectorals to the ripples of his abs, the creases at his hips, and that hard dick standing up, ready for my attention, this man turned me on. He was nothing like the guys in school. He wasn't even like my other boyfriends. Something about Deke was a little more dangerous feeling, and I liked it.

When he crawled across the mattress toward me, I felt like I was being stalked. The man moved like I'd imagine some special forces soldier would. His eyes held me like a wolf's. The strange thing was how much that turned me on. I liked that he wanted me this much. I didn't have to chase or beg. This man was willing to chase me.

His mouth landed on my thigh, just above my knee. Then he kissed higher, taking his time about it. I reached for him, trying to use his shoulders to pull him over me, but Deke resisted. He just kissed my leg again, letting his left hand slide up the other side, his palm caressing my skin.

When his hand reached my hip, his fingers closed, holding me there, and he looked up. "Tell me what you want, doll."

The moment he said that, every sensual idea I'd ever had vanished from my mind. Suddenly I couldn't imagine a single thing to ask for, and if I did, it certainly wouldn't sound sexy. Trying to bluff my way through this, I pulled at his arm, wanting him closer.

Deke moved, but only to press a knee between my legs. Just one, making him straddle my thigh. His grip on my hip got a little tighter, his lips curled a little more, and his right hand moved to trace little circles on my belly.

"I think my girl's the shy kind, hm?" He moved his hand a bit lower. "Ever had a guy talk to you in bed, doll?"

"Yeah," I admitted, feeling myself growing wetter as he took his time about this.

Deke's finger began to tease the short hair at the top of my mound. "But you're the good girl who just lets him play with you, huh? You ever ask for what you need?"

"Yeah, well, kinda... I mean, maybe..."

He chuckled and bent lower, kissing the swell under my belly button. "Well, I think it's hot as fuck when a woman knows what she wants." His next kiss was a little higher, his eyes lifted to look at me. At the same time, his finger was moving lower, making my skin shiver with excitement. "What do you want, Jess?"

"Kiss me," I breathed.

"Is that all?" he asked, lifting his hand away from my pussy.

I whimpered, unable to help myself, and his lips curled - and then found mine. He'd let go of my hip to keep his balance, that hand now by my head. I could feel his hips against the insides of my legs, and his hand was back, but not quite on my pussy. Now, he was teasing the crease of my leg, so fucking close that I was ready to beg.

Which was what he wanted.

"Please," I breathed against his lips.

"Want me to finger you?" he asked, his voice a sensual rumble. "Fuck you? Eat you out? Gotta give me more, doll."

"Yes!" I groaned.

Deke kissed me again, fast and hard, but he refused to obey. "Gotta pick one. Pretty sure I can only contort so much to get you off." He chuckled, sliding his hand lower, but still on my fucking leg! "Knowing what you want gets me so fucking hard," he growled, moving to kiss the side of my neck. "I don't even care how you say it. I just want to give my girl what she wants."

"Then your mouth," I gasped, "and hand."

"You want me to fuck you with my hand while I go down on you?" He began to move lower. "I can definitely do that."

But he stopped to suck on my breast, flicking his tongue across the nipple. At the same time, the backs of his knuckles slid over my folds. The sensations combined into the most erotic tease I'd ever experienced. I arched into his mouth and spread my legs a little wider, just wanting him to make me feel good.

"Say it," Deke demanded as he moved even lower.

"Fuck me with your hand," I repeated, "while you go down on me."

"Fuck, that's hot."

Then his mouth found my pussy. His tongue parted the folds to press against my clit. His hand came right after. Two fingers slid into my body, then curled. I pressed down, wanting him deeper, and Deke seemed to understand. He pumped his hand into me again, sucking at my clit in time. I'd never imagined asking for what I wanted, but he made it feel so good, like a reward as he drove me higher, and then higher still.

"Breast," I panted.

He groaned against my clit, the sound vibrating straight up my nerves in the best way, but his free hand reached up for my breast. Pinching and flicking my nipple with that hand, his other worked me faster and faster. Needing to hold something, I grabbed the back of his hair, tangling my fingers in the molten colors.

My hips were rocking, riding his mouth, and I didn't care if he liked it. The bed began to creak, the sound too soft to carry outside my room, so neither of us cared. My only concern was the pleasure building, growing, and so close to release. This man knew exactly what to do with his mouth and tongue, and he was showing me all of it.

When I came, it was hard. My back arched off the bed and I groaned without shame, pulling him even closer. His hand slowed, but Deke kept sucking, giving me all he had until the last wave of pleasure released me. With a satisfied sigh, I relaxed onto the bed, removing my fingers from his hair.

He removed his hand, kissed the inside of my thigh, then wiped at his face. "Oh, did I wear my girl out?" It sounded like a taunt.

"Oh, no," I promised. "Benefits of youth, or something."

With a chuckle, he crawled closer, making his way up my body. "So what am I doing to you next, doll?"

"No," I whispered, catching the back of his neck to pull his face to mine so I could steal a kiss. I tasted myself on his lips, but didn't pull away for that reason. "I want you to show me how you like it, Deke. I want to see what gets you going."

"Yeah," he breathed, reaching down for my hip, "I can do that."

Gripping my side, Deke lifted, guiding that thigh up, and slid right into my body. When his hips settled against mine, he slid back out, taking his time about it while he watched my face. My hand was still on the back of his head, balancing me in some way. I also couldn't manage to look away from his face.

The scars on the left side added to his appeal. Beneath that, his full lips were parted slightly, and those silver eyes seemed to sparkle in the darkness of my room. Sexy was the best way I had to describe him, and the intensity of his expression made me feel beautiful and powerful. It made me feel like I was the one in control here, even if we both knew it was a lie.

"I like it when you don't try to pretend I'm someone else," he said, pumping back into me. "That's why I want you to look. I want to see you fight the urge to close your eyes and moan. I want you to know it's *me* making you feel good." The next thrust was a little harder. "And I want to watch your body give in."

He kissed me hard, his tongue swirling around mine, but it was over too fast. His free hand landed on my chest right between my breasts and Deke used it to push himself up. Without slowing his rhythm, he shifted his legs until he was sitting on his knees. The hand on my hip pulled me onto him even as he kept thrusting.

My eyes dropped to those hard abs and the pale lines slashed across them. Every time he rocked into me, the man's entire body flexed, and he stretched me open in the best way like this. I could almost see his dick - or at least the top when he pulled back - and it was sexier than I'd imagined.

But I wanted more. I needed to touch him, to feel him where I could. His head was now out of reach since he was sitting almost straight up, so I grabbed for his legs on both sides. Then I pulled, driving myself deeper onto him. That was exactly what I needed. A little deeper, a bit harder, and definitely faster. Beneath my hands, I could feel his thighs flexing.

"So. Fucking. Beautiful," he grunted between thrusts.

And he made me feel that way. Not like I was some teen fetish - Deke looked at me as if he was starving, and I could help with that. He watched me like he needed something and I just wanted to give it. Even better, the man fucked me like he meant it. Every inch of his dick worked my body, his hands gripped so hard - but I loved it - and he wasn't trying to be gentle. He was trying to make me cum.

My body was still so sensitive. His thrusts were so intense. Combined, there was no way I'd last too long. This man knew what he was doing. Every move of his body hit something that felt so damned good. He didn't need to play with my breasts or torment my clit. Just his dick was more than I expected. So big, like he fit me in some way, and every time I pulled myself onto it felt even better.

"Deke," I whimpered, my fingers gripping hard enough for my nails to scrape against his legs.

So he thrust even harder. "Cum, doll. Fucking cum so damned hard. I wanna feel your pussy grip me."

I tried to say something else, but the word got caught in my throat as my climax hit. Yeah, I gripped him hard. My legs wrapped around his back and my ass lifted even higher off the bed. Both of Deke's hands were on my hips now, and he kept going, driving me higher and higher, until I was sure this would never end. He kept fucking me like he was chasing something, until I couldn't take any more.

A cry of passion came from my lips and my body shuddered around him. For a moment, I forgot the rest of the world existed. There was nothing but pleasure, and wave upon wave of it. When the bliss finally began to recede, Deke flopped forward over me, panting just as hard as I was.

"That," he said, easing himself from my body, "is how I like it: when my girl can't hold back her cries." Then he flopped down beside me and pulled me up against him. "And I really like that my girl is you."

I snuggled into his shoulder. "So, I guess I get to break it to the guys, huh?" I asked.

He chuckled. "Yeah, probably easiest. Think they'll be ok with it?"

"I think they'll be relieved," I assured him. "Even Gavin."

He reached back for the blankets and tossed them over both of us. "Good." Then he kissed the top of my head. "And I'm damned proud of you, Anathema. You did good in there today. The four of you are ready."

"The five of us," I corrected. "Because you are my Sandman."

"Yeah, doll, I am."

CHAPTER THIRTY-ONE

THERE WAS something about sleeping naked, lying along the length of a man, that was amazing. Deke's arm stayed around me all night long, and the sound of his heart beating under my ear was oddly comforting. Even better, the normally violent sleeper was perfectly calm for most of the night.

But when he finally jumped, I woke up faster than I would've liked. My eyes immediately went to Deke's face, but he was looking over my body. The sound of Lars' soft chuckle was enough to make me groan and flop back down on my own pillow. That was when I realized that the blankets were barely covering my ass and pretty much nothing else.

"Well, looks like that's my cue to tap out," Deke said, climbing out of the other side of the bed. "Guessing you came to check on her?"

"And it looks like she's doing just fine. Wild guess, your underwear?"

I rolled over in time to see Deke snatch his briefs from the tip of Lars' finger without slowing. Lars just shook his head, but Deke was headed for my bathroom. When the door shut behind him, Lars pointed at the door and lifted a brow.

"So, how often does that happen?" He didn't wait for an answer before crawling onto my side of the bed and sliding over next to me.

"Hopefully more often." I scrunched up my nose as I met his eyes. "He's kinda boyfriend number four."

"Nice," Lars said. "About time, too."

"You don't think I'm being greedy?"

He cupped the side of my face. "I like the kinky shit. I like seeing you smile. I love knowing that you can have everything you want. These guys? I know they'll treat you right. Fuck, Jess, that's why I came up with the idea."

"Yeah?" I asked, rolling onto my back and pulling him so he ended up leaning over me. "Because Deke said something last night, and I'm starting to think he's right."

"What's that?" Lars asked.

"That you will let me neglect you if it will make me happy. That you love me so much you won't push your way in."

So Lars raised his voice. "You're an asshole, Deke."

The bathroom door opened a second later to show Deke, still naked, rinsing off his face. "I've decided that if you can be the confidant, then I can be the group manager."

"Uh huh." Lars leaned down to kiss me, then shifted so he was sitting on his rump, just out of my reach. "What are the others, then?"

"Fuck if I know," Deke said. "Pretty sure they're still figuring it out. My point is that Jess gets caught up in her own head when she thinks there's a problem. Her whole life, she's been taught that minor disagreements end up being painful. Bax and Gavin can't quite wrap their minds around that. I think you and I can."

"Yeah, having seen it firsthand," Lars agreed.

"Still lying right here," I reminded them.

"Hush, man talk," Lars teased. "So how's this working out with the bed hopping, Deke?"

"Shit," Deke huffed out. "If you had any idea how often that girl comes down to my room in the middle of the night, you'd know I'm not exactly worried about it."

Lars looked over at me. "Now I'm starting to get jealous."

"Usually because I have questions," I pointed out, "and it has never been to get laid."

"Could, though," Deke said, finally making his way out of the bathroom.

"And group stuff?" Lars asked.

Deke shrugged. "I'm not the one you need to ask that."

"Yeah," Lars countered, "you are. Just because you fuck guys doesn't mean you want to be around the rest of us. Doesn't mean you want to have group stuff. I mean, that doesn't even make sense. I'd say there's a chance you're shy, but..." He thrust out a hand at Deke's bare ass as the guy made his way around the room collecting his clothes. "There's no shyness there."

Having made it almost all the way back around the bed, Deke dumped the pile of clothing on the chair for my makeup table, and came back to slide under the covers. He didn't bother lying down, though. He just flopped the blankets over his lap.

"Look," he said, "I'm not shy, I'm not a prude, and I have no problem with the kinky shit you four get up to. Bax doesn't have a problem with me. Gavin does. I don't know what else to tell you."

"So, you're down for group shit?" Lars asked again.

"I'm down for group shit," Deke confirmed. "Bax already started it."

Lars just nodded. "And boyfriends?"

"What?" Deke snapped.

"What are your, I dunno, thoughts? Opinions? About getting a boyfriend. Are you looking, hoping, or what?"

I smacked Lars' arm. "Asshole."

"I'm asking for a reason," Lars assured me. "Because this thing we're doing? It's called poly, and lots of people do it different ways. I've kinda been reading up on it. Some people have nesting partners and secondary partners. Some have clusters. There's lots of ways to do it. One thing all of them agree on is communication, so I'm communicating because I'm trying to figure out what Deke is hoping for."

"Jess," Deke answered. "That's what I'm hoping for. I'm not looking for a boyfriend, and no, I don't feel like I'm missing out without one. *That* girl?" And he pointed at me. "She wouldn't handle her lovers dating someone else. It would send her into a spiral. She'd be sure she wasn't good enough, and I have no intention of doing that to her. She *is* good enough. Not sure how you feel, but I'm not really interested in someone I'd have to lie to about what I do. I also don't want a quick fuck just to get off when I have a girl who I can talk to. I'm looking for a relationship, Lars. Someone who I can fall in love with who just might be able to look past what that demon did to me and love me back. That's it."

Lars nodded. "Cool. Oh, and you should also know that Jess likes two dicks in her at the same time."

"Pussy and ass?" Deke asked.

"I've never done... that."

Deke's brow furrowed. "Never done anal, which means..."

"Yeah," Lars said, dragging the word out while he pulled off his shirt. "That's what she means. Granted, I've only done butt stuff once, so figure that's all on you, Deke."

"Eighteen," Deke mumbled to himself. "Fuck, you kids don't always act like you're eighteen. You know that, right?"

"Pretty much raised ourselves," Lars assured him. "It also means we're adults, seven years isn't that much, and you can get over it already."

"Trying my damnedest," Deke assured him. "I also know that your girlfriend was trying to seduce you a second ago, so you'd better not leave her wanting." Then Deke tossed off the blankets and turned like he was about to get out of the bed again.

"Running off already?" I asked him.

Lars smirked and began pushing his pants lower. "The girl wants two dicks, the girl gets two dicks."

"And she does like a whole lot of hands and mouths on her," Deke agreed, his eyes running over me. "Doll, I think you're about to get pinned down on that bed."

"Now that is a much better way to wake up than being startled," I assured him.

The words were barely out of my mouth before Lars caught my arm on his side and pressed it down to the mattress. A moment later, Deke pushed my other hand up by my head. The guys shared a look, then they both leaned in. Lars aimed for my mouth, kissing me. Deke used his tongue to tease the skin below my collar bones. Someone pushed the covers back down.

I felt my body being exposed, but did *not* try to fight it. And while I knew Deke was naked, I wasn't sure if Lars had managed to get everything off because I'd been looking the other way. I had faith, though, so I kept kissing, using my feet to get the blankets the rest of the way off.

Then Deke's mouth found my breast. He teased that nipple until it felt like a rock, then sucked at it. The mattress dipped, and Lars settled his weight beside me. Sure enough, his entire body felt completely bare. Someone's hand found my other breast. Another moved down to my pussy. The pair of them were working together perfectly, and the only way I could show how much I approved was to moan.

"Yeah, she's wet," Lars said, when he gave up my mouth. "How are we doing this, Deke?"

"I think you're about to be a bottom," Deke decided. "Jess on top."

The decision made both guys release my arms, so I pushed at Lars, rolling him onto his back. "I like this idea."

He caught my waist, guiding me up and over him. The man was hard and ready. He also looked amazing like this, spread out for me to enjoy. When I settled myself over him and reached down to angle his dick, Deke murmured in approval, driving me on. Yeah, it seemed I liked to have someone watch me. Clearly it was another fetish I'd need to play with.

But right now, I needed Lars inside me. The moment I got him lined up, I lowered myself down, feeling my body stretch. Lars' eyes hung on my breasts, but Deke had leaned back. He wasn't helping, and I wanted both of them. Lars didn't seem to care, though. Using the hands on my waist, he began to pump my body onto his slowly, easing into it.

Then he paused, reaching over to the side. I felt both of us jerk when he pulled. "You are supposed to be helping here, Sandman."

Deke responded by throwing all of the blankets off the bed. "Oh, I am."

Then he moved behind me. His lips kissed a line up my spine, making me arch my back. I felt his body move closer as he straddled Lars' legs. Deke kept kissing, leaning me forward as his chest pressed against my back, and Lars pulled me down. When my chest was against Lars, he kissed me hard. For just a moment, I stopped thinking about everything else - until Deke began to push his way into my pussy.

My groan was low, and Lars drank it in. Beneath me, his body tensed as Deke's dick ground against his. I had to gasp as my body stretched enough to take both of them, but I liked it. It hurt just right. The kind of pain that felt so good and made me feel so delicate trapped between them like this.

"Fuck," Lars moaned. "This is officially my favorite."

Then Deke grabbed a handful of my hair and pulled me up with it. "Guess this means I'm fucking both of you. Play with those tits, Lars."

"Oh, that's hot," Lars breathed, but he obeyed.

Both of his hands moved to my breasts, cradling them as his eyes devoured me. Then I felt Deke's lips on the side of my neck.

He kissed, he nipped, and then he pulled my hair a little harder, arching my back to press my breasts into Lars' hands.

"That's my girl," Deke breathed. "Just relax and take it. All of it, doll. You keep clenching us this tight and your boyfriend down there is going to blow his load."

"Maybe that's what I want," I panted.

"Sassy and sexy," Deke teased before sliding back, reminding me of just how good this felt. "If you want to make him lose control, then you have to relax. Close your eyes, doll, and let us play with you like we want."

I whimpered as my eyes slipped closed, but it seemed to be enough. Deke began to move with a purpose. Lars grabbed my breasts, using his thumbs to tease the nipples, but he didn't just lie there. He began to thrust in time, moving in opposition to Deke so that I was always filled with one of them, and sometimes both.

So damned tight, so hot, and I couldn't get enough of the feel of them around me. Lars' lean waist was trapped between my legs. Deke's muscular chest pressed into my back. Together, we rocked, and I let them use me. Deke kissed every inch of skin he could reach. Lars pinched and flicked my nipples, making soft noises when my body began to tremble at the rush of sensation.

Then Deke reached around my hip for my pussy. When his finger pressed against my clit, I bucked, my entire body surging with the sparks that sent across my nerves. Lars just thrust harder, his body trying to follow mine. I had to reach down, pressing my hand to the middle of his chest to keep my balance. The other reached back, holding Deke close to me.

These were my boyfriends, and they were amazing together. I didn't care if anyone else approved of this. I didn't even care if they found out. These guys were my everything, and they always made me happy. They made me feel good. There was nothing wrong with wanting to have all of them, and I deserved this. We all deserved this. It was working.

As they pumped into my body, driving me higher, that was all that mattered. There were five of us, and somehow we would make sure this crazy thing we were doing worked. The demons, the magic, and definitely the sex. I loved Lars. I liked Deke. I didn't need to feel guilty about having them both, or Bax and Gavin. I fucking deserved this!

"Harder," I begged.

"That's a good girl," Deke praised, and then he slammed his hips against my ass.

It was Lars who cried out in passion, giving up on my breasts to cling to my waist. I wanted to see him cum. I wanted to finally be the one pleasing him instead of it always being the other way around, but I could only take. Thrust after thrust, Deke kept going, grinding against Lars inside me until Lars grabbed at the sheets and lost control.

His back arched, changing the angle of his dick inside me, and I liked it so much. Deke just kept thrusting, refusing to let up, his hand working my clit with a little more pressure. The other pulled harder, tilting my head back to expose my throat. Then his mouth found my neck, kissing the side of it so sweetly.

"Ride him, doll," he breathed. "Ride him so hard."

"I want to see!" I begged.

So Deke pushed my head forward, his breath coming hard against the edge of my ear. "Look what you do to your pretty boys."

So I pushed my hips back, taking even more of them both. "And you."

But fuck, I was close. My breath was coming out in heavy pants. My entire body felt like it was on fire, but in the best way. I just needed a little more. Everything he was doing was perfect. This felt so good, and Lars looked amazing splayed below me like that. And then Lars began to thrust again.

His jaw was clenched, but he wasn't ready to give up. This time, it was Deke who gasped, obviously enjoying that as much as I did, but it was too much. Too good. My legs trembled and I whimpered with pleasure, so Deke pulled at my hair again. That matched the stretching of my core so perfectly. The sparks emanating from my clit were growing brighter. The men fucking inside me were amazing, and I completely lost control.

When my orgasm hit, I couldn't have screamed if I wanted to. I couldn't even breathe. I just took it, feeling my body tense around both of them and shudder, with every muscle in my body lost to the pleasure. I came, the sensation almost never-ending. For a moment time stopped, the world didn't exist, and only the feel of their skin against mine seemed to matter.

Then Deke groaned in such a deep and primal way that I knew he was done too. His fingers relaxed on my hair, I felt a wave of warmth flood my core, and I allowed my body to collapse forward onto Lars' chest. Immediately, his arms wrapped around me, holding me to him.

"I got you," Lars promised, "and I am never letting you go." His lips found the side of my face. "I love you, Jess."

"Mm, love you too, Lars," I mumbled.

Deke chuckled as he eased himself from my body. "I approve of the group stuff, Lars. Careful, I might want to do that again."

"Always down for it," Lars promised. "Just know she'll be walking a little funny today."

I tried to slap his chest, but it ended up more like a pat. I also didn't care. Nope, I felt much too good right now to be upset. I only had enough energy left to lift myself off him and roll to the other side, putting Lars in the middle so I could face Deke.

"Thank you," I whispered.

"I promise it was my pleasure."

He reached across Lars to take my hand, but I knew those words were the best we had. I wasn't ready to say I loved him, but I wanted to say something. Lame or not, it felt right. All of this felt so very right.

CHAPTER THIRTY-TWO

LARS ROLLED TOWARD ME, wrapping me up in his arms. I loved when he did that, so relaxed into him, feeling like I could fall back asleep. We'd been up late last night, and I had no clue what time it was, but I should probably get out of bed. I also wanted to just close my eyes for a little longer so I could enjoy this.

Then Lars looked back over his shoulder. "You playing with my tattoo?"

"Was looking at the lines," Deke said. "This is not something traditional."

"Nope," Lars agreed. "I'm all traditionalled out. Kinda why I got it."

"Why?" I asked, hoping he'd finally explain his unique tattoo a little more.

"My life was screwed up because of people trying to chase traditions and missing the mark. My shithead of a father is incredibly pure Cherokee. His wife is close. Like, generations with few or no white men, you know? Well, or women. So they look like American Indians, and people in our tribe seem to think it's a big deal, and I dunno. But that's why they got married. Like, everyone around them was pushing them together. To keep the traditions, you know?"

"Which doesn't make a good marriage," I realized.

"And doesn't sound very traditional," Deke added.

"It's really not," Lars agreed. "Never mind that it makes me feel more like someone was breeding horses or dogs than families. But Dad screwed up, I was born, and I looked just as Native as my sisters. My whole life, I couldn't help but think that it wasn't fair. None of it was fair. The plan to breed these pure kids didn't matter in the end because, except for my eyes, my skin's the same color, my hair is just as black and straight, and all that bullshit. When my hair was long, I looked as much like a 'damned Indian' as my dad."

"Still do with it short," Deke assured him.

"Yeah, but less like I'm stuck in an old western movie," Lars countered. "But I cut my hair at sixteen. Oh, and that's not done. Everyone had something to say, and I guess it just made me hate the tribal traditions a little. I wasn't allowed to be me. I had to be a Cherokee, you know? And that's how the tattoo came about. I do love my tribe, and I'm damned proud of the history, but I don't think I should be forced to be stuck in time. I don't know why I can't have a bad breakup and cut my hair, or shit like that. Dad said I'm rebelling, Pamela - his wife - said I'm trying to find myself, and Mom said I deserved to make my own decisions."

"Which is how you ended up here," I realized.

Lars nodded. "Yeah. Got the tattoo the day after I turned eighteen. Dad got drunk when he saw it. He said that's not fucking Cherokee, and I told him it didn't matter. It should be about the spirit of our traditions, not the letter. So yeah, you were kinda right when you saw it, Jess."

Behind him, Deke was tracing the tattoo with his hand. "These are shackles, right?"

"Yeah. At the time, I thought about how our people were imprisoned. The lines are the anger. The feathers are sharp, like weapons. The style is modern, to show we are still here, but the concepts are from our past."

"It's nice," Deke said just as the door creaked open.

I pushed my chest against Lars to hide from whoever that was since the blankets were gone. Lars moved his arm lower, shielding my ass even as he lifted up to look. That blocked my view of Deke, but when Lars relaxed, I knew it was someone who was supposed to be in here. And still, the person didn't talk.

"You're cool, Gav," Lars said.

"I, uh..." The door clicked as it closed. "So, um, Linda's making breakfast. I, um, thought..." He cleared his throat, and then the blankets flopped over me.

"Better?" Deke asked.

I rolled onto my back just as Gavin thrust his hand out, holding a tumbler in it. "I brought Jess coffee. I can get some for you guys too."

"No, I need to get up," Deke said.

I sat up and scooted back, taking the blankets with me so I could pin them over my chest. "Thanks, Gav," I said as I took the coffee.

"Looks like I missed the fun," he told me, a sweet little smile on his lips.

"And I was not in the middle," Lars assured him. "Nothing gay, Gav."

"No, it's cool," Gavin said, sounding just a little awkward. Then he reached up to scrub at his face. "No, um, Deke? I'm gonna say something stupid, ok?"

"Go for it," Deke told him.

"It's normal," Gavin said. "I'm used to all of us with Jess, and if you're cool with this, Lars, then that means it's not weird, and I'm just being a fucking wuss. Deke's not a pussy. Jess is hot. The stuff we do is good, so if Lars is ok with it, then I'd just be dumb to not be ok with it."

ENTER SANDMAN

"Nothing dumb about it," I assured him. "We're all allowed to have fears."

He nodded. "But this one is dumb because Deke has always been cool. It's just like my dad is in my head screaming that he was right, and I don't fucking want him to be right."

"Trust me," Deke said as he got out of bed and headed for his clothes, "he's not even close to right. You are so fucking straight it's not even funny. Also, I like twinks. Girly little guys, Gav. You're not my type - or Lars, or Bax."

"Really?" I asked, my mouth flopping open. "I totally figured you went for bears."

"Uh, no," Deke said. "I like to be the big man in my relationships. I'm also a top, if you were wondering."

"Somehow, not shocked," Lars joked. "And while you're up, parading around, toss me my pants."

"These?" Gavin asked, picking them up from my side of the bed.

"Yep." Lars caught them when Gavin tossed them over. "Someone find Jess some clothes?"

"Or you can all just get out of my room," I suggested.

Laughing, Deke pulled on his pants, grabbed the rest of his clothes, and headed for the door. Beside me, Lars put on his pants under the blanket, then rolled out on Deke's side. When he made it around the bed, he grabbed his shirt, and followed Deke out. The whole time, Gavin just stood there. When Lars closed the door behind him, Gavin just reached up to scratch at his hair.

"What's a twink?"

"Often young, usually lean, and typically more feminine," I explained, waving for him to move out of my way. "And I have to pee!"

He moved, so I made a naked dash to the bathroom so I could clean up. I didn't hear my door open again, though, so when I was finished and came back into my bedroom, I wasn't shocked to find Gavin sitting on the edge of my bed, waiting for me. His eyes jumped up, running over my body, and one of those sweet little smiles touched his lips.

"You should do that more," he said.

I quickly rummaged in my drawer for a bra and panties. "Do what?"

Gavin just pointed. "That. Get dressed. Walk around naked."

"Pretty sure that would get weird in the living room when Linda comes downstairs," I said, trying to laugh it off.

"But you never do it around us," he countered. "Jess, if you are embarrassed, don't be. You're beautiful, *mi cielo*."

I got my underwear on, and grabbed a shirt. "But I keep thinking about my fat rolls," I said as I pulled it on.

He chuckled once. "I do not see fat. I see muscles now. I see curves. I see a hot girl. My hot girl, and I like that."

"Yeah?" I found a pair of yoga pants.

He nodded, his eyes following as I put those on too. "Definitely. I also don't want you to think you have to choose between me and Deke. I'm ok with it. I mean, him. Like, me and him with you." He closed his eyes and sighed. "Like, we used to," he said, doing his best to explain his rambling.

"Group stuff," I offered. "That's what Lars calls it. Sounds less weird."

"I like group stuff," Gavin promised. "Jess, I'm sorry I was weird. Am weird. I don't even know, but I'm trying, and I don't hate Deke. I don't hate you being with Deke - or anyone else. I just like us, and I don't want to mess everything up with you because I was stupid."

I got the pants over my ass and made my way back to him. "You are not stupid, Gavin. This is hard. All of us dating like this? It's... I mean..."

"Yeah," he agreed. "And I don't know how to talk about things like that. Lars says we have to talk so we don't end up fighting. I've been trying, and Deke and I have been talking."

I reached for the side table to get my coffee. "He's my boyfriend now, so you know."

Gavin nodded. "Good. And I'm still your boyfriend too?"

"Yes." I sat down on the bed beside him. "And I still love you, Gavin. I just feel like I'm trying to be extra careful not to make this weird, and it's making it weirder."

"Me too," he agreed. "Maybe we can just pretend like I wasn't a dick to him - or you - and go back to how it used to be? If things happen, they happen, and if I'm stupid, then Deke can yell at me, but I'm not breaking up with you. I'm not letting you break up with me either."

"Never wanted to," I assured him.

Those words made Gavin's body relax and the tension he'd been carrying since he walked in vanished. "I just don't know why you'd want to be with me when you have all of them."

"Because you're sweet, Gav. Because you're a fucking badass. Because you seem to understand that this is hard when Bax and Lars make it all look so easy. Because I'm not the cool girl, and you don't expect me to be."

"I happen to think you're pretty cool," he assured me. "I also love you more than I expected. Guys don't talk about this. They say they love a girl, and that's it. They don't talk about how she's all they think about, and I thought maybe I was doing it wrong. And then Deke, and I kept thinking I wasn't man enough, and with all those things my dad used to say, I was worried he was right."

"I think about you all the time," I assured him. "You know, we've been dating a few months now, and I still get giggly when you take off your shirt in practice, or when you hold my hand, I end up smiling. I think that's normal."

"Is it also normal to be ok with what we did last night?" he asked.

"I am." I shrugged. "I don't know if that's right, but that asshole tried to kill you. Shit, he would've if I wasn't a cambion! Fuck him, Gavin. Greg is dead, and I'm glad he is. Not because he beat the shit out of Travis, but also. Mostly, it's what he did to you. I just..." Leaning my head back, I closed my eyes and groaned. "He's just like my dad! He hurts people and thinks he has the right to!"

"Thought," Gavin corrected. "He's dead, so he won't hurt anyone else."

" Now we need to make sure we get the next one, and the one after that." I reached over for his hand. "And we're the ones with the power to do that. You can make them fight. I can make them die. Bax and Lars have our backs."

"Deke too," he said. "Jess, I used to think that we only had a few years left, but I'm not ready to die. I don't want a few more years with you. I want decades. I like this. I like having my closest friends dating the same girl. I like all of this, and I'm going to fight for it. I am going to figure out how we can be the quad that lives, because you're right. The Order doesn't care about us. It's almost like they want us to die, but we're not doing things their way anymore."

"And when they get pissed and come after us?" I asked.

The smile he gave me was filled with determination. "Then we'll fight them too. We have something no other quad has." And he tipped his head at me. "You. A reason to fight. Something to bind us together. We're not like the other quads, because we love. They just fought."

"And love is a lot stronger." I nodded. "Yeah, so let's figure out what happens when a quad gets old, ok?"

"You will still be sexy when you're old," he said, easing himself off the bed. "Oh, and breakfast is done. Let's enjoy a day off."

CHAPTER THIRTY-THREE

OVER BREAKFAST, I happened to mention that I had a fourth boyfriend. Bax nodded his approval, but Linda was confused. When Lars pointed to Deke, she had things to say. Quite a few things, which started and ended with whether or not he could be fair to the boys if he was involved with me. In the middle, she brought up his position in our group, but Gavin had that.

"He's the Sandman. Conquest, Vengeance, Judgement, Anathema, and the Sandman. He's one of us."

"And he's not our boss," Bax pointed out. "Just the more experienced fighter. Pretty sure we all have an area of expertise."

So Linda pointed at the three other guys. "If any of you think he's pressuring her, you let me know." Then she turned to me. "And you, young lady, had better talk to me if you need to. One boyfriend is a lot. Four?" She tossed up her hands. "I have no idea how you do it. At least they keep the house clean!"

Tash just pointed her fork at Deke. "Don't be stupid."

"Not being stupid," he assured her.

"I don't want to bury you, little brother. So keep your head on straight when the fighting starts. You try to run in and save her and I'm taking over as their Sandman."

"Not gonna happen," Gavin said, which made everyone at the table pause. So he kept going. "He's the one we're bound to. He shares the silver cords with us. Not you, Tash. Besides, Jess is the strong one. She has magic, and her hand can kill. She doesn't need someone to save her. Fuck, she saves us!"

"That," Deke said. "My girlfriend might be very sweet, but she knows what she's doing. They're ready, Tash."

"And you," I reminded her, "need to find out what the Order is hiding."

"Linda and I are starting on that today," she promised. "Talk to Travis and see if that boy knows anything on Monday."

So we spent the rest of the day watching movies and relaxing. At one point, I ended up on the couch with Deke. Bax made a point of picking on him, but in a good-natured sort of way. When Deke snuck in a kiss on the side of my neck, it was Gavin who noticed, smiling at me to show he approved.

On Sunday, we had to get back to training. If this was what would win our battles, then we needed to be the most well-trained Brethren ever. Deke sent us into the woods with a scrap of cloth in our pockets, then told us to try to steal each other's while keeping our own. The person with the most colors at the end of the session would win an evening of being lazy.

It was actually fun, but also hard. Gavin was stealthy, sneaking up on me just to tackle me to the ground. A push of air and a few vines solved that problem, though. Unfortunately, the noise brought the others toward us, so I ran. Lars took out Gavin, taking his cloth. Bax took out Lars. Lars and Gavin took out Bax, but I was well away from them by that point.

Then Deke hit me from the side, coming out of the trees. Like before, I used air and earth - not wanting to set the woods on fire - but he jumped before my vines could get him, and was back on me. We sparred, and he wasn't holding back. Dodging

ENTER SANDMAN

and blocking, I couldn't overpower him with my body, so I had to work magic in without slowing. Not exactly an easy thing. Yet when I finally dropped him, I got his scrap of cloth as a bonus.

So then I had to go back for the guys. One by one, we beat up each other and took the colored cloth. By the time Deke finally called the game over, we were all exhausted and ready to collapse. I came out with Lars' and Deke's cloths. Bax had mine and Gavin's. Lars had Bax's. Deke declared it a draw, and we all got to rest while he made dinner.

But the next morning, we were back to school. The day started much too early, but Gavin made me a coffee to carry with me. This time Lars was driving, so it was Bax sitting in the back seat with me. When we pulled into our parking space at school, everything seemed completely and totally normal except for one minor difference.

Shannon and Travis were sitting at our regular table - alone.

Gavin and I pulled out our hand coverings, and together, the four of us headed that way. "What's the cover story?" Lars asked when we were halfway there. "Why'd we cancel on the party?"

"Date night with Jess," Bax said under his breath. "Linda was the excuse for everyone else, and since you can't be seen in town with her, we wanted to get lost in the pasture. Linda thinks we were cooking s'mores on the campfire."

"Instead," I realized, "we were having a gang bang."

"Yup," Bax said, pushing a smile onto his face when we got closer. "Hey, you two!"

"So you are alive," Shannon teased. "Have a good weekend? Walking bowlegged, Jess?"

I ducked my head, feeling my face getting warmer. "Uh, yeah, something like that."

But Travis just looked relieved. A little too relieved. "Good to see you didn't break the poor girl," he tried to joke, and yet it fell flat.

"Guess you were worried we got busted or something?" Lars asked him.

Travis just nodded. "Yeah, something like that."

Shannon just leaned over to steal a kiss from him. "Hey, I'm gonna go check up on Tina. Pretty sure she got grounded for the rest of her life." And she pointed across the lawn to where a girl was headed this way. "See you in class?"

"Always," he promised, pulling her back for another kiss. "And if you see Terrance, make sure he's not grounded from the next game?"

"Will do," she agreed, backing away from the table. "Still miss partying with you four. One day, you'll have to come hang again."

"One day," Bax assured her.

Shannon turned and strode toward her friend, and Travis let out a heavy sigh. "Serious as fuck, guys," he said, keeping his voice down, "I did not expect to see you four here today."

"And yet you gave us the name," Bax pointed out.

"Yeah, because you wanted it. He's still... you know... greater."

"Was an easy in and out," I assured. "We also have questions."

Travis checked his watch. "And ten minutes until the first bell, so let me go first. Greg's house was broken into this weekend. The guy's missing, but there was a bullet hole in the wall and blood on the scene. Sounds like they have reason to think the guy's dead. Ted was called into the police station, and I heard he set up a story where Greg was selling meth."

"Which means we're covered," Gavin realized.

"For now," Travis said. "I think Ted was trying to cover your asses, but my mom asked me about it. Wanted to know if I had any idea what was going on since she knows the guy trashed me the other night."

"Demon moms," Bax said. "Kinda cool."

"Not cool," Travis assured him. "Greg was a greater, which means he could've destroyed any normal man. He also wasn't on meth because it doesn't really do shit for us. So, that leaves one plausible explanation." He wagged his finger between the four of us. "And I've been seen talking to you. Mom's pissed because she thinks I'm going to bring trouble down on us."

"We're not after you," I assured him.

"Not you!" he hissed. "Jess, I'm talking about your dad. The other greaters. Here I am talking to the Brethren at school, people know, and that makes me a target. My guardians are going to be next. Mom wants me to cut this off, piss you four off, and make a break."

"So, you're out," Gavin said, nodding to show he understood.

"Fuck," Travis groaned. "No. I'm just saying that this isn't as simple as you think. If the greaters suspect me, they'll torture my parents for information. They're just commons, and while they might not be my real parents, they've raised me since I got out. I don't want them to get hurt."

"Then you need out," Bax said. "Travis, we're not trying to get you in shit. We just need answers, and you're the only one with them."

"I know," Travis assured him. "I also know that you could've destroyed me already. Look, we're cool. It's just that when I tried to tell my folks that you're different, they said I don't know what I'm talking about. Jess, I didn't want to give up what you are, so I'm letting everyone think it's Deke. Cambion can't be Brethren, and they all know Ted."

"Which is a benefit for us," I reminded the guys. "But that's the thing, Travis. Why are we so scary? Tash doesn't want us to trust you, but I do. I dunno, I just don't see why it has to be demons against Brethren. Our job is to close the seals so the Horsemen don't get out, nothing else."

"You're supposed to kill abominations," Travis reminded me. "You and your fancy magic can wipe us from the face of the Earth."

"What fancy magic?" Lars asked. "Because we're not that impressive. I mean, we're immune to your poison, can do a few minor things with our hands, and have Jess."

Travis just looked between us. "And you're supposed to be invulnerable, unstoppable, and killing machines."

Gavin tapped his chest. "Impaled by demon claws, remember? Not very invulnerable."

"What do the stories say?" I pressed. "You mentioned bedtime stories, and we're running on almost no information. Travis, we have to touch someone to affect them. Bullets barely hurt any of you, but anyone can shoot the special ones. What do the stories say we do?"

"They say that together, you can make us as weak as humans," he said. "There aren't details, because we don't know your powers any more than you know ours. Mom always used to say that if I wasn't a good boy, she'd have the Brethren come make me as weak as a real boy. She warned me that I wouldn't be able to get away, and you'd cut me to a million pieces and toss me back into the Pit. Just things like that."

"Shit," Bax grumbled. "So no real powers."

"I just can't believe that we're supposed to hunt creatures with magic and have almost none of our own," I told them. "I mean, Bax and Lars are almost useless in a fight, except for subduing."

"Thanks," Lars joked. "And there goes my balls. Chopped right off."

"Fuck off," I laughed. "You know what I mean. Gavin can pull aggro with his touch. I can kill. You two? There has to be more than just the getaway solution."

"Well," Travis said, "I know there's something about when the Martyr is near is when we need to worry." He shrugged. "That's really all I've got. Invulnerable, unstoppable, and walking death. That's what you four are always said to be. And when the Martyr appears, we have no chance."

"Lovely bedtime stories," Lars muttered. "Also, we need another name."

Travis blew out a breath. "Laura and Martin White." He looked up. "I don't have their address, but I know they live on Mulberry

ENTER SANDMAN

Street. Both are newer greaters. Both were there. A girl I know said that Laura got shot and Martin, her husband, is pissed. Sounds like he's been mouthing off about what he'll do to you four if he gets the chance."

"You gonna give them a heads-up?" Bax asked.

Travis just shook his head. "Nope, but I'm going to make you pay me back for that. Dad got in touch with someone about picking up the kids. You are going to let us go in there, get them, and leave without a problem."

"Done," Bax agreed. "I want you with them."

"I can do that," Travis agreed.

"Look," I told him, "None of us want to hurt the kids. We don't even want to hurt the demons who aren't trying to kill us. We just want to keep the Horsemen locked up. That's it."

"And to kick the shit out of any demons who are true assholes," Gavin added.

"Which is why I'm helping," Travis assured us. "You should also know that Shannon's starting to wonder about what's up. She asked if you were blackmailing me to cover for you or something. I mean, you went from hitting all the parties to none?"

"Got a girlfriend," Bax pointed out.

"Which would work if Jess hadn't enjoyed going to those same parties," Travis countered. "She's covering for you, but she's asking a lot of questions. You need to think of something to tell her. That girl is not stupid."

"No, she's not," I agreed. "So, who wants to say he's an alcoholic?"

Lars pointed right at me. "You are. Runs in families, and Ted is a known drunk. I'm worried about it, so I asked you to stop. That's why we're skipping the parties."

"I can do that," I agreed.

"Ok," Travis said, hopping to his feet right as the bell rang. "I'll make sure Shannon knows not to spread that around. Also, be careful of setting a pattern. They're trying to figure out when and where you'll hit next."

"Thanks," Gavin said, clasping his shoulder. "And if you have problems..."

"I'll call," Travis promised, "because you four owe me now."

CHAPTER THIRTY-FOUR

UNFORTUNATELY, Travis's bedtime stories didn't do much to help us figure out better powers. The names he'd given us, on the other hand, led us to the right people. Laura and Martin White were a pair of middle-class townies that no one really knew. They lived in a nice ranchette neighborhood, in a modest little brick home, with an impressive shop in the back.

Tash and Linda scoped it out for us. Deke spent the rest of the week planning this hit. The four of us trained. We came up with scenarios and ways to counter them. We made plans and backup plans for every position we could find ourselves in. We even tried to be good in class so we didn't get detention all week, which mostly worked. Evidently Lars' teacher felt that not doing homework was a good reason to keep him after school.

Then Friday rolled around. That was Senior Skip Day, and we were seniors. So, just to set Shannon's mind at ease, the four of us made an appearance that afternoon. Deke purchased four kegs of beer, which the group of us delivered. That made us immediately popular, but keeping up my ruse, I waved off any drinks offered to me. Lars did the same.

Yep, Shannon noticed. She brought me a glass of punch, and not like what I usually enjoyed at such things. This was the non-alcoholic kind. Bax snagged it from her, making a production of sampling it before handing it over. An hour later, I caught him talking to Shannon alone, and her nodding sagely. That meant the new rumor had been planted and my previous drinking explained away. So when it started to get dark and the four of us bailed, Shannon was more than happy to cover for us.

That night, we cleaned our weapons and gear. Saturday and Sunday, we spent our time looking at the floor plans of their house, the aerial view of the neighborhood, and the possible ways to get caught. When Sunday night finally rolled around, Linda made a production of cooking us a hearty dinner, saying we'd need it to carry us through the late-night hit and school the next day.

And at one in the morning, we headed out. This time, we took Tash's car - a little green sedan that was old enough to go unnoticed in the area, but new enough not to draw attention either. Deke pulled up out front, and the four of us slunk along a row of hedges that separated the Whites' front yard from their neighbors. Then Deke left to make a lap around the block. Like before, we had our phones and earbuds for communication.

"Ok, our entry point is the garage door on the side of the house," Lars said, pointing to show what he meant. "It's a normal door, not the car type. Jess, the locks are yours."

"Do we know if there's an alarm?" I asked.

"They're inside, so they wouldn't set it," Bax pointed out, his words little more than a whisper but coming through my ear just fine.

"Dogs?" I asked.

"Hate demons," Gavin explained. "At least that's what Travis said, and Tash and Linda saw nothing."

Which meant I was clear to open the lock. Pressing my hand to the aluminum side door, I worked my magic. First the deadbolt, then the key lock. Just like with Greg, once it was open, Bax went first, with Gavin right behind him. Lars and I brought up the rear.

It was weird sneaking into someone's home. Even weirder when I knew they were still inside. All the lights were off. The house was quiet. There was a soft snoring coming from the bedroom hallway, so we followed it. Outside the right door, the four of us stopped.

"Hit the husband first," Gavin said. "He's older, so more powerful. Bax and Lars will subdue the woman. Jess and I will deal with the man."

"And I'm following you," I assured him.

Carefully and slowly, Gavin eased open their bedroom door. Cold air wafted out, making it clear they liked their creature comforts, and the snoring got louder without the wood to buffer it. Gavin peered through the crack, then pushed the door the rest of the way and surged in.

Quiet. That was the trick, and yet it was hard to do with all the gear we had. Gavin rushed right to the man. Lars and Bax went for the side with the woman. The moment they had their hands on them, I grabbed the blankets and yanked them off, exposing their bodies - and the skin I needed to touch.

The man roared, sitting up like he was about to come at me. Gavin shoved him back down and my hand found his arm. I pushed. Beside us, the woman was trying to struggle, but her movements were growing weak, and fast. I tried to ignore it, because all that mattered was that this man needed to die. I wanted him to just be dust, and the sooner the better.

"No!" Laura whimpered. "Let him go! You can't. No!"

"Shut the fuck up," Bax growled, sounding like he was trying to force his power to make that happen.

"We didn't mean to. We didn't *want* to!" she whined. "They don't give us a choice. Just let us go and we'll leave."

My head snapped over, but I couldn't believe her. How many times had my father tried to tell me what I wanted to hear?

Thankfully, the power of my hand had the husband already subdued. Martin was struggling, but it was futile, and Gavin's strength was enough to keep him under control.

"You attacked us," I breathed, forcing myself to care about nothing else. "You came after my guys. Just die."

The husband's breath hitched. There was a gurgle in his throat like he was drowning. I just kept pushing. In a last, desperate attempt to defend himself, the man swung, his arm smacking into mine almost hard enough to break my grip.

Immediately, Gavin was on it, releasing the man's shoulder to grab his wrist. The demon pushed at us, hoping that was how he'd break free, but he was too far gone already. In what felt like minutes but was probably only seconds, the man slumped and began to dissolve.

"No!" the woman screamed.

"Shut her up!" Gavin snapped.

So Lars pressed his hand over her mouth, but she kept going even as her husband turned to dust beside her. "They make us. All greaters have to fight. If we don't, we can't stay and this is the only safe place. No, Martin! No, no, no!" Her eyes were locked on the man as he broke down to nothing. "Let me go!"

"This. Is. Fair," Lars breathed.

And she went completely still, but I was already moving around the foot of the bed. Bax had her legs and body. Lars had one hand over her mouth with his forearm braced over her chest. I grabbed her ankle and pushed, but this didn't feel right. It didn't feel gratifying like Greg had. This felt wrong, almost cruel, and I didn't want to do it.

I also didn't have a choice.

Martin was dead, so Laura had to go next. If I let her live, she'd tell the others what we were doing. If she survived, the demons would all come for us. So far, we'd been walking a very fine line of just enough doubt to make them leave us alone, but if we let this woman go and she told the cops?

We couldn't fight the mundane laws, the supernatural creatures, and the cracking seals. She had to die, so I pushed, glad that she passed out quickly the way my dad had done. It was almost like she gave in, which made more questions than it answered. Thankfully, it also meant that she died quickly, her leg beginning to dissolve in my grip.

"And she's gone," Lars said, leaning back. "Gav, check the rest of the house. Make sure they're alone?"

"On it," Gavin promised.

Then he looked at Bax. "We need to strip this bed. Put it all in the washer to get rid of the dust."

"Shit, that's gonna be heavy," Bax realized. "Pour it in the bathtub?" He jerked his head toward the ensuite bathroom. "Jess can find the washer."

"On it," I promised.

I barely made it out of the bedroom when Deke decided to speak up. "What's the status?" he asked.

"Both done and we're cleaning up," I assured him.

"They never got out of bed," Gavin assured him, "and the rest of the rooms are empty."

I had just made it into the kitchen and tried the door that seemed most like a laundry room. "Yep, and I have the washer." Opening the lid, I found it was filled with dirty - and unwashed - clothes. "Shit. They have a load in here. Let me pull that out."

"Put it in a basket," Bax warned. "These are suburbanites. It'll look odd if it's in a pile."

"Yep," I said, grabbing the empty laundry basket and doing just that. "We'll also need to use extra soap unless you rinse that stuff."

"Shit, we don't want to drag water across the house either," Lars said. "I'd also like to say that demon dust does not drain easily. Bax, take that to Jess."

"Laundry's off the kitchen," I told him.

"On it," Bax said. "Hope you can get all of this into the washer at the same time, Jess, because there's a lot."

"Then we need to make it look like the couple did this on their own," Deke told us. "Was their car in the garage?"

"Yep," Gavin said.

"Get clothes from the drawers and closet," Deke commanded. "Put them in the trunk. Someone find the keys."

"And the wife's purse," I added. "No woman leaves without that. Leave cell phones."

"That's my girl," Deke praised. "Lars, I want you to drive that car over to Ted's house and leave the keys in it. I'll be right behind you. Jess, when we get home, text your father that he can do with it what he wants."

"Nice," I said, deciding that I liked this plan.

Then Bax was beside me and we were stuffing the bedding into the washer. Thankfully, it was a front load, which made all of this easier. I tossed in double the amount of detergent, set it for the longest load possible, and turned it on. The whole time, Lars and Gavin were hauling armloads of belongings to the car.

"Check the light for the garage," Gavin suggested. "Most automatic doors light up, don't they?"

"We'll just unscrew the bulb," Bax decided, heading after them to help. "Jess, find the purse."

Well, most women kept them someplace useful. It wasn't in the kitchen, so I checked by the front door. Not there, which made me try the bedroom. There, I found it in the bathroom, sitting on the counter. I also double-checked the mess the guys had made, and was impressed to find there wasn't much. A few drops of water had splashed on the floor, but the tub had been wiped out and the whole area smelled like shampoo, so clean.

"Got it," I told them. "Headed your way. Lars, make sure you lock the side door after us?"

"So I'm going alone?" he asked.

"Sorry," Deke told him. "My hope is that if you get busted, Bax can get you out or your tribal status will hold things up. I'd much prefer that you don't break any laws and drive like someone's grandmother."

"Can do," Lars promised. "What's your status, Deke?"

"Rounding the corner. I'll be back in thirty seconds. We ready to go?"

"Ready," we all assured him, one after the other.

"Lights off, I'm parked where I let you out," Deke said. "Let's move, people. Lars, I'll pull over when we're out of the neighborhood. Pass me there, and I'll follow. Let's move."

Gavin headed out the door first. I was in the middle with Bax behind me this time. We were barely three feet away when I heard Lars locking the doors, and just as we piled into the car with Deke, I heard the car door inside the garage. We had this. We were doing this. It was working!

I ended up in the passenger seat beside Deke. The guys were quiet in the back. When we reached the end of the neighborhood, Deke turned right and parked on the side of the road. Not long after, the Whites' car headed past, moving nice and slow. Not too slow, but definitely not like he was in a hurry.

Deke pulled out behind him. The drive to Dad's place was easy and mostly on the main roads. When we got there, Lars turned off the lights and coasted to a stop on the curb outside Dad's place. Deke didn't pull over, but just paused in the middle of the road so that when Lars got out, he could slide right into the back seat. Then, once the door was closed again, we were off.

"Send him the text," Deke said as we headed for Bax's place.

I grabbed my phone and scrolled. For some reason, pulling up his contact made my guts clench, but we had this. It also meant we had Dad between a rock and a hard place. He could help me or he could turn me in. Either way, he'd declare his side. Opening a message, I decided to make it clear that I didn't care either way. This, more than anything else, was my act to cut him from my life.

Jess: Dad, the keys are in the car. It's outside. Do what you will. Promise I look a lot less guilty than you do. Time for you to see how it feels to be screwed over by someone you think you love. Should I say sorry now? Does it count if I don't intend to change? Think about that.

There was just one problem: hitting send didn't make me feel better.

CHAPTER THIRTY-FIVE

WE GOT HOME and all hit the showers. This time, I was in the second wave, because Lars and Bax were covered in the dust from the demons. There was no blood, though, so that was good. While I gathered up my clothes for my turn, there was a soft tap at the door before Deke stepped in.

"You ok?" he asked.

"This felt different," I told him. "I'm not sure I like it."

"Yeah," he muttered. "I think Bax is having trouble with it too. Um, I suggest you go use his shower, and that you don't wait until he's done. I'm here if you want to talk, but school starts in a few hours, and you four do need sleep. So, see if you can get Bax to crawl in bed and actually pass out?"

"Did he say something?" I asked, going for sleep clothes instead of simply comfortable ones.

Deke nodded. "When he gave me his guns, he said this is bullshit. He said not all demons are bad, and you're proof of that. When I pointed out that these were supposed to have been at the seal, he told me to fuck off. Jess, what happened?"

"The wife begged," I explained.

"Of course she did," he said, reaching up to pull me against his chest. "Doll, that's what people do when threatened. Demons, witches, humans, or whatever else. We lie, we beg, and we cry, because death is terrifying. But they had their chance to make the right call, they didn't, and now they have to pay the consequences. Otherwise, all those innocent people out there, like your friends at school, would pay it instead."

"Yeah," I breathed, leaning into him for a moment to just enjoy the feel of his arms around me. "I know that, but it still sucks. We're not killers, Deke."

"Neither are most soldiers, but they still figure it out." Then he kissed the top of my head. "Sleep in there with him. I'll tell the other guys I have you doing moral support for the night."

"And you?" I asked, lifting my chin.

He reached up to trace the line of my face. "I'm going to make sure Tash and Linda have a full update, I'll drink too much coffee, and I'll pass out after the four of you have safely made it to school. Damn, you're sexy when you're hunting demons. You know that?"

Then he kissed me, not bothering to wait for an answer. It was hard and fast, the way I expected from Deke, but I liked it. He was not a gentle man, and he didn't try to be. Instead, he pulled my head to the angle he wanted and devoured me like I was here for his pleasure. I could feel my pulse picking up and my panties getting wet just as he pulled away.

"Now, go share Bax's shower," he whispered against my lips.

I just closed my eyes and groaned, hating him a little. Still, I did grab my clothes and head for Bax's room. The water was still running, but the bathroom door was only pushed mostly closed, not completely. After setting my things on the closest dresser, I decided to just do this.

If I could follow Deke into the shower, then there was no reason I couldn't step in with Bax. Never mind that I wasn't ok with what had happened tonight either. While Deke's kiss could get me going, it didn't take away that nagging voice in the back of my mind that was adamant that this hit had been different. Killing these people hadn't made us heroes, but rather monsters.

Stripping my clothes, I left them on the bathroom floor, then eased open the glass door. Inside, Bax had his back toward me, the water running over his head and down his beautiful body. He twitched, lifting his head a bit at the sound of the door, but he didn't turn toward me.

"Hey," I said, moving in behind him just to slide my hands over his wet skin.

He laughed once. "Saying I'm hogging the water, huh?" he asked, finally turning so he could push his wet hair out of his face.

"I thought we could share," I admitted. "I also..." Crap. I didn't know how to finish that though.

"What?" he asked, moving so I could have the water.

"It wasn't the same tonight," I told him. "Dusting Greg felt good. It felt like vengeance. This? Bax, are we the good guys?"

"Fuck," he grumbled, stepping closer to help work the water into my hair. "I think that's the problem. I've been trying to figure out why I just feel like shit after that. It was like a damned mafia hit, you know? With Greg, it was like we'd hunted down the serial killer or something. Vigilante justice. This? It felt like shit, Jess. She begged, and I was about to let her go. I *wanted* to let her go!"

"Me too," I admitted. "But if we did, then what? She tells the cops? The demons? No matter what, that would end up badly. We planned the hit, so we had to follow through. Besides, how many times did my dad say he was sorry for beating me, or that he didn't mean to? Hell, a lot of the time he said it was my fault. He *didn't want to*, but I'd made him since I was being bad."

"Same words that woman used," Bax realized.

"And if someone was going to kill you, wouldn't you say anything they wanted to hear?" I asked.

"Probably," he admitted. "I mean, I'd like to say that I'd spit in their face, fight back, or die like a man without whimpering or crying, but I'm pretty sure I'd beg."

"Me too." I moved out of the water and reached for the shampoo. "But we know they were at the seal, which means they attacked us first. That's what I keep trying to tell myself."

"No," Bax said, leaning against the shower wall while I worked my hair into a lather. "I think you hit on something. Are we the good guys or the bad guys? I think that's the problem, you know? We want to say we're the good ones because demons are evil, right? We're trying to save the world from these monsters, or something, so that should make us heroes."

"Yeah?"

"But we're not," he reminded me. "The Order of Martyrs are trying to push back the forces of evil. They're killing abominations to keep the world pure and good. They're supposed to be the heroes. You, Jess, are an abomination, and what is it *we* really want?"

"To stop the Apocalypse," I said.

He shook his head. "No, babe. We want to keep you safe. We want to protect the abominations that aren't evil." He steered me into the water so I could rinse my hair. "Jess, if the Order is good, then what we're doing makes us the bad guys. I think some demons are worse guys, but if you look at the definition, we're not the heroes. We are the villains."

"No," I insisted. "Look, we're doing what's right. We're fighting for the people - "

"So do most villains," he countered. "They just aren't going about it in the usual sense of the word. They don't use the cops - and neither do we. They don't care about the law - and neither do we. They are willing to do anything in their power to protect what they care about..." He lifted a brow. "And so are we. I mean, what would you do if a cop was about to shoot me?"

"Anything I had to," I admitted, nodding to show I saw his point.

"So we need to figure out what kind of villains we want to be," Bax said.

I thought about that as I worked conditioner through my hair and scrubbed at my body. The whole time, he just leaned against the wall and watched me. Sure, sometimes he checked out my tits or my ass, but mostly he just watched as if his mind was somewhere else. Then again, so was mine.

Because he was right. Our whole thing had been that the rules didn't apply to us. We didn't have to be mean to be villains. In fact, I'd always been drawn to the sympathetic and nice villains in the stories I read. The difference was that we would let the world burn if we had to. Shit, I'd light it on fire myself to protect my guys and my family.

"Tash is kinda like a sister," I said, knowing it came out of the blue. "She's fucking annoying at times, and she's arrogant as fuck, but I think she's really trying to look out for us."

"I can see that," Bax agreed. "And Linda's definitely our mom. What about Deke?"

"Uh, boyfriend, remember?"

He chuckled. "Right. Because for me, he's like a big brother. Gav's my best friend, but Lars is kinda like a twin brother. Probably sounds stupid, but he's neither older nor younger, but clearly family."

"And best friend is more?" I asked.

Bax shrugged. "Yes and no. It's different. Gav's been my best friend for years. It's a different level of trust. You know, like how you wouldn't tell Linda some things because of that whole mom aspect. Like, I'm not going to go to Lars and talk about how I'm worried that I'm being a shit boyfriend or that I lose all appeal when I settle down." He flashed me a weak smile, making me think he was honestly worried about that.

"You don't," I assured him, "but I see what you mean."

"But if this is our family, and what we're fighting for is our family," Bax went on, "then what kind of villains are we? How far will we go, Jess? How crazy do we want to be?"

"Not crazy. We want to be smart," I told him.

"But how? Why?" he pressed.

I blew out a breath and actually thought about that. I didn't feel like a villain. I felt like a liberator, here to fight for the rights of monsters like me, but that was the kicker. I was a monster. I was cambion, and according to the rest of the world, that made me something horrible. Travis was a demon, so he was the same.

We weren't the good guys.

Which meant we didn't *have* to be the good guys. We didn't need to always be nice or try to protect people who didn't give a shit about us. People like my dad came to mind, or Mr. Garcia. We could fuck them over and not worry about feeling bad because this whole world had made us the bad guys - and that changed the rules.

And yet it didn't solve the real issue. "So does being the bad guys mean we should whack whoever gets in our way?" I asked. "Good, bad, doesn't matter?"

"The Whites," Bax grumbled, knowing that was who I was talking about. "Fuck, I don't know. In truth, it feels like I have no idea why we're doing all of this. I mean, why are we risking ourselves for these seals when no one is on our side? The Order wants to kill you, and if we keep fixing the seals, they will eventually see your magic."

"But if we don't close the seals, then Deke says the Horsemen will destroy the Earth. Like, nothing left. Not the good guys or the bad ones. We're fixing the seals to save us."

"Who is us?" he pressed. "See, I think that's why this is so fucked up in my head. It's not like we shot someone and left their bodies, because demons dust. That makes it a little less real." He shoved a hand across his mouth. "Not really my most badass statement of the year, but it's true. I don't want to kill people, Jess. I also don't care if I have to. The blood from Gavin shooting Greg in the face? Yeah, kinda disgusting to wear that. Not really my style to play in it, but I'm not going to worry about getting dirty either."

ENTER SANDMAN

"Makes sense," I said, because I kinda felt the same way. Sure, it was gross, but not debilitatingly or nightmare-inducingly so.

"My problem is that I feel guilty," he said. "I think it's because I don't know who I'm fighting for. I can't say if they were on our side or against us, because I don't fucking *know our side!*"

"So, what is our side?" I asked him. "What do we want it to be?"

"Us," he said without hesitation. "The four of us. Well, five, because of Deke."

"Our family," I added. "I think we should also add abominations who have no one else to stand up for them and never asked for this."

"Like Travis," he realized. "Ok. So what do we have in common with him? What makes up our side?"

"We're all supernatural," I said, ticking it off on my fingers. "We all know about the Order and don't agree with it. We have magic. Um..."

"We're alone," Bax added. "This entire system has somehow pushed our families away. Either that was how we got chosen, or for Travis, it's how he ended up here. For you, it's the battle that pits you against your father."

"Doesn't sound very evil to be fighting for the ones who have no one else to fight for them," I pointed out.

Bax reached around me to turn off the water, since my hair had been clean for a bit. "More *Lord of the Flies*, less Lost Boys. We are the leaders of a growing band of rabid supernatural things who have nothing left to hold them back, and no reason to not use our magic."

"Yeah, ok," I admitted, "that sounds a little more evil."

"Not evil," he corrected. "Evil sounds inherent, as if you're made with it. We're villainous. If history is written by the victors, and those without magic are the ones in control, then we are the rebellion that is trying to carve out our place. The villains who refuse to fall in line and be subjugated. The ones who don't care if it's legal when it's still wrong."

"Wait, what place are we carving out?" I asked.

"We are going to make a world where demons like Travis can live happily ever after," he decided, "and where cambion like you can safely learn how to control your magic. We're going to fight - killing everyone we have to - who won't let us just be our fucking selves."

"And burn the world if we can't win," I finished. "Yeah, I can be that kind of villain."

"Me too. Just wish I knew how the Whites fit into that."

"But if we're the villains," I told him, "then trying to stop us means they deserved it, right?"

He just nodded, but for all our tough words, he didn't look like he was enjoying this any more than I was.

CHAPTER THIRTY-SIX

When we got to school that morning, everything was fine. No one had the chance to even miss the Whites yet, so there were no rumors about what had happened to them. The four of us were wiped, though. We'd made it in bed by three, slept until almost seven, and we all looked like it had been a rough night.

I had the biggest travel mug of coffee in my bag and sipped on it all day long. Bax did too. Lars and Gavin went with sugar as their drug of choice. Somehow, we made it to lunch without getting called out for sleeping in class. Bax gave in and bought all of us a basket of cheese fries from the lunch line. Nasty stuff, since our cafeteria was rather questionable, but the carbs helped. I'd just shoved a forkful of them into my mouth when Bax decided to bring up our shower conversation with the rest.

"Jess and I talked in the shower last night," he started off.

Which made Gavin chuckle. "That is not what you're supposed to do with her in the shower."

"Fuck off," Lars said, smacking his arm. "Like you'd know. Pretty sure the only one she's screwed in the shower is Deke."

"Doesn't mean that can't change," Gavin said. "Jess, you can sneak into my shower any time you want."

I rolled my eyes and retorted with something that sounded like, "Mrumph."

"See," Lars said without missing a beat, "she can't talk with her mouth full." Then he winked at me.

I threw a Snickers bar at his head.

"I'm being serious," Bax insisted. "Was last night off for anyone else? Like, did that feel like what we're supposed to be doing?"

"She would've said anything to save her life," Gavin pointed out.

Lars just shook his head. "I dunno, Gav. I'm with them. It felt different. I mean, sure, we hit them hard and fast, but Greg fought hard. They just... took it?"

"Where was the magic?" I asked. "Travis said - "

"What about me?" Travis asked as he dropped into the last empty chair. I was tired enough that I hadn't even seen him coming over. "And so you know," he went on, "Dad told me when I woke up. Ted let everyone know that Martyrs hit the Whites, made it look like they left town. Will probably take a while before the cops figure it out. I'm guessing that wasn't the Martyrs, though."

"Nope," Bax admitted.

The problem was that the guy had a bruise on the side of his head. It wasn't bad, and it was mostly at the hairline and in his hair, but he was right beside me so I couldn't miss it. Without asking, I reached out to trace the edge of it.

"What happened?"

Travis sighed deeply. "Dad thinks I'm going to bring the four of you down on us. If not you, then Ted. He says I've put them in danger and told me to fucking end it with all of you."

"Shit," I breathed. "He hit you?"

"Not like that, Jess," Travis promised. "I told him he couldn't tell me what to do. I may have said he wasn't really my father, and kinda at the top of my lungs."

"But he hit you," I realized.

ENTER SANDMAN

Travis caught my wrist, moving my hand back to the table. "He also knows what I am, and this will be gone by the end of the day. He's only ever hit me when I act up, and only once. They're not bad people. They're just scared. Fuck, we all are."

"But you're the one that gave us the names," Bax pointed out.

"And Ted won't like it," Travis countered. "I'm not scared of you four. Well, I am, but not like that. I'm scared of Ted. I'm terrified he's going to find out that I'm the one giving you names. Don't you get it? My *parents* will be the ones who pay for that. You realize that, right?"

"So we put the blame somewhere else," I decided. "Maybe lay it at my dad's feet. I mean, I'm sure he has connections, and if we make it sound like we just followed him or something?"

"Could work," Lars agreed. "I'll talk to Deke about it."

"But like I was saying before Travis sat down," Bax broke in, refusing to give up on his point, "something about last night was off. It didn't feel right. We know the Order is keeping stuff from us, because we're not as powerful as Travis seems to think we are. We also know that we're not the good guys."

"Wait, what?" Lars asked.

"The good guys," I said, taking over. "Saving the world, protecting humanity, fighting abominations and demons. That's what the good guys do. It's not what we're doing. We've already made it clear that we're willing to break the rules. Just because *we* think we're right doesn't make us the nice ones. We're not the heroes here."

"You are to some of us," Travis said.

"Which is my point," Bax went on. "Guys, we know that the Order is supposed to be the good guys. We know that Ted and the demons who want to take over the world are the bad guys. So, what are we? By the rules we're using, we're villains, not heroes. The question is what side we're on."

"I like villains," Lars said. "Sounds much cooler than good guys.

I mean, I've always been more of the mercenary type, if I'm honest."

"Bounty hunters," Gavin suggested. "We catch the uncatchable - of either side - and we don't care what we have to do to make it happen."

"Then who are we fighting for?" I asked. "You can't say demons, because we're hunting them. You can't say the Order, because we're avoiding them. Which side are we on?"

"Integration," Lars decided. "Look around, Jess. Bax's family are immigrants. Gavin's an immigrant himself. I'm Native. You're a woman. Travis is a demon. Historically, humans find ways to persecute the newest group. The strong stomp on the weak. Well, that's been demons with humans, the Order with demons, and the Brethren doing the Order's dirty work. It's not much different than white men running my people down the Trail of Tears, or slavery, or Irish indentures. Shit, I don't even know how many atrocities there are in history, but you get my meaning."

"But who are we integrating?" I pressed before he could keep rambling. "How do we decide if someone gets a pass and someone doesn't? This isn't just about us against them. We don't have lines on who is an 'us' and who is a 'them', but we need to."

"She has a point," Travis admitted. "You can't make it a broad group of humans, demons, Martyrs, or such."

"It's not *what* we are," Gavin said, looking at each of us. "It's *who* we are. It's what we *do*. It's not about labels like human, demon, or abomination. It's about the ones who are willing to make a community, be fair, and let others live their lives safely."

"Which doesn't sound very evil," Travis pointed out.

"No," I corrected. "I fucking hate that word. People keep trying to assign it to groups like we're destined to be a certain thing, and fuck that. I'm the daughter of the Devourer of Hell. He's the most evil thing I can think of, but I'll be damned if that has to pass to me. I'm not evil. I'm also not a fucking good girl!"

"What makes a villain?" Lars mused. "In her books, it's the

person who knows no limits. I'd say that assassinating our enemies in their homes, using magic, and breaking all the rules we're supposed to follow counts."

"But you have limits," Travis pointed out. "I mean, are you going to sacrifice each other for greed?"

"No, but we would for each other," Gavin said. "I'd gut Lars to keep Jess safe."

"Thanks, Gav," Lars told him, but from his tone, he wasn't really offended.

"We fight for the ones who want to just be left alone," Bax said softly. "The humans who don't know about all of this, well, they're the reason we're going to keep closing the seals. The demons who just want a chance at a life? They're worth saving. The abominations who never asked to be made? They deserve to be people too."

I nodded because I liked that. "We're fighting for a world where we all get a fair chance."

"I'm in for that," Gavin said.

"Same," Lars agreed.

"I'm not a part of this," Travis said, "but I'm in too. I didn't ask to be born a demon, and I certainly don't deserve to be locked in a pit to feed something bigger and older than me. I don't want to spend my life running in fear and hiding in dark corners. I want a fair chance, just like you probably do in the normal world, Lars."

"Because I'm Native American?" Lars asked. When Travis nodded, so did Lars. "Yeah. I think that's why this works. Jess gets shit on for being a woman. Gavin for not speaking English as his first language, and Bax because he's rich and the kid of rich immigrants. Shit. That's why we're all so fucking adamant about this."

"Yeah," Gavin said. "We've all been the one getting shit on in one way or another."

Bax was bobbing his head in agreement. "And now we're the ones with power. If the system is broken, then it's time to dismantle it. That's what we've been doing. So, how many greaters do we have left, Travis?"

"Six that I know of," he admitted. "I'll get you a list before the end of the day, and - "

"Eating over here again?" Shannon asked, surprising us all when she wrapped her arms around Travis's shoulders in a hug from behind.

"Uh, yeah, I was just saying hi," Travis told her.

"Uh huh." Shannon pulled back and looked at me, lifting a brow in an unspoken question. "Just figured this was where all the fun was at."

I shook my head, making it clear I didn't know what she wanted. "Going to sit?" I said, gesturing for her to pull up a chair.

"No," Shannon said. "Don't want to cramp my boyfriend's style. Just hadn't seen you all day, Trav. We still on for later?"

"Yes, we are," he assured her. "I promised you a date."

"If you're not too busy," she said, looking over at Bax.

"He's just trying to get us to hang out sometime," Bax said. "Evidently, we were lame on Senior Skip Day."

"You were," Shannon said, reaching over to clasp my shoulder. "I heard you're not drinking?"

"Don't want to be like my dad," I admitted.

She nodded. "Well, it's cool. If you come to the next party, we'll both be soda girls together, deal?"

"No, Shannon," I groaned. "I'm not trying to kill your fun."

"My fun," she said, "is not feeling like my boyfriend shuts up when I walk over here. I'm starting to wonder if I pissed you off or something."

"Me?" I asked, looking at the guys to see if I'd misunderstood somehow.

"Well, Bax still talks to me, and Gavin doesn't talk to anyone. Lars only seems to care what you do, but Travis won't tell me what all of you talk about. I mean, unless someone wants to fill me in?"

"Just normal shit," I told her.

"Like how we should hang out more," Bax added.

"And that you know about Jess not drinking," Lars said.

"Ok, so what list?" Shannon asked.

"Drinks," Travis said quickly. "Um, some stuff that's not just soda for Jess to drink if she comes to hang out. Stuff Bax can pick up for her so no one asks and makes her feel embarrassed."

"Oh." Shannon looked at all of us, then rubbed my shoulder. "I think you should own it. Just say you don't want to drink and fuck anyone who doesn't like it."

"Not that easy," I told her. "In case you forgot, I've never been cool enough to get away with that."

"You are now," Shannon assured me. "And Jess? I'll keep your secrets too. You don't have to cut me out, ok? I know half the girls in school are trying to cut down or one up each other, but I don't want to be like that."

"You're not," I promised. "No, it's just weird. I'm sorry, Shannon. I wasn't trying to cut you out. I just don't think about asking you."

She nodded. "Ok. Just tell me if I piss you off?"

"I swear," I told her. "You're kinda the only girl I know who hasn't tried to stab me in the back. I'm just pretty bad with this."

"Then you're sure I'm welcome here?" she asked, this time looking at Travis.

He simply leaned back to pull a chair over. "Always, baby. I kinda like having you around."

"And yet you keep running away," she teased.

Which meant he'd been spending a little too much time with us, and she'd noticed. Fuck. We'd have to do something about that. The real question was what could we do? Shannon was human. Completely and totally human, and the last thing she needed was to get dragged into the middle of this. Between the Order, the demons, and the four of us, I wasn't sure she'd survive it.

CHAPTER THIRTY-SEVEN

TRAVIS GOT the list to Bax before school was out. Evidently, they had the last class of the day together, which made it easy. When we all met up at my locker, I saw Travis and Shannon further down in the hall. The pair were talking a little intently, and Shannon looked like she was upset about something. Not that it was any of my business.

I didn't say anything until we were in the car. Then, "Guys?" I asked. "How are things with Travis and Shannon?"

"I dunno," Lars said from beside me. "He really likes her, though."

"Yeah, but she's clearly frustrated with him ignoring her to talk to us."

"She is?" Bax asked.

Rolling my eyes, I flopped back in my seat. "Gav?"

"I don't pay attention to Shannon," he admitted. "She's Travis's girl."

Which meant that all three of them were oblivious idiots. In other words, they were typical guys. Yeah, that probably had a lot to do with why Shannon was freaking out. My guys didn't have a clue that there was a problem, and Travis was so busy trying to fix the demon issue that she kept getting ignored.

"Ok," I told them. "So you know, if you keep avoiding your girlfriend and lying to her about what you're really doing, we notice. Maybe you all think you lie well, but no guy does. You will contradict yourself, leave big gaps that don't make sense, or something that makes us convinced that you're either cheating or going to dump us."

"But we're not," Gavin told me. "We're always with you."

"I'm talking about Travis!" I groaned.

"Not really our place to tell him how to treat his girlfriend," Bax pointed out.

"Nuh uh," I said. "We're the ones pulling him away. We're the reason he can't talk to her. She keeps inviting us to parties, and we're blowing her off. From Shannon's point of view, that probably feels a lot like she pissed off someone and is being punished for it."

"Hence the conversation at lunch," Lars realized. "Ok, so what do we do?"

"I have no idea," I admitted. "Hang out with her more? Talk about something besides demon hunting, maybe?"

"Worth a try," Bax said. "I'll also make sure she knows that you smacked us all upside the head about it."

I leaned forward to wrap my arm around the seat and his shoulders. "See, you're a good boyfriend, Bax."

"Fuck yeah, I am," he agreed, but the guy sounded prouder than I'd ever heard before.

And there still hadn't been any word about the Whites at school. Not that I was sure it would make it there, since they didn't have any kids, which meant they weren't really on the school rumor radar, but town gossip should still travel that fast. It hadn't. I also hadn't heard back from my dad, but I was ok with that. In other words, it was a pretty good day.

We spent the rest of the ride home talking about the names on the list. There were six of them, just like Travis had said. Six more demons we had to hunt down in their own homes, and I was pretty sure our luck wouldn't hold that long. Bax said that the rest of the demons at the seal had been commons, but Travis didn't think they'd show without a greater to stand up for them.

Even if we could just get it down to manageable levels, like two or three, we might have a chance. We just needed to close the seal and run. Granted, the demons would probably start trying to break it right away. There were just too many in town, and Hellam had been too safe for them for too long. The real question was how many of those would actually fight us, and how many times would we have to keep doing this?

We were discussing how long we should wait before the next hit as we headed upstairs. Gav thought we needed to get to the seal quickly. Bax said it made more sense to kill demons on our terms instead of theirs. I thought the bigger issue was the powers we were clearly missing. If we were truly terrifying, then we should have a better chance, but terrifying wasn't the right word for our abilities. More like damned good teamwork.

I said that just as I opened the door to see Linda, Deke, and Tash sitting in the living room, and my words trailed off. Dropping my bag by the door, I moved to let the guys in behind me.

"Is everything ok?" I asked, because Linda didn't usually meet us on our floor after school.

"It's good news," Tash promised, waving us over.

Linda was smiling, so I certainly hoped it was. "Ok?" I asked when I was sitting down, the guys following after me.

"The school board wants to settle," Linda told us. "It's not that much money, but Rafe - Mr. Garcia - would be required to take a course on sexual harassment, and his contract would not be renewed next year. In other words, he'd have to reapply for his position as a teacher. He would, however, finish out the rest of this year, minus the days where he'd be in this course. It's a four-week course."

"Nice," I said, because that meant he would pretty much miss the rest of the year.

"How much?" Bax asked.

"One hundred and fifty thousand," Linda said. "The attorney you sent me to said that I could push for three, but I'm not that worried about the money."

"Put it in a fund for the baby's college," Bax said, "but I think you're right. Money isn't the point. Him not being able to do this again is."

"Exactly," Linda agreed, looking over at Lars. "Honey, do you agree with this?"

"I'm just proud of you for fighting back, Mom," Lars told her. "So yeah. Did you already sign it?"

She nodded. "It is off and done. We won't get the check for a while, but the attorney said that's to be expected."

"And Mr. Garcia is going to do this class now?" Gavin asked.

Linda nodded. "Starting next week. That means you'll have a substitute for the rest of the year." She smiled at me. "He won't be picking on you anymore, Jess."

"Or giving out our final grade," I realized. "Yeah, that's a good thing."

"Well, we have news too," Bax said. "Travis gave us the last six greater demons in town. Everyone else is common or below. He's sure that without the greaters, half the commons won't show up."

"Commons are still tough," Deke reminded us. "And how many commons would we be talking about?"

"No idea," Gavin said. "The problem is that Travis is a teen, like us. People don't always tell us what they're planning. So maybe none, maybe a dozen. It'll still be a fight, probably."

"He's also going to be escorting some commons to my place," Bax said, turning to Tash. "You will not try to stop them so long as they're with Travis, am I clear?"

"For the kids?" she asked.

Bax nodded. "Yeah. They need to be in homes with people who will understand them."

"No, I'm ok with that," Tash admitted. "Hate to admit it, but I like them. They have horrible names that I can't pronounce, but they're cute - and lonely. I told them we're trying to get them help, so this is their help."

"Didn't actually expect that from you," Bax admitted.

Tash shrugged. "Seems we're all trying to accept things we used to hate." And she tipped her head at Gavin.

"I didn't do anything!" he said.

"Exactly," Tash said. "And you haven't in a while. That's an improvement on being a dick to Deke, Gav."

"So," Linda asked, pointing her finger between all of us, "this is still going ok?"

I nodded quickly. "Yep. I mean, besides the training, demon killing, and lack of date nights, it's going great. And no, I'm not telling you how great, Mom." I stuck my tongue out to make sure she knew I was mostly teasing. "But how's the research?"

Tash groaned. "Slow."

"It's hard to find something that doesn't seem to exist," Linda said. "We've all been through Deke's journal. There are a few references we don't understand, but not enough. Tash's records are just as sparse, and everything seems to reset around the 1850s. Anything before that time is from a later reference to what someone had said before."

"They wiped the records," Lars breathed. "Like they tried to do with us. They stopped telling the next generation so the stories wouldn't get passed down!"

"Huh?" I asked, unsure of what he was talking about.

"Most Native kids were taken to Christian schools," he explained. "Taken from their mothers, sent to a school that prohibited us from speaking our own language, and we almost lost it. Some tribes did.

ENTER SANDMAN

Traditions, history, and more were just destroyed. Kids didn't go back to their tribes because they couldn't talk to their own parents, and our people were destroyed with supposed kindness."

"Shit," Deke said, staring down at his toes. "Replace all the Martyrs for the quads, remove the old journals, and wait for the quad to reset. The next group wouldn't know anything they didn't need to. *We* wouldn't know what we didn't know. Same idea, and it would only take one gap. New Martyrs with new quads, and suddenly whatever they wanted to hide is just gone."

"But are we sure there's really anything to hide?" Tash asked. "I mean, the kids have been making quick work on these hits. They *are* dangerous. They're lethal."

"Because Jess is a damned abomination!" Deke shot back. "Tash, if she was an Anathema like Diamond from my last group? They'd have to put a dozen slugs in each demon's head. That's time, and the husband-and-wife pair would've been a massive battle, not an in and out like they did."

"Why would the Order keep something like that from us?" Tash countered. "What benefit would it serve? I mean, if the goal is to keep the seals closed, then maybe the information was truly lost by accident - if it even existed at all."

"Wait," I begged. "Deke's ritual. It was wrong, like discordant. What if the Order doesn't want the seals to stay closed? What if your ritual to secure it again isn't the right one?"

"But why?" Deke asked. "Tash has a point. If the seals crack, then the Horsemen are released."

"And then?" I asked. "Martyrs are abominations too. Maybe you don't count yourself as such, but you said you were descended from these watchers. What were they? Angels?"

"Not angels," Deke assured me. "If demons are evil and angels are good, then watchers were neutral. They simply watched and reported the events. They were supernatural history keepers, basically. They had some ritual-based magic - which is why we do

- that kept them safe and protected the overall health of the world. They were here to protect the future, not the present."

"But you're still abominations," I reminded him. "You're still part supernatural somethings. You have magic, you can do things, and you have those tattoos on your arms that aren't just ink."

"Right?" Deke said, clearly not sure where I was going with this.

"So what happens if the Horsemen get out? Are you immune to them?"

"Shit," Tash breathed. "I don't actually know. The stories just say that all humans and all abominations will be destroyed by them. They will cleanse the Earth, resetting it so the gods can start over."

"But there are no gods left," Deke reminded her. "They were all killed too."

"Wait," Gavin said, lifting both hands to stop us from continuing. "Gods can die?"

"Pagan gods," Deke clarified. "Zeus, Ra, Thor, and the like. They're the only gods we know of - well, those types - and they're definitely gone."

Bax looked over at me. "But Jess is right. None of this adds up. Why are we so weak? Why do the histories all stop about a hundred and fifty to two hundred years ago? Why are the seals cracking so often, and the ritual seems to be fucked up? Why, guys? Because once we figure that out, I have a feeling that everything else will make a lot more sense."

CHAPTER THIRTY-EIGHT

FOR THE NEXT FEW DAYS, we just went on with our routine. With the weather getting nicer, Deke had us out at the berm in the back more often, working on our target practice. Mostly, it was with the frisbees. He'd throw them, call a name, and we had to hit the target. Thankfully, we were hitting more than missing now.

But there was no point in doing the drills in the mansion anymore. We knew it like the backs of our hands - or the scars on them. Our defense training was turning out to be more weight lifting and using the punching bag. It was almost like we'd graduated from being baby Brethren into something a little better. Something Deke seemed to think could hold our own.

Unfortunately, we had one more week with Mr. Garcia in class. He made a big production on Wednesday - which was probably when he got the news - that he'd be out for the rest of the semester because of a personal emergency. The substitute would be responsible for our year-end grades, so he couldn't tell us how finals would be handled. That was ok, though. It gave me an excuse to actually start speaking Spanish to Gavin.

In truth, I was very bad at it. When we practiced in the

evenings, my accent made him grin or laugh, even as he tried to fight it. Still, I was getting ahead, and that was useful. At one point, Lars mentioned that we should all learn Cherokee too, since it was one of the hardest languages to crack, not something most people knew, and would work pretty damned well for code. He had a point, but not now. Not until I at least had my high school diploma, since I wasn't going to college.

Even worse, Linda and Tash weren't having any luck with hints about our other powers. The pair were making a stack of anything that might possibly be useful, and Linda had moved to mythologies and folklore because there was no reason not to. Sadly, without any extra skills, all we had to go on was our training and experience. The next hit would need to be done just like the last, and we really couldn't put it off.

The crack in the seal was getting worse. The basement of the mansion was getting crowded with shadow demons, and something had to change. Thursday, I was thinking about that when I just happened to pass Travis in the halls. I was about to turn and follow him when he beat me to it. Falling in at my side, he leaned in and lowered his voice.

"There's a guy in the office this morning who creeps me out. One of yours?" he asked.

"No," I said, "but I was going to tell you to put a rush on the kids. It's getting full."

"Seal's splitting," Travis said. "Yeah. That's not good, Jess. You don't want what's inside to get out."

"Yeah, I know," I hissed, keeping my voice down so the people around us wouldn't hear.

"Good." He paused like he was going to turn back, then pulled me against the wall. "So, you don't know who's in the office?"

"Maybe the sub for Mr. Garcia?" I asked. "Linda got her settlement."

"No, I think it's..." Travis said before looking up quickly. "Hey, baby!"

I turned to see Shannon headed toward us. "Hey," I said, waving her over. "Do you know if the guy in the office is the new Spanish sub?"

Her brow furrowed and at least three different versions of confusion crossed her face. "There's a guy in the office?" she finally asked.

"Linda got her settlement," I explained. "Travis saw someone. I guess I'll know in third." Then I looked at Travis. "Thanks for letting me know."

"Just keep your head down," he told me. "I gotta get to class, but that guy looks creepy, and we all know Mr. Garcia didn't like you."

The look in his eye made me think it was more than that, but he gave Shannon a kiss and then turned back around. She just groaned and flopped against the locker beside me. Seeing that she wasn't going anywhere, I parked my body beside her.

"You ok?" I asked.

"Yes. No." She groaned again. "Fuck, I dunno, Jess. He's making me insane. I mean, when we're together, he's so amazing, but it's like he's always distracted with something, and I can't figure out if he's trying to blow me off, give me a hint, or has a side piece."

"He does not have a side piece," I assured her. "At least not one that we know about. Mostly, he's just being a stupid guy."

So she turned to face me. "Is that really all it is? Because when I ask him what's going on, he avoids it. Like, he tells me not to worry, that it's no big deal, he's just talking to his friends, or that I'm making too much of it."

"Idiot," I grumbled. "No, Shannon, I asked the guys if there was a problem, and all three of mine seemed confused that I would even think such a thing. They don't get it. Guys are all about what's right in front of them, you know?"

"But I kinda want more than that," Shannon said. "Fuck, I'm going out of state for college in a few months so I shouldn't worry about it, but I'd kinda hoped..." She let the thought trail off.

"What?" I asked.

"He said he wanted to go to school with me," she admitted. "I know, young love never works, we'll break up before the end of our first semester, and all that. Yeah, my parents already gave me the lecture, but I really like him, Jess. I can't even explain why. He's just not like other guys, and he's so excited for me to be a vet. He wants to have kids!"

"Ok, that's cute," I admitted. "So what's the problem?"

She scrunched up her face as she looked at me. "Don't take this wrong, ok? But every time he talks to you four, he cuts me out. You know how when a guy is trying to keep a secret and his story just doesn't add up? Like, things change, he can't explain the huge holes in logic, and that sort of thing? Yeah, that's how he is every time he hangs out with you four. Lunch, after school, or whatever. I don't suppose you want to tell me what this big secret is, do you?"

"I know he's told me that you miss us," I lied. "I mean, you've been so cool, and I feel like a shitty chick friend, but I have three boyfriends, and that's kinda a lot to juggle." I paused. "Ok, that's a lie. I kinda got boyfriend number four, he's older, and yeah. Um, there was a bit of an issue there."

"Who is number four?" she asked.

"Deke. Red-and-blonde-haired guy living with Bax."

Her mouth flopped open. "All in the same house? How the fuck does that work?"

I grinned. "Often, very well. Sometimes, not so much. Um, Gavin wasn't cool at first, and Travis kinda offered him some advice."

"Ok, that's sweet," she admitted. "He told me that Gavin and Bax were his only real friends. The rest of the guys are just someone to hang out with, so yeah, that makes a lot more sense. Thanks, Jess. I really like this guy, and I just don't want him to break my heart."

"Me either," I told her. "The two of you are so cute."

She smiled at me, then jerked her thumb over her shoulder. "Hey, I'm going to be late."

ENTER SANDMAN

"Me too, but friends are worth it," I promised, lifting my hand in a wave before heading the other way.

Hopefully, that would help out Travis a bit. I owed him for the warning, after all, even though I wasn't sure what exactly Travis had been trying to warn me about until third period. I walked in to find Mr. Garcia sitting at the front of the classroom, which meant he was still teaching our class. Of course he was. The man had until next week, and I had a feeling he was going to milk every day he could. Asshole. So who was the creepy guy Travis was worried about?

I'd barely sat down before Gavin tossed his notebook on my desk. This time, the message on it wasn't in Spanish. It was clear and perfect English, but it sent chills down my spine: *There's a Martyr here. Do not let him see you.*

I tossed it back with a nod, but before I could say something, Mr. Garcia started class. Once, I tried to whisper something, but the man stopped and turned to glare at me. Lifting my hands in surrender, I just got back to staring at him blankly, because his version of Spanish wasn't going to help me speak to Gavin at all.

The moment the bell rang, though, I turned to Gavin. "What the hell?" I asked.

"Lars saw him in the halls," Gavin explained, knowing exactly what I was talking about. "The guy reached for something and Lars saw the eye symbol of a Watcher. They're here, Jess, and if they see you..."

"They shouldn't be able to tell," I reminded him. "Deke couldn't. He said he couldn't sense a demon until he matched with his quad."

"But what do their tattoos do?" Gavin asked. "We know Deke's is a doomsday clock. I get the impression that all of them are magical somehow. What if his *can* identify cambion? What if it's like our necklaces? Just... Stay away from him, Jess."

I nodded. "If I knew who he was, it would be easier."

We barely made it to our locker when Bax and Lars joined us. That was not the usual plan, but before I could ask, Bax flopped his sexy self next to my locker, bracing on his arm and smiled. Lars pulled out a candy bar and waved it like he was trying to tempt me.

"So," Bax said, "how do we feel about lunch outside today?"

"Why?" I asked.

"Because there's a Martyr in the cafeteria, looking intently at all the students," Lars said. "So..." He used the candy bar to point toward the front door.

I shoved the last of my things into the locker and closed it. "Has he seen any of you? I mean, what the hell is a Watcher doing here?"

"My guess is that he's either looking for us," Bax said, taking my arm to steer me toward the front doors, "or he's looking for demons, or he heard about Oliver flying through the air and Mr. Garcia spilling his guts. No clue, but the only people my necklace identifies are you and Travis. We don't know what Watchers can do, so how about we don't tempt fate, hm?'

"I am all for a little sunshine," I assured him. "They've started cranking down the air conditioning to 'ice cold' lately, and I need to thaw."

We headed to the same table we used in the mornings before school. There, Lars emptied pockets full of the same chips and junk food that we usually existed on. I grabbed one of the candy bars, needing a little sugar to hype me up through the end of the day. I survived on a caffeine rush in the mornings and a sugar rush for the end of the day. Probably not the best for my figure, but I had a feeling that hunting demons made it a moot point.

I unwrapped it, took a bite, and then looked up to say something to Bax, but paused. Over his shoulder, I could see a car slowly making its way through the parking lot. It was white, and the rental sticker on the back was hard to miss. The side windows were angled just right to catch the glare, so I couldn't see inside, but I was pretty sure I'd seen that car before.

"Guys?" I asked. "Tell me that's a drug sweep and not something worse?"

Lars looked first, since he was sitting on the same side as me.

ENTER SANDMAN

Shaking his head, he got up and moved around the table, positioning himself like he was talking to Bax and Gavin so they could both turn. I was actually a little impressed with how smooth they played it. It was almost like we'd learned a thing or two.

"That's not a drug sweep," Bax assured us. "I'm pretty sure that's the same car the freak from the Slice was in too."

"And I'm sure I've seen it in the parking lot before. At the back. I assumed it was a parent or something."

"Shit," Gavin grumbled. "How long have they been in town?"

"What are they looking for?" I added.

"They can't know about you," Lars assured me. "They probably are just wondering why the seal's been open so long. I mean, if they knew, then they'd be doing more, right? Besides, did Deke even tell them he found you?"

I pulled out my phone. "Let's ask."

> **Jess:** So, seems we have Martyrs at school. One is driving around the parking lot. Another is in the building, hanging out in the cafeteria.

> **Deke:** When the parking lot is clear, bail. Get home. Tell your demon friend to do the same. You see the tattoo?

"What's the tattoo, guys?" I asked.

"Triangle with an eye in it," Lars said. "Kinda looks like the symbol on the back of a dollar."

So I sent that to Deke.

> **Deke:** Do not make a scene. Do not get noticed. Bail as soon as you can and come HERE. They can spot you.

Tossing my phone on the table, I repeated that for all of them, but my entire body felt like it had gone still. I was calm - much too calm. The kind of calm that always came when the worst things happened.

"Shit," Bax breathed, grabbing his own phone to send off a text. "Yeah, if he can tell what Travis is, this is very bad. He needs to get out before - " He paused as his phone dinged with a reply, and then let out a sigh of relief. "He and Shannon are at the back of the building. Same idea. I told him to find an excuse to bail as soon as possible."

"So how do we get Jess out?" Gavin asked.

Lars chuckled. "Give me the keys, Bax. Anyone have anything inside they can't live without?"

"My bag," I said. "It's got my ID and stuff in there."

"I got that," Gavin said, hopping up. "Bax, you stay with her. You can keep them from getting her."

Bax nodded as Gavin hurried back into the building. "What are you doing, Lars?" he asked.

"I'm going to go get the SUV," Lars said. "Once I'm in it, I'm going to drive right up to the curb there, and we're just going to leave like it's normal."

"And how are you getting to the car?" I asked. "Lars, what if they can sense what you are too?"

"They probably can," he admitted. "I have a feeling Watchers are designed for this. So, I don't intend to be seen. Seems my dad taught me a few good tricks after all."

The moment Gavin was back with my bag - which had no books in it - Lars took off. He walked calmly but with a purpose across the school lawn in the opposite direction of the car. That kept plenty of parked cars between them. When it turned to go another row back, Lars jogged across the street and ducked between a pair of parked cars.

"Don't watch," Gavin warned. "That'll give him away."

"And I'm waiting to hear my SUV," Bax promised. "Soon as it starts, we're walking toward the street, and we're piling in. Jess gets the passenger seat this time, Gav. If he has to take off before we're all in, I want her to be in it."

"Deal," Gavin said. "I'll go last."

"You'll go in the back first," Bax countered. "I have the right hand for this." Then he smiled. "Time to go."

Together, the three of us got up and began to meander toward the street, right where the exit was. Lars pulled the SUV out of the lot, then backed up, somehow managing to stay on the exact opposite side of the parked cars from the rental. The moment he stopped, we piled in like we'd just finished a hit, and Lars had the truck moving before our seatbelts were on.

"Did you warn Travis about the guy in the lot or just the one in school?" Lars asked Bax.

"Both," Bax said. "The bigger question is why now? Why are they at our school, and what the fuck are they looking for?"

"Don't care so long as they can't get Jess," Gavin said.

"Same," Lars agreed. "And we will burn the world down if they try to come for her."

I just curled my feet under me and hoped that wouldn't happen. I also hoped Travis got out without a problem. Damn. I should've known this had been too easy for too long.

CHAPTER THIRTY-NINE

When we pulled up at the barn, Linda was lying out on the grass, wearing a bikini and reading a very big book. Like that, her round baby belly was *very* obvious, and starting to turn a little pink, but the sound of the truck made her look up. Seeing us, she sat up quickly and grabbed a shirt from the ground beside her, pulling it on in a panic.

"What are you doing, Mom?" Lars asked as he got out.

"Cooking your sister," she snapped. "Why aren't the four of you in school?"

Which was when Deke came thundering down the stairs. "Any trouble?" he asked us.

"Not that we know of," Bax assured him.

Linda was now on her feet, and Tash came out of the garage. Both of them looked worried, so I quickly gave a recap of the day's events, starting with the warning from Travis and ending with our plan to get out of there. When I was done, Tash blew out a heavy breath, shaking her head.

"They're looking for them," she told Deke.

"Which them?" I asked. "Us, the demons, or someone else?"

"We're doing this inside," Linda declared. "All of you, up." She pointed to make it clear she was serious. "I'm going to get real clothes so I'm not half naked in front of the kids, which means you four have time to eat something."

"We had some candy and chips at lunch," I assured her.

She just sighed. "That is *not* a meal. Don't know why you kids think you can survive on junk food, but you can't. Sandwiches. Now."

The four of us headed for the stairs. Linda and Tash went for the elevator. When we got inside, I headed to change, but Lars and Gavin said they'd make lunch. By the time I was wearing something more lounge-like, the food was made and we headed to the table out of habit. Linda and Tash were already there.

"Let's start with one thing," Deke said. "Your hands do not work on Martyrs." He looked at Bax pointedly. "You should know that."

"I thought it was just our Martyr," Bax said.

Deke pointed to Tash. "What about her? She's touched all of your hands."

"Yeah, but Jess did the fear thing and I did the call thing, and it worked on her. Isn't this the same?"

"Not that we know of," Tash told him. "The theory is that we're immune to the Brethren because we're unactivated Brethren ourselves. It would also be pretty hard to verify what you are if you can just bespell us like that."

"Point," Lars said. "So, how do we fight off Martyrs, then?"

"Bad idea," Deke told him. "First, they can get almost anywhere they need to be. It isn't hard to forge the right documents to convince people we're part of a government agency or something. The Health Department is always a good one, but not the only one. That means no place is safe. Avoid them if you can, but if you can't? The best way to fight them off is to use Jess's magic, and that's letting the cat out of the bag. The other option is to shoot them, but they won't dissolve. That's murder. Guys, there's no good option here."

"Do they know about me?" I asked. "And if so, then what do they know?"

Deke blew out a heavy breath. "I notified them when I found each of you, mostly. For you, Jess, I sent an email saying that I thought I'd found my fourth, a girl, but needed to verify it was a real fit. I never responded after that."

"At all?" Tash asked.

Deke shook his head. "Still, three guys and a girl? That's going to make them want to check her. The only thing we have going for us is that they don't know which girl she is. I sent the message the day before Ted tried to break in. After that, I knew that a check would cause problems. They've been trying to contact me, sending texts saying the seal is still open, asking for an update, and so on. I didn't want to say anything until it was closed, because we both know how this is going to go down."

"They'll want to reset the quad," Tash muttered. "They don't know I'm still here. Before I left, I mentioned that I was coming down to see if I could help with your quad. That got me out of my other duties, but I haven't heard anything since. Clearly, they've decided to check up on what we're doing."

"But we're doing what they want!" Linda insisted. "The kids are taking out demons so they can close the seal."

"The Order is a bureaucracy," Tash explained. "That means the guys at the top look at us like nothing more than numbers. They want results, and we aren't giving them. Linda, they don't care if we die. Not the kids, not Deke and me, and certainly not you."

"So we need to avoid them," Gavin said. "That means we need to know how the tattoos work."

Deke and Tash shared one of their looks, then Deke pushed up his sleeve. "Mine shows how close we are to the tipping point. When the sand is all in the bottom, the Horsemen are released. It's a way for me to know how long we can wait."

But the sand was mostly gone. There was a small amount still in the neck, and just enough in the top half of the hourglass to count, but not much. This was why we had to hurry. If all the Guides had a tattoo like that...

"Will everyone's show the same thing?" I asked.

Deke nodded. "Yep. It's the integrity of the thirteenth seal. I have a feeling that ours isn't the only one that's failing, which is why the sand is so low. I can't do anything about the others, and I think you four actually have the power to fight off the Horsemen, so I'd rather not take stupid risks."

"But we still need to get the seal closed!" I insisted.

Gavin reached over for my hand. "We will. I also won't let you die because they come after you. Any of them."

"We won't either," Linda said. "Now, what about the rest of the Order's tattoos? Tash's is different."

"You have one?" I asked Tash.

She turned her left arm over, showing a book tattooed in the middle of her forearm. I'd seen it before, but it didn't look like something magical. It just looked like the kind of thing a book lover would get, so I'd never thought much of it.

"They're designed to not stand out," she explained. "Hunters have a compass with an arrow as the needle. It points to any abomination in the area, which is why they can track so well. Watchers, as you've seen, have the eye in a triangle. That will point to any supernatural creature. Martyrs, Brethren, demons, and all the way up to angels. The focus of the eye shifts to point it out."

"Which means they wouldn't be able to tell what you are, Jess," Bax realized.

Tash nodded. "Not without a ritual. They're usually the ones who find us as kids. They also keep track of who is what, and what is where. The Hunters only detect supernaturals, though. That means Martyrs and Brethren won't activate their mark. If one of those Martyrs today was a Hunter and not just a Watcher?"

"Then we have problems," Lars said, nodding to show he understood.

"And that's all?" I asked. "I mean, all the tattoos in the Order?"

Deke lifted his hand and ticked them off on his fingers. "Guides like me, Librarians like Tash, Watchers, Hunters, and Directors. The Directors rarely leave the temple, though. They're the ones who make the decisions, and are at the top of the bureaucracy. Their mark is a yellow - called gold - segmented ring. Each segment represents a specific seal, one through thirteen. When a seal cracks, that segment turns black."

"So what does yours do?" I asked.

Tash turned her arm so we could all see, and laid it across the table. "The ink is black when not in use, and a lot of them are like this. When I activate it, I get a glimpse of something I've read before." Tensing her arm, the dark ink began to change, turning from black to maroon, and then into a wine color that quickly brightened to pink.

"Can you feel that?" I asked, reaching out to trace the lines.

But the moment my finger touched her skin, I felt something almost like a zap, but the wrong way around. It was the same surprising sensation as touching the end of a vacuum hose, like a quick and intense sucking. Tash and I both flinched, then looked at each other.

"Ok, no touching," I said, pulling my arm back.

"I don't know if anyone but another Martyr has touched it when activated," she admitted. "That was strange."

"What was?" Lars asked.

"It reverse-zapped me," I said.

"I got a push," Tash said. "Like a rush of something." Then she waved that off. "The tattoos are all magical, made from a specific ritual. The ink is the special part, not the actual tattoo. For mine, all I have to do is want to know something and..." She closed her eyes in a slow blink.

Then her mouth parted and her eyes began to twitch behind her lids. Tash's breath caught, but she didn't move. If this was an example of her showing us how it worked, it was pretty fucking creepy, and yet when it went on too long, Deke stood, leaning over the table to take her hand.

"Tash?" he asked.

She didn't answer, so he pressed his hand over her tattoo. "Tash!"

"I have something," she breathed. "Deke, I'm reading the ritual for making the inks. How am I reading the ritual for making inks?"

"What?" Gavin asked, looking at me as if I'd somehow be able to make that make sense.

All I could do was shake my head, but the rest of us were starting to get worried. We traded looks, turned back to Deke, and still Tash was doing the eye-twitch thing. Linda lifted a hand to her lips as if she knew something had just gone very, very wrong, but we had no clue how to fix it.

Then, just as quickly as she'd started that, Tash stopped and opened her eyes. "I've never read that book," she breathed, looking over to Deke as if he could help her. "It's supposed to only show me what I've read before."

"What book was it?" he asked.

"Deke, only the Directors know those rituals. They don't train us on anything but the seals and our own section of the Order. Of all the things I could've read, the ink is the most restricted!"

"What. Book. Was. It?" he asked slowly, holding her eyes.

"Rituals of the Watchers, volume three," she breathed. "Located in the sacred texts of the temple."

"In the restricted wing," Deke said, nodding to show he understood. "What question did you ask?"

"I didn't," she admitted. "We were just talking about the tattoos, and it hit me."

"The ink of the tattoos," I clarified. "You'd just said that it was the ink, not the tattoo process that mattered, and then you kinda went away."

"To read," Deke explained. "It's supposedly like the memory of a page, but she can read every word."

"Not every one," Tash clarified. "Just the part that pertains to what I'm asking about. Think of it like a card catalogue for everything we've learned. No need to worry about memorizing it all, because we have magical recall. Except it's never worked like that before. It's never recalled a book I haven't read!"

"But one that's in the temple," Linda said. "Could that be it? Maybe there's something about the magic..." She paused, her gaze losing focus for a moment before snapping back. "The kids," she said. "Their hands have different levels of power. Could your mark be the same?"

"Is that the hidden powers?" I asked.

Tash could only shake her head. "Jess, I have no idea. I've never heard of anything like this, and I don't know why it would've happened now."

"Because I'm an abomination?" I asked. "I mean, it has to do with that zap, right? We both felt it!"

"Are you hurt?" Deke immediately asked, looking at me.

"No," I assured him. "The zap didn't hurt. It just startled me."

"Same," Tash agreed. "It was like someone pushed a feather under my skin - that kind of a tickle feeling. Nothing painful, but it was inside, not outside."

"Sounds like we have a lot more to research," Linda said. "And you're both fine, right?"

"Perfectly," I promised.

"Confused, but fine," Tash said. "Very confused, because I actually remember that ritual. It's almost like it was downloaded into my brain."

Bax just tapped at the table, his finger drumming out a beat. "Guys? Maybe it's just me, but isn't that proof that the Order is hiding something from all of us?"

"Maybe," Deke admitted, "and yet it has nothing to do with the Martyrs at your school, and how we're going to deal with them."

"We're going to ask Shannon," I decided. "She'll know if they're still there."

"Immigration," Gavin suggested. "Tell her we think they're here to find me because my visa's expired. It's not, but she'll check for us."

I nodded. "Yeah, she will. I just hate using her like this."

"We'll make it up to her," Bax promised. "No idea how, but we will."

CHAPTER FORTY

THE NEXT MORNING, I sent a text to Shannon. I had to get her number from Bax, but she seemed happy to hear from me. Then I asked her if she'd check to see if the weird guys at school were still there or if it was safe for Gavin to show up. That made her ask why, so I lied my ass off, telling her how his immigration was in limbo, so he was scared they were here for him.

She came back with questions about why Travis had left. The problem was that our weak excuse hadn't accounted for that. I did the best I could, telling her that I knew he'd checked up on Gav last night, but I hadn't realized he'd left. Then I quickly texted Travis so he'd have a heads-up, and told him to delete it so he didn't get busted. He sent back a thumbs-up emoji.

We were stopped at the gas station near the school when Shannon messaged with the all clear. I hadn't honestly expected the Martyrs to be at our school for two days in a row, but none of us wanted to risk it. They *would* do something to me if they realized I wasn't just a normal Brethren. Even worse, our quad didn't make sense because it was supposed to be all men or all women. If they decided to reset us, there was no way we'd be able to fight off both Martyrs and demons at the same time.

But Shannon was right, and for the most part, the school day was boring. The only exception was Shannon chewing out Travis in the halls. I didn't get to hear what she was saying, but from the expression on her face, she wasn't happy. From the look on Travis's, he was doing everything in his power to get out of shit.

I felt bad for them. I really did, and yet it also made me realize why my thing with these guys worked so well. Bax never could've dated a normal girl. First, it wasn't in his nature. Second, the moment she started getting nosey, he'd have to cut her out. Gavin wasn't pushy enough to even try, and I just couldn't imagine Lars with anyone but me. Deke was different.

He didn't go to school or have a regular job, which meant he wasn't spending all day with his girlfriend or boyfriend. That made it easier to leave out what he didn't want them to know. I had a feeling he was also a one-night stand kinda guy. He just seemed the type. He wanted someone to care about him, but he didn't dare give anyone the chance unless they were also in the middle of this - like me.

On the ride home, I asked the guys if there was anything we could do to help Travis with his love life. They laughed. Evidently, that wasn't a thing guys did for each other. Their buddy would either make it work or crash on his own. When I pointed out that they'd been helping each other, the rest of the ride home got very quiet, as if they'd never actually thought about that before.

But Gavin had the answer. "It's our bonds," he said as Bax made his way up the drive. "It's why we can do this. I mean, who shares his girlfriend?"

"I totally would," Bax joked, flashing me a smile in the mirror. "The whole spit roasting thing is a little too much fun."

"What?" Gavin asked.

"His dick in her mouth," Lars explained, "while I fuck her. Could work the other way around. It's like watching porn while getting fucked. Just works. I mean, unless you're too worried about being gay."

"Fuck off," Gavin grumbled as the SUV came to a stop. "Takes balls to be gay. Besides, I'm too manly for Deke."

Then, flashing a devious little smile at the guys, he opened his door and stepped out. I couldn't help but laugh, and more when I saw both Bax and Lars staring after him in shock. Clearly, none of us had expected that, but it made me love Gavin a little more. He'd learned, and he'd made a complete one-eighty to his previous opinion.

"Hey, Gav," I called as I jogged to catch up with him. "You meant that?"

He wrapped his arm around me as we headed up the stairs, Lars and Bax lagging behind while they got their stuff together. "Yeah," he admitted, "I do. I told you I was trying. I think the bonds make it easier. Deke is one of us, and we're all in. There's no holding back, which is why this works." He paused to face me at the top of the stairs. "I love you more than I'm scared of being gay. That's why we help each other. Jess, this makes you happy, and you need all of us. We all need you. If I think about it too much, I get myself confused and try to say something like my dad would. If I stop thinking, all I know is that I love you."

I threw my arms around his neck and hugged him as hard as I could. "Thanks, Gav. I know I'm being selfish, but - "

"So am I," he promised, leaning back to kiss me just as the guys reached us.

"Oh, now that's hot," Bax said, snuggling in behind me. "I would love to see you sucking his dick instead of his tongue, Jess. Just bend you over a little and..." He bent to kiss my neck and grind his hips against my ass while Gavin plundered my mouth.

"And now I'm hard," Lars grumbled. "Cool it down, you three. We still have training, and I'm sure I'll be spending the night in my own room tonight. You can test out the threesome with Gav later. Work first, Brethren."

"No fun," Bax grumbled as his lips moved to my shoulder.

But Gavin's lips curled into a smile, ruining our kiss. He pulled away to look into my eyes. "I'm not scared anymore, Jess. We only live once, right?"

"Yeah," I agreed, swatting Bax away from my ass. "Work, you perv!"

With a laugh, Bax steered me inside, pushing me right past Gavin. He followed, closing the door behind us, but the first floor was completely quiet. It had been a while since that had happened, but the weather was amazing, which meant everyone was probably downstairs.

We all headed to our rooms to change into workout clothes. I never knew what Deke would have us working on next, but training had gone from an all-afternoon thing to a few hours, so I wasn't about to complain. When I was wearing a pair of leggings, a sports bra with a complementary tank, and my hair was in a ponytail, I headed for the elevator.

Lars was already there, leaning against the wall. Once I passed his door, Gavin stepped out. He yelled at Bax, who told us to wait up, so when the car arrived, Lars opened it but didn't get in. Thankfully, Bax didn't take too long. Two minutes later, the four of us were headed down as a group.

We stepped off to find both Tash and Linda crowded around Deke. He sat on the old computer chair that was usually pushed up to the work bench. They were all looking at his arm, and Deke was focusing hard. Linda was holding some old book. The cover was made of soft leather and it had a cord that was meant to hold it closed, but right now, that cord was dangling down between Linda's fingers.

"Kinky," Bax said, making all three of them look.

Then Deke groaned. "Fuck, and just when I thought I was feeling something."

"A tingling in your loins?" Lars joked. "Seriously, that's supposed to be for Jess."

"We are not making sex jokes in front of our mom," I groaned.

Linda just chuckled. "If your loins are tingling, Deke, then you should consider seeing a doctor for that."

The little snort from Tash was what did me in. She didn't want to laugh, but she also hadn't quite managed to hold it in. The sound came out, and for just a moment, everything paused, then we all just lost it. Still sitting in his chair, Deke just leaned back and shook his head, but there was a silly little smile on his lips.

"Thanks, Tash. Not letting you play with my found family anymore."

"My found family too," she countered. "All started with you, maggot."

Deke flipped her off, then gestured to Linda as our laughter died down. "I think Tash is right. There's nothing there."

"Nothing where?" Gavin asked before I could.

"Linda thinks she's found the hidden abilities, but if so, it's not very hidden," Tash explained. "That's a training manual for all young Martyrs. It's equivalent to a sixth-grade history book. Pretty basic stuff, and not where I'd expect to find secret knowledge."

"But it spells out your abilities, Tash," Linda insisted. "Ok, kids, listen to this. *'The power of the Librarian is the page of the book. When the words are known, they can be read. When unknown, they must be found.'* Doesn't that sound like exactly what happened to Tash last night?"

"Yeah, kinda," I said. "She can recall something she read, so that would be when the words are known. And when they're not, they're found, like the ritual that surprised her, right?"

"That's what I'm thinking," Linda said.

"That's not what it means," Tash insisted. "We were taught that explains why we research. Once we've read something, our mark gives us the power of recall and the awareness of what book it was in. When we haven't read it yet, we have to research like everyone else - to find it."

"But you found the ritual," Bax countered. "May have been accidental, yet you still 'found' it. Tash, what if Linda's right?"

"What does it say about Deke?" Gavin asked.

So Linda quoted, "*The power of the Guide is the mark of the time. When the sand is gone, the chance is lost. When the time is nigh, focus on the grains, for they limit the tools of gods.*" Then she looked up. "The first part sounds like his doomsday clock, right?"

"It does," Lars agreed. "I'm curious what the gods have to do with this, though? I thought they were dead."

"Demons and angels are often called the tools of the gods," Deke explained. "And that's about all I can get out of it. We're taught that it means we're supposed to watch the sand to know when the Horsemen are about to break loose. When the time is nigh, or the sand runs out, is when things are bad, so we should focus on doing something before the sand runs out so the gods' nuclear weapon, their biggest tools, are kept contained behind their seal."

"Well, fuck," Bax grumbled. "Both interpretations kinda work."

"Yeah..." Lars breathed, "but Tash did find the ritual. The book was found. She didn't know she could do that, and we've been so sure that we're missing something. What if Deke has more to his tattoo as well? I mean, why would Librarians be the only ones?" And he lifted his hand to prove his point. "Even ours has a secondary ability. The touch and the area stuff."

"Ok, genius, then how the fuck do I activate it?" Deke asked.

I looked at Tash. "How did you?"

"You touched me," she shot back. "Zap thing, you remember that?"

"Yeah, but I don't think that's it. I mean, that's not the activation, is it? You were fine for a bit after, and then you did something, and that was when it went silly."

Lars looked at Deke. "How do you normally activate yours?"

"It's always active," Deke explained. "It just marks the time. The seal integrity is more true. I can't remember the last time it was all the way full, but when a seal is repaired, the sand moves backwards."

So Lars pointed at Tash. "Then how do you activate yours?"

"I focus," she said. "I reach for the inherent magic of the Order of Martyrs and focus on it. I try to push it into the tattoo."

"Like our hands," Gavin realized. "The same way we make our hands glow."

"Fuck, worth a try," Deke said. "Too bad I have no clue what magic feels like."

CHAPTER FORTY-ONE

I MOVED to squat before Deke, resting a hand on each knee. Without me needing to ask, he turned his arm up and toward me. The sand didn't seem to be moving, but it was still dangerously low. Just seeing that made me feel some anxiety, like we needed to hurry, but I was trying to ignore that.

"So, I didn't know what magic felt like either," I told him. "When we were learning to use our hands, you said to either push or pull with them. So, maybe try that?"

One side of his mouth curled up in a boyish smirk. "Gonna touch it first? You know, for good luck?"

I pressed my palm over his tattoo. "Not the first time, Deke. I also think it only zaps if it's on, so... you gotta get all excited before anything fun happens."

This time, Linda made a noise. It wasn't quite a snort, but she was definitely choking back her laughter as she quickly turned away. Weird, but also cool. Best mom ever, in my opinion. So, with my own lips smiling wide enough to make my cheeks tight, I nodded for Deke to try.

"I'll touch it when it glows, big boy."

"Done," Tash said, throwing her hands into the air to follow Linda. "I cannot be mature and respectable around them."

"Me either!" Linda tittered.

Deke made a production of clearing his throat. "I'm getting performance anxiety now, ladies. Thanks."

Together, the pair scampered to the other side of the shop, behind the dividing wall. That did nothing at all to stop the howls of their laughter. Behind me, Lars just sighed.

"I should've moved in with my mom a long time ago. Had no idea she was this cool," he said, trying to make it sound like a complaint, and failing miserably.

"I think having all the rules turned upside down has that effect on a person." Then Deke looked back at me. "What does magic feel like, Jess?"

"Like fireflies in your chest," I told him. "Little sparks of light, but they don't burn or anything. Like tingles, but not tingly. It's like there's something you have no words for, and it's growing, building, and getting excited."

"Not that kind of excited," Gavin said, resting his hand on my shoulder. "It's like when you like a girl and you have the flips in your stomach, but it's behind your lungs."

"Because that helps," Deke muttered to himself. "Ok, I'm going to feel fireflies and butterflies inside my rib cage. Now, how do I get it inside?"

"I just have it," Gavin said.

"Same," Lars agreed. "When I want to use my hand, I become aware of it, but it's always there."

"More when I'm trying to push the power harder or hold it back," Bax added.

Then they all looked at me. "Uh, yeah, I have to open up and suck it in," I explained. "It's like when you're in a quiet room and you try to consume all the peace around you and just meld with it."

"Melding butterflies and fireflies into my chest," Deke said. "No, this isn't hard at all."

"And you tried to make us think it was easy," Bax said, smacking Deke in the back of the head the same way I'd seen Deke do to them so many times.

"Fucker!" Deke snapped. "I'm already having trouble with this. In case you forgot, I'm supposed to be the Sandman, not the Brethren."

"So why do they call you a Guide?" I asked.

"Different branches of the Order," Deke explained. "It's an internal thing, and since most Brethren never get the chance to worry about it, we just go with Martyrs, because that's what we all are. My duty as a Martyr is to guide the Brethren. Tash's duty as a Martyr is to serve as a Librarian."

"I like Sandman better," I told him. "Makes it feel like you're ours."

He looked down at me, and for a moment, his silver eyes found mine. "I'm your Sandman, the Order's Guide." Then he rubbed the tattoo on his arm. "So let's do this."

We all fell silent as Deke closed his eyes and concentrated. Behind me, I heard something scuff, so I looked back to see Tash and Linda making their way back in now that their giggles were under control. Bax lifted a finger to his lips and Linda nodded, but Tash's eyes were locked on Deke.

For a long time, nothing happened. My knees were starting to protest squatting this long. Gavin rubbed my shoulder, and Lars shifted his feet like he was tired of standing the same way. Still, Deke just sat there, breathing. Long, slow, measured breaths. Just when I was sure nothing at all would happen, the sand began to brighten - almost glowing - and it reversed in the hourglass!

Deciding it was worth the risk, I reached out and pressed my palm over it. There was no zap this time, but I still felt something. It was like a gentle suction holding me to him. Nothing I couldn't break away from, but still there, almost as if his skin had become sticky, but without the sticky feeling.

Deke's eyes opened and I moved my palm. He had just enough time to see the glowing blue sand at the top of the hourglass, and then it faded and poured right back down, looking like a cartoon or animation of some kind. Those of us closest just stared, not quite sure what had happened.

"Do it again," Lars said, "and this time don't stop concentrating on pushing it."

"Did it work?" Tash asked.

"The sand jumped to the top," Deke told her. "It was just a second, but we all saw it."

"And did she zap you?" Tash asked.

Deke looked at me. "There was something, but I wouldn't describe it as a zap."

"No, it was different," I told Tash. "Like there was a pull, but a gentle one."

"And I'm sure you've touched him a lot more than me," she pointed out. "Probably even on his mark. Deke, try it again."

Linda moved closer so she could see. This time, it didn't take nearly as long - but that didn't mean it was fast. He closed his eyes and focused, breathing slowly for almost a full minute before it started happening. Tash lightly touched his arm and Deke's eyes opened, locked on his tattoo.

The sand was flowing upwards again. Deke kept breathing slowly, focusing on it. When it was all at the top, the grains once again began to fall, but this time it was slow. Piece by piece, not a torrent of sand, the grains dropped into the bottom. Deke looked at Tash and the flow began to move faster. I sucked in a breath, he looked back to his arm, and it slowed down again.

Until he just gave up and it all went crashing back to the bottom. "Well, that's great and all," Deke said, "but what good is it? I can manipulate the appearance of my tattoo."

ENTER SANDMAN

"The tools of gods," Linda reminded him.

"Uh..." Lars cleared his throat. "When he did that, did anyone else feel something?"

"No?" I said, unsure if that was the right answer.

"Do it again," Gavin suggested.

"Because why not, right?" Deke asked.

This time, it was faster, but the four of us were concentrating on every sensation. The sand moved up, the grains dropped down so very slowly, and I began to see what Lars meant. My knees weren't aching. I wasn't as stressed. It wasn't a big change, but it was as if someone had lightened my mental load, physical one, or something.

"It's like a buff," Bax said, referencing their games again. "A power-up of sorts. Like, I've had this ache in my neck all day, nothing bad, and it's gone."

"I feel stronger," Lars said.

"More focused," Gavin offered.

"Little things," I told them. "Just like a feeling as if this is easier. I thought it was the squatting, but it's more than that."

Deke blew out his breath, released his focus, and pulled me up by my elbow. "Shit, Jess. Then stop kneeling."

"No, it wasn't a big deal," I explained, "but my knees were starting to say it was time to stand up again. I didn't want to break your concentration, and it didn't really hurt, so I figured I'd wait. When you did that, my knees were fine, like I'd just squatted down instead of sitting like that for a while."

"A buff," Bax said again. "A little power boost of some kind."

"How do we test it?" Gavin asked.

"Travis?" Tash suggested.

If looks could kill, the one I gave her would've made her explode into a million pieces. "He's not the enemy."

"He's also a demon, Jess. I'd say you, but it seems you get the benefit. You four don't have to do anything to him, but if Deke tries while he's around, then maybe we can get an idea of what it does?"

"No," Deke said. "Jess is right, and the boy's been helping. Tash, what if it breaks his bones, or suffocates him, or destroys his human skin? None of that is fair to him. I think we should just wait."

"For what?" Linda asked. "For the kids to die trying to hunt demons one by one?"

But her words made Deke sit a little straighter. "No, but that's it. For the next hit. If I'm in the car, I can try it. It won't matter if I'm distracted for a moment if I can hear them. If it does nothing, then no problem. If it does something, then they'll know, right? So, at least we'll get some idea of a range, if nothing else."

"And if being in the car is too far away?" I asked. "You told us that our hands have limits, even the area stuff. What if the same is true for this?"

"Then we've learned something," Tash said, "and we can come up with another test. When's the next hit?"

"Monday night, Tuesday morning," Deke told her. "One in the morning seems to be a good time, and they don't know when we're coming. So long as we change the day of the week and keep picking random targets, then we should be fine."

"Our luck isn't going to hold," I told them. "We need to look at how many we need to kill so we can fix the seal." And I tipped my head at Deke's tattoo to make my point. "It looks like time is the one thing we don't have."

"Better safe than sorry," Deke told me. "These three guys are right, and I don't care what the Order says. I'm not going to get this quad killed when the rest of the seals are falling apart. It's not just you. It's the whole fucking world, Jess."

"It's the rituals," Lars said softly. "A hundred and fifty years ago, the histories were lost. How long ago did the seals start having problems?"

"It's speeding up," Tash admitted. "A hundred years ago, they cracked about once a decade. Fifty years ago, it was half that. Now, it's almost annually."

"The Pit is overcrowded," I pointed out. "Maybe it's not the ritual alone. Maybe it's all of it. The Pit is about to burst at the seams, the ritual is close but not quite right - or the watcher blood in the Martyrs has been diluted too much?" I looked at Tash to see if there was any merit to that.

She just lifted both hands palm up. "No idea. We know that witches don't have that problem. They've been breeding with humans for thousands of years and each witch is born with the same amount of power. It's based on the person, their will, and their training, not the purity of their bloodline. One witch parent or two doesn't matter."

"Well," Deke said, "it matters to what magical abilities they get, since that descends through the bloodlines, but that's it."

"Right," I said, filing that away because it wasn't important. "So, probably not a weakening of the blood thing."

"We don't know," Tash reminded me. "Because that's not true for nephilim. Angel to human is strong. Nephilim to human has some power. Breed to a human again, and they get parlor tricks, as you call them. Enough generations away, and they no longer read as nephilim to us, even if we know what they are."

I just nodded. "So, a million options, no answers, and the best we can do is try to learn the hard way. Sounds like something I'm good at."

Deke just flicked his hand at the weights and punching bag in this section of the shop. "Go work out, you four. I don't feel like loading up and heading to the shooting range, and so long as your muscles are in shape, I think you know what we have to do. We'll call it an easy weekend."

"I'll finalize the plans," Tash promised, turning for the elevator.

"And I'll keep reading," Linda said, following her. "Three demons down, kids."

"Six more to go," Gavin mumbled.

"At least," Bax said. "There has to be a better fucking way. There *has* to be."

"And we'll find it," I decided. "One way or another, we are going to be the quad that's different, and fuck it if the Order doesn't like it."

CHAPTER FORTY-TWO

HAVING school the day of the hit made the time pass a little faster. Travis avoided us all day on Monday, spending his time with Shannon instead, but that was fine. We had what we needed, and there was no reason for him to know when we were making our next attack. Still, the last two classes of the day seemed to drag on, and I felt like I couldn't focus.

Eventually we made it home, and the guys were no better than me. The big question was how this would go down. Would it be fast and easy like Greg? Would they beg like the Whites had? Would something go wrong this time to make up for the first two? There was no way to know, but we wanted to be ready.

Deke suggested we nap to pass the time, but none of us wanted to lock ourselves in our rooms alone, so we all piled into Bax's bed. Well, the four of us. Deke was busy finalizing the last-minute things like gassing up the truck and checking the guns one more time. I ended up snuggled up against Lars' chest, with Gavin pressed against my back, and Bax holding my hand against Lars' ribs. And we actually slept. That would make school the next day a little less painful, but being woken up at ten p.m. was a bit weird.

By one, we were all ready and heading out. The target this time was a guy in his thirties named Daniel Cunningham. It seemed that demons took nice, boring names to blend in. Most of them wore the skin of white men or women, and they came in all ages, supposedly. Daniel drove a truck for deliveries, worked the day shift, and had been the demon on the rocks who'd tried to grab Deke. He was going to pay for that tonight.

Unlike the previous two hits, this demon lived on a small plot of land. Deke said it was just under five acres. There was a wood-sided farmhouse, a metal building that was supposed to be a shop, and a deteriorating barn that looked like it hadn't been used in decades. The distance from any neighbors would be nice, except for one little problem: we couldn't just drive onto the property without giving ourselves away.

Thankfully, the house was on the front side of the property, leaving the back for livestock. Even better, the lot next door was undeveloped, which meant there was no driveway, but also no one to complain when Deke shifted his truck into four-wheel drive and drove through the shallow ditch and onto the raw land. Then, just to be extra careful, he parked it behind a stand of trees, including a bunch of brambles and a few evergreens.

From there, we just had to cross a barbed-wire fence and go straight across the property, but I'd grown up in the country. I knew that was easier said than done. Thankfully, Deke had planned for that too.

"Hold up," he said, his voice carrying through our earbuds. "We're going to cut the fence so it looks like it broke from age. While the four of you are in there, I'll put a few more breaks in the fence so it just looks as neglected as that barn. Be careful approaching the house, check to make sure there are no lights on in the back, and have your guns ready."

"We got this," I assured him.

"And do not get overconfident," Deke chided. "I intend to get laid again, so how about you four help me out with that, hm?"

Bax chuckled. "A man who speaks our language. Ok, ready when you get the fence down, Deke."

He cut the five strands of barbed wire at different places, even between different posts, and then snipped the wires holding them to those posts. When he pulled the strands back, we headed out. Behind us, I could hear the soft rustling of him finishing whatever he had planned, but it didn't carry very far at all.

We moved fast and kept our bodies low to break up the silhouettes. As a group, it was possible that if anyone saw us, they might think we were coyotes or something. Unlikely if they were awake, but possible if they were drowsy, so we bent and ran. The summer grass was quiet, making a whooshing sound under our feet. The weather was too warm for the long-sleeve shirts we were wearing, no matter how thin they were. The adrenaline probably didn't help either.

By the time we reached the side of the house, I felt like my ears were ringing in my attempt to listen to everything. Breathing came over my earbud, but nothing else. We didn't have anything to say, and didn't want to risk being heard, so we said as little as possible. Bax checked the first window we passed, carefully peering into the corner.

"Guest room," he whispered. "Nothing."

So we kept going around. Lars checked the next, which was a bathroom, and also empty. When we got to the back, Gavin looked, finding a laundry room with a closed door. I gestured that we should make a full lap, but Lars lifted his hand and gestured for us to stay before heading that way on his own.

Gavin just grumbled, following a moment later. Bax and I looked at each other, the tension quickly building. When he tipped his head at the back door, I figured he had a point. There was no reason that I couldn't at least start on the locks.

"Unlocking," I breathed, "but waiting." And I pressed my hand to the wood.

"Blinds and curtains in the living room," Lars said. "No visuals."

"Den has a computer on," Gavin said next. "Looks empty."

"Means we're doing this blind," Bax said. "Head back, you two."

"Guns," Deke said, proving he was hanging on our every word.

Bax and I pulled ours, going for the silver ones instead of the black ones that used the blessed ammo. When Lars and Gavin returned, they were both carrying their weapons too. Bax looked at each of us, raising an eyebrow, and we all nodded to show we were ready.

"Entering," Bax whispered.

As quietly as possible, Bax eased the door open. Gavin, me, and then Lars followed, but Bax paused at the next door, the one that led from the laundry room into the rest of the house. Slowly, he turned the knob and cracked the door, peering through the minuscule gap - and we all waited.

Seconds ticked past, and nothing. Finally, Bax opened the door the rest of the way, and we piled through it like spec ops soldiers. Our feet were as light as we could make them, our movements fast and calculated like Deke had drilled into us. Together, in our usual formation, we moved through the kitchen and into the next room

And the lights all turned on.

That was all the warning we had before the first bang sounded. I barely caught a glimpse of a man with a long gun of some kind diagonal from me before I reacted. There was no thought, no intention to what I did. I just pushed with everything I had.

Men flew back. Pellets shifted to the side, shattering the TV and a picture frame. Furniture shifted and something big cracked. I didn't even care what.

"Injuries!" I demanded.

Then the soft pop of silenced guns started going off as all three of my guys aimed and fired.

"We're good," Lars assured me. "Whatever you did, you might need to do it again."

"Melt the guns, Jess," Gavin said.

Well, that was as good of an idea as any, so I tried. First, I tried

ENTER SANDMAN

the one being held by the guy who'd shot us. He screamed and dropped it, so I looked to the next, then the next, working as fast as I could, but that meant I wasn't shooting. I counted six people total, five men and a woman.

"I've got six," I said.

"Retreat!" Deke ordered.

"She's got this..." Gavin said, aiming at another. "Headshots, guys. Knock them out and Jess can dust."

Then someone roared.

Pain flared as weight crashed into my back. One second I was standing, and the next I was on the ground with my face shoved up against a couch or chair. I tried to push, but the man lying on my side was too heavy, so I did the only thing I could, I twisted, pressing my gun against his head as he was struggling to grab my throat, and pulled the trigger.

Gore sprayed, but I was fucking pissed. Without hesitation, I grabbed his limp hand and pushed, wanting him dead and gone as fast as possible. At the same time, I opened myself up, pulling all the power I might possibly need. The rush of the moment made it easy. The terror made it feel like it happened fast. Before I could get out from under the man, his body began dissolving.

"Someone report!" Deke begged.

"One down," I said.

"Six more to go," Bax added. "Jess... *Down!*"

I was already down, but the guys all ducked just as another round of gunfire filled the room. The shots were just over the back of the couch, but I knew it wouldn't be long before they corrected, so I pushed. Like before, I shoved with all I had, not caring where anything went, so long as it all went. In my mind, I imagined things flying into the air, smashing into the demons, and all of it on that side of the couch.

I couldn't see if it worked, but it sure sounded like it. As soon as the shots stopped, all four of us were back up, using the couch as cover - even if it was shit - as we picked our targets. Gavin hit a man in the head, but he was too far away for me to grab. Bax winged one. Lars got another in the leg. Most of our shots just hit the walls.

"Coming in," Deke warned. "Cover the door, and fucking pull back!"

"Can't," Gavin said. "We're pinned behind a - "

He didn't get the chance to finish that as one of the guys ripped out of his human body, revealing the demon inside. Unlike when Dad had tried to force his way into our place, this wasn't a slow process. It was like tearing off old clothes. One second, the man who'd been shot in the leg was down, and the next he was ripping and coming back up with a whole lot more legs.

I tried to make the floor crack under him and wanted vines to reach him. The floor did crack, but he was moving too fast. The vines raced for him, but they didn't stand a chance. Out of the corner of my eye, I saw movement so turned, taking aim before the guy could flank Lars.

My shot winged him, but Lars managed to hit his head, dropping the man like a rock. If only that killed them instead of simply slowing them. The problem was that I'd taken my eyes off the demon. When I looked back, he lunged, aiming right for me. That was when everything happened at once.

The back door crashed open and Deke stormed in. Bax jumped in front of me. Gavin pulled his knife and plunged it into the beast's back as it hit Bax instead of me, all of its sharp legs trying to stab at him. I watched as one hit in the middle of his chest and skidded off, so I grabbed for that leg.

My hand closed on it just as a gun went off and the demon jerked, but I had it. I pushed, ready to kill all of them. These assholes wanted to hurt my guys. They wanted to destroy the world. Most of all, I was not a good girl.

I was the motherfucking villain of this story.

"Jess!" Deke yelled, sounding like he was horrified.

I didn't have time to answer him. Thankfully, Gavin had this.

"Headshots," he ordered. "Drop them and she'll dust them. If we need a wave, tell her, because I'm sure she's listening."

I nodded to show he was right, and felt the leg begin to crumble. That meant this one was dead, so I let it go and crawled for the one on the other side of Lars, now behind me. Just as I was about to reach it, the couch moved. I paused long enough to see that Deke had shoved it over to give me cover, and then I was dusting this guy.

"Two more down," Bax told me.

And this guy was dissolving. "I need to reach them," I warned, pushing to my feet.

"Focus on left!" Deke ordered.

We all began shooting. I heard a click as someone ran out of bullets, and Gavin quickly dropped his magazine to replace it with another. Next, it was Bax, just as the guy dropped.

"Last one!" Deke said.

"No!" the demon cried. "I just want to live. We all just want to -"

It was my bullet that hit his temple, cutting off his begging, and I didn't have time to worry about that. The moment the guys lowered their weapons, I was moving for the next closest demon to dust them one by one.

"I need you to watch them," I said. "If anyone stirs, put another bullet in their head."

That meant each guy took an unconscious demon in human form. They all stood like sentries, with Lars standing over the guy I was working on. I could feel the strain as I pushed harder and faster than I ever had before, but I didn't care. I wanted these guys gone. When one began to dissolve, I moved to the next. Lars and Deke went to check the rest of the house, making sure it was empty, and I just kept going.

Just as I finished, they were back. "We have one problem," Deke said.

"Besides killing seven greater demons like we're fucking badasses?" Bax asked.

Deke just looked at him. "Yeah. This is a mess. If anyone comes looking, it's going to be obvious that something bad happened here."

Gavin pushed his gun back into his holster, and without a word headed for the kitchen. I tried to climb back to my feet, but it wasn't as easy as I expected. Lars grabbed my elbow, helping me up, then wrapped his arm around my waist so we could follow everyone else back into the kitchen.

There, Gavin was looking at the stove. "Leave the burner on," he said. "Gas stove, so easy enough to do. Have Jess light the wall, and by the time it catches, we should be out of here."

"And if it doesn't catch?" Deke asked.

"It'll catch," I promised. "We just need a reason for the wall to burn."

Lars grabbed a roll of paper towels from over the sink, unrolled as much as he could, and propped the rest on the back of the stove. "Best I can do on short notice."

"Which should be good enough if no one's home to stop it," I decided. "Ok, everyone out."

"Not without you," Bax said.

"I'm right behind you," I promised as I turned the knob on the stove, lighting the burner and the paper towel laying over it before turning it down to low. "Just have to tell the fire what I want it to..."

I reached for my magic, imagining a lazy fire that ran across the paper towels, taking its time to devour those, and then moved on to the wood framed walls of this old place. There it would catch, growing quickly, until it could devour the entire structure. It would eat it all, especially the living room. It would burn hot once it reached the top of the wall, and it would burn so fast.

Then I released it.

"It's going," I promised, turning for the back door and jogging with the guys through the laundry room, across the pasture-like yard, and back toward where the truck was waiting.

By the time we'd all piled into our seats, the orange glow was visible in the side window of the farmhouse, and I knew it would grow. I'd put enough magic into that to make sure of it.

CHAPTER FORTY-THREE

BY THE TIME we made it to the end of the rural road, the sky was glowing behind us, so the fire had caught. When we headed back home, I could smell the smoke on the breeze. I had a moment of panic, hoping I hadn't set off a grass fire or something, then realized we were downwind. The little indicator beside the digital compass told me.

When we made it back to the barn, we all piled out and Deke started giving orders. "Weapons and vests in the shop. If you're injured, let me know, damn it."

"I'm fine," I assured him as I started working off the velcro for my vest and walking that way.

"Like, just pile it up?" Gavin asked.

"I don't fucking care," Deke said. "The last time you four faced that many demons, you almost died, Gav."

Gavin just flashed him a smile. "And I thought I wasn't your type."

Deke threw up his hands and followed us into the garage, but the moment Bax had his vest off, Deke grabbed him. Spinning Bax around, he yanked the guy's shirt up, exposing his entire chest -

then pawing at it. Bax just held his hands out like he was being searched. It was Lars who shoved Deke back.

"What the fuck, man?" Lars demanded.

"I saw that spike hit you," he said, talking directly to Bax. "I saw that demon try to impale you, and then Jess grabbed its leg. What the fuck happened?"

"I don't know," Bax admitted.

"And we're all tired," I reminded him. "Not to mention gross."

"Fine," Deke said, giving in. "Upstairs." Then he aimed for the side, hitting the button to close the garage doors.

Gavin called the elevator, which reached the ground floor just as the garage was finally closed. The four of us piled in, waited for Deke, and then headed up. Beside me, Bax had lifted his shirt again, looking at his chest as if he was trying to figure out what had happened too.

"Lars and Gavin get first showers," Deke said. "Jess, you and Bax can tell me what went down in there."

"Jess can go first," Gavin said. "She's got some..." He pointed at my head.

"And what she didn't know wouldn't hurt her," Lars pointed out.

"Gross stuff, huh?" I asked.

The guys all nodded, but Deke didn't seem to care. When we reached the top, he caught my arm, holding me back while he closed up the elevator. But since I wasn't moving, neither were the guys, which meant we all stood there.

"What's going on, Deke?" Lars asked.

"Seven demons," he said. "Travis said there were only six greaters left."

"So one wasn't a greater," Bax said. "We know there were commons there as well, and we saw a woman. Maybe someone's wife or husband was the weaker one?"

"I don't think demons work like that," I pointed out. "Maybe a kid? Maybe Travis doesn't know everyone? Either way, we're all fine."

"You're not fine!" Deke yelled in my face. "You had a demon try to kill you!"

"And there it is," Bax said. "Our big, strong Sandman is worried about his girlfriend."

"In case you missed it," Deke said, "I checked *you* first. I don't even know what I saw in there, but I can't explain it. I watched a demon impale you and not break skin. I saw Jess throw magic without looking. I heard more. How did none of you get shot in that kind of firefight?"

"Came close," Gavin admitted. "Felt a bullet go past my ear."

"Had one hit the couch right by me," Lars said.

Deke looked at me, and I just shook my head. "I wasn't thinking about that. I was trying to block the shots and push them back, and trap them with the floor and vines while dusting them all."

"Which is why you're supposed to stay at the back," Deke reminded me. "Fuck, Jess. If you go down, they do too. I will not lose another quad, and it's clear they've realized that *you* are the threat."

"Which is why I got in front of her," Bax said. "I'd hoped to get my hand on it, but fuck, those things are heavy."

"Like the one that pinned Jess," Lars said. "Hit her from behind, I couldn't get a shot without hitting her under it, and she just pulled out her gun and brained the fucker."

"Let her shower," Bax said again. "She can use my room. Lars can use the main shower since he's got some gore on his legs. Gavin and I will fill you in, and she'll come back so you can see she's ok. Fuck, crawl in her bed tonight, Deke. If that makes you feel better, I'm pretty sure none of us are going to bitch."

"Ok," Deke said, giving in. "Wash the brains out of your hair, Jess. Lars, don't put your pants on anything that will stain. Bax, I want to see your chest, and when you're clean, we'll talk."

ENTER SANDMAN

"And we have school in..." Lars pulled his phone out of his pocket. "Five hours."

We all hurried through our showers. I had to wash my hair three times, because I kept thinking I felt something in it. I didn't, and there were no bits in the water running off, but my mind was convinced something had to be there since the guys had mentioned it. I didn't want to know, didn't want to see, and definitely wanted it off me.

When I got out of the shower, I just wrapped a towel around my body and headed to my room to change. In the other room, I could hear Linda and Tash's voices, along with Deke. Not caring how I looked, I found a long sleep-shirt-style nightie, and went to see if the guys were done yet. Sure enough, I was the last one.

"Get it out of your hair?" Bax asked.

"Don't want to think about it," I said, plopping down in the chair behind the cup of cocoa. "So, you fill in Deke?"

"They did," Tash said before Deke could answer. "I want to know how you moved the bullets."

I blew out a breath. "Air and earth, I think. I pushed them and wanted them to move, but I didn't really think about it. I didn't get the chance. It was bright, and then it was loud. I barely caught a glimpse of a guy with a shotgun, although I didn't even realize it was a shotgun and not a rifle for a bit."

"You did good," she told me.

"Very good," Linda said. "How are you feeling, sweetie? I know that the last time you used a lot of magic, you were exhausted. Do I need to call you out of school tomorrow? I mean today."

"I'll be ok," I promised. "We also had a long nap, so that will help."

Bax just leaned back and pulled up his shirt. "So, how'd you stop this, Jess?"

There, on his chest, was a circular bruise about the size of my fist. It wasn't perfectly spherical or anything, but it was definitely a blob, and right where that demon had tried to spike him. I was starting to think that I really hated the ones with too many legs.

"I didn't," I told him. "Maybe he saw me lunging?"

"No," Deke said. "I walked into the room just in time to see that, and he wanted to spear Bax. She. It! I also think it was the common, because it wasn't as big as Ted. Granted, Ted's special, so I still don't know." He just leaned back and rubbed at his face. "Guys, you scared the shit out of me. I heard the shots both over the phone and across the pasture, so I grabbed my guns and started running." He licked his lips. "And I tried to do the magic thing. I don't know if it helped."

"Was that why it felt like they dusted faster?" I asked.

"The headshots were keeping them down longer, too," Gavin pointed out. "I thought it was just how fast everything was moving."

"That's the thing," Bax said. "There's no way to know, and I didn't know to check for any special feeling. All I was thinking about was how the demons were targeting Jess."

"Same," Gavin agreed. "It was like they saw her and all tried to take her out first. Guess being Ted's kid isn't enough anymore."

"Wait," Lars said, but the guys were still going.

"The one crawled out of its skin without even slowing down," Bax said. "And where did the one come from that hit Jess from behind? That was the kitchen, and I'm damned sure nothing was in there when we went through."

"Outside?" Gavin asked. "No idea. I had no idea it was there until she went down and the others tried to rush."

"Guys!" Lars snapped, loud enough to make them stop. "At the seal, when you shot a demon, how many of them slowed down?"

"None," Bax said, "but they weren't in human form."

Lars was nodding. "But Gavin's knife hurt the one on Bax. It hurt it enough that Jess could grab its leg, and it didn't try to throw her off. It just died, and fast. What about the others? When we burst in, they had the jump on us. How the *fuck* did we walk away from that with bruises and nothing worse? Deke, when did you start the thing? Your magic?"

"When I heard the shots," Deke said. "I was at the truck, though. I heard the shots, pushed at my tattoo, and started running because..." He paused, looking down at the table. "It was like I couldn't imagine being anywhere else. I had to be with you. All four of you. All I could think was that if I was going to lose my quad, I was going down with you because this is where I belong."

"And they started dying easier when?" Lars asked, looking at the rest of us.

"When Deke came in the back door," I told him. "Maybe a bit before, because I shot that one trying to flank you, then the other jumped on Bax - "

"On you," Gavin said. "Bax got in the way."

"Yeah," I breathed. "That."

"So when Deke was close," Lars said. "At first, we were shooting, and I know I had a few good hits, but they didn't care. Deke showed up, and they started dropping. I'm not even sure if Jess dusted them or some were already dying. The guy I was standing over? I swear he started dissolving."

"Takes them a few seconds to do that," Deke said.

"Which means the gunshot killed him," Lars pointed out. "And what did the book say? Something about the tools of gods?"

"Focus on the grains, for they limit the tools of gods," Linda quoted. "What are you thinking, Lars?"

"Deke used his power," Lars told her, "and the demons got weak. We felt stronger in the shop, and Jess got tackled by a demon and didn't slow down. Bax had a spear slide off his skin, it sounds like. We got stronger and the demons got weaker when the Guide used his special ability."

"Shit," Deke breathed. "Are you sure?"

"Not at all," Lars said, "but I think so. I mean, the more I think about it, you showing up was the tipping point for that, and the one big change was your magic, ability, or whatever you want to call it."

"And I have a bruise," Bax pointed out. "It hit me. How could a demon's talon hit me hard enough to bruise and not cut? Ted sliced the shit out of Lars' side. Greg picked Gavin up and impaled him. How did it not kill me, Deke, because that's right over my fucking heart!"

"It's magic," I realized. "Guys, in the middle of that, I had to open up and pull magic. I always have magic now. I don't like to be low, but as soon as I started doing stuff, I felt like I needed more. Why?"

"Not following," Tash admitted.

"Because I touched your tattoo, and you sucked it out of me," I explained. "When Deke's was on, it did the same, but not as big of a pull since I touch him more. It's like you two are drawing in magic from the world around you. Not consciously like I do, but passively like Travis does."

"Like a demon?" Tash asked.

I lifted a hand, holding off her rant. "How do angels do it, Tash? How do witches? I only know how Travis and I work, so that's all I can compare to, but he said something. He said that my ability to draw magic into me was because I'm part human. Makes me wonder if the same is true for the two of you, but you don't know how yet."

"Then teach me," Deke said.

I could only lift my hands, palms up, in surrender. "I don't know how your abilities work. I can tell you that I open up and try to draw the air inside my body through my skin, or the ground in through where I touch it. Things like that. I don't know if that will work for you, or if yours is different."

"We can only try," Tash said. "But on the upside, I can tell you all that I found a way to get Travis in the house. Seems that it's possible to make a key. A symbol that he can carry with him that will make him exempt. I'd prefer it's not something he can lose."

"Phone case," Bax suggested.

"*On* him," Tash said. "Not beside. Must touch skin. They say tattoos or paint. Henna? Body paint? Necklace?"

"Get me the symbol," Bax said. "And what happens if he betrays us?"

Tash smiled at him. "I knew I liked you for some reason. It's easy, though. We just have to change the wards. So long as we make them with the key, he's safe. He screws up, we change the locks."

"Then get me the symbol and I'll see what we can do," Bax said. "After all, I'm going to see him in a few hours."

"Which means bed," Deke ordered. "All of you, and I recommend you sleep."

"You too, Sandman," Gavin said. "Make sure our girl doesn't have nightmares."

CHAPTER FORTY-FOUR

I WAS ALREADY asleep by the time Deke crawled in bed with me. I woke up enough to shift over, but that was it. Then, at some point in the middle of the night, Gavin snuck into my room and took a spot on the other side. I only knew because I woke up with my face pressed against his back and Deke cuddled up to mine.

It was nice, and even more proof that Gavin was actually ok with this. I just didn't want to mess anything up by asking or making too much of it. Instead, I simply got up and started getting ready. I had a moment of hesitation when it came time to change clothes because both guys were awake and moving, but I was tired of worrying about it.

When I pulled off my shirt, Deke sucked in a breath and shifted in the bed so he could sit up. A smile took over Gavin's lips as he headed to the bathroom, but his eyes just darted across me. They didn't linger. It was progress, and while it may have taken me longer to get to the idea of showing off my not-sexy side, I kinda liked how comfortable it felt. More than that, I loved how these guys made me feel like being not-sexy was still sexy - which made no sense.

However, our morning routine was rushed. We'd all opted for a little more sleep, which meant a little less time to get ready. While I tried to do something with my hair and face, Bax made coffee. Lars brought me mine while I finished the little bit of makeup I needed for school, and then we were off.

There wasn't a lot of conversation, but Gavin passed me a bottle of Advil. I took two, and handed it to Lars. When he made it to school, Bax took some as well, because we all hurt after last night. Missing a little sleep was one thing. Getting the crap beat out of us first meant that today was going to be a very slow, very long day.

On the bright side, the new substitute teacher for my Spanish class, Ms. Diaz, was pretty cool. She'd grown up in Colombia, lived in Mexico, and vacationed in Spain. When she called on Gavin for something and he answered fluently with his lisping accent, the woman smiled.

"Were you born there?" she asked.

He nodded. "Immigrating now. Started as an exchange student."

"Nice." Then she looked at me for her next question.

She wanted me to conjugate a verb, so I did my best. The woman chuckled, then looked back to Gavin. "Should I assume you're tutoring Jessica?"

"Jess," I corrected. "I prefer the short version, and my boyfriend's been helping me as much as humanly possible."

"One of them," a guy at the front said. Then fake-coughed, "Slut!"

"You," the woman said, pointing at the door. "Principal's office. Now. We do not bully people in my class for any reason. If you do it again, I will have you suspended."

"But she's dating two guys!"

"I don't care," Ms. Diaz said. "Religious persecution and rape culture have no place in my classroom."

"Whoa," a girl breathed. "I think I love you, Ms. Diaz."

She cracked a smile, but still pointed at the door. "Now, young man. I promise that if you refuse, it will be more than a lecture and detention." When he finally got up and left, Ms. Diaz began to walk across the front of the class slowly as if thinking. "Let me make this clear," she started. "I teach a class on a language spoken by predominantly brown people. Half of the people in here are women. A large portion of all my students will have experienced some form of harassment for one thing or another in their lives. Well, not in my class. I have you all for the rest of this semester, which is only a few weeks, but this will be a safe space for all of you. If you need to talk - about this class, another, or anything else - I am here and available. My job is to teach you, not to judge you. Now, who would like to conjugate the verb for 'to sleep' for me?"

And just like that, we were back to our lesson, but her words hit me hard. I was so used to ignoring the things people said about me. Most people didn't care who I dated, so the few that called me names weren't that big of a deal, but I wondered if this was how Travis felt. Demons were bad, he hadn't done anything wrong, and yet he still got lumped in with all the rest. I at least had my Brethren status to fall back on as 'proof' to myself that I couldn't be evil. He only had us and other demons.

I was thinking about that as we headed to lunch, so I wasn't really surprised to see Travis sitting at our table. Gavin and I took spots on either side of him just as Bax slid a scrap of paper across the table. Travis took it, but from the expression on his face, he had no idea what it was.

"That's a key to my place," Bax said. "I'm trusting you not to hand it out. Supposedly, if you wear that mark against your skin somehow, then you'll be able to cross the wards."

"Like a necklace or bracelet," I suggested.

"Or tattoo," Lars said. "Tash said it doesn't have to be big. It just has to be there. I'm guessing a mark on this skin won't be on the next?"

"Right," Travis said. "So time for the safety pin and India ink thing, huh?"

"Or you can go to a fucking tattoo parlor," Bax said. "There's one in Vinita, which isn't that far away."

"I'll look into it," Travis promised, putting the piece of paper in his pocket. "The bigger issue is the serial killer in town." He looked at each of us pointedly. "Shannon's freaking out. The Whites have been reported missing. That was Friday. Greg is missing and likely dead. Then, last night, Daniel Cunningham's place burned to the ground. Multiple weapons were found inside, including a shotgun and a whole bunch of pistols. Revolvers, semi-auto, and so on. No signs of bodies, and sounds like the fire started at the stove."

"Good," Bax said. "Probably another drug problem, right?"

"Well, rumors say that the cops are worried about a cartel. Granted, that's from Josh Wilkons in my first period class, but his mom's the police dispatcher. Susan Lamore said her dad was at the fire - he's a fireman - and it caught fast. From nothing to inferno in minutes. Thankfully, the grass was green enough that it didn't spread. No cars on the property, not even Cunningham's, so that's suspicious. On the upside, no one is looking at the four of you."

"And the downside?" I asked.

He huffed at me. "Shannon is freaking the fuck out, Jess. Greg and Cunningham seem to both be drug related. The Whites, though? They were pretty normal people who were boring. Nothing at all to tie them to drugs. They just packed up and left, and no one's seen or heard a thing - and we all know why, but think about how this looks!"

"What about the demons?" Gavin asked.

Travis just blew out a breath. "Yeah, they're freaked. Um, a few commons are moving out, which is where the serial killer rumor is coming from. They're using that as their excuse for quitting their jobs. Enough of them are doing it that kids heard before school, and of course it's spreading fast. I mean, that's the best gossip this town has ever had."

Lars leaned in and dropped his voice. "So what are we looking at for the seal? How many could show up if we try to close it?"

"More than that," Bax said, "how many of those fuckers last night were greaters?"

"All of them," Travis admitted. "According to my dad's friend, the greaters started grouping up, and they called in friends from outside town. There are three more here, but they're leaving. We all know it's you four doing it. We also can't turn you in. There's absolutely nothing to tie you to it except the deranged ranting of an adult accusing a high school kid of it. That's more likely to cause problems than fix them."

"So we're safe?" Lars asked.

Travis nodded. "Yeah, but the ones who are staying are willing to fight for this. Trust me, I got a lecture and a half this morning when Dad read the local news online. Something about how we had a community here and I'm helping the enemy, which will bring the rest down on us. Guys, my guardians are panicking. Shannon's losing it. Everyone is on edge, and plenty of them have nothing to lose."

"But we don't want to kill the ones that haven't done anything wrong," I pointed out.

"After you burned a house with the remains of seven demons inside - "

"What?" Shannon demanded, dropping her hands onto the table. "Seven people were in that house?"

"No," Travis tried. "That's not what I was talking about."

"What else burned?" Shannon asked, her attention locked on him.

I just groaned and dropped my head against the table. Thankfully, Bax was pretty damned good at lying. Without hesitation, he waved Shannon down.

"Seven people in the house, probably druggies. Scum of the earth. Travis was talking about the losers they had to be, and what the owner must've been up to."

"Bullshit," Shannon said. Her head whipped around, looking at all of us. "You all know something. People are fucking disappearing

ENTER SANDMAN

in this town, and no one knows who's going to be next, and you know something. For weeks now, the five of you have been meeting up, whispering where no one else can hear, and acting seriously suspicious. It all started when you loaned Travis that money, Bax. And that wasn't long after Jess and Lars moved in with you. Now, I owe you a lot, but it sure as fuck looks like you're blackmailing people to help you with something, and I *will* call the cops."

"It's not like that," Lars said. "Bax gave us a place when Mom needed it."

"No one's being blackmailed," Gavin insisted.

She just turned to look at me. "You want to try?"

There was something in her eyes. She wasn't being a bitch; Shannon was actually scared. Travis was right, and she was in full freak-out mode. She also had a damned good point, and it probably wouldn't take long before someone else noticed all the connections. Not necessarily from us to the victims, but just that there was something going on.

Plus, she was my friend, and I knew how much it had hurt when Megan lied to me. Reaching over, I grabbed Bax's left arm, holding his hand in his lap. Then I pulled in a deep breath and decided to do the dumbest thing I'd ever imagined: tell the truth.

"You read the same kind of books I do, right?" I asked.

Her brow creased and she shook her head in confusion. "Yeah, some, but what does that have to do with this?"

"A lot," I admitted. "Shannon, you know how sometimes the guys can't tell the main female character something because it's too dangerous?"

"Uh huh..." She stood back up and crossed her arms, making it clear she wasn't buying this. "Like being a vampire, running a gang, and so on? Mafia?"

"Not mafia," I assured her. "Yes, the five of us know what's going on. No, we really don't want to tell you because you aren't even remotely involved. It's not the mafia, a mob, or a gang."

"Then what?" she demanded. "You don't fucking expect me to buy vampires, do you?"

With my hand still on Bax's wrist, I tugged, guiding his arm up and onto the table so she could see his palm. My eyes darted over to Lars, who did the same. Letting go of Bax, I pulled off my sleeve and laid my hand down the same way, palm up. With a heavy sigh, Gavin pulled off his glove and showed his palm too.

"We've all had these scars for years," I told her. "It's crazy, it's complicated, and I'm begging you to trust me until we're out of school, ok?"

Shannon's arms had relaxed to fall back to her sides and her eyes were jumping across the marks. Bax's crown, Gavin's sword, Lars' scales, and my strange letters. Pulling in a breath, she tipped her head at mine.

"What's that supposed to be?"

"The number of the beast," I told her. "Not the usual one, but that's Greek for six hundred and sixteen."

"Shit," she breathed. "Who put them on you?"

"No idea," I admitted. "Can we at least have the rest of today?"

Shannon nodded, looking over at Travis. "What about you? Do you have some freaky scar?"

"Not exactly," he admitted. "Baby, it's complicated."

"And she deserves to know," I told him. "How many times has she gone out of her way to be cool to us? How often has she covered for us?"

"Shit," Bax muttered. "Yeah. You're right, Jess, but this is going to blow the fuck up."

"Deke's going to be pissed," Gavin pointed out.

"And I'm going to get dumped," Travis said, scrubbing at his face. "Well, I knew this was too good to be true. After school."

"My truck in the parking lot," Bax said. "We'll all talk there."

"I'm holding you to that," Shannon said, "because if you fuck me over, I'm calling the cops."

CHAPTER FORTY-FIVE

THE REST of the day crawled by, and I was caught between trying to think of the best way to explain this, a great lie to tell, and thinking it all sounded stupid. I imagined the conversation with Shannon a million and one times in my head before school was finally out, which meant I'd thought up and discarded the worst ideas. Unfortunately, that didn't mean I'd come up with any good ones.

When we all met up at my locker, Travis was with Bax, and the guy looked like he was freaking out. I didn't really blame him, but what else could we do? Shannon suspected something. Her fears couldn't be any worse than the reality, and likely would end up with the cops coming to ask too many questions. Considering the number of guns, artifacts, and other weird things at our place, it wasn't a risk I was willing to take. The guys didn't necessarily agree.

"Are you really going to tell her?" Travis asked. "Jess, she's going to dump me!"

"Is that really your biggest worry right now?" Lars asked. "She's talking about calling the cops, Travis. She thinks you're involved."

"Yeah, but I'm clean," he insisted. "I have an alibi for every incident."

"No, you don't," Bax countered. "You have your parents saying you went to bed, they went to sleep, and they didn't see you until the morning. Easy enough to say you snuck out and did something without them knowing. I mean, unless you sleep in bed with your mommy?"

"Fuck you," Travis grumbled. "Yeah, you're right, but still."

Gavin was just watching me. "Do you have a plan?"

"A bad one," I admitted. "I'll try telling Shannon the truth. If I have to, I'll show her some tricks. If it doesn't work, then I'm hoping that Bax or Lars can fix it."

Both guys began to nod slowly as if considering that. Bax answered first. "Pretty sure I got this one, Lars. Not that different than what I usually do."

"Then I'll play backup to the backup," Lars agreed. "And here's hoping that Jess can keep her from freaking out."

"What about me?" Travis asked. "No matter how this goes down, it all comes back to the fact that she's going to find out what I am."

"And?" I asked.

He sighed in frustration. "Demons are evil, Jess. Demons are ugly. Demons aren't boyfriends."

"Lucky for you, Shannon reads the same books I do," I assured him. "Demons are hot, with big dicks, and when they fall for a girl, they don't hold back." Then I winked, closed my locker, and turned for the door with a lot more bravado than I actually felt.

"Please read smutty romance books," Travis begged as he followed.

When we made it to Bax's SUV, Shannon wasn't there. Most of us threw our bags in our seats, leaving the doors open so the heat would dissipate. Travis just dropped his bag by the tire and leaned against the front side of the vehicle. I took a place beside him, both of us watching the main doors to the school.

ENTER SANDMAN

It took a while, but eventually Shannon headed over. She was alone, thankfully, but looked braced for the worst. Her arms were crossed, her shoulders were tight, and the expression on her face could only be described as a scowl. Still, I respected her more for coming alone, even if this had to be nerve-wracking for her.

"You ok?" I asked her.

"No," she admitted, dropping her bag beside Travis's. "Just tell me you don't have anything to do with the missing people in town?"

"Let's start before that?" I begged.

She licked her lips nervously, then jiggled her head in a weak yes. "What's before that? Your hands?"

"Yeah," I breathed as the guys started to gather closer. "Guys, give her some room? She probably thinks she's about to be jumped."

"Kinda was wondering that," Shannon admitted.

"Well, you're not," I promised. "Shannon, you're my friend. Probably one of the only girls who hasn't been shitty to me. I mean, I used to think Megan was a great friend, but she lied to me, and I never want to do that to you. That's the only reason I'm telling you this, and it's probably the worst idea ever, and I'm sure you'll think I'm crazy, but I can prove it, ok?"

"Ok..."

"The supernatural is real," I said, just laying it out there.

Shannon's head canted to the side and she gave me a very good 'go to hell' look. "Uh huh."

"Just hear me out," I told her, "and then I'll prove it. No, there aren't vampires and werewolves. I mean, not that I know of?" And I looked over at Travis.

"Shit, I wouldn't know about that," he scoffed. "But no, I'm pretty sure that's just chick porn."

"Ok." I turned my attention back to Shannon. "Angels, demons, witches, and some other things are real. Not real the way you expect, though. Magic is real. I know this sounds crazy, but it is."

"And you're going to pull a coin out from behind my ear to prove it?" she asked.

"No coins," I promised. "My magic is elemental, so earth, air - "

"Fire and water," she finished. "Yeah, I know about that."

"And spirit," I added. "I'm shit at using it, and I'm still learning, but I have a few tricks."

Holding out my hand, I called a flame into my palm. It sparked up easily, burning on nothing, and hovering in the air. Shannon's entire body heaved like she was trying to decide if she should laugh or run. Instead, she just stared, her mouth falling open in surprise.

So I dismissed that and called water. It took a little longer, but the drops condensed in the same place the fire had burned. I kept pulling until it was about the size of an orange, then pushed it to the ground a few feet away. The glob hit the ground and splattered like a water balloon bursting, leaving a wet spot to prove it wasn't an illusion.

"I can do the others, but they aren't as easy," I said, "but is that enough?"

"There has to be some kind of trick, right?" she asked.

"Probably," I admitted, "but fuck if I know what it is. All I know is that I inherited this from my asshole of a father. You see, I'm a cambion."

"Don't know that one," she admitted.

"Dad's a demon, Mom was human," I explained. "The result is a cambion. Our magic is elemental in nature, like a demon's, but more spell throwing and less world altering. I mean, if I understand that right. Like I said, still learning."

"And this is because of your hand?" Shannon asked.

It was Bax who answered. "Not exactly. Our hands mark us as something called Brethren. Supposedly, we're descended from a supernatural thing called a watcher."

"Angels," Shannon said.

Travis shook his head. "No. Angels are angels. They're a

personification of order. Demons are chaos. Watchers were neutral, but they're extinct. Only the blood that runs through their hybrid offspring is left. Those four somehow activated it, which makes them Brethren. When it's not activated, we call them Martyrs."

"We..." Shannon said, picking up on that word. "So how do you fit in, Travis?"

"Shit," he grumbled, turning away. "I didn't do anything, Shannon. I just tried to help my friends with something they're not supposed to talk about. I wasn't blowing you off. I just didn't want you to get caught up in this mess, because you're just human and..."

"And what?!" she demanded.

"It could get you killed," I finished for him. "The five of us have some kind of protection. Magic, resistances to stuff, or supernatural strength. I mean, we're not technically human, but we also kinda are. The four of us grew up thinking we were just like you, but something happened to turn it upside down. For me, that was when my mom got cancer. She was dying, and suffering, and I wished for it to be over. I wanted her suffering to end, even if mine would start, and I got that mark on my hand. I didn't know what it meant, but I quickly found out that when people touch it, bad things happen."

"What kind of bad things?" Shannon asked.

"They die. Heart attacks. Bad things."

"Which is why you've always worn the sleeve," she realized.

I just nodded my head slowly. "I didn't understand until the night my dad hit Linda. I was in bed. I was in my pajamas! I tried to stop him, and I didn't have my sleeve on, and Linda was unconscious, so he dropped. I thought I'd killed him, but it seems I just knocked him out. Well, I ran, Bax found me, and Deke - the other guy at the house - explained it all. He's a Martyr, you see. His job is to find the four of us so we can work together to stop the mythical Apocalypse. Yes, the one with the Horsemen. Yes, it's real.

We have to keep these seals intact, and other things want to break them, and those things? They're what died."

"What are they?" she asked.

"Demons," I told her. "Full-grown, pissed-off, and evil demons. Not all of them are bad, though."

Shannon's entire body went still for a moment, then she slowly looked over at Travis. "What are you?"

"Baby, you don't want to know."

"What are you, Travis?" she pressed. "Not all of them are bad, Jess said. They've been talking to you a lot lately, and now all this weird shit is going on, and you don't want to talk about it. You don't want to tell me what you are, so do we really have to have a Twilight moment right now?"

He looked at me in desperation. "What is a Twilight moment?"

"You tell her to say it," I explained, "and she states the obvious, implausible, but correct answer."

He just sighed and hung his head. "Ok, fine. I'm a demon. They know, and I've been helping them because I just want to live a nice, normal life."

"As opposed to...?" she asked.

"Hell isn't a realm," he explained. "It's a pit, and it's overcrowded because demons breed. There are no damned souls. There's just us, the demons, and the bigger ones eat the smaller. My real mother got me out when I was a kid, my current parents basically adopted me so I could grow up, and this?" He gestured to his body. "It's made of magic. I have elemental magic like Jess, but I'm basically a juvenile demon, so pretty much powerless. Well, in the scheme of things. I'm physically stronger than most humans, I heal faster, and that's why I'm so good at sports. I really do want to go to college, have kids, and just pretend to be human."

"A demon," Shannon said, looking at him for a long time before turning to me. "Like, are we talking wings and prehensile tails type?"

"No," Travis said. "We're talking more like a horror movie

monster. Um, there's some magic involved in packing my real form into this one, but I'm about two hundred pounds in my real body. I have six legs, a tail with a bony blade, and four horns. Fur."

"You have fur?" I asked, a single chuckle slipping out because I hadn't expected that.

"Most lessers do," he admitted. "Minors are shadows, lessers are fuzzy since we don't have clothes or blankets down there. Commons start to scale up, so they may have like a mane down their back or something, but it's more like an exoskeleton, and greaters are just some conglomeration of whichever parts grew."

"Not the sexy incubus I was hoping for," Shannon said.

"Not sexy," Travis admitted. "Kinda why I tried to make myself decent-looking, you know? I mean, the body grows too, so I only have so much control, but I tried."

"And you have magic?" Shannon asked.

He nodded. "Weak, pathetic elemental magic. I could fluff your hair with wind, and that's my strongest power right now. Um, I can make sure a campfire always lights. I suck at earth and water, though, and I've never had a reason to use spirit."

"It's mostly healing," I explained.

So Shannon turned to the guys. "And you? What do you do, and what does all of this have to do with the people going missing?"

"Our hands have power," Bax told her. "I'm Conquest, Gavin is Vengeance, Lars is Judgment, and Jess is Anathema. She's not supposed to be one of us since she's part demon, so it's complicated."

"Not ICE agents looking for Gavin because his visa is expired," Shannon realized.

I shook my head. "Martyrs looking for us. All five of us. Travis because they want to kill him, those three because they want to know what's taking us so long, and if they find me, they'll 'reset' our quad."

"Which means kill," Lars clarified. "Our duty is to kill the demons who are trying to open the seal that will let all the demons in Hell spill into Hellam. There are too many here, though, so we have to take them out in smaller groups. When they die, they turn to dust, so no bodies. Yes, we killed them. Yes, they were truly evil. No, Travis isn't."

She nodded her head, looking a little lost but a lot less terrified. "So you kill the bad guys, and other bad guys are hunting you, right?"

"Good guys are hunting us," Bax corrected. "The problem is that the good guys have no wiggle room in their rules. Because of who Jess's father is, they will kill her. Because of what Travis is, they will kill him. We're not the good guys, Shannon. We're just the ones fighting for our friends."

Her eyes jumped to Travis. "Ok," she told him. "I'm not going to say I'm in, but I think you should spend this afternoon explaining the rest to me."

"Yeah?" he asked.

She just shrugged. "I mean, Jess has magic! The scars. It makes sense, but..."

"It's a lot to believe," Travis said. "I just didn't think you'd, you know, want to be with me anymore."

Shannon laughed once. "I like the demon romance stories the best. Why not, right? I mean, it's not like I haven't been alone with you before. Also kinda makes me think that this serial killer isn't coming for me."

"I will kill anyone who tries to hurt you, Shannon," Travis swore. "And I will call in all my debts to make those four help."

"That's the kind of demon I'm talking about," she said, reaching down for her bag. Slinging that onto her shoulder, she looked at the rest of us. "But we're not done with this. I'm trying to believe, ok? The proof is there. The story makes sense. I'm just not going to be the girl who gets killed because she's stupid. No more secrets."

"No," Gavin said. "We can't promise that."

"We're not the good guys," Bax reminded her. "I will lie, cheat, and even steal if it means I can keep the people I care about safe.

That includes you, Shannon. So, I'm not taking anything off the table."

"I can actually respect that," she told him. "Travis, take me home? And by that I mean yours."

"Yeah, my parents are demons too," he admitted as he grabbed his own bag.

Shannon hooked her fingers with his and towed him toward the other side of the parking lot. "And I'm probably not supposed to know that, right?"

"Right," he said.

When they were out of earshot, Bax let out a heavy sigh, sounding as relieved as I felt. "You were right, Jess. That was a little tense, but I think she's going to be ok."

"And they'll be better for it," I said as I headed for the back seat. "Now, I just want to go home. I figure Tash will yell at me next."

"Probably," Lars agreed, climbing in beside me. "That's how all good days end, isn't it?"

"Pretty much," I agreed, "but I'm good with it."

CHAPTER FORTY-SIX

I STEPPED through the front door of our place to find Deke reclined in a chair, his feet propped up, wearing nothing but his underwear. There was a bottle of Pepsi on the table beside him, and an empty plate as if he'd just finished eating. All signs pointed to him not being awake for long.

"Did you get some rest?" I asked as I headed for the closest cushion on the couch beside him. They guys kept going toward their rooms, most likely to change.

Deke reached for the remote and muted the soccer game he was watching. "Yeah. I took a nap this afternoon and just got back up. How are you doing, doll? Ready to drop?"

"No, I'm fine," I assured him. "Had a little incident at school that you should know about, though."

He immediately sat up. "More Martyrs?"

"No?" Because that was not what I'd expected him to say for some reason. "Actually, um, it's about Travis."

He groaned. "Don't tell me he's flipped sides."

"No!" I promised. "But his girlfriend did catch us talking and she heard a little too much. It's a mess, but Travis was helping us and ignoring her, and she was trying to figure out what was going on. Now, with the fire, it seems everyone knows that there's something. Most people think it's drug related, but Shannon's not stupid. She's also my friend, Deke. We, um, kinda told her."

"Fuck," he groaned. "Ok, so what is she?"

"Normal."

He closed his eyes and just sighed. "How much does she know?"

"Pretty much everything," I admitted.

"You can't do this, Jess!" he snapped before catching himself and lifting a hand. "Sorry. I didn't mean to yell at you, but you still can't do this. The more people who know, the greater the chances of you getting caught."

"She was going to call the cops," I explained. "She thought Bax was blackmailing Lars, me, Linda, and Travis. I mean, she's Bax's friend, but her logic does add up. From what she's seen and what she knows, it makes the most sense. So we explained that it's not like that."

"And she lost her shit," Deke guessed.

I had to think about that, because Shannon hadn't just accepted things blindly, and I got the impression that she was still making up her mind about all of this, but 'losing her shit' wasn't how I'd describe it either. She'd listened to us. She'd accepted that my magic was real. She was confused and a little unsettled, but holding it together. I just didn't know a good phrase to explain that.

"She's smart, Deke. Shannon believes us, she's talking to Travis to learn more, and she just found out that she's dating a demon. Not a hot, sexy one, but a horribly terrifying one that has nothing to do with God, you know?"

"And I've seen enough people smile, nod, and call an insane asylum," he countered. "Jess, what are you going to do when she starts telling everyone about your crazy stories?"

He didn't even finish the sentence before Bax stepped into the room. "I'll fix it," he said, moving to claim the chair beside me.

"And Jess is right. Shannon's going to vet school, Deke. She's smart, she's driven, and she's not closed-minded. Yes, she was freaked out, but not as bad as I expected. When Jess said she wanted to tell her, we all thought it was the wrong call, but she was right."

"And there's nothing we can do about it now except clean things up when they go sideways," Deke said. "Trust me, things always go sideways." He paused when Gavin and Lars joined us, then groaned. "I'm guessing you're all on Jess's side in this?"

"Yeah," Gavin said. "Shannon has been helping make excuses. She knows, Deke. She didn't know what, but she knew something."

"And what does it really hurt?" Lars asked.

"Martyrs!" Deke snapped. "Don't you four get that? They're here! They're already in Hellam, and they were at your fucking school. They are looking for you, trying to figure out why the seal isn't closed, and you're just parading around - " Again, he paused, took a breath, and then started again in a calmer tone. "The four of you seem to think you're invincible, but you're not. We burned down a house, and that's going to be noticed."

"It was," Lars admitted. "It was also assumed to be drug related."

"Which means more cops patrolling," Deke said. "I'm also going to make a wild guess that your little demon didn't have another name since you got his love life all screwed up."

"Yeah," I admitted as the elevator opened down the hall. "That's a little too accurate. But he also doesn't know who died. He can't tell us who to hit unless he knows who is gone."

"No hits," Tash said as she stormed into the room and shoved her phone into Deke's face. "We're laying low for a bit."

"We can't!" I insisted. "The sand is almost empty, Tash!"

Deke's eyes just tracked across the screen. "And shit just hit the fan," he said, but this time he didn't yell. No, Deke sounded much *too* calm.

Bax leaned forward. "What's going..." He paused as feet tromped up the stairs, and then Linda came in through the front door. That made this a full family ordeal. "Seriously," Bax tried again, "What's going on?"

Deke just pushed to his feet. "I need pants." Then he left the room.

So Tash turned to face me, of all people. "I've been ordered to Hellam to check on the status of this quad. There are concerns that it needs to be reset, and the Martyr assigned as the Guide hasn't been responding to communications from his superiors."

"So they know," I breathed.

"They guess," Tash corrected. "Still, it's why they're here. The seal is open, Deke has been ignoring the fucking Order for months now, and - "

"Stop." Deke said as he walked back in wearing athletic pants and carrying a t-shirt in his hands. "Tash, I wasn't about to *confirm* that I have a quad with three males and a female. Regardless of age, the gender difference would cause concerns. That I already mentioned I was worried about it? All we can do is avoid them because If they try to test her, she'll be found to be cambion, and none of us would be able to stop them before they killed her."

"Which leaves us fucked," Lars said, glancing over to his mom to make sure Linda was keeping up.

She nodded. "Yeah, I got that. So what do we do?"

"Nothing," Deke said. "The four of them know how to spot a Martyr. Adding Travis and Shannon to their group might just be an unforeseen benefit." He sighed. "I'm hoping you're right about her, Jess, because if you're all in a group, it'll make it harder to figure out who and what is triggering their tattoos."

"And," Bax said, "if we see them, we're out."

"You'll see them," Tash said. "It seems someone noticed magic at your school."

"Oliver," Gavin grumbled. "Fuck!"

I just leaned forward and pressed my face into my hands. They knew magic had happened. They knew there was something wrong with our quad. We'd known this would happen, and yet I'd assumed we'd have enough time to close the seal first. Or at least to make sure the greater demons had all been handled.

"Deke?" I asked, looking up. "If we're in the middle of closing the seal, would they still try to kill us?"

"No," he admitted. "They'd wait, but only if we are actively in the middle of repairing it. The ritual would have to be in progress."

"New phones," Bax mumbled. "We let the batteries run out on all of these and throw them in a drawer. Each of us - including you, Linda - gets a new phone. That's plausible deniability. Could buy us some time. If asked why, it's because I have the money to do it, we thought we were being tracked by demons, and we're trying to lay low."

"Could work," Deke said.

"You need to reach out to them," Linda said. "Go into town. Let them find you, and give them the phone excuse. Point out that Hellam is crawling with demons, and you've been a little busy."

"Both of us," Tash said, "because I'm not letting you walk into that without backup."

"And why are you here?" Deke asked.

Tash smiled. "Because you needed to have your fourth tested. I verified that she is, in fact, your Anathema, and we ran some tests. It was discovered that she has, um, one of those disorders where her sex genes don't match up."

"Which means research," Linda realized.

"Yeah, but it might buy us time," Tash said. "That's all we need - time for us to get the seal closed and get out of here."

"But it won't work," I pointed out. "If the seal cracks again, they will know that we're coming back. We have to keep them closed, guys. If we don't, the Horsemen come out."

"So what do you propose?" Tash snapped.

"Is there any way to fake these tests?" I asked. "You all keep saying that no one can tell what I am unless I cast magic, so is that still true?"

"It's complicated," Deke told me. "If a Hunter is called in,

ENTER SANDMAN

happens to be looking at his tattoo when you're close, and nothing else is around, then it will point right at you."

"So would they have Hunters here?" I asked.

Deke and Tash looked at each other, then they both shook their heads. "I don't know," Tash admitted.

"Assuming they don't," I tried, "can we fake the tests?"

"Say she's trans or intersex?" Lars offered.

"It's best to just say you don't know," Linda said. "Make those guesses, but that Jess herself didn't know. How many Olympic athletes have had their medals stripped because of genetic testing after the fact? They never knew before. Jess wouldn't have a reason to guess, and you'd have a hard time getting her to submit to that sort of invasive testing, right?"

"I think it's a blood test," Bax pointed out.

"It's mentally invasive!" Linda snapped. "The point is, if Jess is stubborn, then they can't make her. If they can't make her, and we're being hit by demons - or hitting them - then there hasn't been time to try to talk it out. We'll say that Ted is a demon, he was her father but not the biological one. He told me that her mother had an affair. No reason to doubt it, plenty of questions, and it might just be enough."

"But we need to talk to Travis," Deke said. "We need a check on the other demons. More than that, you four have to be careful. Tash and I will start going around town to see if we can spot any other..." He let the words trail off. "Shit! The necklaces."

"A present I gave my kids," Linda explained. "You both will need to lose yours."

Tash clasped Deke's shoulder. "We can make this work for now. We can hold them off long enough to get the seal closed, but we need a plan for when they figure it out, because if the entire Order comes after her? If they try to reset this quad?"

"I know!" Deke barked. "Fuck, Tash. I know, ok? We have four Brethren - one of whom has magic - two Martyrs, and a pregnant mother."

"Plus a lesser demon and a human girl," Bax pointed out.

"Which isn't enough to stand against thousands of Martyrs," Deke said. "If this fails, we will be on the run. The problem is that I don't see how this can do anything *but* fail."

"So we fake it," Gavin said. "Like *Mission Impossible*. We get someone to send a message back. Or when they talk to you, someone turns on the old phone numbers and tells them it's a mess, we're slowly making progress, and here's the deal. We have someone lie, and if we have to..." He glanced at Bax. "We kill every Martyr in this town."

"We let the demons do it," Lars corrected. "Because the only greater demon that I'm sure is not dead? It's her dad, and he's going to be pissed if they come after her."

"This isn't going to work," Deke said.

I just shrugged. "It's a hell of a lot better than doing nothing, right?" Then I pushed myself to my feet. "I'm going to see if Travis has news, and hopefully things are going well with Shannon. The sooner we get this done, the sooner they stop watching us, and the sooner we can pretend to be normal Brethren."

CHAPTER FORTY-SEVEN

For the next two days, Shannon and Travis were attached at the hip. They also were waiting for us at our table with a ton of questions the first morning, and sat with us at lunch to ask even more. Shannon wanted to know everything, and we did our best to tell her, including how the Martyrs were in town and not to be trusted.

It was a little hard to make her understand why Travis and I were supposed to be bad, though. When I pointed out that demons were evil, therefore *we* must be evil since Travis was all demon and I was half, she still didn't get it. It seemed that Shannon thought the same way I did. We weren't bad people, we hadn't chosen to be born like this, and we weren't cruel for no reason. That meant we weren't "evil." Then she took it a step further: Martyrs were just racists.

It sounded so easy when she put it like that, but it still wasn't quite right. It also didn't matter, because it seemed that Shannon was all in. She and Travis had been working together to keep track of who was still in town and what level of demon they were. Not surprisingly, Travis wasn't the only demon kid in Hellam. There were more in the lower grades, but he was the only one in high school right now.

Even better, the known greater demons were all gone - except my father. Then on Friday, Shannon passed me a USB drive, said that there was a spreadsheet on it, and that it should have the current copy of what they knew. It was a lot better than the scraps of paper torn from Travis's notebook, and the truth was that I couldn't wait to see if we stood a chance yet. With this, we'd have a working picture of the demonic community in town.

I was feeling pretty good about all of this when in the halls between fourth and fifth period, Shannon grabbed my arm and pulled me into the bathroom. There was no talking, no telling me this was important, or anything else. The girl all but shoved me in before her, and I wasn't dumb enough to resist.

"What the..." I asked.

"Travis just sent me a text and said to find you," she told me just as my own phone went off, but she didn't stop. Instead, she walked the length of the bathroom, making sure no stalls were occupied, before she continued. "He just had some man stop him in the hall and ask him his name. He gave him Oliver's, but said he had that same overly-official look as the ones the other day."

"Where are they?" I asked as I swiped at my screen, but Bax had just sent me the answer, and the message was to all of us in a group text.

Bax: Martyrs in the building. Trav says some guy tried to stop him. I saw that freak from the Slice down the hall. Get out of sight, and we're cutting class.
Lars: I'm with Gav. West side. Jess?

Jess: Girls room with Shannon. East.

Gavin: Where R U Bax?
Bax: Library, telling Travis to meet me here.

ENTER SANDMAN

Lars: We're headed that way. Jess, stay there.

Jess: Well, ok then. Someone tell Deke.

Gavin: On it.

I huffed and relayed to Shannon what was going on. "So, the guys are meeting up in the library, but want us to wait here," I finished.

"No, we need them in the locker room," she said, sounding like she'd just had an idea. Pulling out her own phone, she began to type as she talked. "The five of you need to leave. I'm normal, which means I won't set off any alarms, right?"

"Right..."

"So if Travis can get them into the boy's locker room, it has a door leading right to the football field." She pointed to the far wall of the bathroom to make her point. "It's the next set of doors down from this one. I can go get my car and - "

"No," I said, having a better idea. "Last time, Lars snuck through the parking lot to get Bax's SUV. If you can get his keys, then get his truck?"

Her face lit up. "Tell him to wait for me up there."

So I quickly sent a text telling him that. "Ok. There's a road back there, right?" I asked. "Like, for the band busses?"

"Also the football team, and the cheerleaders," she agreed. "Yeah, I know it well. I'll jog upstairs, get Bax's keys, and bring his SUV over. When I text you, I'm here. The five of you can give Travis a ride home, I'll get his car, and then we'll worry about mine later."

"Are you sure?" I asked as Bax replied that he was waiting.

She nodded. "My parents are used to me catching a ride with someone, so they won't care about picking it up. We don't live far. Gets all of you away, and they won't mess with me, right?"

"They might ask what you're doing and try to pressure you," I warned. "I know from experience that they can be pretty intimidating."

She just grinned and put a little fake-happy into her voice. "Cheer stuff. No biggie. Megan sprained her ankle, so I was bringing her SUV around." Then she patted the air between us and began moving to the door, allowing her voice to return to normal. "Stay here. If someone comes in, you're having a period emergency, and I'm getting you something."

"Ok," I agreed, refusing to point out that the someone could be a Martyr.

Because I didn't want to think about that right now. Instead, I just smiled at Shannon one more time before she left, deciding that she was a much better friend to me than Megan had ever been. Shannon didn't make me feel like I wasn't as good as her. She was just on my side, always standing up for me and helping me out. It was so different than everything else I'd known that it hit me right in the chest.

This was what I'd been missing for my entire life. Not just the love of my guys or the trust they gave me. Not simply the freedom that Linda allowed me. It was the respect they all gave me, even when I didn't always deserve it. After Mom had died, I'd learned really fast to keep my head down, say nothing, and behave. My opinions weren't valid, I was a burden on those around me, and any disagreement could end up as a beating.

Now, I felt free. I felt powerful, and not just because I'd been learning how to use magic. I felt like I actually had control of my own life, and I'd be damned if I was going to let these Martyrs ruin it. Fuck them. If one came in here to find me, I'd do whatever I had to so I could survive, because I was not the hero.

Bax had once told me that this was war, and our missions weren't about murdering people. They were simply orders, and I was the best damned soldier the Order had never realized it had. Hell, Deke had probably thrown away everything he had with the Order to keep me safe, and he'd never once mentioned it.

ENTER SANDMAN

No, the man had simply bent over backwards to take care of me. He'd stopped charging at me the moment he realized it made me scared. He'd stopped yelling when he saw me flinch. He'd completely changed his mannerisms to make me feel more comfortable, and that was before he'd known I was a part of this quad.

He'd simply done it for me.

As I sat there in the achingly quiet bathroom, waiting for a text that said Shannon had the truck, my mind just kept spinning. I loved Bax because of how hard he tried to be good to me. The guy was an idiot about women half the time, and a player the other half. I loved Gavin because he made me feel like he saw me, even when no one else did. I loved Lars because he was my rock, the thing I could always cling to when I felt unstable.

Now I had Deke, and as one of the sinks dripped and the building creaked with the silent halls beyond, I couldn't help but think about him. He'd been out risking himself for me over and over this week. He did everything possible for me, and I hadn't even noticed because of how easy he made it seem. He held me at night when I needed it, took my body with such passion when he had the chance, and then he always got out of the way so Bax, Lars, and Gavin didn't feel like they were missing out.

And right now, I just wanted to get back so I could see him.

Yes, I was scared. Who wouldn't be, with some unknown number of potential enemies in the same building? I was also mad that they had to be enemies. Mostly, I just hated that the guys were somewhere over there while I was here alone. We were a team. We were supposed to be together, and it wasn't their fault I was hiding in the girls' room, but I still hated it. I hated feeling like I was weaker without them than I was with them, because I was supposed to be the badass heroine - but it was true. I was weak without them. Their mere presence was the strength I needed.

I was just starting to get paranoid when my phone finally dinged with a message.

Shannon: Here! Use the side exit. Texting the guys.

Grabbing my bag, I opened the bathroom door, turned up the hall, and walked like I was supposed to be doing this. I stretched my legs, using every inch of them I had, and walked quickly. I also kept my head down, letting my loose hair hide most of my face while I scanned everything around me through the strands of it.

Thankfully, the walk was short, and in mere seconds I was hitting that metal bar to open the door and stepping outside. Bax's SUV was parked at the curb halfway between both doors. Feeling overly exposed, I jogged over just as Shannon got out of the driver's seat.

"You may have to move it back," she warned, "but the guys are coming. I already warned Travis that I need his keys, so we'll make a handoff, you'll get him out of here, and we'll all meet at Travis's place, ok?"

"And if things change, we'll text," I promised. "With the guys, we'll know if we're being followed."

I hopped behind the wheel. Shannon wasn't a short girl, but I had a few inches on her, so she was right; I had to move the seat back. I'd just gotten that into place and my seatbelt on when the guys came out from a boring metal door. Inside, I could see the racks for sports equipment, which meant that definitely led to the locker rooms. Considering that the football field was on the other side of this road, it made sense.

Then they all piled in. Travis was last, pressing his keys into Shannon's hands and a kiss to her lips before taking the last spot in the back. I didn't even wait until they were all buckled in before easing my foot off the brake and following the path around the far side of the building and out toward the main road.

"Travis?" I asked. "She's going to meet us at your place."

"She sent me an update while she headed to get this," he assured me.

"The rest of you guys," I said, "need to keep an eye out to make sure we're not being followed. I do not want to lead them right to Travis's house."

"And Deke's heading back home," Gavin told me. "He and Tash were out trying to identify the demons. You still have that USB drive, right?"

"In my bag," I promised.

"Which is between my feet," Bax said. "The bigger problem is what we're supposed to do next. If they stopped Travis, that means they know he's something, just not what."

"Close the seal," Travis said. "Once that's closed, they'll leave again, just like they always do. Until then, I'll just keep my head down and get very good at staying in a pack."

"Fuck the Martyrs," I grumbled. "Fuck all of this. I'm getting really tired of playing nice. I'm supposed to be the one hunting, not the one being hunted."

"So it's time to change the rules," Lars said. "We have all weekend to go over the spreadsheet and make some plans."

"Just don't cut me out?" Travis begged. "I've come this far. I want to see this done."

"Then you're in," I decided, "and fuck it if anyone else doesn't like it."

CHAPTER FORTY-EIGHT

No one followed us to Travis's place. In truth, the Martyrs probably hadn't even known we'd left school, and no one was home at his house. We waited in the SUV until Shannon got there with both Travis's car and his keys, then I traded with one of the guys so he could drive. Lars accepted, which meant I ended up sitting in the back with Gavin again.

When we got back to the barn, all of our cars were there, and no one else's. Tash was with Linda at the side of the house, pretty much under the stairs that led to our place, which was weird. That was why it didn't surprise me at all when Lars called out the moment we were out of the vehicle.

"What are you doing, Mom?" he asked.

It was Tash who answered. "Wards. We're redoing all of them with the key. If Martyrs were at your school again, I want Travis to have a bolt-hole, and right now, this isn't it."

"How long is that going to take?" I asked.

"Not long," Tash promised. "Almost done, actually. We just have to mark the corners and sides of the perimeter we want. The trick is to put them someplace that isn't easy to see, so they won't be pushed aside or destroyed too easily."

Then she showed us a common rock like all the rest on the gravel drive. On the bottom of it was a symbol, and a very detailed one. I wasn't sure what it had been painted with, but I had a funny feeling that it was not just ink or normal paint. There was a smell to it that I couldn't describe, and I wasn't sure I sensed it with my nose.

"Magic?" I asked.

"Watcher magic," Tash clarified. "It's also a ritual, and it seems that Linda can do it if we have all the ingredients for her. We'd always been taught it required the proper bloodlines, but it seems that was another lie."

"And we should be able to make the ingredients," Lars realized.

Tash flashed him a proud smile. "Exactly. Thus, if something happens to both myself and Deke, you will not be helpless. I've already given Linda a copy of all of our training books, along with the necessary recipes for this stuff. Often, the secret ingredient is a drop of our blood."

"Least it's not a gallon," Bax joked. Then he pointed up. "Is Deke upstairs?"

"Waiting for you," Tash promised. "He's also grumpy and probably pacing. Don't be shocked if he has that sword out. We'll be up in a second."

So we headed upstairs. The moment Gavin opened the front door, Deke must have heard or something, because he came storming up the hall to greet us. Then he pointed at the couches.

"Sit, all of you."

Yep, we sat.

"I want to know exactly what happened," he demanded. "They were back? Did they notice you?"

"They saw Travis," I explained. "One of them demanded to know his name, and he lied. He told them he was the guy that got pushed, Oliver."

"I saw the creepy guy from the Slice, but he didn't see me," Bax added. "So there were at least two, because Travis would've recognized him. Well, the five of us warned each other - "

"Six," I corrected. "Travis told Shannon, who pulled me into the bathroom."

Bax gestured at me to show I was right. "Then Shannon got my keys, walked to the parking lot, drove my SUV as close as possible, and we all headed out. Travis went with us. We took him back to his place while Shannon went back for his car and met us there. We all made sure we weren't followed."

I twisted to get into my bag and pulled out the USB drive I'd been carrying since lunch. "Shannon also gave me this. She and Travis made a spreadsheet with all the demons they know of, and their, uh, rank? And all the other information they have on them."

"Useful," Deke admitted, taking the drive.

"But we haven't looked at it," Gavin said. "Don't know how many more hits we'll need, and this is the second time the Martyrs have come hunting for us."

"They're not going to stop," Lars pointed out.

"Fuck," Deke growled under his breath. "Sounds like they *know* you're still in school. I can't remember if I actually told them that."

"So we should quit," Lars said.

All of us just stopped. We'd talked about it before, but Deke and Tash had been adamantly against that idea. They said it would bring too much attention. Never mind that it was the middle of May. We had less than a month of school left and then we'd graduate!

And yet, he had a point. I couldn't count the number of times I'd skipped a class this semester. Three? Five? More? That was going to get noticed. Plus, if we got into a battle in the middle of the school, it would definitely draw a little attention. Even worse would be not fighting back and letting them take us. Well, me, since I was the problem here.

"What if it's just me that quits?" I asked.

"No," Bax said.

"Guys," I tried. "C'mon, the problem is all of us quitting. If I'm the only one who does it, and they've all been saying I'm off the rails, then people won't even bat an eye. The three of you stay in school, get your diplomas, and then we're off to whatever we need to do next."

"No," Bax said again. "Jess, you're the one that cares about this shit. The three of us couldn't give a fuck. You're the one with the dreams of college."

"Yeah, but I'm not going to college now, am I?" I countered. "No, I'm hunting demons and saving the world. I'm fighting Martyrs because they won't just accept that the mark on my hand is good enough. If we want a low profile, then you three should graduate for me."

"I'm with him," Gavin said.

"What about your immigration?" Deke asked.

Gavin scoffed. "Covered. Bax is my sponsor and employer. Did you know I'm the farm manager? It's on the paperwork. I already have a student visa, and now I'm doing a change of status to resident."

"Ok, so that's at least handled," Deke said. "Lars?"

"I'm not leaving Jess alone all day with Martyrs who might jump her," Lars said. "I know you're good, Deke, but you're still just one man."

Deke dropped down into the chair he always used, and then sighed. "I know I should be trying to talk the four of you out of this, but I won't."

The last words were barely out of his mouth before Tash walked in, with Linda right behind her. "Won't what?" Tash asked.

"The kids are dropping out of school," Deke said.

"No," Tash told him, "they aren't."

"Why?" Linda asked.

"Martyrs at school again, Mom," Lars explained. "Shannon got us out without a problem, but how many times can we do this?

People show up at school and we fuck off?" He looked over at Tash. "Like that's not suspicious."

"No," Tash said. "Bax has a home here. That makes this easier than normal. Usually we blow into town, rent hotel rooms, and then leave when done. You four? You can live here and watch this seal. You guys already *live* here - with everyone else in this town, who are all going to know that you dropped out together, are in some freaky sex orgy, and never leave the property. That's called drawing attention."

"And how many kids drop out every year?" Lars asked, looking at his mom.

"Twenty or more," Linda said. "Hellam High doesn't have the best retention rate for students. With that said, it's late enough in the year that dropping out would make a scene. Instead, I think the four of you should just stop going. When the school calls, I'll let them know that something has come up, a family thing, and give you an excuse. They'll want notes from doctors or whatever lie I tell them, won't get it, and you'll just be quietly removed from the rolls."

"They're being hunted by Martyrs," Deke added, watching Tash.

"Which means we've already been noticed," Bax pointed out. "They know where we are. If we slip up once, all of this is over. They will find out what Jess is and kill her. Once she's dead, the demons will come for the rest of us. There's no way I'm going to keep going to school, get the diploma that Jess wants so bad, rub that in her face, and think that she won't resent me for it. There's no way we're going to leave her here alone, with both Martyrs and demons looking for her."

"And the seal," Gavin said. "It's almost been a year since we met Deke and he said it was cracked back then. How long will it stay just cracked?"

"I don't know," Deke admitted. "I've never known of one left alone for this long."

ENTER SANDMAN

"Because you're bending the rules for me," I said, thinking back to my epiphany in the bathroom.

"No, because we failed," Deke said. "I lost my last quad. I had to rebuild one, and that usually happens when repairing a seal. I mean, it did, but this one cracked almost immediately. There was no downtime to recover. There's no support. I can't keep throwing bodies away until a miracle happens, so yeah, I'm fucking trying something new!"

"So we quit," Bax said again. "It won't be long before the Martyrs figure out where we live. The demons already know, but the wards are keeping them away. We quit, we close the seal, and then we're going to need to move."

"What?" I asked.

Bax licked his lips, staring at the ground. "It just makes sense. I mean, the farm is a tax write-off, and Linda can live here, but us? We can't. We can stay for a visit, but we can't just live here like Tash is thinking."

"Shit, you're right," Lars realized.

"No, I'm confused," Linda said. "Why can I stay here, but not you?"

For a long moment, the room was silent as we all thought about that. It was Deke who finally answered. "Once the Martyrs know where we are, they will come - and keep coming - until this quad has been reset. Once they find out what Jess is, she will never be safe again. The same reason they can't keep going to school, Linda. They can't be where the Martyrs can prove that Jess is an anomaly."

"An abomination," Tash corrected.

"Both!" Deke snapped, his head twitching as he glared at her. "A girl with three guys? A watcher/demon hybrid? It doesn't matter *why* they want to find her. I'm not going to let that happen, Tash. Yeah, it's comfortable here, and maybe it makes some things easier, but what will that matter if all four of them are *dead?!*"

"So we quit," Lars said, looking over to me. "Jess, we'll figure something out so you can still get a diploma, ok? There are night courses, and online courses. I mean, even for college."

I waved him down. "It's ok. I mean, it sucks, and I spent so many years just wanting to graduate that it's hard to imagine dropping out, but Bax and Deke are right. I'd much rather live than graduate."

"And we'll make the Order pay for fucking up our lives," Gavin grumbled.

"It's not the Order's fault," Tash tried to tell him.

But Gavin slammed his fist down on the arm of the couch. "Yes, Tash, it is. The Order made these rules."

"And the Order didn't pick you! That's destiny or something. It's because of choices that *you* made. This isn't the Order's fault!"

"Who wants to kill Jess?" Gavin asked. "Who wants to reset her because she doesn't have a dick? Who hates her because she has magic? Who has hidden the information we need to actually survive being picked for this? I didn't. We didn't. The Order did."

"He's right," Deke said, his voice calm and resigned. "That means the four of you had better figure out what you need from school. If we have to, Linda can go pick it up. Anything in your lockers, classrooms, or whatever. Starting tomorrow, you're no longer high school students."

"Which means we need to look at that list," Lars said.

"No," Deke corrected. "You four need to shoot better, fight better, and Jess needs to keep working on her magic. I want you studying the Brethren, not English literature. You're not done learning. You're just changing subjects, because I have no intention of letting any of you die. Not now. Not in ten years. So let's get this right."

CHAPTER FORTY-NINE

WITH THAT DECIDED, Deke gave us the afternoon off while he and Tash went to look at the spreadsheet. Linda followed them, saying she could help. Gavin and Lars went to change clothes, talking about a head-to-head match in some game they wanted to try. I was about to do the same when I heard Bax sigh. I glanced back just as he headed to the front door and slipped outside.

Confused, I followed him. Who cared about comfortable clothes? That sigh had sounded serious, like something was weighing on him. Sure, it sucked to be quitting school, but he'd never really seemed like he cared about it. That had been *my* thing, not his. Then again, I'd also thought Bax didn't *want* a girlfriend when it had been the other way around.

Of all the people in the house, Bax was the best at hiding his true feelings. It was as if he'd learned how to play the little social games better than anyone else I'd heard of. He had his public image, and he was so good at being the rich asshole that it was hard to think of him as anything else. And yet, underneath all of that was this sweet, amazing guy who was scared of the dark.

I made it out the front door just as he reached the bottom of the stairs, but I didn't call out. Bax didn't need to feel like he had to entertain me, and he was clearly going somewhere. I just wanted to make sure he was ok. I hurried but didn't even jog. Still, Bax was in the middle of the gravel parking area when he just stopped.

"Thought you were going to change?" he asked, turning around to smile at me.

It was good. It was so close to the real thing that I probably would have missed the hints if I hadn't heard that sigh. His eyes were just a little too tired and his shoulders were a bit more slumped than normal. So instead of answering, I made my way over and took his hand. That made the smile turn a little more real.

"You sighed like you were upset," I told him. "I thought you might want someone to listen as you talk." Then I shrugged because that was probably stupid. "Or I can leave you alone, if that's better?"

"I just know this has to be hard for you," he admitted.

"Not as much as I expected." I tilted my head toward the trees, inviting him to keep walking. "Hard was those few moments when I was sure I'd killed my dad, Lars would hate me, and that I'd be alone. This? It sucks, but does it really make a difference?"

"Does to you," he pointed out. "Jess, you had such dreams. We're eighteen years old. This is the time of our life when we're supposed to be thinking about conquering the world and figuring out who we'll be when we grow up. Instead, we're putting aside our dreams - and for what?"

"To live," I reminded him. "Plus, if I'm honest, I never wanted to get a business degree and spend most of my life in an office. I thought I had to, which is very different. This? Saving the world, saving demons whose only crime was being born, and having the chance to actually change something? It doesn't even matter if our names won't go down in history. It's kinda like that poem about the starfish, you know?"

"Don't know that one," he admitted.

ENTER SANDMAN

"The guy was throwing starfish back into the ocean, and someone said it was pointless because there were millions on the beach. The guy said that it mattered to that one. This? It matters to Travis. It matters to the shadows in your basement. It matters to the ones we help, and that means more than some shitty job that sucks away my life."

"I like that," Bax said, but he didn't sound any happier.

I waited until we'd crossed into the tree line, picking my steps carefully without letting go of his hand. Then I asked, "So what's bothering you about this?"

He just ducked his head and laughed once. "Jess, you're supposed to pretend like everything's ok and not try to fix me."

"I'm just trying to listen," I assured him. "So spill."

He kept walking, but he didn't say no. This felt more like he was trying to figure it out himself. Eventually, the barn and cars were hidden by the woods around us. Above, leaves rustled softly, and a bird was singing in the branches. Unfortunately, it wasn't a pretty song. Bax just slowed down and sighed again.

Then he turned to face me. "I always thought that this place was the one thing that would always be here for me." He forced out a dry laugh. "Stupid, right?"

"No, it's your home."

"But it's not," he insisted. "Fuck, I won't even live in the house. I'm scared shitless of the basement. I mean, knowing that it's kids down there has helped, but I'm still afraid of the dark, Jess. That's going to take some therapy shit to get rid of. I hate the memories in that house."

"But the barn is yours," I realized.

"And this," he said, gesturing around us. "Friends stabbed me in the back. When it happened in elementary school, I came home and cried about it. My nanny would tell me they were jealous, or some other bullshit excuse that mothers are supposed to tell their kids. She tried, but I knew better. Then, in middle school, it was the cliques. I didn't want to play sports, so I was lame. I wasn't this or that, so I didn't fit there. The girls would giggle and smile at me, so I figured that was cool, but the guys wanted to punch me for it."

"Because middle school sucks," I reminded him.

"Fuck yeah, it does," he agreed. "And yet, when I came home? The barn was always fun. I had games to play, the staff would talk to me, and I could lose myself in these woods. I mean, it's only a few acres, but it always felt like the biggest forest in the world."

"I like it," I said softly. "It's peaceful out here."

That earned me a real smile. One of the sweet kind. "Yeah," he breathed. "But that's the thing. When the girls didn't want anything serious with me, when the guys wanted to use me for my money instead of really being friends, I had home. I had my own place. I had this, Jess, and now I'm going to lose it. I've never lived anywhere else!"

"We can come back," I tried, hoping to make him feel better.

Bax just shook his head. "No. That's the thing. We can't. So long as they want to hurt you, we can't live here. And if I have to choose, I'm choosing you every single time. I used to think that Gavin was the only person who'd ever understand me. That's why he's my best friend, because he knows that I'm more than wild parties and easy fucks. He gets it when I feel like shit, even though I supposedly have everything."

"You don't have parents," I said without even thinking.

Bax just met my eyes and nodded. "Yeah. You get me too. Somehow, you understand that I can know how fucking lucky I am and still accept that I miss the things I don't have. That I want my mother to fucking care! That when my nanny quit, it hurt like hell because I'd almost convinced myself that she liked me for more than the paycheck. Shit, I've never told anyone else half this shit, and now I don't even care who knows."

"Because being the rich player is a mask," I pointed out. "The guy at those parties? That was you escaping reality for a bit. But, since I've gotten to know you, I've kinda realized something." I chewed at my lower lip, hoping I wouldn't upset him by saying this. "It's easier to lock people out than it is to let them in. That was why I was ok with being invisible at school. If no one saw me, then they wouldn't pick on me. You do the same thing."

"But I saw you," he said softly.

I nodded. "And I see you, Bax. We will come back. Maybe for a visit. Maybe we'll fix this shit and get to live here. I don't know, but we'll come back, because this is my home now too."

He draped his arm over my shoulder, and we began walking again. "Can I say something really stupid?"

"Ok?" Because that didn't sound good.

Bax leaned in to kiss my temple. "I'm going to miss home. I really am, but I won't regret leaving. If I have to choose between my safe place and my girl? I'll pick you every single time."

"That's not stupid," I assured him. "Bax, that's sweet. That's..." I leaned my head against where his arm met his shoulder. "That's the kind of thing a girl always wants a guy to say."

"Yeah, that's not the dumb part," he promised. "This is. See, I used to have a different girl in my bed every single night. I was living the dream, right? It's what guys say they always want, and yet I like this more. Maybe you crash with Deke, or sneak in to fuck Gavin, or I have to work to get my time with you, but that's ok because of this."

"Which this?"

"The part where you listen to me." He shifted his arm to play with the ends of my hair. "The part where I feel like you're as much my friend as a hot piece of ass I want to brag to all my friends about. The part that makes me sure that even though I've never done this before, I really am in love with you, and it's not a puppy love thing, and it's not because you give good head."

"Bax!" I laughed, slapping playfully at his abs. "Wait. Do I?"

"You do," he promised. "I mean, don't get me wrong. I love that you're a kinky girl, and the group stuff is fun. I just like this better. I like the quiet moments."

"Think it's because we're not kids anymore?" I asked.

"Fuck that." He chuckled. "Nah, I'm going to be an irresponsible kid as long as possible. You know, blowing money, playing video games, and chasing girls. Might be either my girl or a demon I'm going to cut down, but still counts, right?"

Now I was giggling. "Sure. If you say so."

Then he sobered again. "Just tell me that I'm a good boyfriend?" He paused again and pulled his arm away. "I'm serious, Jess. I don't know how to fucking do this right, and I'm trying to make sure I'm not pushing too hard or taking advantage of you. Deke says that you're going to try to fix everything because that's what girls are supposed to do." He winced. "No, I mean that's what you were taught, not that it's really..." Then he groaned. "Shit. See? I suck at this."

"You are amazing at this," I promised. "Shit, Bax. You're like romance novel boyfriend material. You don't try to hide things from me, you put in a real effort, and you're not afraid to be more than a two-dimensional set of abs with a dick."

"Oh," he said, making a playful production of it. "Yeah, I think I read that one." Then he changed his voice to something a little deeper and a lot more bland. "Lady, I will save you. Here is my twelve-inch cock the size of a coke can. Please drop to your knees in thanks and I will bail out your failing bakery."

"Yep, you read one of them." Then I caught his hand again. "Sadly, there are plenty like that. I like the ones where the guys are flawed, still amazing, and the kind of people I'd actually like to talk to."

"Like... me?"

"Like you." Then I tugged him toward me, lifting my face for a kiss. "See, that's why I - "

The crash of underbrush cut me off and we both spun toward the sound. I caught a glimpse of movement and then Bax shoved me back, once again putting his body between us. I didn't have the chance to think. There was no time to dodge what was coming.

Something crashed into Bax's raised arm and side, then wood splintered over me.

That was when I pushed, forcing whatever it was back.

And there, crouched before both of us was my father in his human body. He looked pissed, and his gaze was locked right on Bax. "She is still my daughter," he snarled.

"Fuck you, Ted," Bax growled, falling into his natural fighting stance. "There are some things worth dying for. She's mine."

There was just one problem with all of this. We didn't have any weapons - just me.

CHAPTER FIFTY

"I won't let you have her," Bax said, flexing the fingers of his left hand.

I was pulling off my support sleeve to bare my own palm. "Dad, if you hurt my boyfriend, I will use this on you, and this time I'll do it to kill!"

"You've ruined her!" Ted roared, but he also stood up a little more. "She used to be good!"

"She's still good!" Bax yelled back. "She's just not weak and scared anymore. She's not hurting because we love her enough to take care of her - not *use* her."

"Lies!" Ted grumbled. "You think I don't know what you're doing with my daughter?"

"Stop!" I screamed, trying to push around Bax to stare down my father.

But Bax pushed me back, keeping his body before me as a shield. "Jess, he will hurt you."

"Oh, sure, hide behind the invulnerable one," Dad huffed, lowering his arms. "That's how you always deal with things, isn't it, Jessica? You run. You hide."

"Fuck you, Dad," I snapped. "This? It's why I left. You hurt me, and you never care. Doesn't matter if that's words, fists, or your damned belt. You drive me away and then get pissed when I go. Well, guess what? You did this to yourself!"

"You. Are. My. Daughter!" he roared.

"And I'm my own person," I taunted. "I grew up, Dad, and there's nothing you can do to get me back. I'd rather die."

"But I'm trying to help you," my father insisted. "Jess..."

"No!" I moved to Bax's side simply because I refused to cower behind him. Thankfully, Bax didn't try to push me back again. "You're probably so sorry about what happened, right? It was all a misunderstanding, and somehow it was my fault. Somehow, it's always my fault. Next, you'll tell me how hard you're trying, but this? It proves that you haven't changed at all. Not all demons are evil, Dad, but you are."

"Oh, and that's why you brought the Martyrs to town?" he asked. "Do you honestly think they can kill me? Do you really think that I'll use my protections to shelter this army you're building?"

"I don't fucking want your protection!" I screamed back.

"How many are you hiding in there?" Dad sneered. "Think ten is enough to kill me? Waiting for more?"

"More what?" Bax asked. "Fuck you, Ted. Love isn't something that comes with hoops to jump through. Either you're a good dad, or you're just a bad memory that we'll help Jess put down."

"I've killed tougher things than you, boy," Dad warned him. "And I will kill every Martyr you bring into Hellam as well."

Wait. Martyrs? He wasn't talking about Tash and Deke. I wasn't sure why, but it didn't feel like that. Dad was talking about the ones at school and in town.

So I grabbed Bax's arm, pushing it down so he'd relax. "How many Martyrs have you seen, Dad?"

He scoffed. "You think I'm going to make this easy for you?"

"Because they're hunting *me*!" I screeched. "Fuck, you self-absorbed idiot."

My father's face completely changed. The rage vanished, surprise took over, and he made a half-step in my general direction before stopping himself. Beside me, Bax tried to shift before me again, but I still had his arm.

"They're looking for her," Bax explained. "Jess isn't supposed to be Brethren. She's an abomination, they say. They want to kill her and reset the quad because we can't close the seal. Because of what she is, Ted. If they see her, then they will try to kill her, but we're not going to let that happen."

"Shit," Dad breathed, turning to pace two steps to the side. "Do they know what you are, Jess?"

"They know the quads are supposed to be either all male or all female," I pointed out. "They know this one doesn't work like that."

"And the two in that house?! They know what you are." That came out in a low growl, sounding like a threat. "What will *they* do to you?"

"Deke and Tash," I explained. "They're not Martyrs. They're our Sandmen. They're ours, and they're protecting us."

"Her," Bax clarified. "Deke is training her to fight. Tash is helping her learn her magic."

Dad just nodded, his eyes on the ground like he was thinking as hard as he could. "And Linda? Do those two know about her?"

"About the baby?" I asked. "Yes. Linda's helping us figure this out. She's researching."

"Good," he said. "She'll love that. She's a good woman, Jess. Too good for me. That's why I'm going to learn. She's going to raise the baby, and I'm not going to hurt it because I'm trying. I'm doing everything you asked."

"No, Dad, you aren't," I pointed out. "You just tried to attack my boyfriend!"

"Because he..." Dad closed his mouth. "I'm sorry."

Bax and I looked at each other since that was not at all how my

ENTER SANDMAN

father was supposed to react. Dad never apologized like that. Sure, he said he was sorry all the time, but it was always an excuse, never with honest regret.

"Is the other boy ok?" Dad finally asked. "The one Greg tried to kill?"

I nodded. "Yeah. I healed him."

"All five elements?" Dad asked next. "Can you use them?"

"I've been learning," I promised. "I have a friend helping me."

That caught Dad's attention and his head snapped up. "The boy. Travis?"

"Don't answer that," Bax warned.

"It's Travis," Dad said. "He will be a strong one when he molts again, but he's causing problems. The weak ones think he's betraying them. The strong ones think he's a traitor. Someone will try to remove him."

"Greg already tried," I snapped. "I put him back together too."

Dad just smiled. "Then I'm glad Greg's dead. I told him not to touch my little girl, but he didn't listen. If you hadn't killed him, I would have."

"But you didn't," I shot back. "Greg tried to kill Gavin, and you just pretended like it never happened."

"I helped you escape!" Dad roared, slinging an arm through the air to make his point. "I lied for you! I put protections around this house to keep them away - or did you think we don't know where you live? Do you honestly believe that we couldn't get in there? Without me, you'd all be dead already. I have been helping you, Jess! I didn't go when they wanted to stop you!"

"But you didn't try to stop them either!" I yelled. "No, you think it's enough to bury your head in the sand, because it's all about you, isn't it? Just ignore the shit you caused and it'll all go away, right?"

"You don't understand," he grumbled.

Bax gave me a nudge, breaking in before I could reply. "Why don't you explain it then, Ted? Don't you think she deserves that?

You're the reason why demons and Martyrs want to kill her. You taught her nothing, beat her down until she couldn't remember how to fight back, and then get pissed off at those of us willing to do something about it. We are the ones protecting her. Not you. The *least* you can do is explain it."

Dad reached up to scrub at his face, and then it was like he just gave in. "Ok. What do you want to know?"

"Why are you trying to break the seals?" Bax asked.

Dad shook his head like that was a stupid question. "To get out."

"But you're out," I reminded him.

"And I'm not trying to break the seals. The ones inside are. You don't understand. In there? It's kill or die. Being 'nice' isn't an option. We learn to fight, and we learn to attack anyone and everyone who comes near us. No one is safe. Not our mothers, not our brood, and certainly not other demons. We fight, we kill, and we devour the dead for what little magic we can get. Strength is the only thing that matters, so I learned to be strong - and cruel. I had to!"

"And now you're out and don't need to be that way anymore," I pointed out. "Never mind that you're strong enough to protect others, but you never think of that, do you?"

He sighed heavily. "Habits are hard to break."

"More when you aren't trying," Bax grumbled.

"I am trying!" Then Dad stopped himself again. "I'm just not good at it. Jess, I spent centuries fighting. I tried to help the other kids. More than that, I tried to raise you to be something else. I just wanted you to live a normal life as a human girl. No one would know. Cambion aren't easy to detect. Your magic doesn't take over. If you were never trained, you would've been able to grow up, have a family, and - "

I would not let him play the hero. "That's a shitty excuse for beating me, Dad."

"I never hit you that hard!"

"You broke bones!"

ENTER SANDMAN

"Because I'm used to demons!" Again he stopped. This time, it was to pull in a breath, like he was fighting the urge to keep yelling. "You're right. I was wrong, and I'm trying to make up for that. I'm trying to be a good father."

"But that's more than saying sorry," I reminded him. "You proved to me that you were a piece of shit. Now you're going to have to prove that you're not, and it's going to take years, Dad. One nice gesture isn't enough. Being my dad isn't enough. This is going to take a long time, so if all you want is the quick and easy fix? Well, you're going to be disappointed."

"I know," he admitted. "I just heard that Martyrs were in town, and I wanted to see what kind of army you were making. I'm supposed to guard the seal, you see. That's why we live here. It wasn't your mother. It was me."

Which gave me the opening to ask what I'd always wanted to know. "Did Mom know what you are?"

"No." He shook his head. "I wasn't brave enough to tell her."

"So how can you say you loved her?" I asked. "If you didn't even tell her the truth, then how could you call that love? If you didn't trust her, then were you using her? Can you even feel *anything* for someone else?"

"I loved her as much as I love you," he swore. "As much as I know how to love. Jess, your mother was the one good thing in my life. In my very long, very violent life, she was my spark of light. Then it was you, but you weren't an easy child. You were too demonic. I thought that if I could just make you more human, then we'd be happy, and it worked for a bit. Until your mother got sick."

He sounded so sincere, unlike when he'd growled out the words the last time. This time, Dad sounded like he'd honestly cared, and it made something inside me change. No, I couldn't forgive him, but the fear that my entire life had been a lie vanished. It hadn't exactly been the truth, but my parents had cared about each other. My memories were real. It wasn't much, but it was exactly what I needed.

"She was a watcher," I told him.

Dad nodded. "Which is how you're Brethren. Has to be, because it couldn't be me." Dad made a weak gesture toward my hand. "Anathema?"

"Yeah."

"You've already learned that you can kill. Most can't." Then he looked at Bax. "And you seem to know that you're invulnerable."

"What?!" Bax asked.

Confusion swept my father's face. "Conquest cannot be defeated. Demon claws will not pierce. Our venom will not sicken. Bullets will not hit. Conquest cannot be defeated, which is why I thought you jumped in front of her."

"I did that because I love her and I won't let you hurt her anymore," Bax said.

But I heard what Dad didn't say. "What else? Dad, what do the others do?"

"Vengeance is unstoppable. When he wields the Sword of Vengeance, nothing will block it. In his hands, it will cut through anything. Judgement returns us to our state of being."

"What does that mean?" I asked.

Dad smiled wryly. "Ashes to ashes. Dust to dust. It's all about order and chaos, Jess. I know the phrases. I've seen it in action. I have no idea how you use them."

No, he wasn't getting out of this so easily. "But we have powers that terrify you, right?"

"You do," Dad admitted. "The touch of your hands can change or persuade minds. The area around you can influence us. The push of your power will destroy us. That is what makes the Brethren so deadly to our kind. The Martyr will wait. He will be the sacrifice. His job is to repair it all when it's over, and to hold you up while you battle."

"Hold us up?" Bax pressed.

"When the Martyr is there, we become weak," Dad explained.

"His - or her - power makes us no stronger than humans. The blessed bullets and swords will kill."

"What blessed swords?" I wanted to know.

"I don't know," Dad explained. "But the Brethren's weapons were always blessed. Different ones, but they burned with power, the wounds refusing to heal for far too long."

"What else?" I demanded. "Dad, we have to close that seal or the Horsemen will get out. We need to know everything you can tell us!"

"That's all I know," he insisted. "Jess, I don't *talk* to Brethren. I kill them or I run from them. This? Our limited knowledge about your powers? It's what has been passed down from those who ran fast enough to survive. It's nothing more than stories, but it's all I have."

I nodded. "Ok. And when we try to close the seal again, you still won't try to stop us?"

"No," he promised. "I'm going to prove to you that I'm learning how to be better. Linda said it will take at least four years, so I've been trying." Then he grunted. "And failing. I'm not good, Jess."

"I know, Dad. I'm just hoping you can learn how to be, because I'm not ready to forgive you."

"But this," Bax said, "helps. It might be enough to keep her alive long enough for you to have a chance."

Dad bobbed his head. "That's all I can ask." Then he looked up, right at me. "I really am sorry, Jess."

"Yeah, I know, Dad. You keep saying that, but it doesn't change a damned thing. Your guilt isn't worth more than my pain. That is the part you need to learn."

Then I turned and walked away. Bax followed, catching my hand to lace his fingers through mine. The surprising thing was that Dad didn't try to follow us.

CHAPTER FIFTY-ONE

WHEN WE GOT BACK to the barn, Bax and I headed up to the third floor. Linda, Tash, and Deke would be there working on the spreadsheet. Neither of us talked about it. It was like we both knew that we had to tell them what we'd learned, so we simply headed to the elevators and all the way up.

When we got there, Lars had joined them, and we walked in on the middle of a conversation. "...For what? It's not like I'm going to have time to worry about a job, Mom. We'll be fine, and if we have to, the four of us can get online diplomas or something."

"Ok, just so long as you're sure," Linda said. "I just don't want you four making a decision out of fear when it could affect the rest of your life."

"School?" Bax asked as we stepped off the elevator.

"Yeah," Lars said. "I think it's the right call, though."

"Been saying that for a bit," Bax told him, using my hand to tow me after him, into Linda's living room. "You should also know that we just bumped into Ted."

"Where?" Lars growled, instantly in protective mode.

"The woods behind the parking area," I said. "We walked out there to talk - "

Deke broke in. "Everything ok?"

"Adjusting," Bax assured him. "But it seems Ted was out there. Sounds like he knew about the Martyrs in town, so he was trying to get a look at how many there were. He assumed they were gathering here."

"Because Brethren go with Martyrs," Tash agreed.

"And he tried to attack Bax!" I said. "Hit him with something."

"A log," Bax said. "Well, branch, but a thick one. It was also rotten."

"Are you sure?" I countered. "I mean, he said you're the invulnerable one."

That had everyone's immediate attention. Tash closed the laptop before her. Linda twisted in her chair to look at us, and Deke stood halfway up before he caught himself. Lars just twitched his head like he was trying to make that fit in his brain.

"What?" Lars asked. "Invulnerable?"

"Long story short," I told them, "Dad mentioned those powers we've been trying to find. He doesn't know much, but that makes sense. Tash only had the smallest amount of information about my magic because she's not a cambion. Dad only knows what we do to them, not how."

"What can we do?" Lars asked.

It was Bax who answered. "I'm invulnerable, evidently. Gavin can cut through anything with some Sword of Vengeance. You're supposed to be able to return something to their base, and it seems our dear girl has already tapped into her ability to kill with a touch."

"Jess, the overachiever," Lars teased. "But what base? What does that mean?"

"And what sword?" Bax asked. "Because Ted also said something about how Brethren used to bless their swords. Always different, but the wounds didn't heal, or something like that."

"So there's a ritual to make it," Deke murmured to himself. "Not a specific weapon, but his power?"

"I don't know," I admitted. "I just figured that with Tash's tattoo, maybe she could see if there's anything about it?"

"It will probably take time," Tash said, "but I can try. I just have to get the right question to find the answer. This thing is like the worst Google search ever."

"On the upside," Linda said, "it looks like the only greater demon left is Ted. That means the next hit needs to be him. Are you going to be ok with that, Jess?"

"Are you?" I asked back.

"No," Bax said before she could respond. "We leave Ted alone." He lifted both hands when everyone looked at him as if he'd lost his mind. "He said some helpful stuff out there, and he let us leave. So, I'm thinking he's trying to make amends with Jess. He also seemed honestly worried about Linda."

"You don't think that asshole is doing more than lying to try to get his way?" I huffed.

"I think it doesn't matter," Bax told me. "Jess, I know you're not ready to forgive him, and I agree with you. I also think that we can use this."

Lars began to smile. "Oh, that's a good idea."

"How?" Deke asked.

So Bax laid it out. "Ted wants to get his women back. Look, the guy's still a dick, but he's also a guy. I can't count how many of my friends have been complete dicks to their girl, but the moment she dumps him, it's like he wants to suddenly change. He'll do anything she asks, bend over backwards, and make a big production over winning her back. Usually, it's because he thinks he can go right back to being a dick once she gives in - but that's beside the point. Ted is in the proving himself stage. He will bend over backwards to get Jess and Linda to say they forgive him."

"Which includes helping us," Lars added. "He won't let anyone else hurt them. Not demons, and not Martyrs. Guys, he might even protect us when we try to close the seal."

"And then we can take him out afterwards," I realized, nodding to show I approved. "Yeah, that's actually not a bad idea."

"But can we trust him?" Tash asked.

"Not at all," Bax said. "Ted hasn't changed. He's just saying what Jess wants to hear. If he'd changed, then he wouldn't have snuck up on us. He wouldn't try to beat the shit out of me for almost *kissing* her. That man still thinks the same fucking way. He's just trying to make a show of how much he's changed without actually doing the work."

"Yeah," I breathed, shocked that Bax actually understood why I was still so mad at my father.

"Ok," Lars said, heading to me to wrap his arm around my back. "That means we can't rely on him, but he might make a good backup. Start figuring out what comes next. I'm going to make sure that Jess actually changes out of her school clothes."

Bax looked over at him and jerked his chin. Lars nodded, even though no words had been said. I wasn't dumb enough to ask what that was about, at least not in front of everyone. Although once Lars took me to the elevator and had us closed in, I couldn't take it anymore.

"Ok, what?" I asked. "The little man thing back there. What was it about?"

"You," Lars said as he pushed the button for our floor. "Seeing your dad messes with you. You're too damned strong to complain about it, and Bax is worrying about you. I know how much you hate your dad, so I'm going to make sure you're honestly ok and not just ignoring it."

"Because you think I can't talk to my dad without breaking down or something?"

That earned me a laugh. "No. Because I think that you're pissed off at him. In a little bit, you're going to start wondering if he may have been telling the truth. After that, you'll remind yourself that he always lies. That's a spiral, Jess. It also happens to be one I know a little too well, because I did it with my own dad. When I don't see him, I'm fine. When I do, it's like all the trauma is brought right back up."

"Oh," I breathed, because he was kinda right.

"And I'm still your best friend."

The elevator stopped, so he opened the door. I got the outer one, and then we closed it all back up. Without needing to say a thing, I headed to my room at the other end of the hall, and Lars followed. My loyal, sweet, wonderful and amazing Lars, and he was right. I couldn't just ignore everything my dad had done to me. How many months had it taken for me to stop flinching when Deke was around? How many other things did I do because of him?

And now Dad wanted me to simply forgive and forget? Not fucking likely. The man had broken my arm. He'd made my life miserable. Even worse, he'd been the only family I had left, until Linda came along. While she might not be related to me, she was family. So was Lars, and everyone else here.

But finding happiness did not erase what I'd suffered. It didn't just go away because my father said he was sorry. Plus, Bax had said something else when we were outside. He'd pointed out that I'd wanted to fix things because I thought I had to. The truth was that I wanted to fix it because I still lived in fear that if I pushed one of these guys too hard, he'd lash out, or maybe he'd turn into an asshole. I didn't know, but it was so ingrained in my mind that I had to be good or I'd lose everything, because it was always my fault.

It wasn't. That was from Dad's rants in the back of my mind. Maybe my bones and bruises had all healed, but not all scars were the physical ones. My father had abused me for *years*. He'd ruined my life, chased off my friends, and had convinced me that I was worthless. How did saying "sorry" fix that? It didn't!

It never would. I'd spend the rest of my life with the nightmares of him chasing me, hitting me, and making me feel like I'd be better off dead. Every time I wanted to do something fun, I'd have a moment of hesitation because he'd taught me that I didn't deserve it. He had changed me forever, and a half-assed apology wouldn't undo that. No, if he was truly sorry, then *he'd* change, and until he proved that, I was standing my ground.

"Jess?" Lars asked when I started pulling out clothes without saying a word.

"I'm ok," I tried to assure him, then stopped. That was another thing left over from Dad. "No." I tossed my clothes on the bed and turned to face him. "You're right. I know you're right. I also hate how weak and broken it makes me feel when all of you know how I'm going to react. It's like I'm this delicate little damsel in distress, and I need the big strong hero to come in and take care of me."

"Nope," Lars said, shaking his head. "This is nothing like that. This is your best friend being in awe of how much you've gone through, and how you keep pushing your way forward. This is your boyfriend hating that he can't do anything but listen, and being all too aware that you, and you alone, are the one fighting this battle. Jess, I'm worried about you, but all I can do to help is this, reminding you that I will always be here when you need a shoulder to lean on or an arm to hold you when you have to rest."

Two steps were all it took to close the distance between us, and then I threw my arms around his neck. "I love you, Lars. Thank you for making me feel like I'm not broken."

"No, Jess. What I'm trying to say is that if you are broken, you're still beautiful. Like those Japanese bowls that are put together with gold. It's ok to break. It's normal, even. I'm just going to keep putting you back together, making you more beautiful in the process, because you are that amazing." He kissed the side of my head. "Just don't try to hide it from me, ok?"

"I don't mean to," I promised.

"I know." He leaned back to look in my eyes. "I just want to help, and I feel useless when it comes to your dad. This is all you, baby, but you are the strongest one in this quad."

For a second my heart forgot to beat. "What? Me?"

He nodded slowly. "You. That's why we put you at the back. Not to protect you. It's so you can protect us. Deke screams that at us in practice. We can fall. We can be fixed. You are the key to all of this, and so long as we will stand with you, then you will make sure that we survive." He cupped the side of my face, then slid his hand back, caressing the hair at the back of my head. "So let us help, ok? Even just things like this. Lets us guys save our pride a bit."

I ducked my head, pressing it into his chest. "You're so full of shit, Lars."

"Yeah, that's the thing," he said softly. "I'm really not. You're just not ready to believe me yet, but I'll keep saying it until you are. I'm also not going anywhere. None of us are. We love you too much, even when you're feeling a little broken."

There were no words to respond to that. Instead, I just let him hold me. His arms moved around my back and shoulders, and we stayed like that for a long time. I didn't count the minutes, because it didn't matter. Lars believed in me. Bax, Gavin, and Deke did too. I wasn't weak and useless like my father said.

I was strong. I was powerful. I was going to learn how to be a hero, but that didn't mean I wouldn't feel every step of the way. And this? Trying to mentally escape my father's hold on my life? It was probably the hardest step of them all.

"I couldn't do this without you," I finally mumbled into his chest.

"You will never have to," he swore. "I'm not going anywhere, Jess. I love you too much to live without you."

CHAPTER FIFTY-TWO

THE NEXT DAY, Deke put us to work. At nine in the morning, he walked down the hall and banged on all the doors. It didn't matter if anyone was in them. When we made it out to the living room, he had coffee made for all of us, and said we'd need to be out in the yard in an hour. It was time to put all of our lessons together, and we needed to figure out these extra powers.

First up was testing Bax's supposed invulnerability. Bax didn't believe it existed, but Deke was convinced that explained how the demon hadn't stabbed him in that hit that went crazy. Clearly the guy could still hurt and get bruises, but when asked, he couldn't remember the last time he'd been cut. Neither could the rest of us, even though I knew he'd been torn up pretty badly at the seal battle.

"It's the bonds," Gavin said out of nowhere. "When I died, they weren't all secure yet, but I think they are now."

I nodded. "It seems like that. When I healed Travis, I could see us all bound together. All five of us."

"So, we needed Deke to lock in?" Lars suggested. "Like, most quads thought they were four, but they forgot about their Sandman."

"Fuck," Bax grumbled, "I don't think most quads *have* a Sandman. They have a fucking Martyr. A babysitter."

"So what is Tash?" Deke asked. "Sandman or Martyr?"

The four of us glanced at each other, but from the looks on their faces, we all agreed. "Sandman," I said. "Both of you are all about fighting for the right thing, not just following orders."

"I'm good with that definition," Deke said. "So, who wants to stab Bax to test this?"

"Yeah, no!" Bax said. "Never mind that being invulnerable would suck if I needed surgery."

"We need to know your limits," Deke pointed out.

"And stabbing me is out," Bax told him.

"How about a cut?" Deke suggested. "Nothing deep, and just to see."

Pushing out a frustrated breath, Bax pulled his own survival knife and tried. Then he sucked in a breath and showed the nick on his arm that was starting to bleed. "Invulnerability disproven."

"Ok," Deke said, before inhaling slowly and tensing. "Now try?"

Bax shook his head, but he did it again. And again, he winced at the pain. "Still cuts. You using your power?"

"Trying to," Deke said. "Fuck. None of this makes sense, and we're working on nothing but guesses. Ok. Let's get back to tactics, because if I'm supposed to be a part of this, then I'm going to be in the middle of you four. Just remember that I do not have the resistance to demon venom, and while I can shoot, I have no magic at all."

We spent the next few hours learning new formations. Like always, I was put at the back or near the center. Thankfully, Deke was even more protected. He became the guy to watch my back, shooting around me if something tried to sneak past the guys or flank us. Then we began learning how to move like that. It was a mess and chaotic, yet we all knew enough to improve quickly.

Just as I was getting tired, the sound of a car made Deke wave us down. Immediately, I bent over to catch my breath. The guys, however, went on high alert, and Deke headed toward the drive. A moment later, Travis's little black sedan parked beside Lars' Mustang. When Travis stepped out from the driver's side, he lifted both hands at Deke.

"I just need to talk to my friends real fast. Not spying, sneaking in, or anything else."

"There a problem?" Bax asked.

Those words made Travis deflate. Closing the door to his car, he headed over, and we moved to meet him halfway. As we gathered around, Travis reached up to scrub at his mouth, looking for all the world like he didn't want to say whatever he'd come here to tell us.

"Um, I'm headed out," he finally admitted.

"Out where?" Gavin asked.

"Of town," Travis explained. "Yeah, um, seems my parents heard about the Martyrs in town. All of us are talking about them, actually. There's two in town that we know of, and possibly more. Well, they say four, but Deke and Tash are in that. Plus the four of you."

"Ok?" I asked, not quite following.

Travis just bobbed his head, nodding like he was hyping himself up. "And my guardians told me before to stay away from you four. I didn't. They're convinced that I've put them in danger, so they told me I need to go. They gave me the weekend to get my things together and find a new place."

"Shit," Bax breathed. "Where are you going, Trav?"

"I have a bit of money saved up. I figured I could head to some boring town, get a job, and try my senior year again there."

"That's not cool," Lars groaned.

"They fucking kicked you out?" I asked. "What the fuck?"

He just shrugged, trying to act like it was no big deal, and yet he was failing. From the look on his face to the way he swallowed a few times too many, it was clear that this bothered him.

"Yeah," he managed, but his voice broke, so he cleared his throat. "They pointed out that they aren't really my parents, we all knew it, and my dad didn't want to risk my mom's safety. That was his excuse. I mean, I get it, but they don't know you, and - "

"So move in," Deke said.

We all turned to look at him, but Bax was nodding. "Yeah. Tash re-warded the place. You just need the key and you can come in, right? Then you can finish school and go to college like you wanted. Probably get a football scholarship or something."

"I can't go back to school," Travis said. "Guys, those Martyrs want to kill me even more than they want to find Jess. Once they know who I am, it's not a stretch that they'll figure out what my parents are. I mean, they're right, and I'm already packed..."

"And Shannon?" I asked.

He turned away, walking two steps before reaching up to wipe at his face. "I'm going there next. I didn't want to do this over the phone."

The problem was that his voice sounded strained. He was on the verge of tears, struggling to hide it, and we could all tell. Surprisingly, it was Gavin who grabbed his arm, pulled Travis around, and hugged him hard. They both slapped backs, and Travis blinked a few times too many.

"We have a room," Bax said while Gavin hugged him. "It's the least I can do for you helping us, right? Stay. School, no school, doesn't matter. I mean, we're quitting too. Linda said not to withdraw because it will draw too much attention, so we're just not going back. Makes sense for you to do the same."

"And when they come here?" Travis asked.

"Then we kill them," Lars said. "If they come here, then they're coming for Jess. If we can keep our heads down, then fine. If we can't?"

"We burn the world," Deke said. When we looked at him again, he chuckled. "What? You think I'm opposed to that? There's a reason why Tash and I are still here." Then he flicked a finger at Travis. "So, think you can handle a little pain?"

"Excuse me?" Travis asked.

Deke chuckled. "I'm assuming you need the key still. Tash said a scar will work, or a tattoo. We've got a few knives here, and I'm pretty sure we can find some ink."

"Will something from a pen work?" Bax asked.

"Have a sharpie in the car," Travis offered. "Probably not the most sterile, but I'll survive, right?"

"Exactly," Deke said. "Grab the marker and let's go into the shop."

Just like that, a plan was made. When we got into the shop, Deke started rummaging around, looking for something. He came back with a typical ballpoint pen, then gestured to the chair by the work bench. Travis took it, looking about as thrilled with this idea as the rest of us.

"This is stupid, right?" he asked.

"Yes," Deke said. "It's also not going to last as long as a normal tattoo, it's more of a scar, and if you were human, it could kill you. However, it's also a quick way to get you into the house until you can get a real tattoo."

"Benefits of being a demon, I suppose," Travis said. "Where is this going?"

Deke grabbed his arm and pulled it across the table. "Middle of the forearm. That's enough room to fix it later, and enough flesh that I won't hurt you too bad." Then he pulled out his knife. "How good are demonic immune systems?"

"Good," Travis assured him.

So Deke started cutting. There was no poking and imbedding the ink. He just carved the symbol to get through the wards. When that was done, he set down the knife, picked up the ballpoint pen, and pulled out the ink part. Opening that up, Deke dropped the ink onto the wound, then rubbed it in.

"I suggest you take that sharpie and follow the cuts," Deke told Travis. "Keep doing it while that heals, and it should be enough."

"Shit," Bax breathed. "He could've gone to town if you hadn't cut him open."

But Travis had the pen and was drawing the mark. He also looked like the whole process hurt like a bitch. "Nope," he grunted. "This works."

"Demons are tough," Deke told us. "They heal fast, and they can take a lot of pain. Just keep in mind that Jess is half. That's why her dad didn't kill her." Then he tossed the ruined pen in the trash. "I suggest we use the stairs so he's not trapped in the elevator."

"Sounds like a plan," Travis said, capping the sharpie, standing up, and then putting it into his pocket. "I'll still have to tell Shannon about this."

"Might as well invite her over," Bax said. "Unlike you, she can come in and out, and I have a feeling the crew would like to meet her."

Travis nodded. "Yeah, and, um, in the fight we had? I mean my fight with my parents, not me with Shannon. Um, I..." He paused to lick his lips. "Guys, I fucked up."

"How?" I asked.

He hadn't taken a single step toward the stairs. "Do you really want to know?"

"Know what?" Lars asked.

"Yes," Gavin told him. "We want to know."

"Remember that couple?" Travis asked. "Husband and wife. I think it was your second hit? Yeah, they were at the seal battle. They really were there. I just didn't know that they were there to get the kids. They weren't trying to fight. They simply wanted to get the kids out. One of the greaters made them show up, so they decided that if they had to be there, they'd make the most of it, and all I knew was that they were actually there, which was why I gave you their names..."

We'd all gone silent. That had been the hit that didn't feel right.

ENTER SANDMAN

The one where we'd all hated it. The wife had begged, but I'd still killed her. I'd been the one to kill both of them. It had been so easy, and they'd barely fought back, but they'd been innocent.

A shiver ran down my spine as the reality of this news hit me. I'd killed someone. Murder. It was everything I didn't want to do, because I wasn't supposed to be evil. For a moment, I was sure I was going to puke, but I just breathed through it, reminding myself that dozens of people had died, and more would if we didn't try to do something.

"They were still demons," Deke said, gesturing for us to get moving.

"No!" I snapped. "No, you don't get to do that, Deke! You don't get to make it sound like being a demon is a death sentence! Not to me, you don't."

He grabbed both of my arms and shoved his face right in front of mine. "And you aren't the good guys, Jess. That's what you keep saying, right? Well, you don't get to have it both ways. People are going to die, and I will not let you melt down on me. You are nothing like your father, because you tried. It's not your fault that Travis was wrong. It's not his fucking fault that they were there! This is a fuck-up, and it sucks, but they were still greater demons! They could've still killed you!"

I jiggled my head in something like a nod. "But I killed the good guys."

"Not good guys!" Deke said before pulling me up against his chest. "Oh, doll... The world isn't that simple. None of you deserve this, but you're still the only ones who can do it. Good people are going to die - whether by your hand, because you didn't act fast enough, or anything else. Good people will die, and I don't ever want you to think it's because of what you are. It's because four people aren't enough to save the world."

"Five," I breathed, looking up at him.

He leaned in to kiss my brow. "Yeah, five, because I will be with you every step of the way." Then he caressed the side of my face.

"But don't cry for strangers, doll. Get revenge. Fix the problem. Do something, Jess. That's what you're best at. Be the villains, even when it isn't easy, but be the villains the world really needs."

"Yeah," Travis said. "I like that. How do I help?"

"Oh, trust me," Deke said, "I'm going to use you."

CHAPTER FIFTY-THREE

OVER THE NEXT FOUR DAYS, Travis settled in and we started packing. When Travis asked why, we broke it all down for him, explaining how the demons and seals were only a small part of the problem. The Order would be coming for me, and there were a lot of them, so staying in one place was a bad idea. Bax then insisted that Travis could stay. Someone needed to keep an eye on the place, especially the big house with all the little demons using it for sanctuary.

Travis wasn't so sure, but the talk was the push for him to text his parents, letting them know where he was and that he could get the guardians into the house to pick up the kids. That was scheduled for Tuesday. Then, first thing Monday morning, Bax and Deke headed into town to pick up new phones for all of us, because we were still planning to avoid the Order when we could, and lie our asses off when we couldn't.

Between all of that, we trained, researched, and planned. The sand on Deke's tattoo was still getting lower. Too low, in my opinion. Time was running out, and it was like we could all feel it. Tash found some obscure references to the Sword of Vengeance, but nothing that said what or where it was. Naturally, Bax asked what Deke's sword was called. Evidently, it had a name too. It was the Martyr's Sword of the Eighth Quad. Yep, because *that* just flowed off the tongue.

However, we did learn that Deke's ability did something that made Travis feel different. Since we didn't want to hurt the guy, testing was hard, although it seemed like any of his inherent magical resistance vanished. Now, I couldn't figure out why Deke's tattoo would cause that to happen, but at least it was something beneficial. It was also something I'd need to keep in mind, because there was the very real chance that as a half-demon, I'd be more vulnerable as well.

By Wednesday, we had all we were going to get. The details of the demons, our abilities, and the Martyr's powers were discovered, the pieces had all been found, and all that was left was to put it together. Linda and Tash came down with books, papers, and the laptop, then called a meeting in the dining room. There was a little confusion as we worked in enough chairs, and then Deke started off.

"I want to do this tomorrow night," he said. "I'm thinking around three in the morning, so that those demons who have jobs will be deep asleep. The delay might be enough for us to finish this."

"How many demons total?" Bax asked.

It was Linda who answered. "According to Travis's notes, sounds like we have forty-two. Of those, at least thirty-six are expected to show up, but the rest could too. They're the ones like Travis, though, who don't want to release the Horsemen."

"Then I doubt they'll come," Travis said. "With the greaters gone, the pressure to fight is even less."

"But it's still thirty-six demons," Tash pointed out. "There are only six of us."

"Seven," Travis said. "I'm helping."

ENTER SANDMAN

"No," Gavin said. "You told us that you aren't strong enough for that. That they'd tear you apart."

Travis just slapped the table. "And I'm still here to help. Fuck. You guys have had my back. I'm sure there's something you're going to need out there that I can do. Drive a truck, carry ammo - I don't even know."

"Actually," Tash said, "that might work. You'll have to lose your skin, though."

Travis's eyes jumped over to me, then away. "Yeah, I'm ok with that."

"What?" I asked.

He shook his head, but I wouldn't let it go that easily. That look had been a little too intentional, and almost like he was hiding something. Now was not the time for secrets.

"Travis, spill," I insisted.

"Sometimes, when you touch me, I get a rush of magic. Like a refuel. I don't think I'm pulling it from you, and I've never heard of a demon being able to do that, but I'm fine. I mean, I'm completely full, you know?"

"Really?" Tash asked.

Deke seemed to hear something in her voice. "What are you thinking?"

"The zap," Tash said. "My tattoo was activated when she did it, and lately it's been like I can barely get it to work. Like the battery's drained."

I stretched out my arm. "Wanna try?"

So she focused on her tattoo. The black ink quickly turned pink, so I pressed my hand over it. Sure enough, that sucking sensation was back, but this time was a little different. Less intense. In truth, it was more like how it had felt when I'd been "stuck" to Deke's that first time.

"Chaos magic," Travis said.

"Explain?" Tash asked.

Travis made a little grunt like he wanted to, but needed words.

"Ok, so demons and cambion work on chaos magic. Nephilim and witches work with order. There used to be druids, who were the chaos version of witches, but they've been hunted to extinction, and watchers are gone too. That's because the Order kills chaos magic abominations first. Us, Jess. Thus, the world is filled with plenty of order magic, but free and available chaos is limited."

"So where do I get my magic?" I asked. "I mean, it's like it's always out there."

"You're half human," he pointed out. "Jess, you change order into chaos. That's why I can absorb it from you. Probably why she can too, and from the smell of it, her sigil there is consuming chaos."

"Fuck," Deke breathed. "What about mine?"

"Right now, it smells foul, like order."

Which made me think of something. "Could that be the problem with the seal ritual? It stinks because it's order magic?"

"Shit," Travis breathed. "But using order magic on a demon seal is going to weaken it! It's like flexing a piece of metal too much. Eventually, it will..."

"Crack," Deke finished. "Fuck. That's why they're not staying closed!"

"But watcher magic is supposed to be neutral," Tash insisted.

"There is no neutral magic that I know of," Travis said. "Watchers are also gone, so there could've been. I just don't know of any now."

"Which means we need a different spell," Lars pointed out.

I shook my head. "No. There's no time to find out, learn it, perfect it, and be sure it will work. This? At least we know it will close it again. *Then* we can find the right spell."

"I agree," Tash said, smiling at me proudly. "The abomination is right."

For some reason, that felt good. Even just the way she said abomination was different, as if it no longer left a bad taste in her mouth. Mostly, it just proved how far we'd come since the last time we'd tried this. The time when we'd almost lost Gavin.

"Ok," Tash said, looking back at Travis, "if you can shed your skin, then I'll have you cover for me. I'm going to perform this ritual, which means I'll need eyes to let me know if we're going to be attacked, and hopefully someone who can take a hit."

"I can do both," Travis promised.

"It'll be three in the morning," Gavin said. "Do you really think there will be as many demons?"

"Yes," we all replied in unison.

But Bax kept going. "We know someone's always watching the seal. We know that the last time, it took mere minutes for more demons to show up. They probably have groups close by on standby."

"They do," Travis said. "People volunteer to watch the seal, and groups wait at any house close enough." He looked over at me. "They used to hang out at your place about a decade ago. That's why Ted would never move. He said when you went away to college, he'd be a safe house again."

"Fucker," I grumbled. "Ok, so that means they'll be on us fast."

"As soon as you start moving," Travis admitted. "Sounds like they watch for cars to leave here. The problem is that they never know where you're going to hit."

"How did they know to be at Cunningham's place?" Lars asked.

"I don't know," Travis admitted. "I'm not really in that crowd. I do know that I was picking the ones who'd actually attacked you all, so that might be why. He was the last greater who'd caused known damage?"

"Regardless," Deke said. "They will be there, and we need to be ready. I'm going to be moving with you four. Tash is going to do the ritual. Travis will cover her."

"What about me?" Linda asked.

"No," Lars said. "Mom, this is where I draw the line. You are pregnant."

"I'm not useless!" she snapped.

"No, but you're worthwhile," Bax said. "Linda, I know it's hard, and I know it sucks, but we need you to stay here. We all need you to be safe, because we can't risk being distracted."

"And someone is going to get hurt," I told her. "You'll need to have a place for us to heal up."

She looked at each of us like she wanted to say more, but thankfully gave in. Pressing a hand to her belly, she nodded. "Ok. I'll have bandages and water ready. Just..." She gently rubbed her stomach. "Please don't die?"

"We can't promise that," Deke told her. "We will try not to, but I don't want the last thing they tell you to be a lie."

"Ok," Linda breathed. "Then how are you dealing with these demons?"

"Focus fire," Gavin said. "We've learned that hitting them in the head knocks them out. It doesn't kill them, though."

"So," Lars said, picking up the idea easily, "we'll call targets and clear the area, moving Jess to each so she can dust them."

Travis flicked his fingers up. "Um..." He waited until we all looked. "That might not hold true in demon form. These human bodies slow us down because they take magic and compress us. They'll heal a lot faster in their real forms."

"How much faster?" Deke asked.

"Seconds?" Travis guessed. "Maybe minutes. A headshot won't drop them for long. See, it's not really the brain that's there. Well, not always. It's just a magical approximation..." He let the words trail off. "Yeah, not important. Mostly it's like being dazed, because the mind space shatters, but not the actual brain. In their real form, you have to actually hit the brain, and that means getting through some of their skins."

"Because Dad's was rough," I reminded them. "Still, the idea is a good one. I'll keep pushing, and we'll stick as close to Tash as we can. If they can't get to her, then they can't stop the ritual, and none of the rest matters, right?"

"Except getting out," Deke reminded me. "Jess, they aren't going to go away when the seal is secure. They'll try to break it again."

"Shit," Gavin breathed. "We have to kill all thirty-six?"

"Yeah," Deke said. "I lost my last quad *after* the seal was closed. It's when we'll be the most exhausted, drained, and distracted."

"And there are Martyrs in town," Tash reminded us. "The problem is that we have no idea what they will do. Will they show up? Will they help us or try to kill us if they do?"

"They do know where the seal is," Deke warned.

"But not when," I said. "Three in the morning means they should be sleeping. Getting ready to, waking up from, or deep in the middle of it. The chances of them being there are slim enough that I think we can plan around them, right?"

"Kinda what I was thinking," Deke agreed. "I just need you four to think long and hard about what you'll be willing to do if they make an appearance. Jess will use magic. They will see it. They will not dissolve. The demons are easier that way. Their deaths feel a little less real because there's no body to worry about."

"And each demonic death will fuel Jess," Travis said. "Me as well, but less than her. When we break down, it releases chaos magic. That's free and easy power for her to keep casting, and should mean she can work bigger spells."

Bax was nodding. "So we wing it. I say we drive Deke's truck right down to the seal, jump out, and use it as a shield."

"I fucking like my truck!" Deke snapped. "Do you have any idea what the demons will do to it?"

"I'll fucking buy you a new one," Bax told him. "Look, it's big. Bullets won't go through it, so that makes it harder for Martyrs. It gets us there before the demons can hit us, and it will put us in a choke point."

"Too many fucking video games," Deke grumbled.

"But he's right," Tash said.

"I know." Deke just nodded his head as he gave in. "Tash, you drive. Pull up so the driver's door is right there. When you open that, it's a little more protection."

"And watch the rocks," I told Travis. "Someone climbed on them last time to get to Deke."

"Yeah," he agreed. "Most importantly, guys? I mean, the biggest thing you have to remember? I can heal Jess. It's not as strong, and it might use all I have, but I can do it - because she's the key to making this work. She's the one who can save all of our lives, and probably the only way we'll survive this. Try not to let her get hurt?"

"So we all keep Jess safe," Gavin said. "We die first."

Deke nodded. "Yes. We die first. Hopefully, we might even live."

CHAPTER FIFTY-FOUR

THAT NIGHT, I lay in bed, alone. I didn't want to be alone, but I was stuck trying to decide whose room I should go to. Gavin? Deke? Bax? Lars? I'd ignored them all a little too much lately, but I didn't really want to spend what might be my last night alone. I was beginning to spiral through the reasons why I should pick one over the other when my bedroom door opened.

The silhouette that slipped into my room was clearly Lars. I reached over and turned on the bedside light. A dim glow filled my room and Lars chuckled, realizing he was busted. He also didn't seem to care.

"I'm actually surprised you're alone," he said, making his way around the bed to crawl in beside me.

He didn't even make it all the way under the covers before the door opened again. "I saw the light," Gavin said - and then paused. "And I wasn't the only one."

"I was trying to figure out which room I should visit," I admitted. "I hate deciding where to sleep. More when it could be our last day, you know?"

"But is it worth it?" Lars asked me.

"No," Gavin said. "None of this is worth it. We also didn't get another option. I'm not ready to die again."

Grabbing my waist, Lars pulled me over on top of him. My legs naturally found a spot on either side of his hips. He stopped, making it clear he'd intended to put me in the middle, but a devious smile touched his lips. His hands moved down to my thighs, and then he shifted both of us in the bed.

"Well, I was going to say that I agree with Gav, and now I have a much better idea."

"Oh yeah?" I asked, tossing back the blankets so I could sit up. "What's that, Lars?"

He pressed his palms flat on my thighs, fingers pointing upwards, and slipped under the edge of my sleep shorts. "Gavin, are you still worried about doing something gay?"

"Fuck you," Gav grumbled.

"I'm being serious," Lars said. "You see, our girl has a little kink. She likes to see if two dicks can fit at once. Spoiler: they can. Feels fucking amazing, but I'm not sure if you're into it."

"Like, same hole?" Gavin asked.

"Yep," I said. "Kinda like sex on steroids."

Gavin just pulled off his shirt. "How?"

Lars all but dumped me off his lap and onto the bed beside him. "Naked, Jess." And while he scrambled to get his own underwear off, he told Gavin, "Easy. She's on top of me, and you're behind her. Your dick might touch mine. Promise I won't think anything of it."

"And it doesn't hurt you, *mi cielo*?" Gavin asked me as he pushed his own pants down.

"Not at all," I promised, tossing my shorts across Lars to the floor and bending to get my shirt off.

But before I could climb back on Lars, Gavin grabbed my ankle. "Fine, but if we could die, then I want to do this first."

One tug was all it took to slide me to the opposite side of the bed. I also shifted so I was more sideways than right-ways on the bed. My feet were pointed at the side, my head toward Lars, and

Gavin climbed closer. His lean body was bare, begging my eyes to follow all of his muscles down, right to his quickly hardening dick, and he made his way toward me, right between my knees.

"Oh, I like this idea," Lars said as he turned so he could reach my neck, kissing it while watching Gavin bend toward my pussy.

Lars sucked at my pulse, then I felt Gavin's breath down there. Gavin's tongue came next, parting me just to slip inside. My breath caught, my legs relaxed, and then Gavin flicked his hardened tongue across my clit. The rush of sensation made my back arch and I reached out, grabbing Lars' side for stability.

That was when the door opened. Tilting my head up a little more let me see Deke. The man paused before finally coming in and closing the door behind him. The problem was that he didn't come closer. There was a moment of hesitation as both Lars and Gavin noticed him, and then I felt a hand on my breast, flicking my now-hard nipple.

"Should I go?" Deke asked.

Gavin took his time, sucking at my clit until I was struggling not to whimper with pleasure. Only then did he lift his head. Trying to catch my breath, I looked up at Deke again, aware of the tension quickly building in the room. Deke was ready to walk away. Under my hand, Lars felt tense, as if he was ready for this to blow up. Then I looked down just as Gavin slid two fingers into my body, his complete attention on Deke.

"All in," he said, glancing down to my pussy then back up to Deke.

Of course, that was when Bax decided to join us. He strode through the door with a grin on his face and his mouth open like he was about to make a smart-ass comment, but he shut it as soon as he saw the scene. Gavin pumped his hand into me slowly, taking his time about taunting me, refusing to let me relax and deal with this.

I thought about telling him to stop, but I really didn't want him to. I needed him to move a little faster, because that felt so good, and yet I couldn't focus completely on what he was doing to me either. Not with the guys all trying to decide if this was ok.

"I won't touch you," Deke promised.

"No," Gavin said, pausing again. "I'm all in, Deke. This is us. I have to learn, and I promised that I would. It may be weird, but..." He glanced over to Bax. "It's not gay. It's us being all in."

"Oh yeah, it is," Bax agreed. "Make her cum, Gav. I wanna watch."

Deke groaned deep in his throat. "Yeah, me too. Fuck, she's hot."

"Like watching porn while getting off," Lars agreed before moving to suck at my breast.

"Great," I told them. "But if you stop again, Gav, I'm jumping on someone else's dick."

Gavin didn't bother to reply. He just bent down and started sucking. While his hand worked me higher, his mouth drove me insane in the best ways. Lars teased my nipple, licking it, swirling his tongue around the aching peak, and then nipping at it gently. I could hear clothes rusting, but I couldn't look. I couldn't let myself be distracted, because these two men on me were gorgeous. Every move they made had some muscle flexing or bulging. Even better, there was something hard that I could actually reach.

Shifting my arm, I managed to reach for Lars. His hips were up by my head as he curled around me, but I could work with that. I wrapped my fingers around his shaft and was just about to move so I could get that in my mouth when someone grabbed my other arm. Then, another mouth was on my other breast.

"Oh, that is hot," Deke said, his voice moving back toward the door. I looked up to see him lock my door. He caught my eyes and smiled sweetly. "I'm just here for the show, doll." Then he pulled off his shirt, tossed that onto the floor and moved to lean against my dresser.

Gavin must've been watching, because his hand began to move faster, almost like he was trying to prove something. I didn't care if it was an ego thing, because it felt amazing. His fingers fucked me nice and hard. His mouth sucked and his tongue tormented me, bringing me higher just to back off. I couldn't help but moan, and the overabundance of sensation was making me unable to think.

Three men. Three mouths. All of them worked at a different pace, seducing and pleasing me in their own way. I didn't have to work for it. I didn't need to do anything but take, so take I did. My fingers were still wrapped around Lars' dick, but I couldn't do more than fondle, not even really stroke. My mind was simply too overwhelmed by pleasure.

I could feel my knees trembling. My muscles began twitching, and I knew I was making stupid noises. I also didn't care. I gasped, I moaned, and I even whimpered. At one point, I huffed out something a lot like, "Yes," and that seemed to encourage them even more. My body was so close, and I didn't even know how to ask for what I wanted, so I just took.

The pleasure just kept building, though. Someone's hand caressed my thigh. Another was on my belly. One held my wrist a little too hard, but I liked it like that. That was when I realized that my eyes had closed. All I could think about was the sensations on my skin, taking over my control and making me feel the most amazing things. That pleasure was like a wave, growing ever bigger, more intense, and then it slammed into me, sending me right over the edge.

I came, and hard. My hips bucked off the bed. My fingers released Lars' dick so I wouldn't grab too tightly, and the hand over my head clenched into a fist. After that, all I knew was the intensity of my orgasm as I rode Gavin's face, thrusting my hips to grind against his mouth while my nipples exploded with sensation.

Then it let me go and I felt like I crashed back to earth, panting harder than I ever had before.

"That," Deke said, his rough voice even deeper than normal, "was amazing."

Lars chuckled. "Oh, we're not done yet. Gavin's doing some very not gay stuff."

I managed to crack my eyes open to see Deke lift a finger and head into my small bathroom. The cabinet opened, and then he was back, tossing a bottle to Lars. "Lube. Use it."

"Cool," Lars said, popping open the top to pour a large dollop into his palm. "Gav? Still in?" And he lifted the bottle like it was an offer.

"Yep," Gavin said.

Lars tossed the bottle over, and Gavin did the same. Yep, I tried to watch them both stroking themselves, because that was hot. There was something about a man's hand on his own dick that I loved seeing. My eyes drank them in, aware of the differences in how they touched themselves.

Then Gavin lifted the bottle toward Bax. "You?"

"Nope," Bax said. "I have every intention of sticking my dick in that hot little mouth of hers."

"Deke?" Gavin asked.

"Watching," Deke said. Then he made a little noise. "Yeah, I'll take it. Gonna have to face this way, though."

The mattress shifted. Lars moved, all but reversing his position. It took me one whole second to figure out what they were doing, but when Lars lay down with his head at the foot of the bed, I figured it out. I also didn't need any encouragement. Before he could even reach for me, I was climbing on. The mattress moved again, this time the weight getting closer, and then I felt a hand on my back that didn't belong to Lars. Gavin's, I realized, because I could see Deke and Bax.

"Ease down on that, Jess," Lars said, catching my waist and guiding me onto his dick.

While I felt him fill and stretch me, Bax said, "You're going to have to straddle his legs, Gav. Jess, lean forward."

"Oh, we won't fit," Gavin said.

"You'll fit," Deke promised as he pushed his sweats lower. "It'll also feel like the tightest pussy you've ever had."

I barely had Lars all the way in before Gavin moved closer. His hand was braced on my back, low, like he was expecting me to push against him. Then I felt him. Lars wasn't a little guy, and Gavin pushed in above him, not beside. My body tried to protest, these two being a little thicker pair than the others had been.

"Breathe," Deke said softly.

My eyes jumped to him working a handful of lube across his fingers. With his other hand holding his sweats down, he lowered his slick hand and slid his fist down his length. The whole time, his eyes held mine almost like he was taunting me.

My body stretched. Deke's dick did too, the skin tightening as he gripped himself hard. I breathed. My core relaxed, and Gavin's hips pressed up tight against my ass.

"Oh, that's my girl," Deke praised. "Let her adjust. We don't want to hurt our little play toy, do we?"

Gavin leaned closer until his lips were right beside my ear. "No, we want to take care of our slice of heaven."

Then Bax grabbed the base of his dick and moved to the side of the bed, right next to me. "You suck this, babe, and they're going to fuck you so good. I want you to swallow my cum as you lose control."

"I think I like this game," I taunted, twisting so I could reach him.

One of my hands landed on Lars' chest for balance. The other wrapped around Bax's shaft, and my lips followed. I licked at the head of his dick, swirling my tongue around him, and then pressed lower. That was when Gavin began to move. Slick from the lube, he glided through my body, but it was so amazingly tight. Below me, Lars groaned in approval, and then began to shift his hips.

Lars might not be able to thrust hard, but Gavin clearly felt it. He made a noise, something between surprise and amazement, and then he pushed back into me. The next thrust was harder, and I felt Lars' fingers tighten on my waist. Bax's hand landed in my hair, pulling me down on him the way he wanted, and Gavin grabbed my shoulder.

Each guy had a hold somewhere on my body, and he used it to make himself feel good. It was like they were using me, and yet it felt like so much more. All in, Gavin had said, and this definitely counted. There was just one thing I was missing. Tilting my head slightly, I could still see Deke as he stroked himself, his eyes hanging on my body. With each thrust from Gavin, I could feel my breasts bouncing, and Deke was watching them intently.

"Fuck," Gavin huffed.

"So good," Lars said, seeming to agree.

I didn't have to do anything. I just took, feeling like a greedy little slut, but in the best way. These were my guys, and I loved them all. Each of them was different, fucking me his own way, and it all came together perfectly. Gavin's hard thrusts contrasted with Lars' deep penetration, while Bax was fucking my face so gently. Still against the dresser, Deke pleased himself slowly, taking his time about it, yet the drop of pre-cum on the tip of his dick kept getting bigger. He'd stroke it down his length just for another to appear.

I might have the three hottest guys in school, but I also had the sexiest Sandman in existence. They were beautiful examples of male perfection, and I had them all. They were also so much more. Loving, caring, intelligent and just amazing. These men were perfect, in their broken, angry, and flawed ways. Maybe the rest of the world wouldn't agree, but these four were perfect for me.

And I loved them.

I never wanted to lose them. As they used my body, driving me higher, that was what I kept thinking about. If there was anything worth fighting for, it was them. I would kill a million more innocent people to protect them. I would let the world burn. I didn't care if it was good or right, so long as I never lost this. The pleasure, the love, and the safety of being in all of their arms.

"Lars!" Bax panted, his voice sounding strained.

"Oh, that hot little mouth is gonna make you cum?" Lars taunted, his own words rough with passion.

"Clit!" Bax all but begged.

And Lars complied. His hand moved lower and he splayed his fingers on my belly as he used his thumb to rub circles on my clit. I bucked, shoving my hips back and driving Gavin deeper. That just made him fuck me a little harder. The first cry of passion broke free, forcing me to let Bax fall from my lips. I tried to bite back the sound, aware that we weren't alone on this floor. And yet, the more I struggled to stay quiet, the harder all three of them worked me.

"Scream," Gavin whispered against my ear. "I want to hear you lose control, *mi cielo*."

He didn't even care how close that put him to Bax's dick. For this one moment, none of that other stuff mattered. Our bodies rocked. The guys all grunted and groaned when it felt good, and I just let go. Holding nothing back, I moaned around Bax's shaft, sucking him back as deep as I could.

Then Lars let go of my side with one hand and pressed that onto the bed for leverage. He began to thrust up. His other hand simply pressed hard against my clit, the motion of our bodies doing all the grinding I needed. Behind me, Gavin was ruthless, fucking me as if nothing else mattered. It was hard. It was crazy. It was all so fucking good that I couldn't help myself.

I tried to pull away from Bax's dick, but he grabbed my head and held me there, thrusting into my mouth even as my body lost control. My core clenched, gripping both guys together inside me. My back wanted to arch, my breasts swung below me as Gavin and Lars kept going, riding me through my orgasm, and Bax thrust a little deeper.

I came, and I kept coming even as Bax swelled in my mouth, throbbed, and then exploded. Warmth filled the back of my throat, but I didn't care. It felt so good. So amazingly perfect. So much like heaven that I barely remembered to swallow before Lars groaned in completion. Hot liquid filled my pussy, and that was more than Gavin could take. His rhythm faltered, his hips slammed into me, and the sound he made was the epitome of primal male glory. Deep, raw, and uncaring, he growled out his climax before wrapping an arm around me - and everything stopped.

The bed rocked with our breaths. I could feel a trickle of sweat sliding down my back. I also didn't care. Of all the fantasies I'd had about multiple dicks, not chicks, none of them had ever been as good as the reality.

CHAPTER FIFTY-FIVE

DEKE SHOVED his pants to the floor, stepping out of them as he made his way toward the bed. "Now, it's my turn," he warned, pushing Bax aside as he caught both sides of my face between his hands.

I heard Bax chuckle as Deke's mouth crashed down onto mine, kissing me deliriously. He didn't care that I'd just swallowed another man's cum. Deke's tongue explored, took control, and claimed my mouth as his even as he lifted me higher, encouraging me to slip off the men still inside me.

Gavin withdrew and moved back. Lars helped me off him even as Deke pressed me back. Without lifting his mouth from mine, Deke leaned in, following me to the other side of the bed. He crawled across Lars' body, guiding me onto my back diagonally with my head up near the pillows, and still kept coming.

I could feel Gavin's leg against mine. The mattress shifted as Lars moved to lie across the foot of the bed. Deke just kissed me again, then again as his body settled over mine. I could feel his dick, so hard against my belly, and I spread my legs to make room for him.

He lifted his mouth to suck in a breath, then found my neck. I arched into him, skin against skin, but mine was so sensitive that it felt like it was tingling. Caught in the glory of my afterglow, I had no intention of resisting this. Not at all, and since the other guys weren't complaining, I could only assume it was ok.

Then hands guided my arms up, holding them against the pillows. I felt Deke's lips curl against my skin right before he shifted his hips, angling his dick to my entrance. Then, in one hard thrust, he pushed in.

My leg curled around his ass and I gasped at the rush of sensation. He began to withdraw, so I curled my other leg around his thigh, keeping him exactly where I wanted. When Deke pumped back into me, I pressed into him, taking more, deeper, and greedily.

"Yeah, that's hot," Gavin admitted.

"If he'd spread his legs a little more, I could see him sliding into her," Lars said.

The surprising thing was that Deke adjusted, giving Lars his view. Then he thrust hard, rocking both of our bodies with the intensity of it. This time, when I cried out, it wasn't around a dick to muffle the sound.

"I will share," Deke growled against my throat before kissing me again. "But I will not ever give you up."

Then he slammed into me again. Hard and fast, he fucked me. After the intensity of two men, it felt just right. This man was taking my body, putting his claim on me, but it worked for him. This was the only way Deke knew how to love. If this was our last night together, if we might possibly lose something, then none of us wanted to hold anything back.

Not even me.

I wanted to wrap my arms around his back, to drag my nails down his skin, but I couldn't. It was Bax holding my hands, his eyes watching me, devouring me like he was trying to burn every moment into his memories. I couldn't see the others, but I felt them. Gavin's hand slid along my calf, caressing it where it wrapped around Deke's ass. Lars leaned in to kiss my hip, so close to where Deke was thrusting into me with wild abandon.

Hands touched. Bodies moved, and while this was just me and Deke, it also wasn't. No sooner did I realize that then Bax leaned in to suck at the other side of my neck. I groaned with desire, closed my eyes, and took it all. A hand moved up my side, sliding between me and Deke to toy with my nipple. That was Lars, and his mouth was now on my waist, pressed against the bed, and still Deke fucked me.

It felt like a tangle of arms and legs, as if all of the hesitation was finally gone. No one cared who touched where. They all just wanted to touch me, and I loved it. I was the trophy, the thing they couldn't get enough of. I was their desire, their love, and more than all of that, their need.

I could feel the bed rocking. I could hear the headboard clank against the wall every so often. Paired with the sound coming from deep in my throat and the primal grunts from Deke, it didn't even matter. Hot, slick skin slid so perfectly. My pussy was dripping with the cum of two men and my own desire. Deke just rolled his hips, using his pelvis to grind against my intensely stimulated clit.

I knew I wasn't going to last. I also didn't care. I'd already come twice. Each one had been better than the orgasm before. I had no idea how good this would feel, but I wanted it. Shoving myself onto him with each thrust, I chased that feeling, knowing what I needed, and I could feel my core clenching, tensing, and so very close.

"That's my girl," Deke grunted. "Oh, fuck me back, doll. Just like you want it."

So I pushed harder, thrusting in time with him. Our bodies crashed together in the best way, the intensity of contact matching these emotions growing inside me. All of it, from fear to passion and lust to love. I needed them. I would die for them. I also never wanted to lose any of them.

Then I felt Deke growing thicker inside me, swelling, filling me a little more. "I," he growled, pumping his length deep into my body. "Love." His breath caught on the word and he thrust again. "You!" And he rocked his hips, grinding against my clit just right to ignite my climax. "So fucking much," he finished in a rush as he lost control with me.

I came, pulling my arms free from Bax's grip to throw them around Deke's back. He tried to keep moving, to ride me through it, but I didn't even care. I'd heard the words. I was lost to the pleasure. Every nerve in my body lit up, screaming its approval, and my mind agreed. I'd heard the words. They were on repeat in my mind as my orgasm washed over me.

I pressed my face into the side of his neck as the pleasure began to subside, but I didn't have the breath for words. All I could do was nod and hope he understood. Against my neck, Deke was panting just as hard, and no one else said a thing, and yet it didn't feel tense. It felt... right.

"Me too," I finally managed to get out.

And Bax chuckled. "Is this where I chant 'one of us' or something?"

"Shit," Gavin said as he moved over. "Deke, there's room."

Lars just murmured at the foot of the bed, sounding blissfully content. "Hey, Jess? I love you too."

"Yeah, I do too," Bax said as Deke extracted himself from my body and flopped down beside Gavin.

"*Te amo, tambien*," Gavin said.

I just lazily made a gesture that was supposed to include all of them and instead looked like my arm had a spasm. "Yep. All of you," I said, struggling to control my heavy breathing. "That. Good. Must do again."

"And you can't hog the entire bed," Bax said, nudging me over.

Deke grabbed the arm on his side and pulled. Lars took care of my feet, the guys working together to angle me back on the bed the way a normal person would lie. Then Bax slipped under the covers behind my back. Lars sighed, making a production of it, then moved to crawl his way up so he could lie on the far side of Bax.

"Shit," Deke grumbled. "Let me up, Gav, and I'll sleep on that side."

"No, stay," Gavin told him. "I am not my father."

"Get the light," Lars said, his words sounding slow and lazy.

Gavin reached for the light, but Deke was a little too still. When Gavin shifted a little more, Deke rolled onto his back. Immediately, I moved in to claim his shoulder as my pillow. Without thinking, Deke curled his arm around my back, holding me there, but he was looking at Gavin.

When the room turned dark, Deke said, "Are we good, Gav?"

"We're good," Gavin promised. "You were scared of her being part demon. I was scared of you being part gay. We both can learn."

"Yeah, we can," Deke agreed, ignoring the 'part gay' part of that. "Means a lot, man."

"Just don't fuck me," Gavin said, but I could hear that he was trying not to laugh.

"Nah. More likely to fuck Bax. He'd probably like it."

"Me," I said. "I like it. All of it."

"Yeah," Bax breathed, but it sounded just a little too serious. "Guys, I've never really had a family before. I've never had anyone in my life I could trust, but you four? You're it. Without a doubt, question, or concern, I trust you."

"Like brothers," Lars said.

"No, you're too cute to be brothers," Deke joked. "Partners. Let people make of that word what they will. We're partners in all of this, from hunting demons to protecting Jess from the Order. We're also partners in bed, working together for..." He huffed something almost like a laugh. "Let's call it the common good."

"Partners," Bax agreed.

"It works," Gavin said, "and if someone calls me gay, I'll punch them in the face."

"And I'll fucking help," Deke said.

"I'm down with partners," Lars said. "I'm also thinking that we're going to need a bigger bed. Wherever we go next, we need one of those Alaskan or Californian kings. Room to work."

They all murmured their agreement, but I was just watching them, taking in how their silhouettes moved in the darkness. There was a new comfort between us. An acceptance, I supposed. Gavin wasn't worried about Deke. Deke wasn't being insensitive to everyone else. Bax felt loved, and Lars felt treasured.

It was perfect. My problem was that it felt too perfect. Maybe it was the high of so many orgasms wearing off, or it could've just been my own paranoia, but this felt almost final, and that made me worried. I tried to ignore it, letting my fingers play across Deke's skin as a distraction, but as the guys fell quiet and began to grow still, I knew this was my last chance to say something.

"Guys?" I asked, my voice a whisper.

"Mm?" Gavin responded, and the others made similar noises.

"Promise me that the world can burn before we'll lose each other?" I begged.

"Shh," Deke breathed, kissing my hair. "We can't know, Jess."

"No, but we can also refuse to give up. I just..." I shifted onto my back so I could see all of them by just turning my head. "I don't care what happens to the rest of the world. I don't care how many people I have to kill. I don't care about anything else but us. Well, all of us. Linda, Tash, Travis, and even Shannon. Mostly, the five of us. I don't want anyone to give up. I don't want you to be heroes. I don't want us to decide that since Brethren don't live very long that we might as well go out in a blaze of glory! I want to live. I want to do that again, get pissed off when people call me a slut, Bax a whore, Gavin a fag, and anything else they might say about Lars and Deke. I want us to fall asleep beside each other tomorrow morning, and still be five. I want us to swear that we will at least try!"

"I promised to teach you Cherokee," Lars said. "That means we're not done yet."

"I'm not ready to die," Gavin promised. "I already tried that."

"I won't have you all saying I was the weak or shitty one," Bax promised. "So, sorry. You're stuck with me."

Then I looked at Deke. He was staring up at the ceiling, and his breathing was slow and measured. Slowly, he nodded. "I will gladly die to protect all four of you. I will swear to you that I will not have another quad." Then he looked over at me. "I also will do everything in my power to make sure it's because this one is still going. I won't lie to you, Jess. I won't promise to survive a battle with demons, but I will swear that I will not give up."

"That's all I can ask." I told him, once again curling up against his side. "Because we didn't survive that much shit just to lose it when we've only just found happiness."

"I don't think even fate is that cruel," Deke whispered. "But if the worst does happen, at least we had this moment."

"All in," Bax said softly.

"All in," Lars agreed.

"Yeah, all in," Gavin whispered.

"All in," I said against Deke's chest.

He kissed my head again. "Finally, I get to be all in. There's no way I'm letting that go easily."

CHAPTER FIFTY-SIX

THE NEXT DAY, just as night fell, Linda insisted on cooking a big formal dinner for all of us. To enjoy the family time, she said. Bax cracked some joke about the Last Supper, but it fell flat. Mostly because that was exactly what it felt like. Travis's awkward laugh broke the tension, though. There was something about inviting a demon to the Last Supper that was rather perfect for us.

I tried to help Linda in the kitchen, but she chased me out. Bax wanted a beer, but Deke said no. Tash suggested a movie, but the truth was that none of us wanted to waste what might be our last hours with that. So we ended up sitting at the table and talking. There was a new casualness between Deke and Gavin. Even better, Tash joined us and picked on Travis like he'd always been a part of things.

If this was going to be my last memory on Earth, it was a good one. All of the latent resentments were gone. All of the problems had been fixed. These people had become the family we'd all wanted, and while we were far from perfect, it was comfortable. There was a trust that I hadn't expected. We were good - and that made my insides twist in fear.

Because good was how people talked about things at funerals. Good happened when looking through rose-colored glasses. Good was never just good, and if I was honest, I was scared shitless, and a massive meal was the last thing my body desired before we headed out in a few hours.

Which naturally meant that Linda overcooked. There was a whole ham, green bean casserole, stuffing, yams, and just about everything typical in a Thanksgiving dinner. She was a few months early, and she'd gone with the options that could be cooked in an evening, but this was a feast.

"Whoa," Lars said as Linda began setting dishes on the table. "Mom, I think you outdid yourself."

"Is it November?" Bax joked, clearly thinking the same way I was.

"Green bean casserole is my favorite," Travis told her.

"And there's fresh bread," Linda bragged. "I just wanted this to be special." She paused, putting her oven-mitt-covered hands on her hips to look at each of us. "And there will be plenty of leftovers for tomorrow when you're all too tired to even make a sandwich. I can make soup with the ham if someone is hurt..." She paused, biting her lips together. "And I will. I have no problem with that. Just make sure that you're here to eat it all."

"We're going to be fine, Mom," Lars promised. "I mean, we've got Jess. Travis is going to play backup for her. We got this. Now sit down and eat!"

"The bread!" Linda gasped, hurrying into the other room. Then she called back, "Dig in. It's better hot. I just need to get butter!"

"Ladies first," Deke said, turning the serving fork toward Tash.

One by one, we all filled our plates. When Linda returned, she gave us each a thick slice of warm, fresh bread. It was more food than I could eat normally, and with my anxiety kicking up? Yeah, I'd never finish, but I decided to enjoy it anyway. Never mind that Linda was an amazing cook.

"Good," Travis said. "Maybe you can teach me?"

"Of course!" Linda assured him. "And you're going to have to bring that girlfriend of yours around. I've heard good things about her."

Travis chuckled. "Yeah, um, I was telling her about my family situation. I mean, it's weird."

"Having demons as parents?" Tash asked.

Travis shook his head. "No, that's normal. It's the lies. I call them my parents, and I know that's what's expected. So, um, when Jess explained about all of this, Shannon assumed they were my demon parents. I had to go back and tell her my real history. I'm still surprised she hasn't dumped me."

"She likes you," I teased. "Keep that girl."

"That's the plan," he promised. "I mean, I'm not going to college now, it seems, but she got accepted to OSU and Texas A&M. She said that she's going to take OSU, though, so she can be closer."

"And when she gets a college boyfriend?" Tash asked.

He shrugged. "I was thinking that we could have a talk before she goes. I mean, she's talking about leaving in August, right? Well, I'll just tell her that we're officially breaking up, I'm an old pal from school, and that if Jess can make this mess work, then I can too. She can tell me about her boyfriends, and I can pine away for the girl of my dreams."

"Not going to get an online diploma?" Bax asked.

Travis shrugged. "I'll think of something. My bigger concern is that I can't afford college. No parents, no grants. Yeah. I dunno. I figure I can worry about it next week, right?"

"Exactly," I agreed, because we were all thinking about the same thing. There might not be a next week. We just didn't want to say it.

Linda just sighed, making a production of it. "Well, I'm starting to think that I'm a failure as a mother. I've got six kids now, and not one of you graduated!"

"Hey," Deke teased, "I did. I'd like you to know that I was at the top of my class."

"Ok, that's one," she said. "But does a religious school even count?"

"It wasn't..." Then he paused. "Yeah, I guess it does count as a religious school." But he was smiling at her, making it clear he wasn't upset. "Although I think raising five supernatural teenagers should get you bonus points."

"And not freaking out," I told her.

"Or making us feel bad," Lars added.

Linda looked up and smiled at him. "Well, except for that once."

"Never happened," he said. "Mom, you've been amazing. You dove into all of this and made it easy for us. I shouldn't have hidden it from you that I liked Jess."

"When did that start?" she asked. "And I know it's none of my business, but I'm trying to figure out how long all of this was going on under my nose."

"We knew Lars was a part of the quad that first time you invited us for dinner," Gavin said.

Bax nodded. "Which was why we couldn't stay. We had to tell Deke that we'd found Judgement."

"But Jess," Deke said, "was harder. She was supposed to be a guy. I honestly had no idea until the night she made a run for it. She always had on that sleeve, so I never saw the scar. I also never looked because I wasn't searching for a girl."

Linda nodded. "So you were almost as confused as me, Jess?"

"Not quite," I admitted. "I knew what happened when I touched people. For me, it was a relief to know I wasn't cursed. More when I found out that you were ok. I was so sure that all of that was my fault, and that my dad had killed you. So when I heard you were ok and Deke could help me control my hand, it was all good news. I had no idea about Dad, though."

Then Linda sat up, sucking a breath. We all looked over, proving we were a little hyper-vigilant right now, but she waved us down. "Sorry. I just got kicked."

"She's kicking?" Lars asked.

"Little kicks," Linda assured him, "but she's growing fast now. I'm trying to figure out what to name her. Mostly her last name. If she's a Bailey, then she'll share a name with Jess."

"No," I said. "I don't want her to have Dad's name. She should be a McKay."

"Ted made it up anyway," Travis pointed out. "We're told to pick names that won't stand out. The more boring, the better."

"So, McKay?" she asked Lars.

He nodded. "I like it. Shit, she certainly doesn't need to be a Drywater. Besides, it might be easier if we all have different names. Fewer questions about why my sister and my girlfriend have the same name."

"There's that," Tash agreed.

"And she needs a first name with an L," Gavin said. "Linda, Lars, and the baby."

Linda was smiling. "Any ideas?"

"Laura," Gavin said, pronouncing it with his rolling accent in the Spanish style.

"Lyre," Bax said. "Nice, short, and unique.

"Lilly," Tash offered. "It's a little less weird."

"What about Lexi?" Lars asked. "That's cute. I could also scream it at her when she's about to get in trouble."

Then they all looked at me. I just smiled at my plate. "I think she should be Leia, like the rebel princess."

"Yep, I still like Leia," Bax agreed. "The rest of you need to get on board with this."

"She'll get picked on at school," Travis pointed out. "No, I like Lexi. Fits the 'don't get noticed' rules, but isn't boring."

"He has a point," I admitted. "So, I'm changing my vote to Lexi too."

Deke just pointed at Bax with his fork. "I'm going with Lyre. It's pretty."

"Linda, Lars, and Lexi," Linda said. "Linda, Lars, and Lyre. Yeah, they both work." Then she waved that off. "But we have time."

"Plenty," I agreed, trying to make myself believe it.

From the looks on everyone else's faces, they felt the same. We were lying to ourselves and each other - and trying to believe it. But we'd survived the last battle. This one couldn't be any worse. We had more training, more magic, a better idea of what was coming, and weaker demons.

And yet I still couldn't eat that much. When we all had given up with half full plates, Linda made a comment about how she'd clearly made too much, and she said she'd put it all aside for us, because we'd probably be hungry later. Over and over, there were so many reminders of later, tomorrow, and next week being thrown around. It was almost as if we were all trying to work some kind of magic.

The guys got up to help put things in the fridge, telling Linda to just direct. I just sat there, watching the ice slowly melt in my glass. Across from me, Tash sighed, reminding me she was still there.

"It's going to be ok, right?" I asked.

She looked up and gave me a weak smile. "Jess, it's never ok. All of this is a mess, and the more I learn, the more of a mess it seems."

"But are we going to be ok?" I asked.

She nodded. "Yeah. You are the strongest quad I've ever heard of, and I'm a Librarian for the Order of Martyrs, so I've heard of quite a few. The four of you are young, you're strong, and you will find a way to be fine so long as you put your minds to it."

"Then we'll be ok," I told her. "Maybe that will be ok and on the run, or ok and fighting back, but it's still ok."

She paused, glancing over to the door. Everyone was still in the kitchen, discussing how to make room for one of the pans, so she looked back at me.

"Take care of Deke, ok?"

"Promise," I said. "And you too. I might get pissed off at you, but I figure I've never had a big sister before, and we're supposed to fight a lot, right?"

That made her smile turn a little brighter. "Yes, we are," she agreed. "I just know that if someone has to take the fall for this, I'm not going to let the Order blame Deke."

"No," I said, shaking my head just as Bax stepped back into the room. "Tash, we're all in. You are our Sandman too."

"I'm a Librarian," she reminded me again.

I shrugged. "So? You're not a very good Martyr. You're not a blind follower. So, if you're not one of them, then what do we call you?"

"Sandman," Bax said.

"You know," Gavin said, moving around him to return to his chair, "the Sandman also makes dreams."

"*To them is given an hourglass to mark the time,*" Deke quoted as he returned. "*And they shall be tasked to share the ways until the number of their charges equals four.* Tash, what else are we doing but sharing the ways? You are as much their Guide as I am. If anything happens to me, I want them to claim you."

"They can't," Tash reminded him. "Deke, the Order will not recognize this quad. No matter what happens, they will declare that it needs to be reset!"

"Which is why they'll need both of us," Deke said. "No more accepting our demise. No more waiting to die. No more expecting the worst. Not from any of us. We will fight, and we will do our best. If we fall, then we fall doing the right thing, but we will not make it easy. To be a part of this quad, the first real Brethren in history, we must be all in."

Tash nodded slowly. "All in," she agreed.

"All in," Travis said softly from the door. "Because while I might not have a lot to lose, it sounds like there's a hell of a lot to gain."

CHAPTER FIFTY-SEVEN

At midnight, we began loading up the truck. Weapons, ammo, and anything else we might need went in the back. Yes, there was a medical kit included. Tash pulled out the cloth stretcher from who knows where, and put that in the back seat. It was there if we needed it, and wouldn't get in the way if we were all riding in the back.

That took about an hour. When it was done, we all went up to get changed. I made a point of stopping by Linda and letting her know that I loved her, she was the best stepmom ever, and while I wouldn't compare her to my real one, I appreciated all she'd done for me. I had to say it, and she seemed to understand, but her response was simple.

"Just come home safe, Jess. That's all the thanks I'll ever need. Always come home safe." And then she hugged me harder than she ever had before.

Eventually, we'd all changed into our tactical gear. This time, Deke had us carrying ammo in every available spot. The spray paint was gone, as were other potential tools that I'd never used before. I was simply covered in clip after clip of ammunition. The same was true for all of the guys except Travis. He didn't get special clothes. I didn't figure out why until just before we were going to leave.

"I'll catch up in a second," he said, ducking into the garage.

I almost followed, but Deke grabbed my shoulders and turned me back to the truck. "He doesn't want to ruin his clothes, Jess. Let the guy strip in peace."

"Strip?" I was so lost.

"Demon," Gavin said as he climbed into the back and offered me a hand up. "He said he's more deadly in his own body than his magical one."

"Oh." Then I realized they meant he was coming to this as a demon, not a guy. "Oh!"

Lars and Bax both chuckled at me, but that was ok. I deserved it. While we waited for Travis, we all checked our weapons one more time, rechecked our ammo, and found places to sit. No more than a few minutes later, a creature slipped out of the garage and my breath caught.

That had to be Travis. He was bigger in this form, but not by much. His body was shaped almost like an iguana, but covered in thick fur. His legs were more like a cat's, though. Not a house cat, but a panther or tiger. Strong, muscular legs with impressive claws that could rend and destroy. Then there was his tail. Thick and supple, it was about as big around as my thigh, and the last third was covered in something hard like bone, maybe. The edge was jagged - no, serrated - and the tip was sharp, like a blade he'd grown himself.

On the other end was his head. The four horns were hard to miss. Set in pairs on each side, one before the other, those things were long and reminded me of a gazelle. His face was broad, shaped like a lion's or something, but without the mane. Thankfully, he only had two eyes, but his mouth had to be filled with sharp teeth. And all of him was a medium-grey color, sprinkled with white. Not in patches, though. This was like a frosting to the hair behind his elbows and down his spine. Like he'd gotten a little too cold and ice had started to form.

He wasn't a beautiful creature, but neither was he hideous like my father. Travis just looked like, well, a monster. When he reached the back of the truck, he stood up and climbed in, using his body more like a monkey than a dog or person. Then he settled into the empty space in the middle.

"Hey," he said, looking at all of us.

His voice was deeper and almost hollow, the same way as my dad's, but it was still him. I chuckled, trying to get over the difference. When I thought of Travis, I imagined the guy from school, but this was him.

"You're kinda fuzzy," I said.

He huffed out a laugh. "Yeah, I'll lose the fur when I molt again. So, um, please don't shoot this demon?"

"Promise," Bax said. "And if you ever shed those horns, I want them."

"Fuck off," Travis said, laughing for real this time. "But sure."

Not long after that, Deke set one last box of ammo in the back seat, then hopped over the bed. Tash climbed into the front, and it was time. No going back now. No rethinking or replanning this. When the truck started, everyone in the back with me paused for just a moment, mentally bracing, and not a single word was said.

Not until the truck began to move and Deke finally broke the silence. "I want us to hover around Travis and Tash. If we can keep them safe long enough to repair the seal, then we'll be done. If they have to stop and fight, this will all take longer."

"What about the rocks?" Lars asked.

"One jumped on them to get you last time," I reminded him. "Pretty sure Travis can't stand up to a full-sized common."

"No, but I can slow them down," Travis said just as the truck went off the gravel and onto the dirt track that led out to the pasture with the seal.

The ride was bouncy, jostling us all in the back. Travis gripped, his claws screeching on the bed before he reached over to hold the side. The look he gave Deke didn't fit on his monster face. It was guilty, maybe even filled with regret, and I couldn't help but giggle.

"You're fine," Deke promised. "Not worried about the paint back here."

"Good," Travis said.

Then the truck started going up. I twisted to find we were closer than I expected. Tash was making her way around the lowest part of that berm. Any moment, we'd be visible to anyone watching the seal. None of us bothered to check. We just reached down and pulled out our weapons. Safeties were still on, but our guns were in our hands, and this time we'd left the silencers at home.

"Keep an eye out for their spotter," Deke said. "Heads on swivels, people. They hit us hard last time."

I was scanning the trees on the far side of the property, but got nothing. Deke was doing the same. On the opposite side of the truck, Bax and Lars were looking the other way. Gavin was twisted around to look out the front window, and Travis seemed to be watching behind us. We had all sides covered, and Tash was driving as fast as she could without losing us.

A bump tossed my ass into the air. Deke grabbed me, shoving me back into place without taking his eyes away from the trees. There, near the center of the field, was a cluster of rocks. They were a bit taller than the height of a man, no more than ten feet, and wider at the base than the top. It looked like where the farmer had put every rock he'd found on this property for decades, possibly longer.

That was our destination, because under those rocks was the seal, and beneath that was a gate to the pit called Hell. Tash would need to get to the seal so she could perform her ritual. Our job would be to hold off the demons until she was done. While it sounded easy, we all knew it would be anything but.

"Ready!" Deke warned. "Hold on."

ENTER SANDMAN

The truck skidded to a stop, jerked, and then turned off. We were all hopping out of the back by the time Tash opened the driver's side door. Travis headed to her, and the rest of us grouped up. There was maybe twenty feet between the truck and the seal, possibly less. Just enough room for seven people to move freely.

"Jess, move the dirt," Deke ordered. "Gavin, peek around to check the other side. Bax, watch the back. Travis, stick with Tash no matter what. Lars, you're with me."

While I jogged over to where Deke and I had done this the last time, Deke and Lars took up positions against the side of the truck. Deke was watching the berm side of the property. Lars was looking at the tree line that felt like it was much too close.

"Anything?" Bax asked.

"Nothing yet," Gavin called.

I was already working. The dirt I'd moved the last time had partially fallen back into the hole. Another spell cleared that, making it even bigger. Large enough for Tash to jump down into it. It wasn't much cover, maybe eighteen inches, but it might help and sure wouldn't hurt.

I turned to head toward Gavin just as the first roar pierced the air. That was definitely a demon, and it came from the other side of the rocks. The side opposite of where my old house was.

"We have incoming," Gavin warned, backing up a bit.

"I've got a lot of movement in those trees," Bax warned.

"Numbers, people!" Deke snapped.

"Just movement," Bax told him. "Dark shapes in a dark night." Then, "Shit. Ten? Fifteen?"

"More over here," Gavin said.

"Something's in the trees," Lars warned.

I was turning, trying to figure out who was closest. "They're all around us," I breathed.

"You got this, Jess," Travis assured me. "I'll scream your name if things go bad."

I glanced back, still not used to seeing him like this. "We just have to close the seal."

He nodded, and then the first one broke from the trees.

I reached for fear, finding it much too easily. The fear of this place and the terror of what had happened the last time rushed into my mind. It wasn't mine, and I didn't stop to identify who it belonged to, but I was willing to use it. The scar on my hand began to glow purple as I pushed as hard as I could, hoping it might slow the demons.

Then Bax's hand began to glow with a pale blue light as he did his best to keep them away. Lars' was next, the eerie green color most likely working to calm them. Gavin's palm stayed dark. There was nothing he could do but make them fight harder, and right now, that was the last thing we wanted.

"My side!" Gavin yelled.

Like we'd practiced so many times, we all rushed that way. Gavin's gun went off and a demon jerked, proving he'd scored a hit. I took the next shot, making sure I aimed right. Moving quickly, we all formed a line, shoulder to shoulder and firing at will, but the demons weren't slowing down. Our abilities barely discouraged them. They knew we were here, and they wanted to make sure we would fail again.

Then the air began to grow thick. That was Tash's ritual, drawing the available magic to her. A moment later, the noxious feeling began to grow. Order magic, a bad ritual, or something - I didn't honestly know. I just knew that it was impossible to miss, and the demons charging at us roared, proving they could sense it too.

"Deke, use your skill," Bax said, all of us still shooting.

"Jess," Lars yelled, "call the targets."

"Spider thing," I yelled, putting my bullets into that one.

All of the guys shifted slightly, the muzzles of their guns finding the one I was trying my hardest to take out. With five weapons hitting it, the damned thing slowed and the others overtook it, but the demon refused to die. Just when I was about to call a new target, though, something changed.

Travis made a surprised noise. I felt it too, but there were no words to describe the sensation. It was as if my ears popped, but my ears weren't involved. A pressure change, or a power shift. Either way, the next bullet to slam into that spider-looking monster dropped it like a rock, and the body began to dissolve almost instantly.

"Gorilla!" I yelled, and we changed targets as one.

No, it didn't look like a gorilla, but it had wide shoulders, was more upright, and was running on hind feet and fists. It was too dark to be sure what colors these demons were. They were too foreign to anything I knew to have a better description, and while they might have names, I couldn't recognize them like this, so I was winging the fuck out of it.

But three shots was all it took before that one dropped too. The only problem was that just as it hit the dirt, the ground below us bucked. I staggered. Deke tripped to one knee. The guys wavered, but that was all. Lars immediately grabbed Deke, helping him back up, because it seemed our Sandman was very, very distracted.

"Keep shooting," Deke ordered. "They're weak. They're like human weak. Kill them!"

"Fire at will!" I screamed, and they all obeyed.

It should've been carnage. In a movie, dozens of bodies would've dropped. The reality was that aiming at a moving target was hard, and half our shots missed, maybe more. We still kept trying. Some we winged, others merely grazed, but when we actually hit, the demon dusted within seconds.

Dead. We were winning. We were fucking killing them, and all of this was working!

But just as I began to think we had a chance, the demons realized it too. The herd of them stopped and began backing away. The sounds they made were unintelligible to me, but it was like they were talking. We kept shooting, kept trying to even the odds, but there were so many. Thirty-six demons. That was what we had planned for, but it was a lot more bodies in reality than in theory.

Then Travis yelled, "They're going to use magic!"

I had barely enough time to shove wind at them before the first barrage of fire came at us.

CHAPTER FIFTY-EIGHT

STICKS BECAME TORPEDOES, flying at us from the trees. The ground bucked again, a ripple of cracked clay showing where it had come from. The world had turned into chaos, and there was only so much I could do. I still tried. The bucking ground rocked all of us, but I kept it together so we wouldn't be sucked in. The sticks decayed in an instant, leaving us pelted with little more than sawdust. The fire was the hardest, but I pulled water, sucking the heat out and making a wall of ice that served well enough as a temporary boundary.

"The babies!" Tash screamed. "Travis, get them out."

I looked back in time to see her pointing to a gap in the stones and the darkness trickling out of it. No, crawling out of it, and that was a kid. There were more, and they all looked confused and terrified - not that I blamed them. Travis didn't hesitate, though. In his demonic body, he leapt up on the rocks, making his way to the first, then the next closest.

One by one, he helped the kids out, reaching into the gaps to find even more. A collection of them was forming, and the demons outside my ice wall were doing everything in their power to get through. Again the ground bucked, but this time it wasn't a trail from a demon. It was as if the entire pasture was heaving, trying to knock us off. I'd never been in an earthquake, but that was where my mind immediately jumped.

"Close the seal!" Deke yelled.

"We need to get the kids out," Tash snapped.

It was Travis who answered. "You'll never get all of them. That's the gate! They're pushing at it. Close the seal!"

The words were barely out of his mouth before the wall of ice shattered and our moment of peace turned back into a full-scale war. The guys shot, tagging another demon, but the rest were still out of range - then something roared behind us. As a group, we spun just as more demons charged across the pasture.

Deke pulled in a deep breath and holstered his weapon. His right hand pressed across the tattoo on his left arm, and the glow brightened. Through his fingers, I could see the sand moving even slower. Grain by grain, it dropped, proving his power was still working and most likely on a timer.

"Shoot!" I ordered. "Deke has them weak."

But the angle was all wrong. To aim this way, we'd be shooting right over Tash and too close to Travis. Lars rushed around the back of the truck, putting it between him and Tash, then opened fire. Gavin was next, with Bax and me following a second later. Deke, however, was concentrating too hard on his skill. It was like he hadn't even heard me.

So I stopped, going back to grab his arm and tow him with us. Parking him at the tailgate of the truck, he was in my sight and out of range, so I joined back in. Three more demons dropped before that wave figured out they were weak. The pops of our guns were so loud, and my ears felt numb to the concussions, yet just as the demons began to pull back, one last shot rang out.

Tash screamed.

She was on the other side of the truck from us. There was no way a stray bullet could've hit her. We'd been trained too well for that, but her cry was one of pain, and there was no hesitation before we were moving back toward her.

"Deke!" I barked, shaking him from his stupor. "Tash is hurt."

"Shit," he breathed, letting go of his ability.

My eyes dropped to his arm in time to see the sand pour down to the lower half of the hourglass. There was almost nothing in the top and just a bit left in the neck. I'd never seen the clock that low before, which meant we had to fix this, and now.

In the pit I'd made, Tash was on her knees. Blood poured from her shoulder and down her arm, landing on the stones. The miasma of her ritual was cloying, making me want to gag, but I forced my body to ignore it. Tash was down. She was hurt. This was my job.

But Deke pulled me back. "Not now, damn it," he snapped. "Watch the fucking - "

A roar from the top of the rocks was all the warning we had before a demon tried to grab me. I ducked back, the wind of its claws so close it pushed my hair out of my face. Travis launched himself on the beast, his own roar just as deep, but without as much of an eerie echo.

"Don't shoot Travis!" I begged.

No one was listening. Deke had already rushed to Tash's side. Bax and Gavin pushed to the other side, forming a barrier for that wave of demons. Lars moved to my side, pausing to meet my eyes. The demons took a second to figure it out, but the one on the rocks was still going, still alive, and that meant the weakness was gone.

They rushed in. The sound of Travis and that demon fighting was worse than a pair of dogs. Growls, roars, and snarls were interspersed with clacks of teeth and the screech of nails on rock. I spared a glance so I could force vines to grab the enemy demon, and then I only had time for what was coming at us.

Lars opened fire, but I had something more deadly. I had magic. Picking a demon, I set it on fire. The next one was sucked into the ground. Spears of ice rained down on the one after that, and then I turned back to use air on the wave rushing Bax and Gavin. Those were pushed back, but it wasn't enough. They were gaining, and I could only cast as fast as I could think.

Then something slammed into the wave of demons from the side. It was big and moved fast. I caught a glimpse of a whip - no, a tail - lancing through them, and the monster's claws destroyed anything it could reach. When it raised its head, slinging a smaller demon into the air, I realized that was my father.

Like this, the size difference between a greater and a common demon was horrifying. Even worse, my father wasn't fighting fair. He tore a hunk from the side of a demon, and swallowed it. My mouth dropped open, my eyes were bulging, and my mind was spinning, trying to figure out what the fuck he was doing. Was he... helping us?

"Jess!" Lars yelled.

That snapped me out of the moment, and I lit another on fire, but the distraction had been too much. The first ones were on us. Without thinking, we pulled back. The thump of something hitting metal made me look over to the truck just as a demon launched off the back of it toward Tash.

A push of air carried it the other way, but I could already feel the strain. I was casting more than shooting, and I'd never used this much magic before. Not even at that first battle. It was constant as I cycled through my easiest spells. Unfortunately, demons were surrounding me on all sides. I had to know where I was casting - and I couldn't keep up.

Then Travis shouldered me aside just before a demon could slam into me. Travis took the hit instead, and Lars grabbed its side. The demon froze, stunned by Lars' power, so I shoved my palm against its arm, killing it as quickly as I could - which wasn't very quickly.

The ground bucked again just as the demon began to turn to dust. I wasn't ready for it, and this time I fell. Something roared, drawing my eyes, and I realized we were overrun. A demon slashed at Bax, but while the claws tore his shirt and caught on his vest, Bax didn't fall back. He pushed in, clearly unharmed.

"Cover Deke!" Travis roared, using his mass to push both me and Lars back toward the seal.

Demons were coming over the rocks, swarming the truck, and trying to press in on both sides. In that instant, I knew we'd never make it out alive. All we could do was regroup and do our best. Tash was lying in the grass, blood covering her entire shoulder. Gavin was standing over her, so I hoped that meant she wasn't dead, but I couldn't be sure. Deke was focused on the seal, and Bax was doing everything he could to hold back the demons on his side while Gavin shot furiously.

Lars and I turned and ran, rejoining our party. Travis still fought, struggling to keep demons from following, but he was losing. A common bit his shoulder, shaking the younger demon like he weighed nothing. Anger grabbed me, and I had an idea. I reached for the air, but instead of pushing it, this time I pulled.

All the air that demon was breathing went away. I made a vacuum around him, and it was enough to make him drop Travis. Wounded, my friend hurried backwards, aiming for us. Lars started shooting, and I called vines to hold the beast in place. The moment he was secure, I torched that fucker, making the fire burn hot enough to keep the others at bay.

That meant one side was covered, so I spun to deal with the ones on the truck. A burst of air knocked a few off, but it was like they were learning. What I needed was more spells, more flexibility, and more creativity in the moment. Not having that, I resorted to my gun, shooting between bursts of magic, but it wasn't nearly enough.

Another roar made me spin. My father came over the rocks and landed right between us. It was like his limbs worked in all directions, stabbing, grabbing, and stomping any demon he could reach - yet he avoided the two Sandmen he stood over. He was helping! He was actually *helping* us!

Travis seemed to figure it out too, because he rushed in, using Dad's body as a shield while he attacked anything he could. The choke of Deke's magic made it hard for me to breathe. Fuck, it made it hard to even think. Something was wrong, and I didn't like it at all, but the demons seemed to know it too. They rushed in together, pushing Bax back. I tried to blow them away, but they were learning to dig in. They skidded back mere feet instead of yards this time, and once the wind died, they came right back.

I tried to use fire, but I didn't want to burn us. Water took too long. I didn't know what else I could do, but if I was going down, I wanted it to be fighting. I barely had the thought before a demon rushed in, using its tail to stab at Travis as it aimed for Deke.

Travis didn't try to avoid it. Instead, he lunged at Deke, knocking him out of the way, but I was already moving. There was one thing I had that always worked. I just had to get closer. I needed to get my hands on that beast. Jumping at the last second, I hooked my fingers into a ridge on its side and pushed death deep into its body.

The demon roared.

Gavin didn't hesitate. "Deke, do it! We need to clear some space!"

"Tash!" Deke yelled.

"Just do it!" Lars snapped.

I couldn't see what happened, but I felt it. The sensation came again, the pressure changed, and the demon I was holding onto screamed. A split second later, it was dust, but the guns were firing again. I released the handful of dust I was holding, but I'd lost my gun. Without hesitation, I pulled the other. They were weak, and I didn't give a shit if these bullets were hard to come by. They were all I had, so I shot.

We were almost standing on top of each other. Dad's body was in the middle of us, a massive wall of demonic flesh that separated me from Bax, Gavin, and Tash. Since he was fighting on our side, I also didn't care. Travis, being smaller, picked his battles better, scaling the rocks to keep the stragglers off of us.

And we, the Brethren, shot just as fast as we could. Dust filled the air, and the magic came with it. I pulled, taking it in, but right now my gun was a lot more useful. Slowly but surely, we were starting to regain ground. We were winning. We could actually do this, but no one was finishing the ritual, and Deke couldn't do both.

Like I'd summoned it, the ground heaved again, but this time something cracked. Something big, the sound reverberating through my feet. The world heaved one more time, but I couldn't stop shooting. I couldn't waste these precious seconds. We needed to kill them so Deke could get back to it, and -

A boom echoed across the entire world.

The rocks behind us shattered. Travis went flying. My father surged over me, covering Lars and Deke in the process. I'd fallen to the ground, and through Dad's legs, I could see both Bax and Gavin over Tash, using their own bodies to protect her. Rubble rained down. Some were the size of my fist, but other pieces were much, much bigger.

And then a roar came from the hole that had been a mound of rocks only moments before. The hole that was supposed to be the seal. The hole that clearly led straight into the Pit of Hell.

CHAPTER FIFTY-NINE

"Run!" Travis yelled, proving he'd survived.

I turned to follow his voice and found him on his side, pointing toward our place. It seemed the words weren't for us, because dozens of shadows rushed off, the direction being all they needed. Thankfully, the babies weren't the only ones who ran. Some of the enemy demons were pulling back as well, turning and fleeing in all different directions.

Then a foot landed on the edge of that hole. It wasn't black. If I had to guess, I'd say brown or red. The claws were long and so very sharp. They were also huge, nearly the size of my father's. That had to be a greater demon, one who'd been raised in the Pit, and now it was out. The bigger question was what would come behind it.

Dad's dragon-like head with too many eyes swiveled to face me. "You need to close the seal."

"You're on it!" Deke yelled.

But Dad didn't move. "They will come for you, Jessica. You are the enemy now, and I still love you." He glanced back as another foot came out. "You wanted proof?"

The guys were all climbing to their feet, but I was all but pinned under Dad. Gavin dropped his clip and put in a fresh one. That made Lars and Bax do the same. We were all struggling for breath, and that smell still lingered in the air, but the demon was heaving itself out of the pit leg by leg. Another claw hooked the edge, and then a fourth - and fifth!

"Shit," Travis gasped, forcing himself back to his feet - all four of them. Then he tried to rush the gaping maw that led to Hell.

Dad's tail lashed out, blocking Travis. "Take care of my daughter, demon," he growled. "Stand by her, and I will remember it. Betray her, and I will make sure it is the biggest mistake you ever make." Then he looked back to me. "I think I finally understand what love is. I'm going to prove it."

Then he spun, aiming for the closest of the demon's hands.

"Dad!" I screamed.

Thankfully, no one else seemed to care. Deke scurried to get to the bared portion of the seal. Bax, Gavin, and Lars were searching the area, looking for the rest of the demons. Travis headed to Tash, pressing his cat-like hands to her arm, trying to push her shirt up.

"Here," I said, moving to help him.

But I couldn't take my eyes off the Pit, and that demon wasn't getting any slower. Its head came out next, and it looked like some kind of hammerhead shark. Nothing fit. All of it was hideous, and it was massive - but my father was still bigger. The moment it was in sight, Dad jumped on it, his tail lashing down like a scorpion.

"Heal her, Jess!" Travis said, pulling my attention back. "That's just the biggest. It's blocking the entrance, but there are thousands down there, and the gate is wide open. Get her ass up, because if Deke can't get this closed..."

He didn't even need to finish the words. I grabbed Tash's arm and reached, finding her soul so easily - and yet, I hesitated. She was completely unconscious and bleeding badly, but alive. Much more alive than Gavin had been when I'd saved him. The problem wasn't if I could do this, but whether or not I should.

How many times had Tash said this was evil? She'd yelled at me for trying to steal Deke's soul. Now, it was her soul I needed to know so I could fix her, but I'd be damned if I was taking any of it. Instead, I merely touched the silvery color of her and then began to push my own life in.

I didn't need to take to help. I didn't need to be good or bad. All that mattered was keeping us all alive, because this wasn't over. Whatever was wounded inside of her needed to be fixed. Her organs, her skull, her mind, and definitely that massive bullet hole. I pushed, watching as a chunk of silver was pushed out of the wound. Almost immediately, Tash gasped.

"Stop!" she begged, looking around to get her bearings. "What the..."

I could barely hear her over the sounds of two greater demons fighting. The echoing nature of their voices made it come from everywhere and nowhere at once. The remains of that rock pile shifted under their feet. Some of it fell into the hole, but plenty was sent toward us. The air was so murky it was nearly a haze, but that was debris. Just normal dirt and rock dust.

And magic.

"Deke's trying to finish the ritual," I told her. "The gate's open, the seal shattered, and Dad's trying to hold the demon back. How do I help?" I begged.

Tash was breathing hard, clearly disoriented, but my words sank in. "Make sure that demon doesn't get out. I'll help Deke."

She crawled her way toward the open section of seal only a few feet away. I found my gun on the ground and swapped clips. The guys were watching, waiting, all of them ready to act, but this couldn't wait. We needed to make sure that demon went into Hell, and from the looks of it, my dad wasn't exactly winning. At least he wasn't losing either.

"Cover me," I told them as I scrambled over the loose rocks and dirt to get a little closer.

Not too close. I didn't want a tail or random demonic body part to get me. I just needed to see, and there was still enough of a ridge to make that impossible. Yet the moment I could see over it, my entire perception of reality changed. That was definitely a pit. I'd seen photoshopped pictures of sinkholes that looked less intimidating. It was deep, it seemed to go down forever, and it was the size of a fucking house!

Never mind the demons trying to shove each other into it. Dad bit the new one's arm, trying to tear it off. The beast from Hell attacked back, using one of the many pairs of legs it had. The whole time, they both kept themselves braced over the opening. I just needed to figure out how to make that new one slip, or lose its hold, or something. The problem was that I couldn't figure out how without taking Dad down with it.

So I heated the ground, making it as close to molten as possible. I pushed air down, using as much force as I could. Hopefully, something would help, but instead, Dad turned to look at me. All of his eyes met mine.

"I'm proud of you," he said, his words barely audible.

The other demon used his distraction to impale Dad's side, but that seemed to be what my father was waiting for. The moment they were locked together, he simply let go. All of his size and weight bore down on the other demon's smaller, weaker legs. The burning edge was too painful to grab onto, so the beast slipped.

For one horrifying moment in time, they hung there, and then my father pushed with all he had. Together, they both fell, tumbling down into the endless hole. I could hear them hit something. A yelp made it clear that others were now falling with them. I honestly had no idea if Dad could survive that fall, but I knew he couldn't get back out.

"Dad!" I screamed, rushing for the edge of the pit.

I never made it. Lars caught me around the waist, spinning me away. I still struggled, trying to understand what had just happened. That was my dad! I hated him, but I loved him. He'd hurt me so many times, but he was proud of me. Now he was gone, and I didn't know how I felt. I just needed to do *something!*

But the stench was worse. It had gone from a smell to a sound, and a pressure was weighing on me. In my struggles, I couldn't see, but I knew something was happening, and I hated it. I hated all of this. I didn't feel like we were winning, and I wanted to scream out my rage.

Lars just pressed my face to his chest and hugged me hard as the discordant magic reached unbearable levels. My hands went to my ears, but I could still hear Travis screaming in pain, and my voice joined his.

Then it simply stopped.

"It's done," Deke said, sounding like he barely had any energy left.

That was when Lars finally released his hold. I pushed away from him to see the hole, but now it was the seal. A smooth slab of pristine stone covered where that hole had been, making it feel like a bad hallucination. Runes and symbols were etched into the surface, fitting between lines that locked together into amazingly intricate shapes. The seal. That was what it was supposed to look like, and it meant that Hell was no longer open.

"Jess?" Gavin asked, his hand lightly touching my arm.

"My dad's in there," I said.

"Yeah," he muttered. "Are you ok?"

I just nodded, unable to pull my eyes away. "Did we all live?"

"Yeah," he breathed. "I'm sorry."

Those words didn't fit, which made me finally tear my eyes away and look at him. "What?"

"About your dad," he said. "It's so easy to just hate him, but hard to realize that you might love him too."

I threw my arms around Gavin's neck and fought back the tears that stung my eyes at his words. I would not cry for my father. That man had terrorized me, and now he was gone. I was finally safe - but he'd said he was proud of me. He'd said he was going to prove it, and that could only mean that he actually loved me. In the end, he had, and he'd given up everything to prove it.

I just couldn't decide how that made me feel.

"Whose gun?" Tash asked.

I turned to see Bax first, kneeling beside Travis. Our friend was nodding, but he looked like he'd suffered in all of that. Tash had a weapon in her hand, and I was pretty sure it was the first one I'd lost. Letting go of Gavin, I headed that way to retrieve it. I made it two whole steps before Tash's head snapped up, looking behind me. Deke's gaze followed, and from their expression, whatever they saw was bad.

"Demon," a man's voice said. "Cambion!"

I turned to see the creepy guy from the Slice, but this time he was dressed just like us. He was also holding a gun. Behind him was another man, probably the Watcher from school. Both of them looked ready for a fight, not like they wanted to celebrate.

"This quad is defective!" the Watcher snapped.

"This quad works," Deke told them.

The creepy guy just smiled. "Which means you're the Guide. Hello, Martyr."

"Director," Deke replied. "These four deserve a chance. They just fought back more demons than I've ever seen, and the seal is closed!"

"She is an abomination!" the Director screamed, pointing at me. "A beast made from evil! You should've reset this quad long ago, but it seems you've been corrupted."

"Hold on," Tash tried.

But the man didn't give her the chance to finish. "You too. I saw you. Freeing demons! Corrupted, both of you, and the only way to explain the downfall of two Martyrs is the presence of her. And what is that one? Her lover?"

"You fucking - " Gavin growled before Lars yanked his arm, cutting off the words.

"A year!" the Director bellowed. "That's how long it took to close this seal."

"Because my last quad died closing the one in Colorado," Deke shot back. "I had to find all four of them, and I didn't expect a girl."

"You should've reset them as soon as you found her," the Director said. "You know the rules, Guide."

"And then what?" Deke asked. "Let the seal sit cracked until I find yet another quad?"

"This is why they're cracking," the man said. "Evil has infiltrated our ranks. The abominations are so thick in the world that they're among us, decaying our protections on the seals, and trying to corrupt the Earth we were promised."

"No," Tash said.

But Deke spoke over her. "And what about the abilities that the Order has been hiding from us, Director? What about the skills this quad has that haven't been seen in centuries? What about the power our Anathema wields *for* us, not against us? You want to hold back the Horsemen, but your only method is to sacrifice the lives of others to make it happen. Always others, though. Never you, never those in charge!"

"You know what Martyrs do," the man shot back.

Deke just smiled lazily. "No, tell me, because I'm not a Martyr. I'm their fucking Sandman. I renounce all allegiance to the Order of Martyrs and the broken methods it uses. They are the ones with the power, Director. They are the ones doing the hard work. That means they get to call the shots, and it's finally working."

"All of you are compromised!" the man screamed in anger. "I will not suffer a demon to live. I will not allow your corruption to - "

He lifted his gun, his eyes on me, and there was a loud bang. I flinched, but it wasn't me who felt the pain. My body wasn't the one that slumped to the ground. The Director crashed down with a hole in the side of his cheek with blood quickly pooling around him, and Bax's gun was still raised.

Beside him, the Watcher scrambled for a gun, but Lars was faster. "Think hard," he warned, lifting his own gun. "You see, we're not the heroes here. We're the fuck-ups fixing your shit."

The man paused, thinking about it, and then tried to yank his gun up to get a shot off. Two shots rang out, and both of them were close to me. Deke looked at Lars, nodded, then put his gun away. Lars holstered his a second later.

"So," Gavin said much too casually. "they're not going to go away."

Travis just chuckled softly. "How about I meet you back at the barn in half an hour? I'm going to need that key on my skin again."

"I'll be there to give it," Deke promised. "Let me know if you need any help."

"I think I've got this," Travis promised. "Go home. Let Linda know we're all ok." Then he pushed himself to his feet. "And don't look back."

CHAPTER SIXTY

MOST OF US piled into the truck, but Deke headed for the man called the Director. When he reached the pair of bodies, he checked each of their pockets. Finding something, he tucked it into his own tactical vest, then moved to check the men's arms. The Watcher was a quick glance, but when he got to the Director's arm, Deke paused for a little too long.

Then he simply walked away and hauled his weary ass into the bed of the truck. Patting the side seemed to be the signal. The moment Tash heard it, we just drove away. I was worried about leaving Travis out there alone, though. What happened if someone came back, like one of the bigger demons? But when I said something, Deke promised he'd come back for the guy. From the look on his face, he was trying to be very careful about leaving off the why.

"He's eating them," I said. "Ingesting the magic."

"Yeah," Deke admitted.

I just nodded. "Good."

"Hey," Lars breathed from the other side of the truck bed. "Are you really ok, Jess?"

ENTER SANDMAN

I actually had to think about that, and the jostling of the truck as Tash drove it back the way we'd come helped. I wasn't really hurt, that was for sure. I'd been pushed around and I had a feeling that my entire body would start aching soon, but nothing bad. Nothing life-threatening, that was certain.

But he meant emotionally, and there was only one answer I could give him. "I don't know. Dad's gone. He was there to help us, and he said he's *proud* of me, and now he's gone. I..."

"Yeah," Lars grumbled. "That's hard."

"It's ok," Bax told me. "Babe, you don't need to know how you feel about that. I'm more worried about what you think of Travis?"

I blew that off. "Fuck the Martyrs. Besides, it's magic and he's going to need some after making his skin."

"How are the fireflies?" Gavin asked.

I paused to check, but they were still there, like bright little sparks inside me. "Weak, but alive."

"So, she's tired," Deke decided, leaning back against the bed just as Tash hit a good bump. He grunted, proving he ached as much as we did. "But we figured out what my skill does. Makes the demons as weak as a normal person."

"And they couldn't get their claws in me," Bax said. "So I'm invulnerable to demons?"

"Why now?" Lars asked as the barn came into sight.

Tash slowed the truck, parking it in the driveway, as close to the stairs as possible. Gavin immediately hopped out to open the tailgate for the rest of us.

"Jess," he said. "The bonds. I don't know if it's what she is or just that we have a bond, but that's why." Then he held out a hand toward me.

I wasn't too proud to take it. While the trip back seemed so much shorter, every step felt like it was a lot more work. Together, the six of us made our way up the stairs and inside. Linda was standing in the living room, waiting. The woman was actually wringing her hands.

"There's medical supplies in the dining room and..." Her words faded as she saw all of us on our own feet. "Where's Travis?"

"Growing skin," Tash said, leaving off the rest of that. "He's fine, Linda. The boy can take a hit, too."

"He said being a demon was what made him good at football," I pointed out. "He's like a supernatural tank."

Deke just let out a heavy sigh. "We actually have bigger problems, guys."

"Who?" Linda asked.

"Dad," I told her. "He jumped into the Pit. No, let me start over. He was there, and he was helping us. I thought we were going to be overrun, but he started attacking them - not us - and then he shielded me when the seal broke, so the pieces didn't hit me, and when the demon tried to climb out of the Pit, he fought it back, and I'm pretty sure he shoved it in, knowing he'd go with it."

"And right before Deke closed the seal," Tash told me. "He waited, Jess. He used it to block the exit, and he dove in right before the ritual was complete. He made sure nothing else could come out."

Linda's hand went right to her belly. "So, he's gone?" She looked at all of us. "Dead?"

"Ted Bailey is missing," I told her, "and soon he'll be presumed dead. If anyone asks, two men came looking for him." Then I described the Martyrs to her, making sure to mention how they'd been dressed in cargo pants and long sleeves in summer.

Linda nodded. "Who are they?"

"They were Martyrs," Deke said. "And sadly, Ted wasn't the problem I was talking about." He pulled in a long breath. "When those two don't check in, they'll send more. A lot more. Also, the twelfth seal cracked."

He held out his arm to make the point. The sand was higher than it had been before, but not as much as I wanted. There was less than an eighth in the upper half of the hourglass now. It also didn't take a genius to figure out what all of this meant.

ENTER SANDMAN

"Colorado?" I asked.

"Yeah," Deke said.

"When?" Bax wanted to know.

This time, it was Tash who answered. "As soon as we can leave."

"How long?" Linda asked. We all looked at her in confusion, so she huffed. "Are we packing you clothes for a week or a month? We're going to need all the guns, the tools, and the ammo. You'll also need to buy more. We've got the books to pack, because they've been helpful. So, how long?"

"A month," Deke decided. "Probably more. Pack for a long stay, everyone."

"Which cars?" Linda asked. "I can start doing that while you all get some sleep, and -"

"No," Lars said. "Mom, you're not carrying that stuff down."

"Fine," she said. "Then I'll do laundry, pack a month's worth for all of us, and you boys can pick up Tash's and my stuff when you wake up."

"What?!" Lars gasped. "Mom, you can't drive across the country. You're pregnant!"

"And there are doctors in Colorado," she told him. "I am not going to sit here, not knowing if you're alive or dead, all alone and being useless."

"Then there's Travis," I pointed out. "Actually, he can go back to school if he wants. He'll just need an excuse, and his parents kicking him out should be enough. Plus, we'll need her."

Bax just looked at me like I was insane. "Jess. What about the baby?"

"She's not even six months along, and we need her to help research," I pointed out. "Besides, I know how much it sucks to be alone. No, the whole family goes."

Tash chuckled. "And you boys just lost. C'mon, Linda, I need a shower, and we can start..." She paused. "Wait... Travis!"

"What?" I asked, a rush of worry hitting me, because he was still out there.

"He can't go," she said, sounding like she was having an epiphany. "He needs to finish school, and we need someone to watch the seal. Plus, what about the kids? That means it would work out perfectly!"

Bax actually smiled. "Ok. Travis can live in the big house. Shannon too, when she needs a place to stay. I'll get him the keys and everything, then he can watch the kids. I also have a feeling he won't mind. So go shower, Tash. Linda, I'll buy us a nice house or something, ok?"

"Or rent one," she told him. "That's more cost effective, young man."

"Go get the boy," Linda told Deke. "Don't make him walk. Oh, and take him some clothes?"

"The key too," I reminded him.

"I got it!" Deke promised. "Lars, put Jess in the shower?"

Bax waggled his brows at Gavin. "Wanna share, big boy?"

"No, you can wait," Gavin said, heading up the hall before Bax even realized what was happening.

Gavin turned right, but Lars turned me to the left and straight into the bathroom. I was exhausted, completely wiped out, and it was more than just physical. This was mental and emotional as well. It felt like I'd been completely wrung out, so when Lars started helping me take off my guns, tactical vest, and clothes, I didn't fight him at all.

"Go turn on the water," Lars told me before opening the door and setting my weapons and combat gear outside. Then he stripped off his own.

I was inside and under the water before he joined me. There was a dark red mark on his side that was probably going to bruise. I had a feeling a few more would show up in the morning, but I probably didn't look any better. Lars ran his eyes over me, smiled, and then turned me around so my back was facing him.

"I think we should leave your truck here," he said before squeezing shampoo right into my hair. Then he began lathering.

"Why?" I asked, tilting my head back to make it easier.

He made a noise. "I think I may have used too much shampoo. Well, too late now." He then swapped places with me, turning me so he could keep scrubbing while soaking himself. "And because it's the least reliable. If Travis needs something, he'll have a backup. If we have to fly home, we'll have something."

"And we're taking everything else?" I asked.

"Deke's truck should stay," Lars decided. "So my Mustang, Bax's SUV, and Tash's car. Three vehicles for seven people. That should be plenty."

"We can probably take less," I pointed out.

"We'll need them," Lars assured me. "Granted, maybe we should leave my Mustang and take the truck. It has four-wheel drive. I dunno. I'll talk to Deke about it later. I just want you to know that we'll handle this, ok?"

Pulling my hair out of his hands, I waved for him to move. "Lars, I'm fine."

"And you just did three times the work as the rest of us," he countered as he lathered his own hair. "You're also allowed to grieve your dad. You don't even have to like him to do that. Plus what those Martyrs said. Maybe you didn't hear them, but they know what you are, Jess, and what do you think the chances are that they didn't tell someone else? You need to recover that magic, and you need to do it as fast as possible."

"Yeah," I realized, working to get the excessive shampoo out of my hair. "And we're still ok? All of us?"

Lars stepped in, sudsy hair and all, to wrap his arms around my waist. "We will always be ok, Jess. I can't get enough of this. I've never had friends as close as Bax and Gav. I have the most amazing girl, and I actually like sharing you with them. Deke fits too, and watching you fall in love with him has been amazing. I thought I'd be jealous - and I am at times - but I still like it. I still know that we will always be ok, and just because some other girl in this situation might have been willing to pay more attention to him, or Bax or Gav, you won't."

"But I have," I pointed out.

He pulled me a little closer. "You haven't. You are my best friend, Jess. You are also the love of my life, and no matter how long or short that life is, I promise that I'll push if I feel ignored. I also promise that I will spend it right here, with you."

"And them," I added.

He smiled. "Yeah, and them. Now stop hogging the water, woman."

So we turned again, and this time I reached for the conditioner. "I loved you first, you know."

"More?" he asked, the teasing audible.

I scoffed at that. "How about we don't do a 'more' or 'most,' ok? First is big enough for me. And I don't mean first out of my current boyfriends, Lars."

His hands paused and he stepped out of the water. "What do you mean?"

"I didn't know I could love until I met you. I started doubting how I'd felt about my mom, and then there was Dad, and Collin, and Megan. When I found out I was half demon, I thought that maybe I just couldn't, but you were there. Always there."

"And I always will be," he swore.

I nodded, just a little jiggle of my head. "Yeah, and not just physically. Lars, I loved you first in my life, and it's a lot."

"A good kind, though?"

"Yeah," I breathed. "The best kind. But I love Bax, Gavin, and Deke as much. Is that... ok?"

He caught both sides of my face and leaned in to press a kiss to my lips. "It's perfect, Jess. Conquest, Vengeance, Judgment, and your Sandman, because he's definitely yours more than ours."

"I don't feel like Anathema," I admitted.

"Jess, if you're cursed or shunned or anything else..." Lars promised.

ENTER SANDMAN

I finished the last part for him. "You'll still be here with me."
"There's no place I'd rather be," he swore.

EPILOGUE

GAVIN

Deke had hauled clothes down to Travis, and then brought him back. Travis promised that the bodies were gone and would never be seen again. When Jess got out of the shower, she made a point of healing him up, then making sure Tash was perfectly ok. After that, Bax and I pulled Travis aside to see if he was ok with Bax's plan. In truth, the guy was thrilled. He could go back to school, get his diploma, and he'd explain about getting kicked out as his reason for missing part of the week.

Then, the next morning, we started packing. Both floors of the barn turned into chaos, but we made it work. Around noon, Bax said he took Travis over to the big house and showed him the codes for the doors and the security system. Then he gave him the grand tour. Travis got to see all the entrances and exits to the basement, plus the assortment of bedrooms to pick from. When Bax explained that things had changed and he was ok with never living in this house again, that was all it took. Travis was sold on the plan.

We headed out the very next day. Mostly, that was because it simply took so long to pack, and Jess seemed a little weaker than usual. She said she was fine, but we all knew to ignore that. Jess was always fine, and she'd figure out how to make that true. The girl was stubborn and strong in ways I hadn't expected before I actually got to know her. She was also beautiful, even wiped out, without makeup, and wearing a shirt that I was pretty sure belonged to Deke with sweats that had to be Lars'.

Now, we were in Kansas and headed west to Colorado. Deke, Jess, and Lars were in Deke's truck at the front. Bax and I were in the SUV in the middle, with Tash and Linda in Tash's car behind us. We made sure to go the speed limit too, because each of these vehicles was carrying an arsenal of weapons that would probably get us thrown in jail. Thankfully, we had this - and the powers to get ourselves out of anything that happened.

The radio was going off with some special news break. Something about a massive whale problem in Alaska. Dozens dead and hundreds of fish washing up on the beach. Not exactly the kind of thing to put me in a good mood. It felt like the world was trying to go to shit all around us, but this was our life now.

Bax had been much too quiet for most of the drive. I was pretty sure it wasn't because he was tired or hurting either. He just hated leaving his home. Jess was still trying to figure out what she felt about her dad. Lars was fretting about his mom and her baby. Deke? I wasn't sure about him, but if I had to guess, he was worried about Jess. He always was, and that actually made me not care about the rest of his mess. Then there was my issue.

"Hey, Bax?" I asked, breaking the silence of too many straight miles.

"Hm?" Bax asked, reaching over to turn down the satellite radio.

"Is it weird when it's just you and Deke with Jess?"

Bax laughed once. "Nope. Gav, I don't give a shit where he sticks his dick. If he wants to lick or stroke my junk in the process, then less work for me. I mean, it's not like no one's ever seen it, and most of the girls at school jumped on it." He glanced over. "Why, still freaking a bit?"

"That's the part I'm confused about," I admitted. "I'm not. Deke didn't look at me. He didn't try to touch me." I almost left it there, but this was Bax, and he'd always helped me when I needed it. "Lars did."

"You mean inside her?" Bax nodded. "Feels amazing, right?"

"Is it supposed to?" I asked.

This time, Bax's laugh was real and drawn out. "Man, why the fuck would you want to have sex if it didn't feel good?"

"Because it feels good for her," I said.

Which made Bax's laughter die off. "Yeah, ok. That's a pretty good point. But it's *supposed* to feel good. Shit, makes me understand why some guys are into guys. The way I see it, though, is that this doesn't count. See, there's like the real world where demons aren't a thing and Jess is just a cute girl we managed to convince to try poly. Then there's the supernatural world where magic exists and grinding my dick against another guy's doesn't count because she's in the middle. I don't need to tell anyone else about it but us, and neither do you."

I just nodded, liking his version of separate realities. "My dad made me scared of it. I thought that Deke would, you know, force me in my ass."

Bax snorted something meant to be a laugh. "And you'd beat the shit out of him. You might be the shortest and leanest of us, but you're also the meanest, Gav."

"Jess is," I corrected. "And you. I didn't shoot, Bax."

"It was my way of burning the world, nothing more," he assured me. "If they come for Jess, I will kill them all, and I know you'll be right there beside me."

"You, Lars, and Deke shot," I reminded him. "People, Bax."

"I fucking know that!" Bax told me. Then he thumped his hand on the wheel. "I do, Gav. I killed a guy, and you know what? I'll do it again and again. I know that I should feel like shit about it, but

I don't. I feel worse for feeling nothing than I do about killing him. He was going to kill Jess. He didn't care if we died, and no. She is everything. All my money, all my... whatever I have! It's for her. I love her, and I think it's kickass that we all can make this work, but if someone has to be the bad guy, then I'm damned good at it."

"Me too," I agreed. "I hate that I didn't shoot."

"You'll shoot next time," he assured me.

I just nodded, but something about that - all of that - was tickling my mind. There was a connection there, and I couldn't quite find it. Summer-brown crop fields passed on either side of us, the highway going on forever, and I leaned back in my seat. The sun was straight ahead of us, blinding in its intensity.

The seal in Colorado had supposedly cracked at some point while we were in the middle of that fight. Deke said he wasn't sure when. He just knew that once everything calmed down, he could tell. It was a sense he had, the same way our necklaces made us aware of the abominations around us. He knew, and he didn't know how he knew, but he was going to be right.

But Jess thought the ritual was wrong. Travis said it was order magic that was weakening the seals, and that meant the one in Colorado would probably shatter too. From the sounds of it, they'd both been repaired about the same number of times. They were brittle, and the magic the Order was using was weak stuff. Not powerful like what Jess threw around.

That was it!

"Bax, do you think Tash hating Jess for being a demon was the same as me hating Deke for being bi?" I asked.

Bax's brow furrowed. "I want to say no because you're cooler than Tash," he admitted. "Gav, man, do not take this wrong, ok? But you being freaked out by who Deke fucks is dumb as shit. Like, stupid, paranoid, moron shit. I get it, though. You didn't know anyone like that."

"You didn't either," I pointed out. "No one at school is gay."

"Ok..." He made a murmur of a sound like he hadn't expected that. "But I wasn't raised being told it was wrong either."

"That," I breathed. "The demons. The Order. I think that's how they do it. Deke said they took him as a kid, right? Young, so they could teach them and make it stick. They made Tash as scared of demons and cambion as my father made me of being gay. It's evil, weak, and a vulnerability. The Order is making people so afraid that they don't dare listen, so why did Deke?"

"Jess," Bax realized. "C'mon, we all knew he was into her on New Year's. He asked how old she was, and that meant he was considering it. I think he was pissed that she kissed me."

"Fuck," I laughed. "I was pissed that she kissed you. I would've fought Collin for her."

"It was Megan," Bax reminded him. "Megan wanted to fuck me, and that's the only reason Jess picked me. Otherwise, we both know she would've gone straight for Lars."

"Fucker." But I grinned as I said it, because he'd brought her to us. That also wasn't what I was really wanting to talk about. "I wish we could use Jess against the entire Order. She made Deke reconsider. We made Tash. Well, you made Tash."

"The kids made Tash," Bax corrected. "Jess just proved they weren't flukes."

"But the Order won't see that. They're scared, Bax. All they know is fear, and they have to kill to protect what they love - the Earth. The Order, maybe? I don't know. But they start young, don't know anything else, and they won't give her a chance to 'corrupt them.'"

"But when we get the seals not only closed, but also repaired, they'll - "

"No," I said, breaking in. "Listen to me. They don't care. She's a threat. She might help once, but she will turn on them, she's evil by nature, and we need to be reset. Life has no value to them. It's all about something else."

"The seals," Bax said, sounding like he understood where I was going. He was also wrong.

"No, it's something else," I insisted. "If they cared about the seals, they'd care about the ritual. They'd care that they're getting weaker. They'd even care that the history is missing. That's not it. What are they doing, Bax? What do they care about?"

"No fucking idea," he admitted. "What do you think?"

"I think my father convinced me to hate being gay so I wouldn't embarrass him. I think Ted convinced Jess to be good so he could control her. Those are the same thing. I think the Order is using the Martyrs for something."

"What thing?" he pressed.

"The seals are weak. Jess can be blamed." Then I paused. "They want to let the demons out. They're letting the seals break in a way where they can't be blamed! They'll kill Jess, reset the quad, and the demons will be free until another Guide and quad comes together. A new Guide, who doesn't know what he's doing, because they want us dead too."

"Shit," Bax breathed, looking over. "Gav, we're supposed to take the fall for this."

"For letting the demons out," I said.

"No," Bax said, sounding like he was honestly shaken. "Not all seals have demons, but all of them are cracked. Six for demons and six for angels, Gav. They're all cracking! What if there's a quad out there with a half angel in it? Shit, even if there's not. It's not the demons they're trying to release. It's the fucking Horsemen."

"But why?" I asked.

"I have a feeling we'll figure that out in Colorado," he said. "Gav, this is going to be bad."

"And the Order will be waiting," I added.

Bax just nodded. "Yeah. We just have to keep Jess safe, and this will all work out."

I looked out the window, amazed at how gold the fields looked.

That had to be wheat. Maybe oats. Not that I really knew which was which, but it didn't matter. It could be hay, for all I knew. It was still beautiful, rural, and wonderfully peaceful. At least for now.

"Hey, Bax?" I asked. "You know they made us into the villains, right?"

"Fuck yeah, I do," he agreed.

"So let's be some damned good villains."

He just held out his fist for me to tap, so I did. "That's what I'm talking about," Bax said. "When we stop next, we'll fill Lars in. Fuck the Order. They picked on the wrong quad this time."

"Yep," I agreed, and this time when I leaned back in my seat, it felt like my mind could finally relax. We had this. One way or another, we'd make sure of it.

BOOKS BY CERISE COLE

End of Days - Auryn Hadley & Kitty Cox, writing as Cerise Cole
(Paranormal Reverse Harem):

Completed Series

Still of the Night

Tainted Love

Enter Sandman

Highway to Hell

Cowritten by Auryn Hadley & Kitty Cox
Gamer Girls (Contemporary Romance):

Completed Series

Flawed

Challenge Accepted

Virtual Reality

Fragged

Collateral Damage

For The Win

Game Over

ABOUT THE AUTHOR

Cerise Cole is the pseudonym for the combined efforts of Kitty Cox and Auryn Hadley. After writing the *Gamer Girls* series together, the pair decided to join forces on a more permanent basis.

Kitty and Auryn are best friends in both real life and the literary kind. Living in Texas, they come up with their next crazy book idea while riding horses or drinking margaritas and martinis. Together, they combined Auryn's world building with Kitty's character depth to create stories that you will not forget.

For a complete list of books by Cerise Cole, visit:

My website -
www.CeriseCole.com

My Amazon Author Page -
www.amazon.com/author/cerisecole

Books2Read Reading List -
books2read.com/rl/CeriseCole

You can also join the fun on Discord - https://discord.gg/Auryn-Kitty

Visit our Patreon site
www.patreon.com/Auryn_Kitty

Facebook readers group -
The Literary Army
www.facebook.com/groups/TheLiteraryArmy/

Merchandise is available from -
Etsy Shop (signed books) - The Book Muse - www.etsy.com/shop/TheBookMuse

Threadless (clothes, etc) - The Book Muse - https://thebookmuse.threadless.com/

Also visit any of the sites below:

facebook.com/CeriseColeAuthor
goodreads.com/CeriseCole
bookbub.com/profile/cerise-cole
amazon.com/author/cerisecole
patreon.com/Auryn_Kitty

Printed in Great Britain
by Amazon